HUDDLESTON HOUSE

Denis Mackail has also written:

NOVELS

WHAT NEXT ?
ROMANCE TO THE RESCUE
BILL THE BACHELOR
ACCORDING TO GIBSON
SUMMERTIME
THE "MAJESTIC" MYSTERY
GREENERY STREET
THE FORTUNES OF HUGO
THE FLOWER SHOW
TALES FROM GREENERY STREET
ANOTHER PART OF THE WOOD
THE SQUARE CIRCLE
DAVID'S DAY
IAN AND FELICITY
CHELBURY ABBEY
THE YOUNG LIVINGSTONES
THE WEDDING
SUMMER LEAVES
BACK AGAIN
JACINTH
MORNING, NOON AND NIGHT
UPSIDE-DOWN

COLLECTED SHORT STORIES

HOW AMUSING
HAVING FUN
LONDON LOVERS

BIOGRAPHY

THE STORY OF J.M.B.

PERSONAL OBSERVATION

LIFE WITH TOPSY
HO!

FOR CHILDREN

TALES FOR A GODCHILD

HUDDLESTON HOUSE

A Period Piece

by

DENIS MACKAIL

HUTCHINSON & CO. (PUBLISHERS) LTD.

LONDON : NEW YORK : MELBOURNE : SYDNEY

First Published November, 1945
Reprinted   December, 1945

MADE AND PRINTED IN GREAT BRITAIN AT
THE FLEET STREET PRESS
EAST HARDING STREET, E.C.4

CHAPTER I

FIRST THERE HAD BEEN FLAT, OPEN COUNTRY. THEN THERE HAD BEEN FIELDS. Then, not far away, there had been a house, with a large garden, and a brick wall round it. Then there had been more houses, not quite so large, yet helping to cover the ground. And then, of course, came the streets.

As they spread, they ate into the gardens, and mopped up the fields as well. One by one the original houses drew back their skirts, and then gave up the struggle, and vanished or at the best could but pass on their name to another new street. It was all part of London now, and in only a few more years not even of outer London—though once it had been so far away as to be considered a rustic retreat—for still it seemed that the monster must grow and grow.

It did, what is more. It leapt and sprawled, and no one could stop it. But here, so near to the heart of things now that a fast taxi could get you to Piccadilly within a matter of minutes, the growth must inevitably take on another form. Down came some of the humbler houses; in other words, more gardens were overwhelmed; and bigger houses were built. Would they do? Not quite, apparently, or only as a stopgap, as more and more citizens became determined to inhabit this same, small part of the globe. Big houses weren't enough, however closely and tightly they were jammed together. Of course there must now be blocks of flats as well.

So again more sites were cleared. Huge holes were dug in the earth, and steel frameworks began rising as fast as the riveters could clatter. The brickwork followed. The pipes, the wires, the concrete floors, and the thin partitions, of breeze-blocks and quick-drying plaster, that transmitted almost everything but light. Immense ingenuity was shown in obeying the letter of all by-laws and dodging what may possibly have been their spirit. House-dwellers who were curious enough to come wandering over these up-to-date erections could hardly believe that they were habitable.

"Is this a cupboard or a kitchen?" they would ask. "But where," they would inquire, "could one *keep* anything?" "Just look," they would exclaim, "at the size of that little bath!"

These, in fact, were not yet prospective tenants, and never imagined that they would be. Yet from somewhere mysterious characters appeared, and seeped into the new flats; so that sometimes one might even see lace curtains here and there while workmen were still hammering and banging on another floor. Impossible, of course, to guess from outside what sort of life they led or how they managed to cram into these constricted quarters. Most of them had cars, whether paid for or not; and some of them, which was even more amazing, had children and perambulators as well—or perhaps instead. There was seldom any question that they had radio sets.

5

But who *were* they ?   Where had they come from ?   And was it they and their inexplicable requirements that had caused these flats to be built, or had the whole thing started at the other end ?   Was it the builders, that is to say, who had developed an extraordinary sensibility towards the shape of things to come ?

The house-dwellers, who in those days all had servants—though not necessarily the same ones for more than a few weeks at a time—and all had possessions, too, just couldn't make it out.   For the flats weren't even cheaper, if you went into the whole thing thoroughly; and though you were saved a little trouble, no doubt, just look what you lost in space, and privacy, and the feeling that you were the owner of a good long lease.   There may have been a chuckle from the Spirit of Irony when this last thought occurred to the house-dwellers.   But they couldn't hear it.   Still there was a gulf, for nearly all of them between houses and flats.   And they no more dreamt of crossing it, in those days, than of changing their profession, or religion, or anything else that was fixed.

Yet the flats still sprung up, and if they weren't immediately filled to overflowing, they were anything but empty, either.   Their lifts continually glided from floor to floor.   Smart young porters stood in their halls, continually ready to be tipped.   Milk-bottles were ranged outside their innumerable doorways.   Postmen came regularly tramping along their countless corridors.   Tons of solid or liquid fuel were poured into their vast cellars.   And whatever had drawn the inmates here, there were certainly enough of them, it would seem, in almost every instance, to return some form of interest on the capital involved.

Nothing stands still, though.   For a while there was a kind of balance or equilibrium between the house-dwellers and the flat-dwellers—though already, if you had looked closely enough, you might have noticed that hardly anyone left a flat for a house; and then, there could be no question now, it was the houses that were beginning to give way.   Some of them did this so thoroughly that they were turned into flats, of a sort, themselves.   Others, it might seem, were resolved to hang on.   But suddenly it was no longer the least unusual to have an agent's board attached to your area railings.   Of course, you said, you wouldn't dream of moving unless you could get a really good price.   And of course, at this epoch, there was very little chance that you would ever get it.   But what had once appeared to be solidity and security were now revealed, with thunder in the offing, to be nothing of the kind.   Some of those long leases began looking rather like millstones round their owners' necks.   And the owners certainly began inspecting the flats—and tipping the smart young porters—though still they returned, far oftener than not, with the conviction that it was impossible to cram themselves into anything like that.

It might have been a long, slow process of adjustment if there had been no war. But there was; and though it started, as it now seems, mildly enough—at any rate so far as London was concerned—it didn't add to the sense of either solidity or security when all the lights went out, and children were being evacuated to the country as fast as they could be packed into trains. The great discovery was made that if you emptied your house entirely, you were no longer responsible for rates or taxes. Where house-holders hadn't already rushed further afield, there was a rush for the flats, with their short leases and fixed charges, whether it was impossible to live in them or not. There was a pause for breath. There was some very bad news. There was worse news still. There was the most glorious summer weather. People's friends were all telling them that no bomber could possibly get through the London defences, but the sirens were certainly wailing a good deal.

The bombers had got to Croydon. One evening, as the days relentlessly drew in, the whole of the eastern sky was as bright as though the lights had come on again, though also a good deal redder. And then the bombers were over London indeed.

Some people couldn't leave, and some people wouldn't leave, while some, of course, were no longer people at all. But a lot of them did leave; more and more, as the row went on and the bombs came down; for as they were explaining all over the country now, they couldn't do without sleep. A very centrifugal autumn and winter. Even freeholders shut up their houses and beat it. While as for the flats, you could have had your pick now, and practically fixed your own rent. On the whole, though, very few people were taking advantage of this change.

Yet most of the flats were still there. It was true enough, also, that steel and concrete, though anything but immune to high explosives, could still take a good deal of punishment without actually dissolving into rubble. There were pock-marked flats, and flats without windows, and flats with gaping gaps here and there in the walls. But on the whole the main part of the fabric stood; and at length, as the tempest eased—and then even seemed for a while to have ceased for good—there was something more than a trickle of tenants again.

They weren't necessarily the same tenants as at the beginning of the war; for some still clung to the country, few of the little families were still of the same size, and though rents had come down a bit for the time being, almost everything else had gone up. There were traces, indeed, of a flat-aristocracy now, in which those who had stuck out the whole thing looked down on those who had gone and come back; while these, in turn, rather tended to despise the ones who had never been in the block before. But this didn't last. Time dealt with it; and the remains of that breakdown of the old stand-offishness which had come with the sirens' song. Once, it was true, you could live even in the smallest flat without knowing or even nodding at your neighbours, as had always been the habit of house-dwellers. But if you had to fire-watch together, if you stood in queues together, if it was even your duty to keep calling on each other for subscriptions to a Savings Group or the Red Cross; above all, perhaps, if each one of you, whatever your claims to distinction, could no longer hope to dispense with a shopping-bag, why, then even flat-aristocracy was of little value, and all, whether they wished it or not, were merged into a strange sort of metropolitan, village life.

Yet quite apart from this it can hardly be said that the flats were what they had been before that song began. At Huddleston House, for instance, though no scars could be seen from the street in front, the paintwork of the many windows was now very shabby indeed. There were no smart young porters now, either, but a small selection of slipshod veterans, not one of whose uniforms seemed to fit. The entrance-hall, which had once been the showiest part of the building, was dimly lighted now, some of its electric fittings were even broken or missing, and no attempt had been made to keep that list of the tenants' names up-to-date. Once they had been neatly painted on a varnished board. But no one could do that sort of work now, and anyhow the tenants were always shifting and sub-letting. They stuck their own names on with gummed paper if they wanted to; or they just did nothing, and were content, apparently, to be described as Col. and Mrs. Matthews when in fact they were nothing of the kind. It didn't really much matter nowadays.

The lift, too, which had once been quite remarkable for its speed and silence, was a lumbering sort of vehicle now. It had been overworked, its mechanism had been patched rather than repaired, and it had had a nasty jar when what was popularly known as a land-mine had fallen in Crofton Street, and all those little houses had been more or less blown to bits. It was on this occasion, also, that the back of Huddleston House had been peppered with fragments of flying masonry, and had acquired that crop of scars. It had also, naturally, had a quantity of windows broken; but though these had been replaced now, the scars remained. Partly, no doubt, for a number of other very adequate reasons, yet chiefly, perhaps, because the back of the block was something that had never been planned or intended for public view. It had loomed over the narrow gardens of those little houses, and had cut off a good deal of their light and air, and to this extent had of course been visible. But its own tenants seldom saw it, and neither did any ordinary wayfarer, so long as the little houses still stood. When they vanished, its functional indentations were revealed as a mass of drain-pipes swarming over yellowish bricks; quite a striking contrast in every way to the faintly Georgian flavour round at the front. But it had survived the so-called land-mine, which was the great thing in those days, and no one expected any more to be done to it now.

And no one expected a new carpet on the main stairs, though it was badly worn owing to its original quality, and to the number of times that the lift had broken down. With all the furniture that had been moved in and out, too, there was many a scrape and smudge on the passage walls. On the other hand, there was very little light now in these passages, either—for the landing windows had been blackened, so as to dispense with curtains, and were generally closed, at any rate right through the winter, so as to keep out the cold; and again nobody expected more bulbs or fresh paint so long as the war went on.

It is true, quite apart from such signs of the times, that the tenants all hated the landlords—or the Syndicate, as this elusive and also technically bankrupt body was generally known; and that few of them, unless out for some particular advantage, concealed this emotion from Mr. Todman, the Syndicate's thin, bat-eared, and melancholy representative, whose office was in the newer and much larger Bessingham House on the other side of the street. It is true, also, that the longer anyone lived in either of these so-called Houses, the more he or she became aware of their curious physical short-comings. Of the partitions, that's to say, through which sound passed almost as easily as through paper, though at the same time they were so hard and tough that it was impossible to knock in a nail. Of the odd projections, in almost every room, which were in fact part of the invaluable steel framework, yet effectively prevented you from placing any piece of furniture where you wished. Of the windows which admitted draughts whether they were open or shut. Of the plumbing so arranged that you always seemed to be getting someone else's gurgles; not to mention such phenomena as an uprush of old tea-leaves, sometimes even into the bath itself. Of the fragility of all fixtures and fittings. Of the miniature bedrooms in which there was often, quite literally, no space for a life-size bed. Of the cupboards for dustbins—how ingenious they had seemed at first—which discharged their vapours back into the tiny kitchenettes. Of the essential, inevitable, and resourceful meanness of the whole aggregation of cells.

Yet what, at this epoch, would anyone gain by moving, and how could they move when every such block was full? For none of them wanted a house now, except in their dreams, and even the larger and older flats would need more than a daily maid. Cling, then, to the thought of constant hot water—though sometimes it was cold, and sometimes the taps only gave forth a hollow gasp—and to the knowledge that though of course you couldn't afford even this method of life, it was virtually all that was left. And sometimes the radio through the wall, or ceiling, or floor, would be stilled for a while, and the lift would stop whining, and children would stop screaming in the street outside, and for a moment even this strange little room was again your castle and home.

Take courage, then. Think of the others who were so much worse off

Forget, perhaps, the past that was lost, and particularly any principles that had once been instilled about what might be spent on rent. You've got a roof, though it is a bit chipped here and there with fragments of anti-aircraft shells. You've got a front door, though anyone can open it, with a lock like that, by giving it a sudden kick. You have fed tonight, which is always something, and never more so than in this present year of grace.

Rest, then. Relax. Take up that book that you've been reading, or trying to read, for so long. Sit back. Cross your legs. Now, then . . . .

The radio again. Two radios; or more, for all you can tell by now. They have broken that very faint spell, though, and back goes the book on the table, as you glance at your own little set. There *might* be something tonight; something wonderful and tremendous at last. Curse the radio! But it's better to hear it properly than to strain after muffled words. So as this composite, imaginary tenant of Huddleston House is always—like all the other tenants—just a little on edge, he (or it may be she) slides from the chair, in a slightly tormented manner, and turns on the well-worn switch.

The set begins humming. It falls into line with the other sets—or with some of them—in the final bars of a song. A woman announcer starts speaking, rather hurriedly, and is wafted at once off the air. The familiar chimes come hot, as one might say, on her heels. And the familiar pause, which is always and invariably a little longer than anyone expects.

Then the first boom of Big Ben. One counts, because one can't help counting. Millions of people are counting, consciously or otherwise, not only all over these islands, but all over the world. And then, of course, there is that faint, preliminary sound in a masculine announcer's throat, followed forthwith by the full blast of his voice.

In other words, the nine o'clock news has begun.

CHAPTER II

"AND THIS," SAID THE SETS—FOR NOT YET HAD THE SHORTER FORMULA BEEN discovered, nor the absence of need for any such preface at all—"is William Whippenstall reading it."

When Providence created Man—unless, indeed, this was some kind of accident which has not yet been put right—he was given eyes and facial muscles with which to mark or modify his other gift of speech. But when Man created the microphone, he swept all this aside. The voice and nothing but the voice came through it. All other trickery was stifled at the source. Loud-speakers, henceforth, became—for anyone with ears to hear—an absolute and infallible test for sincerity; and as William Whippenstall had read the news now for months and indeed years on end, he was quite incapable of striking that authentic note.

He could emphasise, he could accelerate, he could pause—one could almost hear him counting five after announcing that the next-of-kin had been informed—and at what he conceived to be the right moments he could even sneer. He was a whale at pronouncing Russian place-names, whether the Russians would have recognised them or not. But after all those months and years, his soul, if he had one, had long ceased to be involved. He was performing a task, with a good deal of technical skill. But the microphone knew it. The loud-speakers knew it. And the listeners, however little prone to this kind of analysis, must still supply any real emotion for themselves.

Not many of them did; and least of all on a night like this, when the whole bulletin—though still dealing with death and destruction all over the face of the globe—was almost a formal parody of itself. After the first, inevitable disappointment—for not a listener but had a faint hope that the war might miraculously have ended five minutes ago—attention and patience both wavered. Some, though Heaven alone knows why, thought it right to hear the complete text. Others, less scrupulous, perhaps, would begin talking after a while, though they still kept the thing turned on. While others, again—aware, it may be, despite the narcotic effect of Mr. Whippenstall's accents, that he was merely repeating what they had read in their evening papers—would suddenly come to their senses, and switch the contraption off. This was easier to do if you were alone, though. For wherever two or three were gathered together, one at least of them would always be a bulletin-addict, and would beg for a continuance of the all-too-familar feast.

In the small sitting-room of No. 18—not that there was a really large one, either here or anywhere else in the block—it was Mrs. Geoffrey Margetson and her daughter June who were paying a certain amount of attention to the punctual voice. Mrs. Margetson was about forty-five, had once been pretty, and still wasn't exactly plain. Anxiety, however, adds to nobody's good looks; and with a husband, to whom she was still devoted, indefinitely detained in America, and a son, whom she frankly adored, in the Royal Navy, there were reasons, no doubt, why Mrs. Margetson should be anxious at times.

Again, she detested air-raids, though she had never yet said so. And she detested standing in queues, though she had never mentioned this fact to a living soul. To a minor degree, she detested both cooking and housework, of which she now did a good deal. Whenever she awoke in the morning, at this epoch, it is a fact that Mrs. Margetson groaned. Yet she didn't complain, for this wasn't her way. She knew, also, that she had been remarkably happy and lucky for a considerable number of years; and that t ough she wasn't happy now, she was lucky to have an income, and that it was right—this was the great thing—that she should be here to look after June.

Hope, also, must surely have entered into a part of Mrs. Margetson's spirit, or why, otherwise, should this little flat be so overcrowded with furniture and other objects which could easily be sold—or at least re-sold—for a great deal more than they had cost ? The answer, of course, is that Mrs. Margetson had been a house-dweller once, and still dreamt of being a house-dweller again. The longer she waited, the further—if one faced things squarely—such a future appeared to retreat. Yet even to lighten the dusting and polishing—of which she did so much more than Mrs. Goosey, her Daily Help—Mrs. Margetson was unable to get rid of any of these personal effects. There were a lot more in a very expensive repository; but still the same rule applied. For even if one never returned to Wallington Gardens, one might possibly sell it some day, and move into a smaller house. After the war, of course. Or, again, if June got married——

"Blast!" said June, at this moment, with some emphasis.

"What is it, darling ?" asked Mrs. Margetson.

"I darn and darn and darn," said June, employing a fierce inflexion, "and these stockings just ladder and ladder and ladder. Look at *that*, mother!"

Mrs. Margetson looked. Again she was half-moved to apologise for the state of the world, though this certainly wasn't her fault, while at the same time wondering if a few bracing words wouldn't really be more to the point. However, it was June who spoke.

"Why," she inquired, indignantly, "can't Daddy send me some ? Just *look* at these rags. I *ask* you!"

"Well, darling," said Mrs. Margetson, "he's very busy, you know. I mean, I'm sure he would, if he thought of it; but—— Well, haven't you got any coupons ?"

"Of course not!" said June. And: "Oh, damn!" she said. She was twenty-two, and though prettier when not scowling and cursing, could hardly—owing to the cunning of her creator—look really repulsive even now. Her mother's heart was wrung, though never could she have dreamt of speaking to her own mother like that. Again she was torn in two. I ought to say something, she thought, when she uses those words; and she's getting worse and worse. But then think, she thought, what a day she's had. Getting her own breakfast, fighting her way on to that bus, working in that office without any heat, not having a proper lunch, working again, fighting again—and then, after all that, I burnt the potatoes. It's worst for her, thought Mrs. Margetson, again thinking of her own, original, comfortable, well-staffed home, than it is for me. I *must* be patient with her, she thought.

"Can't you let me help you ?" she asked.

"Oh, mother!" said June, contemptuously. "Your darning's *hopeless*!"

Quite true. Mrs. Margetson knew it. There was evidence of this on her own much thicker stockings; but of course June must wear what she wanted to wear, and must have, as she had already had, the bulk of her mother's coupons as well as her own. According to Mrs. Margetson this was only fair, and of course she wouldn't dream of making any allusion to it now. Instead, though this was the last thing that she had meant to do, she found herself thinking of Wallington Gardens again, and of June in a perambulator. And then of Robin, a little earlier, in the same perambulator, where she couldn't help wishing to Heaven that she had got him now.

She was silent, in fact. And June, frowning rather than scowling over her handiwork now, was silent, too. But of course William Whippenstall was still going strong.

"Addressing a meeting at Wolverhampton this afternoon," he continued, "Mr. Lionel Haycock, Parliamentary Secretary to the Ministry of Utility, stated that the Enemy was now on the defensive everywhere; on land, at sea, and in the air. But, added Mr. Haycock, the heaviest part of the struggle still lay ahead. He warned his audience that there must be no complacency——"

"Good God!" said Miss June Margetson, as she reached over the back of the sofa, where she was surrounded by stockings, and switched the apparatus off. "That's better," she added, defiantly. And then, passing swiftly, as she so often did, into another mood: "Oh, mother—do you mind? Did you want to hear it?"

"No, darling," said Mrs. Margetson, not altogether truthfully, for even the dregs of a bulletin, she believed, might still bring some message of hope. But she was touched, and she must be patient. "Of course not," she said.

"No, go on," said her daughter. "I'm sick of these stockings, anyhow. I'm going to bed."

She rose, she picked up the stockings—or all but one, which she had overlooked—she turned on the set again, she bent over her mother and kissed her, and went out and slammed the door.

Mrs. Margetson didn't start, or even blink, for she was as accustomed as it is possible to be to this method of leaving the room. Besides, there was something about the way the doors were hung at Huddleston House that made it almost impracticable not to slam them. Her thoughts, moreover, were far away now; in Washington, D.C., and somewhere—though she didn't know where—on a light cruiser at sea. The set hummed again, and indeed had got well away into a resumption of the musical programme before she fully realised that it was emitting any sounds at all.

When she did realise this, she sighed, and got up, and turned the thing off once more. Naturally the music didn't cease altogether, for it could still be heard from a number of other flats. But Mrs. Margetson didn't mind. In fact, she was rather pleased on the whole, for as long as the music continued, it was almost a guarantee, that autumn, that no sirens would wail. An omnibus, in the main road, gave its well-known imitation of the preliminary, chromatic howl, but Mrs. Margetson remained calm. Those nerves near the midriff—closely connected, it would seem, with the nerves that made her swallow—hadn't been stirred. When they weren't stirred, sometimes in some extraordinary way one wanted them to be stirred; perhaps so as to test one's courage (which would instantly fail) or so as to get the whole thing over. But the bus proceeded on its dark and distant way, and Mrs. Margetson dismissed it from her mind.

Another day, she was thinking; and it was an exhausting thought, though at Wallington Gardens she had seldom gone to bed before eleven. But at Huddleston House there was always work, with a background of queues and shopping-bags; and, besides, though June never took this seriously, Mrs. Margetson did part-time, unpaid work in an office, too. She had thought she ought to, before she had realised quite what an additional strain it would be. It had been intended—selfishly, no doubt—as a kind of anodyne, but had turned out to be nothing of the sort. She was constantly irritated there. She was constantly on the verge of unseemly clashes with other part-time, unpaid women, though of course it was perfectly true that she had had no training.

No training. As she bent over to straighten the loose cover of the sofa, which her daughter had a peculiar gift for corrugating by the mere act of sitting on it, she couldn't help thinking how she had spent nine years at various schools, six months in Paris, and—after a short interval of admitted self-indulgence—the best part of twenty-one years in running a house. It hadn't been run so badly, either; but of course this didn't count. Or not now, thought Mrs. Margetson, a little sadly, as she picked up that flimsy stocking and simultaneously caught sight of the stain on the carpet where Mrs. Goosey had upset the ink.

Dreadful and indispensable Mrs. Goosey, she thought. And was ashamed, because Mrs. Goosey, though slap-dash and incompetent, was so much more adjustable, and had had—there could be no doubt of it—so very much harder a life. On the other hand she was incessantly boasting of all the money that her sons and daughters were making and spending—with the exception, that's to say, of Jim, the Black Sheep, who had quarrelled with his girl and gone into the Air Force—while even the Goosey homestead (in Block D of what were locally known as The Dwellings) was as large and as well-equipped, from all accounts, as No. 18, Huddleston House.

No wonder, then, that Mrs. Margetson was in constant terror of losing her helper and bugbear. That she bribed her and flattered her. That she had said nothing about that pool of ink on the carpet, but had got down on all-fours to deal with the disaster herself. And no wonder, perhaps, that she was so tired by half-past nine now that she, too, was quite ready for bed.

Besides, if one slept, one forgot it all; unless, of course, one was awoken by the wailing without. So Mrs. Margetson put her own sewing away—which wasn't so fanciful or feminine as it had once been, for she had been patching one of the bath-towels—and turned off the gas-fire (for no central heating was yet permitted in Southern England, though it had been bitterly cold for the last ten days), and switched off the light, and hung the stocking on her daughter's door-knob (for the smaller a flat, the more one must still try to respect privacy), and so passed, with a slight ache in her back, into her own little room.

She looked at her husband's photograph as she undressed, and at her son's, too. And again, as she neatly folded her clothes, she thought what she thought at this hour every night.

But you mustn't suppose that Mrs. Margetson was unpatriotic. Indeed not. Nothing could possibly have been further from the facts of the case.

CHAPTER III

HUDDLESTON HOUSE HAS NO SECRET FROM US; UNLESS IT SHOULD BE WHY A building with twenty-five separate flats in it should be described as a house at all. For us every wall is transparent and no door is locked. We can hover over the roof, if we like, observing those curious excrescences—one of them shelters the lift-gear and the other a big water-tank—which the architects hoped would be unseen from the street below. While up here we can also quite realise why fire-watching takes place in the entrance-hall; for even in daylight this roof is about as dangerous and precipitous as a roof can well be.

Or, again, we can plunge into the basement, whence the constant hot water proceeds. At the moment, owing to the law of the land, only one of the big boilers is working, and even this is a bit sulky, for it was meant to burn oil and has never quite taken to coke. Next week its brother, or possibly its sister, will come into action, too, and a certain amount of warmth will emerge from the radiators when various air-locks have been cleared. This mechanism is in charge of a character called Eldritch—(Is this possible ? Well, at least it is how he is always addressed)—who conducts an almost entirely subterranean existence in a suit of very old overalls. But he will come up, when tempted, not only to deal with air-locks, but with washers, and electrical fittings, and obstructions in waste-pipes, and even—though not always so successfully—with the refrigerators that are built into the twenty-five kitchenettes. As he copes, or endeavours to cope, with these cases, he not only leaves prints of his hands on the walls but often contrives to break something else.

Nevertheless, it is Eldritch or no one for the tenants when a crisis crops up. He is elderly—or he wouldn't be here at all. He is ill-mannered, or at least he despises the tenants, and never conceals this contempt. But he, and everyone else, knows that he is here, in all probability, for the duration, and that whenever he likes he can make the constant hot water even cooler than it already is. So he collects a lot of tips—especially as few of his repairs can be more than temporary now—and even Mr. Todman, though admittedly no hero, treats him with care and respect. As for the Syndicate—who bit off more than they could chew when they built Bessingham House, and though still functioning have been in a state of official insolvency almost ever since—they know well enough that if Eldritch should leave they could whistle before they found anyone to replace him. So if a tenant complains about the constant hot water, they attack Mr. Todman, and he cowers, and his bat-like ears turn pink. But as he is no hero, and still more, perhaps, owing to the number of jobs that he has lost during the last thirty years, he absorbs the shock, and everything goes on as before.

Besides, the boilers need cleaning, and there's no one to clean them. In the last resort, as when bearded, for example, by Mr. L. Wilson Barker (No. 5), who can develop a somewhat hectoring manner at times, Mr. Todman will plead this technical point; and then even Mr. Barker must realise what he's up against. There's a war on, and if you don't like it, or its effects, you're not patriotic. Much virtue in war, then ? Well, it serves quite a number of purposes, apart from whatever its principal purpose may be. Mr. Barker is quelled. Mr. Todman has another brief triumph. He hasn't pointed out that he was gassed in the last war and that Mr. Barker has still managed to avoid any active participation in this. But these truths are in the background, and the boilers remain uncleaned.

If we peer at them once more, on this autumn evening, there is a very good chance that we shall see at least one of the porters down here as well. Freeth, it may be, with the stiff leg and the long, crooked nose; or Popham, with that false air of briskness and slightly alarming squint; or Truelove— no figure of romance, despite his name—who "doubles," as they say on the stage, at the bigger block, and thus enables both staffs to permute their shifts. In a sense, therefore, Truelove is invaluable; but in another he isn't. For not only is he, by nature, far and away the stupidest of the whole lot, but this "doubling" business is a justification—or so he would appear to believe— for instantly forgetting any message with which he is charged. He is a bit of an idiot, in fact, and not even particularly good-natured. Yet if he goes, and isn't immediately replaced by someone equally ready to play this rather complicated role, it is almost certain that there will be more resignations among the rest of the staff. So he stays, and they all take advantage of him, and he is of singularly little use to anyone else. He seems to suffer a good deal from catarrh.

Strictly speaking, of course, no porter is supposed to lurk in the boiler-room. But they do, for though it is dirty, it is warm, and no one can say that they are exactly off duty when they can still hear a shout from the hall. If they don't always answer it, that is because they know well enough which shouts, from their own point of view, are really important. They judge them, it must be admitted, in terms of prospective tips, and though they come scampering up promptly enough at a cry from Major Hurst or a call from Mrs. Wardrop, they prefer, it would seem, to affect a slight deafness when summoned by Miss Tuke or Mrs. Musselberg. For an intermediate class of client they will sometimes come half-way up; while in the mornings, of course, when they are sweeping, or banging doormats, or hurling buckets of water in the general direction of the gutter, they are clearly at anyone's mercy. In the colder weather, however, they make little use of the niche, behind a counter, to the right of the entrance-hall, which is where they are supposed to be. This was all very well for the smart young porters, who would frequently spring from it, in days gone by, just to open or close the lift-gates. But times have changed since then.

Next door to the boiler-room there is a cellar full of trunks, cases, and other property belonging to the present occupants, or to others who have failed to remove them. There is a certain amount of furniture here, too, which can't be crammed into the flats, but to which people like Mrs. Margetson are still hopeful or unpractical enough to cling. Everything is more or less thickly coated with a deposit of grime, which analysis would reveal to have come chiefly from the furnace; and the whole place is so hot and dry—even with present restrictions on fuel—that many of the effects are in a state of unsuspected dissolution. Glue ceases to perform its office down here, fabrics crack where they are folded, wood warps, and leather turns into dust. In this unnatural atmosphere, moreover, moths seem unable to distinguish one season from another, while their grubs are as skilful as ever at choosing the richest diet. Nevertheless, this store-room, as it is called, is undoundtedly regarded as a convenience; and without it one can hardly imagine how some of the tenants could turn round in their flats at all.

Beyond it is an apartment or cavity known as the Shelter. This wasn't designed as such; any more than the architects, as we have seen already, were concerned with Alerts when drawing their plans for the roof. Well, the point wasn't mentioned; so the roof is hipped and unparapeted and would be a bit of a death-trap even in day-time; while some people say that the Shelter is a death-trap, too.

That rather depends, of course. Certainly, if the whole building collapsed it would take a long time to dig anyone out of this furthest cellar—who's original purpose, if any, has now been forgotten—and by that time, perhaps, it would not contain very pure air. Yet at the beginning of the aerial war it was no less certainly used, night after night, and at first by nearly all the tenants who still remained. They didn't much like it, but they preferred it to the immediate alternative, or what they conceived this to be; and there they sat quaking, or trying not to quake, through an autumn and winter that left a mark on them all.

But the full test never came. The block wasn't hit; not even, strictly speaking, on the night that the alleged land-mine came down. Yet other blocks were, and the shelterers couldn't help noticing first that even steel and concrete weren't all that they had been led to suppose, and secondly that bombs had a freakish habit of exploding against the bottom of a building quite as often as they came through the top. This knowledge, and the longer lulls now, rather altered their frame of mind. Some became fatalists, some were just sick of the cellar whether it was safe or not, while others, returning from the country, had failed to acquire the burrowing habit at all. The Shelter was almost deserted. It was quite deserted during the very long lull that followed the first great assaults. And now, though the sirens had begun wailing again—though more fitfully as yet—the Shelter was quite out of fashion, and only a couple of residents used it at all.

Mr. and Mrs. Champion, from No. 11. They were old, and small, and dry, and dull. They had been in the block since the year after it was built, which was also the year when Mr. Champion had retired from work. They were conservative, both in politics and in everything else; or, in other words, though it took a great deal to make them alter any of their customs, it took even more to make them alter them twice. They had been right through the first great assaults, though there was no reason why they should live in London more than anywhere else, and they had originally descended to the Shelter only after their kitchen window had been blown in. This, however, had apparently convinced them that there was something to be said for the idea; and though it was a wrench, no doubt, to make this decision, they stuck to it once it was made.

They were very slow. They never emerged from No. 11 until they were completely dressed, so that sometimes they only emerged to the sound of an All-Clear. In this case, of course, they turned round again, and undressed, and went back to bed. But otherwise, as the guns banged and thumped and rumbled and roared, you might still see Mr. Champion (with a cushion under his arm for Mrs. Champion), and Mrs. Champion (with a torch in her hand in case the lights went out) conscientiously making their way to the Shelter again. They sat quite alone there, nearly always, and what they thought as they sat it would be hard to say. They didn't read, they didn't talk, they didn't sleep. They just waited until the signal released them, and then, a shade more slowly, they made the return trip. As they were both over the age at which they could be required to perform any other services, and in so far as anyone in this category should be tolerated by the State at all, they might be described as perfect citizens. Yet Popham or Freeth, or even Truelove, had been known to wink as the Champions went by. And though perhaps there was just a trace of pride in these winks, as though in some sort of way the Champions were doing them credit, the general legend, we're afraid, in Huddleston House was that the Champions were a bit soft in the head. Perhaps they were, too. And so, perhaps, was the World.

We mustn't, however, spend all our time down here in the basement ourselves; any more than our immediate post is up on the roof. Rather, with a wave of the wand, it was our purpose, as those radio chimes rang forth, to glance at the whole building—regardless of brickwork and breeze-blocks and black-out curtains—and, treating it as a kind of giant doll's-house, to see such other tenants as this glimpse revealed. That was the task; and since time can stand still for us, or move in such direction as we choose, now is the moment when we peep and peer. The five floors are all laid open to us, more clearly than in any architectural elevation or plan, and wherever there is light—or, in other words, wherever a tenant is now at home—we can not only see but listen, if we like, as well.

On the top floor, then, with its sloping outer walls, amidst which five flats have been ingeniously dovetailed, three rooms are visible at once. In the first a dark gentleman of foreign aspect—his name is Mr. Vardas—is writing in a concentrated manner and also in a cloud of cigarette-smoke. One might judge him to be about forty. He is in slippers. There is a large, bald patch in his somewhat bushy, black hair. On the corner of the table at which he is scribbling so hard there are the remains of a simple meal. There are pamphlets and papers all over the floor, while more papers have been stuck on the walls. He doesn't look healthy, and he doesn't look wealthy either. How, then, do we account for his presence here, in a room which apart from the afore-mentioned details, is far more suggestive of the female of the species, and of the British species at that ? That pale-yellow paint, those mauve curtains, that pouffe on the hearthrug, that *bergère* settee, those pictures, those ornaments, that shelf of mildly intellectual English fiction—how can we associate all these with a man like Mr. Vardas ? The answer is, of course, that we needn't, except in a fortuitous fashion. If there had been no war—or perhaps it would be more accurate to say if there had been no threat of war—Mr. Vardas would still be living in Central Europe, and Miss Cicely Pattinson might still be living at 22, Huddleston House. At the moment, however, she has hurled herself into the fray at a branch of the Ministry of Priority now situated on the sea-coast of Lancashire, and Mr. Vardas isn't actually paying her any rent.

He did once. But she is mildly intellectual, or in other words not at all

business-like. And Mr. Vardas isn't at all business-like; and, again, there
is something faintly corruptive about being a refugee. He has a job. He
works for a periodical, composed in his native language and published at the
ultimate expense of the British tax-payer, which is supposed to circulate
among those in the same boat as himself. But though he has been doing
this for quite a while now, it is also quite a while since he last bothered to
send a money-order to Miss Pattinson—nominal as is the monthly sum
involved—and he hasn't exactly paid for the telephone, either. Miss
Pattinson can do little or nothing, and perhaps doesn't want to do much,
for in a sense she regards Mr. Vardas as part of her war-effort; and anyhow
she let him in without consulting her lawyer, and she has more than a rough
idea what the lawyer would say if she admitted that there was no written
agreement.

So you can call it lease-lend, if you like. But Mr. Vardas is undoubtedly
a victim of aggression, and knows it, and has a distinctly continental
conscience. He isn't saving his money, either, for he is no miser. It just
slips through his fingers, or sometimes through the lining of his pockets;
and he smokes and works like anything up here, when he isn't at the
editorial office, or shouting and gesticulating, in an underground tea-shop
near Holborn, in the tongue that he still knows best.

He has got Miss Pattinson's radio turned on tonight, though, for he
likes to work with a good deal of noise in the room. And when William
Whippenstall announces Mr. Lionel Haycock's declaration on the subject
of complacency, Mr. Vardas looks fierce and very much in favour of it
indeed. He writes, in fact, with even more frenzy now, so that his pen
spirts, and more drops of ink appear on Miss Pattinson's table, already well-
scarred by the stubs of his cigarette. For Mr. Vardas may be unbusiness-like
in some matters, but he is just as patriotic as Mrs. Margetson. Or even
more so, perhaps, when you consider that absence is said to make the heart
grow fonder, and that he hasn't the least intention of returning to his native
country—or to his wife and family, either—so long as he can contrive to
subsist elsewhere.

So much for No. 22, then. Click! and we find ourselves looking into
No. 24. Another two-roomed flat—that's to say if you don't count the
bathroom or kitchenette, which in truth, even if joined together, would still
hardly hold an ordinary taxicab. No light in the sitting-room here, though.
The sole illumination comes from a small lamp on a table beside Miss
Kenton-Hinksey's bed. The rest of the vision, however, is not the least
immodest. Miss Kenton-Hinksey is certainly in the bed herself, but she is
wearing a bed-jacket—because of the intense cold, no doubt—not to mention
a species of net-work helmet over most of her head. Even the garments
that she has removed are chastely covered with a large silk kerchief, while
her shoes are symmetrically arranged and neatly treed.

There is nothing, in fact, for Miss Kenton-Hinksey to be ashamed of; and there never has been if it comes to that. No cream, as it is called, is smeared on her face; and though of course she would scream and duck under the bedclothes if she saw us, there are other signs that display no lack of courage. A much solider helmet is hanging from a hook on the inside of her door, and below it is a bifurcated costume, of a brownish colour, which would seem to have seen some use. If the sirens start, it will be the work of a moment for Miss Kenton-Hinksey to slip into both helmet and costume, not to mention a pair of ancient, cloth overshoes, and to descend, in this rather formidable outfit, to the entrance-hall. For tonight Miss K.-H. is, as she would say, on duty.

Does this surprise you? It might, if you judged her age by her face, and recalled the ruling of the Ministry of Home Security. But then this Ministry —which curiously enough only came into being when most homes were being broken up and security no longer existed—has never forbidden any active woman of about forty-nine to share in the defence of the realm. So Miss Kenton-Hinksey, who is extremely active, and never walks when she can hustle or bustle or even run, has insisted on joining the fire-watching gang (under Party-Leader W. Popham); and the better to fit herself for this task, hasn't only attended a number of lectures—which have left her in considerable confusion about the different types of bomb—but has even crawled through a hut full of smoke and flame in that bifurcated apparel.

Why is she in bed, then? Well, it all comes back to the roof once more, as indeed has already been explained. Nobody can go up there, because it isn't safe. So the fire-watching party meets in the hall, where if anything happened it would be distinctly baffled by all the contradictory instructions that it has received. Once, for instance, it was supposed to summon the Fire Brigade; but now it mustn't, for the Fire Brigade hasn't only changed its name but has become involved in a web of remarkably complicated instructions, too. The theory now, in fact, is that the fire-watching party should itself make use of some apparatus that hasn't yet been delivered; and this being the case, we can't see why its communal vigil should begin before the guns go off.

If they do go off, it will be there in almost a flash—that's to say if it hasn't excused itself on grounds approved by Party-Leader W. Popham—and will continue to sit on a row of chairs like Casabianca himself. But at this phase it can hardly be expected to do much more; and since Miss Kenton-Hinksey is now working in a shop all the week—where if there were anything to sell she would perhaps be of even less use than she is—and in a canteen on three evenings as well, her feet, if we may mention them, are feeling the strain, and that's why she has gone to bed.

She isn't asleep, though. The energy which has made her hustle and bustle all day may temporarily have affected her arches; but her soul is indefatigable, her keenness, as she would describe it, is quite untouched, and she isn't only reading a report on atrocities—which the bulk of the population have been quite content to have boiled down for them in their newspapers—but is listening to William Whippenstall as well. She nods when Mr. Haycock is reported to have alluded to the Enemy's plight. But she nods still more vigorously when she learns of his views on complacency. For the curious thing is that though Miss Kenton-Hinksey has so far succeeded in getting no nearer the heart of affairs than a shop, and a canteen, and periodical membership of a fire-watching party, she has absolutely swallowed the legend that this war only came just in time to save us from moral collapse.

She has never been near such a condition herself. There is evidence all round her that people are no happier or better for what they have undergone. If she really looked back, she would see herself hustling and bustling—which she has always done—with far more contentment than she hustles and bustles today. But some people are like this; they help to form, presumably, what is known as the Mass Mind; and Miss Kenton-Hinksey would far sooner that the war went on for ever than that a single pledge from the Front Bench, however hasty or capricious, should fail to be fulfilled.

Is she complacent, then? But of course not, when not only has she been warned against the vice so often, and not only is she in that secretly disturbed frame of mind which comes from believing everything that one reads—her views on France, alone, for instance, would be enough to give anyone a headache—but when her feet have begun giving her such a lot of trouble as well. One can't help rather admiring her in a way, in spite of her sharp, red nose. But if one is feeling good-natured, one can't help pitying her, too. Her mind is in a muddle and her feet hurt, because she has tried to do what she thinks right. There ought to be a better reward than that for women like Miss Kenton-Hinksey.

By the way, that coloured photograph over the chest of drawers represents her father, who rose to the temporary rank of Brigadier-General in the last war, and died shortly afterwards, mainly from a surfeit of drink. But though before he did this he wrecked her one and only love-affair—by frightening both her and the young gentleman in question more or less out of their wits—she has since become intensely proud of him, and is always alluding to him as the General, whether others are interested or not. Yet if this sounds complacent, there is another aspect as well. It can't be denied that most people *aren't* interested; and she feels this, though she won't admit it; and she becomes irritated, and difficult, and dangerously touchy—in a world, moreover, where plenty of other characters are now in very much the same state.

Then there is another thing about Miss Kenton-Hinksey. She had a great friend once, a Miss Smallwood, who was no beauty, either—being short, and stout, and square—but to whom she had linked her life for many years; even to the final and triumphant point of sharing a small seaside cottage. It was the apple of their eye, though they couldn't use it very often, owing to the necessity of earning a living elsewhere. But they went there for week-ends about once a month, and of course they both used it for their summer holiday, and it was their plan, if they could ever afford to retire at all, to settle down there one day for good. However, what actually happened was that it was blown to blazes in the winter of 1940, with Miss Smallwood inside it—though not, as you may have gathered, with Miss Kenton-Hinksey, who was preserved by having missed her train. So then Miss Smallwood's remains were extracted and buried in the new annexe to the local churchyard, and though there was no cottage now, Miss Kenton-Hinksey still went down there from time to time to see that the grave, for which she had paid a good deal, was properly kept, and to place flowers on it, and to think of the past.

After about eight or nine months of this, another bomb fell in the annexe itself, and now there was no trace of either Miss Smallwood or that expensive headstone, but merely what had come to be called a crater, with a diameter of about fifteen yards and a very considerable depth. And though it was better, no doubt, that the bomb should have fallen here than among the living, it is at least intelligible that Miss Kenton-Hinksey, who had worshipped her very plain friend, should henceforth be a little mad. Quite secretly, again, like lots of other people; and with unaltered courage, like lots of other people, too. But proud as she had become of her father, it was Miss Smallwood whom she mourned, and could never mention. Something would snap here, perhaps, one day, if the war went on, as it looked like doing, and if she now refused, as she did, to take any sort of holiday at all.

Poor woman. But we can't help her; and it is time to leave her—though of course she has neither seen nor heard us—and to pass on to the flat next door.

No. 25. Mrs. A. C. Amberley. Young, or certainly no more than about twenty-five. A good deal of paint on her face, or more than seems really essential; but of course that means nothing in these days, or certainly not what it did. Mrs. Amberley, who returned from the factory, where she is a part-time worker, at about half-past seven this evening, has had a bath, and has eaten—though not much—and is now attired in a brightly-coloured wrapper, with a brightly-coloured scarf round her head. She is smoking, she is ironing, she is cursing under her breath when the smoke gets in her eyes or the ash drops on the ironing-board, but she has switched on the radio, too. Her movements are quick and skilful, though she is very tired, and would look it if she hadn't carefully repainted her face after having that bath. But she is expecting no visitor; she has merely taken this trouble because she is now horrified by the appearance of her face when it isn't painted—having rather lost her eye, as they say, for her own features in their natural state.

She has a bit of a cough, too, for she has just had a bit of a cold. But she isn't weeping, though tears are undoubtedly oozing from her eyes. This, however, is due partly to cigarette-smoke and partly to mascara, for in fact Mrs. Amberley has quite given up weeping, even though she has done a good deal in the last few years. It doesn't pay, she has decided. It isn't worth it. It makes one look old. It's better to be tough, or to pretend to be tough, when one's husband has been a prisoner of war since Calais, and God only knows if one will ever see him again.

Is she in love with him still? Don't ask her. How can she tell after all these years, and when the only link is the letters that take weeks or months to go to and fro, and are read by other people on the way, and in any case must always be guarded and never—because one mustn't be selfish—come too near the truth? But she *was* in love with him, she has never dreamt of being in love with anyone else, and it is only, perhaps, because there are bars to certain thoughts that the question must be evaded now.

If the bars go down, she's finished. For from the beginning she has been fighting against Time; trying to dodge it, because she knows she can't bear it; clinging to the past and ignoring the present—though no one, of course, can ever really do that—and never, so far as possible, for she has become very superstitious, giving more than a glance at the future. On these terms, which are enough to account for anyone turning a little queer, Mrs. Amberley thinks she can manage. But of course, another very important thing is that she, too, should always be busy and never relax or rest.

She wasn't always like this. She wasn't the least like it as a child or before she married, when indeed she was frequently held up as an example of sloth. Even at the outbreak of the second world-war she was still more of a slightly resentful onlooker than anything else. But then came the sudden engagement, the hurried marriage, the swift, short, passionate, and uncomfortable life as a camp-follower; the parting; the agonising anxiety; the two telegrams—but with a dreadful pause between them; and Mrs. Amberley had entirely changed.

Not that she could remember very much about that summer, when she had been so miserable as to be virtually stunned. But towards the end of it, when her parents left London, she insisted on staying behind. Suddenly, now, she had got to *do* something; and she did it indeed, in a dark-blue uniform, during the autumn and winter of that year, and the early spring of the next. Unimaginable nights of noise and horror, yet with little or no self-approval to help her through. She wasn't even particularly frightened, for she rather wanted to be killed, which was why, she supposed, she hadn't been. Nor was she drawn into a companionship of valour—or of drink, either, which was largely concurrent at the time, and can be well understood —for she remained remote and was thought stand-offish while constantly risking her life.

All this time her parents, in Berkshire, and her parents-in-law, in Wiltshire, were as constantly urging her to join them. But she wouldn't. She couldn't. She had to go on. In fact, she only turned up at her parents' retreat, looking more like a ghost than a girl, when the news came through that her brother, in Coastal Command, had "failed to return" from patrol. She couldn't remember this journey, either, though she remembered arriving and saying that she was all right. She was desperately ill, however, for the next six weeks; and then, having put on a pound of the stone she had lost, and having shown enough vigour to quarrel violently with her father and mother—though afterwards, of course, they would all know that none of them could help it—she had left them abruptly and gone back to her sand-bagged Post.

But there were no bombs now, and she couldn't stand this, either. Furthermore, she had acquired a habit of fainting from time to time, and was presently discharged. But she couldn't be idle. She couldn't be quiet. It may be pointed out by those who object to her painting her face so brilliantly that she still had a private income, and that her husband wasn't dead—as her brother undoubtedly was—but merely detained in a foreign land. Nevertheless, and though she never spoke of it, Mrs. Amberley's rash though well-founded hopes of motherhood had also been dashed, at a very early phase, in the summer of 1940; and though others might hold that this was no world into which to bring children—or even one child—neither celibacy nor sterility was necessarily good for her nerves.

She was in and out of a lot of odd jobs, while the State, having all but lost the main war, embarked on its campaign against women. But she didn't resist it, though she could be stubborn enough. Some of its instructions she obeyed, and others she blankly disregarded—for we are not pretending that she was an ideal member of the community that it was trying to create. She was generally and often deliberately behindhand in dealing with its buff forms; but she was now working quite as hard as her health would allow in a not very conveniently-situated factory, and if she didn't know or much care what she was helping to make, no one could ever say that she slacked.

In spite of this she wasn't exactly unpopular with her colleagues, to whom she was always polite, though she either couldn't or wouldn't make friends with them. They called her Primrose, to show that they weren't afraid of her. But they were, just a little, for there was another barrier here. Not of class, though some of them tried to believe this, for Mrs. Amberley had got over all that. Something else. Impenetrability, as Humpty-Dumpty might have said.   So she was accepted, though again she didn't much care whether she was being accepted or not.   The noise, and the artificial light, and the monotonous routine, helped to stop her thinking and to eat up time.   That was the real point.

But she still had her hair done at an expensive shop, and still wore smart clothes when she wasn't at work; for this, however it is all to be explained, seemed very important, too.   And she went out at night, as often as not; for this, and running her own flat with the very minimum of help, might partly achieve the same ends.   She had also given up fainting; though, as we have noticed, she still coughs.   Such, then, is Mrs. Amberley, at the moment, with her painted face, and her electric-iron, and her radio, all in the rather harsh rays of a hundred-watt lamp near the ceiling.

"—— still," says William Whippenstall, or his voice, "lay ahead.   He warned his audience that there must be no complacency——"

But Mrs. Amberley has no time to react to this familiar phrase, though it might possibly be interesting to see how she does.   For her telephone has started ringing, and though she doesn't stop smoking, she quietens William Whippenstall to an inaudible whisper, tilts up the iron so that it will burn nothing but current, and takes the receiver (or whatever it is now called when it transmits as well) from its rest.

"Hullo ?" she says, in a distinctly impenetrable manner.

Another voice addresses her.

"Oh, it's you, is it ?" she says.   "Well ?"

The tone is still not particularly encouraging.   But we are bound to admit that she is now sitting on the arm of a chair, and has reached for an ash-tray, so that it looks as if she were at least prepared to listen for a while. She listens; but her expression is quite inscrutable; the other voice still seems to be doing nearly all the talking.   So perhaps it would be as well if we now move on once more.

Down to the third floor, or fourth storey, into which no less than six separate flats have been crammed; while some of them, owing to the outer walls being perpendicular now, and again owing to certain projections, on this level, at the back—are even a shade larger than those overhead.   We have been in one of them already, of course; No. 18, where (by some successful experiment with time) Mrs. Margetson and her daughter June are still and again in their rather congested sitting-room.   No cause for us to pause, though, for we know now what will happen here next.

We may remember also, though, that through the wall, or in No. 17, there is a tenant who would appear to own quite a loud loud-speaker, too. Here he is, in his own, much barer sitting-room, just preparing to turn it on. He is not very skilful at this, though he has had practice enough.   He is, indeed, the kind of licence-holder—for in all the block there is no one of whom we can be more certain that he has bought his licence, and even knows where it is—who must always fumble a bit; who must eventually light on the desired station with the very maximum volume, so that as it comes roaring in he is even more startled than his neighbours, and frequently loses it again as his fingers jerk. With a full set of chimes and nine booming strokes, though, even Mr. Everard has the chance to correct quite a number of errors, and he is generally there by the time that William Whippenstall or one of his colleagues has in fact begun to speak.

Thus it is this evening, and since we have heard the news already ourselves —or such filleted and filtered intelligence as is thought fit for us to hear— we can again concentrate on yet another listener.

Mr. Ernest Alfred Everard, then, is a Civil Servant, but there is nothing temporary about him. He is mortal, of course, that's to say—in the sense that even he must eventually pass from this scene—but in all other respects he is a very permanent phenomenon indeed, who has moved on a plotted orbit from the day when he passed a largely irrelevant examination and so entered on his present career. Nay, even when it technically ends, he will still know just where he is. For Mr. Everard—or perhaps Sir Ernest by then—will of course have a pension when he at length retires, and only the complete breakdown of the very strongest part of our present system can interrupt these regular payments, though he should choose to survive to any age you like. This knowledge tends to make him take a long and on the whole hopeful view of most things, and to discourage him from hurrying over anything that it is possible to delay.

At the moment that pension is still about eight years off. But Mr. Everard is far from impatient. Once, when he had just passed that examination, there was another war, in which he was then even ardent enough to wish to take part. But on its being pointed out to him by his father—who is now Sir Alfred, and has been drawing a pension for all but a quarter of a century— that this sort of thing was shilly-shallying and would prejudice his advance-ment, he hesitated, and was either lost or saved.

He was saved, as one might say, from the discomfort and danger of a long and often murderous campaign; for though the Comb, as it was called, kept passing through the Office, and with some vigour towards the end of the struggle, its teeth seemed blunted whenever they came near him, since one only had to look at him to see that he was indispensable at once. Perhaps this was heredity. Perhaps even the Comb must waver in the presence of such a chip of the old block. Yet Mr. Everard was lost, of course, as a complete human being; if no more so, possibly, than if there had been neither war nor Comb.

He was a type, you see, and doomed to be a type; or at least it was unimaginable now that he should ever have been anything else. He was already a little arid and elderly at the age of twenty-six, which was when that other war ended. He became no younger with the return of peace. By thirty-five he was almost completely bald, though still lean enough, for he was a great walker, and heredity again would have had a job to make him really stout. By forty there was only a short fringe round the back of his head. When he laughed, which he only did at his own small selection of stories, or when somebody else in the Office made a harmless mistake, he appeared—though this wasn't the case—to be merely gasping for breath. When he spoke, it was with a succession of odd interruptions; not a stammer so much as the interpolation of meaningless sounds. He wore spectacles now. His clothes seemed strangely old-fashioned; or perhaps it was their material, or the way he wore them, for there had been little change in men's wear since his first grown-up suit. He was pedantic, of course; he was always correcting other people, even when he wasn't at work. He played no games. He had developed several rather irritating habits, such as sniffing as a method of emphasis, or thrusting his little finger into his ear when engaged in thought. The backs of his hands, and, indeed, the rest of his skin so far as it was visible, were curiously scaly and dry.

Nevertheless, at the age of forty-three Mr. Everard got married. Surprisingly, perhaps, yet not suddenly; for he had been weighing the pros and cons for a very long time—though he hadn't actually addressed minutes or memoranda to himself on the subject—and having chosen his intended mate, had still taken nearly eighteen months to come to the point. She was the daughter of a more elderly colleague, who was now drawing a pension, too. She had been very well educated, and was the possessor of a university degree. At the time when her great happiness came to her she was aged thirty-one, had rather a queer figure, and an eager expression which may or may not have reflected some quest in her soul.

Certainly it had alarmed a number of young men, who at the same time had hardly regarded her as nubile at all. But Mr. Everard either saw something else there, or was governed, as a Civil Servant, by laws that fail to apply to the rest of the race. His own quest, at any rate—though it had never been very active or urgent—was now over. The day came when he declared himself, in a cautious manner, and was accepted. He was married. He took a little house in London. An amazing sequel—though perhaps it was less amazing to Mr. and Mrs. Everard than to the average onlooker— was that they became the parents of a little boy. They named him Cyril, after Mrs. Everard's old father, and seemed satisfied that one miracle was enough.

In any event there were no more children; and within very few years there was no little house, either. It had vanished as completely, and for much the same reason, as Miss Kenton-Hinksey's seaside cottage or the houses in Crofton Street. But the Everards had left it by now; for Mrs. Everard and

Cyril had withdrawn to the country, as advised by the State, while Mr. Everard was sleeping—when he couldn't get down there, too—at his Club. It was someone else's trouble, in fact, that the little house was reduced to rather less than its component parts. But as the storm grew less, and the trains worse and worse, Mr. Everard took a lease of this flat. And though he sometimes went down to the country now, and Mrs. Everard sometimes came up, he saw very little of Cyril in these days, and was at least half a bachelor again.

Perhaps he had never really been anything else. There was no sign that he pined for the little house—in the sense that Mrs. Margetson still pined for Wallington Gardens—or for any great change in the life that he was leading now. His thoughts lay almost entirely with his work, and it was convenient to be comparatively near it. He had secured the succession—for it would be more surprising than anything else if Cyril didn't eventually turn into yet another Civil Servant—and he never felt lonely because he always had papers (by which we don't mean newspapers) to read. Again, he was always a parent, though hardly a husband, in his attitude towards the general public. They were there, that's to say, to do what he told them, to be punished if they didn't, and never to question his rule. He hadn't exactly declared war himself, but the Government had, and he was part of the executive, and therefore it was his duty to keep it going as long as he possibly could.

If this point of view strikes you as exaggerated or inhuman, we would invite you to glance at Mr. Everard again. *Now* do you believe us? Yes, it's true he looks tired—for in these days he is generally at his Office until eight, and quite frequently on Sundays, too; but if there is no trace in those features of mercy for himself, there is still less for anyone else. That document on his lap—as we can see, if we approach still closer—contains little to encourage the victims to whom it will presently be circulated, and Mr. Everard's pencilled corrections aren't tending to make it any milder now. Why "Servant," then? Why "Minister," if it comes to that, which should mean exactly the same thing? Indeed, and in truth, this has become an astonishing planet.

Yet it doesn't appear to astonish Mr. Everard, as he also listens to William Whippenstall without a flicker of expression on his face. For the news is just what he expected it to be. He even knows already that Mr. Haycock has been speaking at Wolverhampton today. And when he hears that little piece about complacency, though he thoroughly agrees with it, he doesn't even trouble to nod.

For it is meant for others, of course, and is a very necessary warning. He has never, he is convinced, been the least complacent himself. One can't be when one knows what Mr. Everard knows; or so Mr. Everard thinks.

Now, then, Fate! Are you going to do anything about this? Are you watching, are you listening, are you waiting ? Or are you still just a shade too busy elsewhere ?

No answer. We scarcely expected it, of course, for Fate can be remarkably mum. Like Mr. Everard, as he picks up that pencil again; and as we, who have really had quite enough of his dull company by now, are drawn towards yet another flat on the same floor.

CHAPTER IV

THERE ARE VOICES HERE AGAIN, AS WELL AS LIGHTS AND A LOUD-SPEAKER. But you can't call No. 15 tidy. This is the flat at the end of one of the short, windowless corridors that branch off from the landing; and in the original design, one is led to suppose, a bulb was intended to burn just outside it by day and night. If it didn't—and it doesn't at present, because it perished some time ago, and has thus become a token of economy—no one could see the number on the door, or the bell-push, or the orifice for letters, or even the lock. However, not only have people grown used to such difficulties—though the wood round the lock has certainly been scratched a good deal where latchkeys have made bad shots—but we ourselves, of course, can enter as easily, and as silently and invisibly, as we have already entered elsewhere.

This is another two-roomed flat, with the same qualifications as before. The bedroom, which is dark at the moment, belongs to the actual sub-tenant, who is a girl or young woman named Bryony Bretton, though customarily addressed as Bugs. The name of the official tenant, who has no intention of returning from the Lake District while present conditions prevail, is also Miss Bretton; customarily addressed in this case as Aunt Babs. While the name of the younger Miss Bretton's friend, or companion, or lodger, who is slightly younger again, and sleeps on a divan (as it is called) in a corner of the sitting-room, appears on her Identity Card and other such documents as Jemima Marsham. But in this case, for some reason that will no doubt emerge, she is customarily addressed as Echo.

Echo, of course, was the name of a nymph; and as she is slim and fair, and still under twenty-three, the word may seem apt enough. No nymph, on the other hand, so far as we are aware, was ever called Bugs. It is a name, moreover, which to the ear, and even to the eye, is distinctly lacking in both glamour and charm. Yet anyone seeing these creatures together would almost certainly look at Miss Bretton first.

We do it ourselves. We can't help it. It may be that it won't last, of course—for it is with this sort of thought that we are caddish enough to attempt to defend ourselves—but Bugs (if we, too, may allude to her thus) is certainly very good-looking. She may know it. We somehow feel that she does. And it may be, again, for some cause that we can't quite expound, that we should prefer her to be less sure of the fact. But one can't get away from it. She isn't only good-looking, but she sparkles with something, even when she is alone with her friend. Vitality; self-assurance, or a close imitation; a certain bossiness, perhaps—but it can't, at first sight, be resisted. Echo looks pale rather than fair for a moment, and thin rather than slim. It is true that one of her eyebrows attracted our very honourable attention for an instant, for it was really rather an interesting effect just now when she lifted it without a trace of a wrinkle on her forehead. But one can't go on looking at her with Bugs in the room. Echo, in such circumstances, would seem to be an echo indeed.

We can listen, though; which is more than these tenants are consciously doing to the little scarlet, American radio-set that splutters and crackles— for it is long past its prime—on a shelf by the side of the fireplace. The tenants, we should be quite right in supposing, employ it as a kind of permanent background when they are both at home after their day's work; and that is the main function that it is performing now.

There is also a small sofa in the room; but neither tenant is sitting on it, nor on any of the absent Miss Bretton's chairs, nor even on the divan in the corner. They have preferred, it would seem, on this cold evening with a cold radiator under the window, to sit on cushions in front of their electric fire, with the lower part of the sofa as a support for their backs. From conscience or economy they have only turned on one bar; but as this flat is to a certain extent their castle, of course they can sit on the floor if they choose.

One of them—and again it is naturally Bugs whom we take first—having spent some nine hours today in a branch of the Ministry of Redirection, has now draped a face-towel across her lap and is carefully painting her nails. That, of course, accounts for the smell of pear-drops, or whatever the correct chemical name, which at the moment has almost taken our breath away. We are unable to decide, however, whether Bugs is adorning herself like this so as to fascinate men, so as to compete with other women, or merely in order to strengthen her own morale. Perhaps she doesn't even know herself; for no man—and she knows quite a lot—has yet said: "What beautiful blood-red nails you've got," few women have alluded to them beyond occasionally asking her what that colour is called, while in the matter of morale we can as yet detect no sign of any shortcoming. She's full of it, we should say, and of all that goes with it, and as often as not would really be better for something in the nature of a sedative.

Nevertheless, she is making a very good job of this particular if possibly pointless task; and we may observe, also, that, as with the ancient Chinese, the nails in question are kept remarkably long. In ancient China, or so we understand, this was meant to show that the owner was absolved from manual work. Miss Bretton, however, hasn't only spent nine hours—apart from the luncheon interval—toiling in the service of the State, but helped to cook the breakfast here, and the dinner or supper as well. If she didn't do quite as much as her friend Miss Marsham, then Miss Marsham—whose own nails, we note, are much more normal—has not been heard to complain. And if neither young woman has washed up the dishes or so far done any housework today, then this is partly because of the State again—for Echo has spent just as many hours in another branch of the same Ministry—and partly because a rather rough-and-ready character called Mrs. Garrison (also from The Dwellings) comes in at about eleven o'clock each morning, except Sunday, to deal with as many of these duties as she sees fit.

Any questions? Of course. Is it true, you ask, that young women of this age are paid so much for whatever they do that they can afford to share a flat in Huddleston House and to have a charwoman, if only for a couple of hours, to keep it in order, too?

Indeed not. The whole of their joint salaries, allowing for deductions, would barely cover the rent. But they have parents, though again not in London. These parents, like almost everyone else in their class, are now necessarily living on their capital. But this doesn't imply that they are mean. On the contrary, it seems to make them more generous, or reckless, or anxious to spend whatever is left before the State takes it away. In fact, then, they are subsidising their children—who are also heavily taxed; but whether this is reasonable and justifiable or not is for none of them here nor there. It is what is happening. History is on skids now, and the future must look after itself. One does what one can, say the parents. One takes what one can get, say the children, or these children, who were certainly never brought up or prepared for the life they are leading now.

They are leading it, though. They can't and don't try to get away from it. They are tired, in spite of Mrs. Garrison; they're nervy, like everyone else in the block and elsewhere; one of them rather bullies the other, whether she means to or not, while the other seems curiously content with this arrangement, and returns, so it appears, admiration instead. She has even allowed her name to be changed, for it was Bugs who first called her Echo, when they were both at school. She doesn't mind—though she is so sensitive that her eyes often swim at thoughts she could hardly describe. For Bugs, so she believes, is wonderful. She would do almost anything in the world for Bugs. And indeed, on this so far quiet and peaceful evening, the filmy garment which she is attempting to repair is not her own, but her friend's.

Bugs has a habit of saying: "I say, you might just do this;" or: "Be an angel, Echo, and do that." Then Echo, who never argues, does it. A bit dreamily, sometimes, and not always so very efficiently—whereas Bugs, if she chooses, can slap-dash her way through practically any job. If two young women, however, find themselves sharing a flat, they can't both take the lead. Again, there can be no question as to which is endowed with the greater proportion of foot-pounds. Technically, moreover, though each pays her whack, Miss Bretton remains the lessee.

"I say, Echo."

" 'M ?"

"Have you done the coffee ?"

"Oh, bother! No."

If the coffee is made overnight, and left in a saucepan, this doesn't only save time in the morning, but even adds—or so some people say—to the flavour.

"I'm awfully sorry," Miss Marsham goes on. "I'll do it now."

"No, finish that other thing first, darling. I'll remind you. By the way . . ."

" 'M ?" Miss Marsham has subsided, and is sewing again.

"Do you want a bath tonight ?" asks her friend.

"Well, I would *rather* like one. But not if *you* would."

She doesn't add, and perhaps there is no need to add, that, owing to a further peculiarity of the plumbing, not to mention the fuel and the boiler and the State, it is extremely unlikely that a second bath will be anything but tepid before tomorrow morning. And if it comes to that, Miss Marsham looks perfectly clean.

"All right," she says, agreeably. "That'll remind me." She means, of course, that her colleague's bath will remind her about the coffee. "I'll do the hot bottles, too," she adds; "though I think mine's just going to burst. It's got an awful blister."

"Well, you won't get another," says Bugs, with some truth. "There!" She looks at her left hand, which she has just finished, with considerable satisfaction. "Could you make some cocoa, too ?"

"No milk," said Echo, with a faint air of apology. "I'm awfully sorry."

"What! But we didn't finish it this morning."

"Well, I looked just now. There's only an empty bottle in the sink."

"Smashums!" says Miss Bretton, in a venomous tone. It is quite clear, however, that she hasn't suddenly begun playing Up Jenkins, and that she couldn't while her nails are in this state. Smashums is what she calls Mrs. Garrison behind her back—as does Echo, but it was Bugs who thought of it—and for a very good reason, too. "It's too bad!" she exclaims. "Just because I once said she could take that bottle that was a bit off. She's *always* doing it now. I shall *murder* that woman one day."

Not yet, though. Echo looks paler than ever at the threat—or is that just our imagination, because Bugs is looking pinker ? But even Bugs daren't really face Mrs. Garrison, or not on a matter like this. And whether

Echo knows this or not—and perhaps she does—some practice has enabled her to produce the right soothing mixture.

"How," she inquires, sewing steadily still, "was Mr. Haggerston-Hawksworth today ?"

"The same as usual," says Bugs ; but she bridles—just a little—too. "He blew in when I was alone after lunch, and wanted to know if I was cold. Well, of course I was ; but I was busy, too. So I just turned him out."

"Did you ? Oh, Bugs—how ?"

"I gave him a look," says Miss Bretton. She gives it again now, as a kind of illustration. One would call it provocative rather than alarming. It would seem to demand some such answer as "Soho, my proud beauty," though as Mr. Haggerston-Hawksworth bears a certain resemblance to Mr. Everard, this is the last thing that one can imagine him saying to a junior member of his staff. It is more likely, in fact, for whatever reason he returned to his own desk, that he received no such look at all. Yet Bugs, thanks to Echo, has regained her poise ; and as there is also an implication—perhaps not wholly unfounded—that Mr. Haggerston-Hawksworth may be ranked as an admirer, too, she is able to pass, without further delay, to the favourite topic of all.

This is herself, of course, as perhaps you have gathered. Or herself as a siren—though not the kind that wails—and as a collector and breaker of hearts. There may be something in it, for she is decorative enough, whether proud or not ; and war, as has been noted, does little or nothing to turn young men into monks. Should she boast, though ? One wonders. Is it really necessary to have quite so many photographs of Lieutenants, and Sub-Lieutenants, and Flying Officers—interspersed among cards from the smaller night-clubs—in this sitting-room which is also, by the way, someone else's bedroom ?

She didn't go out and buy them, of course. They have all been given to her, and they are nearly all most affectionately inscribed. With Christian names, naturally, for that is all that anyone has now, and it is many a long year since the last young man said : "Miss Dalrymple—may I call you Dahlia ?" The truth is, in fact, that she is a bit shaky over some of their surnames ; but she would call these phantoms her friends—alas, some of them are now phantoms indeed—and of course she has been out with all of them.

"Going out" means a night consisting partly of Cimmerian darkness, partly, quite often, of considerable danger, partly of a plush *banquette* or a scrap of parquet in a cellar, partly of shouting for taxis, and partly of saying "What do you take me for ?" inside them. It is also apt to make one rather sleepy at the Ministry of Redirection. But the squire always pays, Miss Bretton knows well enough how to protect herself, and so far there have always been more squires. Leading to what ? Only to the same sort of night again, of course, with Guy, or Alister, or Chips (if you call that a

Christian name), or Hugo. Echo takes their telephone-messages. Echo
gets up at four, or five, or even six in the morning, when Bugs has again
lost her latchkey. She doesn't much care for such nights herself, though
occasionally she is also involved. But she thinks, and is right in a way,
that it must be wonderful to have Bugs's spirits. Only she can't attain them.
She would rather be quiet, and look on, and dream, and wait for she doesn't
quite know what. The young gentlemen sense this, and though a few of
them have noted that lifted eyebrow and smooth forehead with traces of
passing interest, too, on the whole they prefer high spirits and a girl
who laughs. For *they* can't dream or wait. Their leave's up on Tuesday,
and anything may happen before they get any more. Taxi!

". . . at Wolverhampton this afternoon," says the voice of William
Whippenstall, combined with some splutters and crackles, "Mr. Lionel
Haycock . . ."

At this point Miss Bretton suddenly interrupts not only the announcer
but some story of her own about Alister as well.

"I say, Echo!"

" 'M ?"

"The laundry, darling. Did you ?"

"Yes, I rushed in this morning—" yet somehow one can't see Echo
rushing—"and they said it would be Saturday now."

"Damn! Hell! What a khurse!"

(That means "curse," of course; but "khurse" is much nearer the sound.)

"I'm awfully sorry," says Echo, almost as though it was indeed her own
fault.

"Oh, well." Bugs can take it. "If you finish that thing tonight, I can
wear it tomorrow. Saturday, though. Help! What was I saying?"

"About Alister knocking that American down ?"

"Oh, yes. Well, you see . . ."

The somewhat self-centred saga goes on. In the interest of Allied
Unity you may also be glad to learn that this part of it is rather exaggerated.
What Alister actually did was to say afterwards that for two pins he *would*
have knocked the American down; and if you had seen the size of the
American, you might have thought this rather a frantic boast. But the
other version at least puts Bugs (who is supposed to have been insulted) in a
more romantic light. And if her friend doesn't quite or altogether believe it,
she would much rather have things that way. For she is loyal, as well as
patient and self-effacing. Or again, perhaps, we have all got to cling to
something, when the whole world is on skids.

In any case, neither young woman hears anything—or at the best they
only hear it half-consciously—about Mr. Haycock on the subject of complacency. In any case, also, they have both heard it before. Nor are
they complacent, though on the whole they are far better off on their parents'

capital than if they were in a hostel or a Nissen hut. But one of them must now secretly toil—though it all seemed fun once—at the part she has chosen to play; while the other, so used by now to her minor role, must still lift that eyebrow at times, as though seeking the answer to some teasing and insoluble puzzle. Or even the puzzle eludes her, though she knows all the time that it's there. For she is one of those—far more than Bugs—who has been in a kind of nightmare since it all began. "It" being the war, of course, which, whether it is mentioned or not, can never be far from her thoughts.

All right, then—though it is anything but all right. Let's leave them now. Down to the second floor.

There are five flats here, so that again some of them are a little larger than those on the floor above. No. 10 is in darkness, for the tenant is out. In No. 11 we can certainly see Mr. and Mrs. Champion, who are also listening to the news-bulletin. But as there is no expression on either of their faces, as they are both completely silent, and as there is nothing to suggest that they are ever going to move or speak, we just look, and leave them. If the wailing starts, we know what they'll do—and there, on a third armchair, is the cushion that Mr. Champion will take down into the Shelter, so as to soften the seat for his wife. But there is no wailing yet. There seems nothing to keep us. We shake off a slight if unworthy sense of oppression, and flit into the flat next door.

No. 12. There is a light here; but as we glance again, we see that there shouldn't be. Someone is helping the Enemy, though perhaps not very much. But they have forgotten or omitted to turn off the switch in the little lobby, though it is clear, from all the open doors, that no one is now at home. There are two bedrooms; one of moderate size, and the other distinctly minute. The usual bathroom. The customary kitchenette. But quite a good sitting-room, for once—gained, we should say, at the expense of the smaller bedroom—which appears to be rather abnormally full of books. As one can't buy shelves nowadays, we are not surprised that many of them are on the chairs and the floor. But there are certainly a lot of them. Do we scent literature, and if so does this tempt us to pause? No; for we are in search of tenants tonight, not of signs from which to reconstruct them.

So we leave No. 12, dart through No. 13—which is let, and sub-let, and even re-sub-let, but at the moment is empty, too—and direct our gaze into No. 14, where we find Mrs. Musselberg.

This name, for some reason, hardly suggests a blonde. Yet Mrs. Musselberg *is* blonde. Or her hair is, though not always near the roots. Her figure, again, is technically passable for a woman of her age—for as she has turned all the lights on, we can't help seeing that she is at least on the wrong side of thirty. Yet somehow, even though she is seated just at present, it suggests something rather powerful in the way of belting. It looks as if it might pop if you stuck a pin into it—though of course we shouldn't dream of doing that. We don't find her hands very attractive, either, in spite of their rings; while it can't be denied that her insteps bulge a good deal from her high-heeled shoes. She is wearing the best silk stockings, though, that we have seen as yet. Her eyes, by the way, are brown, and so is her dress, which doesn't look cheap, either. Her lips are painted, though there is nothing strange in that. But she keeps tucking them in, or sometimes her tongue flickers round them, rather as though she were still trying to decide whether she likes the taste of the paint.

This can't be the real reason. In fact, it is probably just a habit by now, however it first arose. Another habit, we should say, is to keep on patting the back of her hair, which she has done three times already since we first caught sight of her here. A little restless, then, perhaps; or perhaps a little self-conscious. Very likely; yet somehow—and as she can't see us, there is nothing rude about this—we don't want to look at Mrs. Musselberg for very long. Quite frankly, she's not our type.

Nor, by Gum, is this room, though everything in it seems new. That's rather a mystery, when hardly anything new is obtainable now. It strikes the eye. We suddenly realise how shabby all those other rooms were, though we took this for granted at the time. It must be admitted, also, however, that everything is in the worst possible taste. The colour-scheme— for it is definitely a room with this pre-war attribute—is buff, and orange, and pale-blue. It makes us blink. We don't, though this may be fastidious, much care for the irregular geometric design on the carpet. We don't like the zebroid stripes on the curtains, despite the depth of the pelmets. We can't bear the lamp-shades. We have never much cared for coloured prints a very long way after Gainsborough or someone like that. There are too many cushions, we should say, and they have too many frills on them. There are too many articles that can only, and disparagingly, be described as ornaments. The disposition of the furniture—which is mostly of satinwood or some close imitation—is to our mind maddeningly, and even provocatively, asymmetrical; nothing, by any chance, being at right angles to anything else. This can't be an accident. Surely it must imply some twist in Mrs. Musselberg's mind.

We glance at her again. We glance away. Pouf! it's hot in here; for both bars are burning in an enormous electric fire, which is made to look even hotter by some glowing, artificial coals. Mrs. Musselberg, one may gather, has her own views on how to interpret the almost piteous appeals of the Ministry of Fuel and Power.

That Gothic radio-set, for instance, which is also blazing away, and the dials of which are almost as bright as the wall-brackets, must be getting through a power of watts. It isn't the only musical instrument, though. There is a baby-grand—placed cock-eyed, of course, in the corner, and supporting not only more ornaments but a vast vase of fainting flowers. Involuntarily, we find ourselves thinking of Mrs. Musselberg's hands. Is it possible that she plays on those keys ?

It isn't. She doesn't. She can't. But she is proud of her piano—which is also now the only one in the block. Nor is it merely a symbol; for not only do her visitors perform on it from time to time, but her maid—for, believe it or not, she has a maid as well—quite frequently strums on it in the most frightful manner when Mrs. Musselberg is at the pictures or out shopping. Not that Mrs. M. goes forth with a string bag. Oh, dear, no. The maid does all that, and anything else arrives by the pool delivery. It is true that the maid—who doesn't actually sleep on the premises—has a glass eye and slight curvature of the spine, and if she hadn't could hardly be holding her present post. Yet such is the magic of the name Musselberg that even Maggie, as this maid is known, is seldom disappointed by any tradesman, and hardly ever wastes her time in a queue.

If there should be any difficulty in her marketing, she reports to Mrs. Musselberg, who reports to her husband, who then steps round, at the next opportunity, and the difficulty is at once removed. We don't know what he says, or how he does it, for it is a fact that the tradesmen don't like him; even if at the moment they don't much like anyone else. Perhaps it's a knack, then. Or a gift. But it works. And it, or something like it, has already brought Mr. Musselberg from somewhere on the wrong side of Aldgate, *via* Perivale—that was quite a leap—to Huddleston House; while even this, so his ardent spirit tells him, is but a step towards higher things. Yes, he's certainly quite all there.

Not here, though. Or not this evening. This evening Mr. Musselberg is in Manchester—though he will be telephoning before long, without much doubt, for he is devoted to Mrs. Musselberg, though he would like to have some little Musselbergs too. This, however, has so far been his only disappointment; and there is much on the credit side. At thirty-five, for instance, which is his present age, he is a welcome figure in a number of Ministries—or at least he is seldom kept waiting—he is a director of several companies (albeit with a total paid-up capital of about five hundred pounds), he has other irons in the fire as well, and enjoys the very best of health.

He has no fear, moreover, of the Ministry of Labour and National Service, for it has been established that he is quite indispensable to the war-effort where he is. In Manchester, that is to say, tonight. In London, perhaps, tomorrow. And then in Liverpool, Cardiff, Glasgow—oh, all over the place, and every one of his journeys is necessary. Who says so ? He does. And when has Mr. Musselberg been wrong ?

Oftener than not, when he goes away, Mrs. Musselberg has someone in for company. A female relative—again oftener than not—of whom there appears to be an almost inexhaustible supply. To them she boasts of her husband's importance, and as they are all on lower rungs of the ladder they are much impressed. Or at least they affect to be, for this, of course, is how they pay for their supper—which as a rule, indeed, is well worth payment. It is one of them, a flushed-looking cousin called Connie, who strikes those semi-classical fireworks—she is very strong on Hungarian Rhapsodies— from the baby grand, while the ornaments jingle and even the vase jumps up and down. She can also be heard quite clearly in a number of other flats, where her strains are found anything but soothing, and have occasionally led to rather unneighbourly bumps on floors and walls.

"Go on, dear," says Mrs. Musselberg, when this happens. "I have a piano. You play it. More rudeness, and Mr. Musselberg shall take it up. We pay the rent same as them, don't we ? Go on, Connie, with your piece."

If this happened every evening, there might be more than bumps and threatened retaliation, and poor Mr. Todman might find himself dragged into another conflict between tenants—with immediate effect on the hue of his bat-like ears. Fortunately, however, these musical sessions are much more infrequent than that. Passions die down in the quieter intervals, even though there is a kind of cumulative irritation in the other flats ; and no one has so far indulged in a written complaint. If they do, Mr. Musselberg will deal with it, and we have a strong idea that it is he who will come out on top. For he is a stubborn adversary, and though he has never been articled or called to the bar, he has learnt a good deal about the law.

On these longer and darker nights, however, that have come with the approach of winter, even female relatives with hearty appetites need more persuasion to leave their own homes. At the moment, therefore, Mrs. Musselberg is alone. She doesn't much mind. She has had a good dinner. She has had a cocktail or two, and even—more magic here—a glass of authentic port. Presently Jake, as she affectionately calls Mr. Musselberg, will be speaking to her from Manchester, and almost certainly he will hint at some gift—another ring, perhaps, or an ornament, or it might be more food or drink—that he will be bringing her back to-morrow. Meanwhile, there is a lot of light here, a lot of heat, and a lot of noise. She likes that. She hears Mr. Lionel Haycock's message to the people of Wolverhampton, and she quite agrees with it, though she, too, in some mysterious manner, seems immune from all personal effort. Jake has fixed it. Jake can fix anything. But if people start slacking, because they think it's all over, that *would* be a nice state of affairs.

She shakes her head. Her tongue flickers again. And some impulse causes her to pat the back of her hair. Thus we leave her—without much regret, perhaps—and descend to the first floor.

Here's Mr. L. Wilson Barker, in No. 5. Mr. Barker is also a company-director, and a managing director, too ; but—unlike Mr. Musselberg—is concerned with only one firm. Once it made mangles and mowing-machines, in a southern suburb and in rather a small way. Now, of course, it is engaged on war-production; not as profitably as might be, owing to this infernal E.P.D., but on a very different scale from the distant days of the slump. In fact, though still one firm, it now controls a secondary plant in a north-western suburb as well. Mr. Barker, therefore, is also indispensable—though if it comes to that he is a year or two older than Mr. Musselberg—and in addition to this has petrol to run a car. The nuisance is, of course—or one of the nuisances is—that all the nearest garages have now gone over to war-production, too; so that Mr. Barker must either walk the best part of a mile to reach his somewhat rusty and battered vehicle, or must risk leaving it in a kind of alley by the side of Bessingham House. Mr. Todman, on behalf of the insolvent Syndicate, rather objects to this latter arrangement, since he says, with some truth, that it obstructs the Borough Council dustmen. So far, however, Mr. Barker has adopted his hectoring manner, and has continued to use the alley whenever he feels like it. "How else," he has asked, "do you expect me to get to my work?"

So far, also, Mr. Todman has been diplomatic—which, after all, is partly what he is paid for—and has kept his own thoughts to himself. To-night, for instance, that car is certainly in the alley again, which is a source of satisfaction to Mr. Barker. Yet when we watch him alone, as we do just now, there is not much triumph on his face.

He is tired, of course, like all the rest, but that isn't the main trouble. The main trouble is, and always has been, that Mr. Barker's hectoring manner is nearly all, as you might say, façade. Unlike Mr. Musselberg, once more, he suspects that he should really be doing something else; and of course he could, if he chose. If he never went near either of the works again, they would soon get over the loss; and Mr. Barker—as an anti-aircraft gunner, perhaps—might find peace in his complex soul. But then he can't face this. At the beginning of the war, with almost unconscious foresight in those days, he put up a bluff that he couldn't be spared. It was accepted, and now he just daren't turn round. He would look a fool, he thinks, if he did. People would point at him, and ask why he hadn't gone before. This doesn't mean that he isn't fully convinced that a lot of them are pointing at him now. But this is what it has come to, and the hectoring manner, which was once merely a mask for self-mistrust, has now passed to something much more resembling the offensive. Strike first, is its motto and Mr. Barker's. He does. He can't help it. He's a terror at those works in the two suburbs; though terror of some sort is almost certainly needed to keep their output up.

That isn't all, though. Why, you may be wondering, if Mr. Barker has so little idea of sparing either himself or others, does he live so far from his jobs, and not even on the direct line between them? We can tell you. Once he lived within half a mile of the original works, in a gabled, neo-Georgian

Tudor house (called *Charlcote*), in a road of such houses, each with its half-acre of garden; and Mrs. Barker (Doris) had a couple of maids, and shared in driving the car—which was quite new then, and had its own, asbestos garage; while Miss Barker (Maureen) had a little bicycle, on which she went tearing along the pavements—to the great danger of pedestrians, but even they would rather not see her run over elsewhere—to quite a superior day-school. An Englishman's home, as you might say. Ugly, and not too well-built. Fitted with gimcrackery and fumed oak. Its overhead just a little more than Mr. Barker was justified in spending. Yet he wasn't unhappy or unduly anxious. While the hectoring manner, in those days, scarcely disguised a good deal of benevolence too.

At the beginning of the war his wife and daughter went off to his mother-in-law's house in Worthing. Both maids left, and Mr. Barker conducted rather an uncomfortable and lonely existence with the help of a hag. Sometimes he went down to Worthing for week-ends—which was as safe then as going to Ireland—but he was too busy to go often, owing to the change-over at the factory, and anyhow he had to sleep on a very hard folding bed. So he kept begging Mrs. Barker to come back, which she did now and then, though never for more than a nervous night or two, and always accompanied by a gas-mask.

On the other hand, there were no air-raids. And rumour had it—though Heaven knows why—that our defences were now so immensely strong that the risk was as good as removed. The Government, it was said, was determined at all costs to protect London, and there were rings of guns all round it which nothing could pass. There were also mysterious contraptions —this rumour was probably based on radiolocation—which would destroy the electrical equipment of all enemy aircraft. While in those days it was also quite widely believed that the barrage-balloons were as good as a defence in themselves.

Nevertheless, Mrs. Barker was still nervous, and became more so, in the following summer, when gun-fire from across the Channel was audible even in Worthing. Her mother, who was rather deaf, couldn't hear this, but Mrs. Barker jumped and blinked whenever the windows rattled, and suddenly decided that it would be safer to return to her home. She didn't exactly desert her mother, because her mother refused to leave. But she was back now, and Mr. Barker was delighted to have her back. The hag gave notice, of course, but a substitute was found. Maureen was delighted to go bicycling along the pavements again, and not even to school now, for there was no longer any school to attend. It was a wonderful summer, as you remember, and as we have said before. But for the presence of Maureen —and he was curiously fond of her—Mr. Barker almost felt that the clock had been put back; and that with his wife doing the cooking once more, this was again the beginning of their married life.

He told her repeatedly about the guns, and the contraptions, and the power of the balloons, and teased her a little about her nervousness, which was perhaps a mistake. The truth is that he was getting a bit nervous himself—though not about bombs yet—for no one could pretend that the war was going too well. But it was certainly a complete surprise to him when—slightly anticipating the sirens—a bomb fell, one late afternoon, about three roads away, and entirely demolished a fortunately unoccupied house.

He was decidedly disturbed. He was coming home in his car at the time, and for a moment he almost imitated his daughter by steering it on to the pavement. But he was still more disturbed when he did get home to find his wife in a state of hysterical frenzy, to be told that he wanted to kill her and Maureen, and that the whole thing was his fault.

Maureen, of course, was howling, too; being distinctly imitative herself. The tempest continued through most of the night—though there were no more sirens or bombs—and by the following evening Mr. Barker was again alone. Where do you think Mrs. Barker and Maureen had gone to this time? Rhyl, in North Wales, where the Barkers had spent their honeymoon. It came out afterwards that Mrs. Barker had been in correspondence with some lodgings there for some time; they were ready for her, for she had even paid a deposit; and there she and the child remained.

Naturally, Mr. Barker must continue to support her, and he visited her whenever he could. He didn't think her a coward, though, and still less did he call her one. She was a woman to whom he had been married for ten years, and he had learnt in that time that women aren't governed by reason. Or at any rate not by what men call reason. In this case, of course, she had been governed by an instinct for self-preservation, if also by maternal solicitude, which were stronger than anything else. Can one blame her for them? Isn't the first instinct implanted in us all, and isn't the second supposed to be a virtue? Had Mrs. Barker ever been trained as a target for aircraft, or had the State even pretended to consult her as it drifted, unprepared, towards war?

Mr. Barker was both loyal and generous, though it was about now that his hectoring manner became much more marked. It was a shock, also—though again he said nothing—to find, on his first visit to Rhyl, that his wife was regarded as something of a heroine there, and to hear her telling another lodger that she had been "bombed out." But she was his wife. She was taking care of Maureen. And he had been rather scared himself.

The truth is, in fact, that after a fortnight or so of augmented alarms in his deserted house, and still under the illusion that the Government was capable of defending London itself, Mr. Barker had made a quick deal with a business acquaintance of less sanguine temperament, had emptied *Charlcote* and stored its contents, and had stepped into this hideously-furnished first-floor flat at Huddleston House. Shortly afterwards he would have given a good deal to step out again; but he hadn't. Partly, perhaps, because one place—or one place in reach of his work—seemed as bad as another; and partly, it may be, for the same psychological reasons which had made him stick to his job. One must be consistent. One mustn't chop and change, even, so it would appear, during a world war. If one took a flat on grounds that no longer existed, this didn't mean that one could admit to being fallible, or could risk being quoted as a man who changed his mind.

This very British outlook—which was also to be found in much higher circles—kept Mr. Barker where he was through the first great air assaults, which he disliked quite as much as anyone else. Towards the end of them his home in the southern suburb, on which he was still paying interest to a Building Society, lost most of the tiles on its roof and nearly all the glass in its windows; so that there seemed less reason than ever why he should return. There was also less reason than ever why his wife or child should return. In fact, they had moved into a little furnished bungalow, near their lodgings, for which he was also paying. They seemed to be fixtures there; and Mr. Barker, so far as this could be said of anyone, had become a fixture at Huddleston House.

He still corresponded with Mrs. Barker. He still occasionally went to see her. She appeared to have made a number of friends up there—well, that was all right, for she had always liked company—yet her husband rather wished at times that Maureen didn't address them, or some of them, as "Uncle." He didn't say so, however. He was generally too much occupied in resisting a conception of Mrs. Barker's that he was having a high old time in London, and that it was he rather than she who was responsible for their present separation. For some reason even the hectoring manner wilted a bit, when faced with a charge like this.

For what reason? Well, at first because he was fond of her, and didn't want to waste time in quarrelling with her, and because of the general state of his conscience about something else. But then, when he tried to salve it by becoming a Home Guard, Mrs. Barker was now openly contemptuous, and laughed at him with the support of a particular Uncle who was a real soldier, though he never seemed to leave Rhyl. Mr. Barker was slow to wrath, even when Maureen was encouraged to join in the mockery, too. The very last thing that he intended was to avenge himself, especially as he would still have trusted his wife with a far more attractive rival than Captain Tubbs. But one wasn't meant to live entirely alone. He was in what you might call a slight mess now with his secretary, who was engaged to a conscript in Iceland; or he would be, at any moment, if he didn't take jolly good care.

He was terrified. He was drawn on. He made resolutions. He broke them. So far he had only patted her shoulder twice—well, perhaps three times—and if he called her Ethel when they were alone together, why on earth shouldn't he ? Yet even this constituted a mess for Mr. Barker, who had always despised men who went on like that, and must now—once more —despise himself. Thank God, he thought, he'd had to put her off, that time he'd been taking her to the pictures. But he knew that, sooner or later, he was going to do it. And then . . .

Poor fellow. Not really lovable, you know. He can't be, with that hectoring manner ; and he's not a very good shape ; and sometimes, in these days—though this isn't so easy—he drinks just a little too much. But he is a man with a variety of troubles, every one of which, as it seems to him, has come since the outbreak of war.

" . . . He warned his audience," says the five-valve superhet which Mr. Barker took over from his business acquaintance—who might have returned by now, only that he has been snapped up by the Army— "that there must be no complacency. . . ."

"Thanks," says Mr. Barker, in a distinctly mordant tone. We are afraid he doesn't seem the least grateful for the fact that his firm is busier now than it has ever been since he joined it. Perhaps we had better leave him, then—for it's never much help to count somebody else's blessings— and drop in, with another brief switch back in time, on Mrs. Wardrop.

That's No. 7, and the only other first-floor flat, at the moment, with any sign of life. We shan't be here long, though, for having told you already that Mrs. Wardrop has a habit of tipping the porters, we haven't much more to add. She is about sixty. She has been a widow for about fifteen years, and subsists—as widows in what was once known as her class are supposed to subsist—on provision made for her by her late husband.

Unfortunately, however, and though he made quite a nice little pile in the City, he failed to provide for the present scale of income-tax or for the recurrence of world-wide war. So Mrs. Wardrop had to clear out of a much larger and smarter flat in Muncaster Mansions, and having then withdrawn for a while from the London scene, returned, as things quietened down, to Huddleston House. This means, of course—as in the case of Mrs. Margetson—that she has too much furniture and that much of it is too big. It also means that she has no cook or house-parlourmaid now, but relies on yet another Daily Help named Mrs. Trudgeon.

But she isn't broke ; though she will be if she and conditions go on like this for long enough, since of course Mrs. Wardrop is now living on her capital, too. But she doesn't give this impression. No one suspects it, as she still trails certain clouds of glory from the flat in Muncaster Mansions. And because it was her husband's habit, and therefore, subsequently, her own habit, to keep tipping the porters there, she still carried on with this tradition, and is none the less popular for that. She gets little or nothing in return, apart from some cap-touching which has been pretty well abandoned in the case of most other tenants; and it may even be said that the recipients of those shillings and florins regard her as slightly touched, too. But they don't refuse them. They spring about with an air of unaccustomed activity, when they see her coming; and if again they wink as she goes on her way, they quite like the old girl, and only wish there were more of her sort.

Thus does Mrs. Wardrop pay tribute to the memory of a somewhat self-indulgent husband who gave her a good deal of trouble while he was alive. But she likes to do it. She is buying back a bit of the past, in a way, which—whether we enjoyed it at the time or not—is what we should all like to do. The money is being wasted in a sense; but in another it isn't. For each time that it passes into a momentarily subservient hand, Mrs. Wardrop again breathes the air of Muncaster Mansions. And there, she has come to believe, she was always happy. What possible harm can there be in an illusion like that?

At the same time, although living on her capital, and at first sight, perhaps, a mere idle mouth in our fortress island, Mrs. Wardrop is no mere dreamer or onlooker at this extreme crisis in its fate. For not only does she still take in *The Times*, which in itself is almost enough to dismiss such a notion, but it is Mrs. Wardrop who goes round for the Red Cross, and the Savings Campaign, and for the Prisoners of War as well. She knocks and rings; if anyone answers, she shows her little book and says her little piece; and because she has still not lost her old air of grandeur, or because, at her age, a slight awkwardness and shyness produce much the same effect, it is seldom, indeed, that she is refused. It is seldom, either, at the end of each month, that her accounts aren't a little bit mixed. But she is scrupulously honest. She dips into her capital again so as to get them straight. And though she knows no more about money now than she did in the days when poor James used to get so cross with her sometimes, as she goes on her rounds she isn't only doing what has apparently got to be done, but is even as good as convinced that she alone could do it.

To-night, however, she isn't collecting, and she isn't even trying to check the receipts. She is tired. She has turned on the wireless, for she doesn't rely exclusively on *The Times ;* she has put a shawl round her shoulders, because of the intense cold; and she has also placed her feet—which have been aching, as a result of queues—on another and smaller chair. Her head tilts back, as Big Ben prepares to boom. Her eyes are closed. Her mouth is slightly ajar. You couldn't believe now that she was a pretty, gay little thing once, in the days when her husband came wooing her, forty years back. It is almost impossible to picture her with a child in her arms, though another and still more secret part of her never forgets what were truly the six-and-a-half happiest months in her life. Ought we to be gazing like this?

It makes no odds. For one thing, we are still invisible. And for another, as William Whippenstall rounds out his periods about Russia—though in vain, through that tell-tale microphone, does he affect to know where any of the places are—and at least a couple of minutes before he gets on to Mr. Lionel Haycock and his encouraging though cautionary speech, we are fain and indeed compelled to observe that Mrs. Wardrop is now whistling, very gently and from some part of the thorax, herself. She will be colder still when she wakes up, and has to go to bed. But she is asleep now; poor old girl.

CHAPTER V

THE GROUND FLOOR AT HUDDLESTON HOUSE, AS MAY HAVE BEEN HINTED before, was originally designed—whether consciously or subconsciously—as a species of man-trap. The idea, if there was one, would appear to have been that if the entrance-hall was showy enough—if something that looked like marble, for instance, was used for the pilasters, if something resembling mahogany was employed for the panels between them, if the carpet was moderately thick, or at least had thick felt underneath it, if the lights burnt behind something in the nature of alabaster, if there were extra curly-wiggles round the grille of the lift, and if the grille itself, in this case, was painted to look like bronze, then anyone who saw all this would entirely overlook the very economical construction of the flats themselves.

We shouldn't say, either, that this thought—if it actually occurred to anyone at the time—hadn't something to recommend it. For first impressions are notoriously important; and in those days, when competition was much more keen, it was everything to overwhelm a prospective tenant, if possible, at the first glance. Nothing, after all, could change the size of the rooms. Let the hall, then, appear to promise far more than the rest of the block could hope to perform. Besides, as a still further justification, the hall would be used by everyone—or at least they would have to pass through it—whereas the separate flats were a purely private affair.

This evening, however, we shan't linger here. Partly because we have seen it already; partly because, with its present faint air of shabbiness, its dim lighting, and those thumb-marked shutters that have now been affixed to the glass-panelled swing-doors, it is scarcely calculated to uplift the soul; and partly because the only reason why it has been mentioned at all, at this juncture, is to account for the fact that on the street-level here—or, to be perfectly accurate, at a height of two steps above it—this generosity in the matter of atrium, ante-chamber, or vestibule has only left space for four flats.

They are numbered, as might be expected, 1 to 4. No. 1, to the left and at the back, is empty and silent at the moment; or silent save for occasional, uneasy sounds from its electric refrigerator. But No. 2, at the front, over-looking the street, has all its three inmates at home.

These consist of Mrs. Tuke, who is old and rather foolish, and has been knitting to the accompaniment of a good deal of muttering below her breath; of her daughter, Miss Tuke, who is in the middle thirties, is wearing a dark-blue uniform—which doesn't really suit her, though one might doubt, with some reason, if anything else would—and is standing in rather a manly manner on the hearthrug, inhaling a cigarette; and of Lulu, a middle-aged, miniature poodle, who just at this moment is in the arms of Morpheus, not far from the younger of her companions' feet. In addition to these living creatures there is the voice once more—though no one appears to be listening to it particu-larly—of William Whippenstall.

Another domestic scene, then? Yes and no. The dog is all right, though it's snoring a bit. The old lady, as a background figure—for we can see at once that she would never be anything else—might fit into a thousand contemporary interiors. Miss Tuke, on the other hand, sticks out. Not only behind, as is clearer than ever when she stands like this with her hands in her trouser pockets. And not only in front, though as she doesn't stick in again here, her figure is more like that of a somewhat squat sergeant-major than, for instance, even a Juno. She sticks out—that's our point—metaphorically but quite unmistakably. She focuses our attention, though she hardly enchants our eyes. Domesticity, one would say—and again one would be both right and wrong—can have no connection with anyone looking like that. And how on earth her old mother has produced such a daughter is possibly as much of a puzzle to the worthy if slightly witless creature as it must be to anyone else.

If there hadn't been a war—— But it's impossible to imagine Miss Tuke without a war, even though she must have been more than a chicken when it started, and surely must always have been a very queer shape. Nature, perhaps, was looking ahead. Women must be wardens, she may have felt—for "Warden" is the word emblazoned on both shoulders of that uniform—and she had better prepare the right type. So she did, or tried to—in any case there were now thousands of Miss Tukes in the world—and if she had been wrong in her forecast, Miss Tuke and all the others might have been hard put to it to find their niche; since there is a much more limited demand for games-mistresses, and there are, or were, economic reasons why only a very few women can drive big racing-cars. But Nature was right, of course, as she always is. According to some people, in fact, it is she rather than the British Foreign Office that is actually in league with Mars. We don't know about that; or we wouldn't know about that, to use a topical expression which suggests that we know everything above everything else. But we do know that when the hour came, Miss Tuke was there; dauntless—and we mean that—but decidedly unfeminine in at least four parts out of five; tireless, but not very gentle; conscientious, but not very adaptable; and bulging out of her uniform in a fashion calculated to strike terror—that is to say, if they ever saw her—in the very boldest of our foes.

Has she fulfilled herself, then? Poor dear, she can't. Notwithstanding the fact that there is no longer anything the least exceptional about her appearance, and that while the war lasts she will always—if she survives—have work to do, her real aim must remain as confused as ever. It's that fifth part that dishes her. She has set herself to ape men, and to some extent she has succeeded. But she also despises them; and no one should ape what they despise. In addition, moreover, she despises women—or what were formerly regarded as women—yet of course is unable to avoid being one herself. If there is war between the sexes—and again some people would have it that there is—then Miss Tuke isn't only on both sides at once, but is also rather uncomfortably placed in the middle.

She walks like a man, or so far as she is able. She talks like a man, so far as intonation and language go, and has even been gifted—by Nature once more, perhaps—with a contralto that is half-way to a baritone. But her mind, quite clearly, isn't a man's mind; so that what she says can still only sound like some kind of impersonation.

Or observe the manner in which she wrinkles her forehead just now, as the cigarette-smoke gets into her eyes. We can quite see what this is based on. It is what men do without thinking. But with Miss Tuke it is obviously a conscious bit of acting, however often she may have practised it in the past. Though she is standing with her back to that mirror in the overmantel, we just *know*, somehow, that she is watching this particular contortion, and with a good deal of approval, too. Well, men don't do that, or not when they have been smoking for fifteen years, however despicable they may be.

We note something else. Miss Tuke's complexion appears at first sight to be slightly sunburnt, or even more than slightly; which is odd, seeing that summer is well over, that the greater part of her work is done indoors, and most of it at night. But if we look again, we see that this is art. Miss Tuke has carefully applied some substance of the colour of brickdust to the whole expanse of her face. And though admittedly we have seen a few men who have achieved this naturally, Miss Tuke has gone further and put on some lipstick as well.

And though her hair is cut and parted like a man's—if not like most men just now, for it is anything but a Service trim—not only is she wearing a couple of small pearl ear-rings, but there is even a little diamond clip in that beret on the table. Can't she help this, then? Is it intentional? What is her object?

Of course we can't ask her. Yet we doubt very much if even Miss Tuke knows the answer. Something has drawn her half-way out of her sex, but something else has compelled her to cling to some of its visible characteristics. Plain by nature, and plainer still as a result, one would say, of considerable thought and care, she must yet go in for these details of self-adornment. One suspects turmoil somewhere, past if not present. And perhaps one is right. Perhaps, whatever it is or was, it also accounts for her treatment of old Mrs. Tuke.

For she can be dashed sharp with her. She calls her "Mater," which in itself is a kind of rebuke to anyone so little like a Roman matron. She orders her about. She commands or forbids her to do this or that. And one of her instructions, which is still in force, is that the old lady must remain here in London—where her daughter says she can look after her—instead of clearing out, as she would much sooner do, to some distant and safer retreat.

"Nonsense, mater," is one of this tyrant's favourite expressions, and the victim always obeys. In revenge—but she doesn't even know it's revenge—Mrs. Tuke addresses her bulging child as "Sylvia"; which on occasion has caused her to grind her teeth, for at the Post she is called "Tuke"; among her friends—you must try not to feel sick—she is known as "Richard"; and it is a pain in the neck now whenever her real name is used. On the other hand, even she can't deny that it *is* her real name, and even she can hardly request Mrs. Tuke not to use it. More turmoil, then. Even audible turmoil, sometimes. For Tuke, or Richard, or Sylvia has splendid teeth—clean, white, and strong; proud as she is of that nicotine stain on her left forefinger.

There are links, though. Indeed, there are almost bound to be links, with the same blood in both sets of veins. One of the two chief links is Lulu, who belongs to Miss Tuke, but has spent so much time with her mother as to be equally and trustfully devoted to both. Sometimes, it must be confessed, there has been bickering about Lulu; for the daughter says that the mother spoils her, while the mother says that her child is unduly harsh. That isn't quite true, though it is interesting to see how reciprocal devotion can make even the mother, in one case, stand her ground. It is true, that's to say, that Miss Tuke often shouts at poor Lulu—rather as though she was a boy-messenger at the Post—and is curiously fond of remarking: "Damn that dog!" But, bless you, Lulu doesn't mind. It rather amuses her to put her tail down and pretend to cower; but if you watch it carefully, there's always a quiver at the tip. She worships both occupants of No. 2, with only slightly distinguishable varieties of the same passion. She has reason, for in fact they both spoil her. Indeed, they are engaged in an endless struggle as to who can spoil her the more. Her only sorrow is when they both take her out, and then part from each other in the street. Poor Lulu is nearly torn in two, then, as she attempts to follow both at once, and then—whoever attaches her to the lead—makes a further attempt to dig her claws into the pavement, as she turns her head and exhibits the whites of her eyes.

"Good Lulu," says Mrs. Tuke, if it is her turn to pull.

"Damn that dog!" says the Warden, in similar circumstances, though of course she is only pretending to jerk at the lead.

So this is one link, strengthened—as it can be with dogs—rather than weakened by jealousy. But the other link is, if possible, stronger still.

Gossip. Now, that is a distinctly feminine practice, particularly on the subject of neighbours. Men aren't so good at it. You may call them stupider or less observant, but they are definitely inferior at noticing and reporting what their fellow-creatures are up to. Men—we are only generalising, of course—seem governed to a considerable extent by some hidebound tradition about minding their own business. Alternatively, if they see another man wearing a new hat—and even this is unlikely, as they won't be looking out for it—they feel no urge, as a rule, to keep passing the intelligence on to others. Why, men have even been known to forget to tell their wives that their half-sister's second cousin has had twins.

With women, however, it is otherwise; though of course we don't know why. Yet the fact remains—if we may once more generalise—that some of them do seem to notice and report quite a lot. They do hear things, in cases where men would appear to be congenitally deaf. And though it may not surprise you that Mrs. Tuke is an adept at all these arts—for it has been noted, too, that an air of foolishness here can be curiously misleading —the point, whether surprising or not, is that her daughter is just the same.

Naturally she says "Nonsense, mater," to a great deal that the old lady tells her. But she laps it up. She remembers and stores it. While in the matter of keeping her own eyes and ears wide open, and transmuting the results into human speech, she is no mean performer herself. Yes, this much she has certainly inherited, together with a much sharper nose than you might suspect for other people's affairs. The Tukes, in fact, are quite a team here, as well as competitors in the same sort of game. They don't boast of it. It may even be possible that they are unconscious of it. But again it acts as a powerful link. And again it shows that Miss Tuke, in spite of that deep voice and addiction to trousers, has still got a feminine side.

For the purpose of keeping in touch with what doesn't directly concern them, they are in rather a good situation, too. For not only does their front door open almost directly on to the entrance-hall, through which every tenant must pass—so that slight fumbling with a latchkey enables them to spy or eavesdrop in the most natural way in the world; but from the window of this sitting-room, which is next to the entrance itself, they can see almost everyone approaching or leaving the block. Since the black-out, of course, this side of their activity has been rather seriously curtailed. But on the other hand, since the black-out, there has been much less reserve between characters such as Mrs. Goosey, Mrs. Garrison, and Mrs. Trudgeon; and what they don't know and don't tell Mrs. Vowles—from whom, in turn, it is extracted by the elder of her two employers at No. 2—might be described as nobody's business.

Mrs. Tuke is the principal extractor because she has more time for it; just as she has more time, at present, for lurking behind the lace curtains in that window overlooking the street. But her daughter certainly makes the best of her opportunities—in addition to such gossip of her own as she brings back from the Post—and many a time, though Mrs. Tuke has actually provided the evidence, it is her child whose deductions have turned gossip into scandal as well.

Are they a nice couple, then? Well, listen to them. It is the younger who is speaking.

"Nonsense, mater," she booms. "They both ought to be interned, I say."

"Who, dear? Mr. Vardas and Miss Pattinson?"

"Oh, I've nothing against Miss Pattinson—though it's rather queer in a way. Besides—" a short, meaning laugh here—"you can't be interned for *that*. No, I wish you'd listen to me."

"I am, dear."

"No, you're not. I'm not even talking about 'em now." Violent absorption of cigarette-smoke, which then comes out through Miss Tuke's nostrils. "It's the Musselbergs, I mean."

"Oh!" Mrs. Tuke is still looking foolish, but to a certain extent she contrives to look cunning as well. "Why, have you heard something more?"

"Only what you've just told me, mater."

"Oh, I see. About Mrs. Vowles saying he'd gone up to Liverpool—heh?"

"It was Manchester just now," says Tuke. "But that's not the point. They're both in it, if you ask me."

"Both in what, dear?"

"Something," says the daughter, darkly. "Don't you remember the last time he came back? Besides, no one's called Musselberg for nothing. A whole case of gin!"

"Where?" Mrs. Tuke looks startled and puzzled; yet eager, as it were, as well.

"Oh, don't be so stupid, mater! You told me yourself. You saw him taking it out of the taxi."

"Oh, yes; so I did." All the same expressions again. And this time a lowered voice. "Do you think they *drink*, then?"

"Drink?" An absolute explosion of smoke. "Who *wouldn't* drink, if they had the chance, I'd like to know? But where do they *get* it?"

"Do you mean you've found out, dear ?"

"Not yet," says the Warden, criss-crossing her forehead with a multitude of lines. "But mark my words, mater. There's dirty work up there."

"Oh, Sylvia!"

But this, as you might say, has torn it. Miss Tuke has never yet forbidden her mother to use that name. She can't, very well, without giving some reason that can't be put in words. But she always resents it. She blenches, she scowls, and immediately takes her revenge. It is true that since she has been standing and smoking here, very few of the other tenants have been spared the lash of her own or her mother's tongue, and that gossip for this evening has pretty well run out. It is true, also, that she hasn't the faintest idea, nor any means of discovering, where Mr. Musselberg gets his gin. It is even true that when she shocked her mother by alluding to dirty work just now, she certainly wasn't suggesting—as Mrs. Tuke seemed to think and half-hope—that No. 14 was being conducted as a house of ill-fame. Indeed, she has no grounds for this charge whatsoever—though she has got, as she said ten minutes ago, her eye on Mrs. Amberley and that Bretton girl.

But she won't be called Sylvia. Or, rather, if she is called Sylvia, then Mrs. Tuke—who is so foolish that she still hasn't noticed this—must at once be punished. How ? Quite easily. By putting a temporary end to the endless game.

Mrs. Tuke flutters, and drops a stitch. "You're not *going*, dear ?"

"Must. Late already. Can't you see the time ?"

". . . But, added Mr. Haycock . . ." says William Whippenstall.

"No, but *do* tell me what you meant, dear. About the Musselbergs . . ."

"Can't. Oh, don't be absurd, mater. Lie down, Lulu! Grandma'll let you out."

Mrs. Tuke must be content with this rather insolent and second-hand endearment, as Tuke hurls her cigarette-end into the fender, heaves herself into a great-coat, and—another flash of femininity at the last moment—turns to the mirror before adjusting the dark-blue beret.

"There!" she announces. "I'm off. G'night."

Mrs. Tuke, like Lulu, has now risen to her feet.

"Do you think——" she begins. But Tuke is sick of that question, too. Hasn't she told her mother a thousand times that even at the Post they don't know if there's going to be a raid or not now, until it has practically started ? She doesn't even appear to be touched by that faith in her war-like appearance. Both links are dissolved—for but for that sudden change of mood it would have been she, almost certainly, on a dark night like this, who would have coped with the miniature poodle. She has gone, though. She stumps away with that swinging stride. And in another moment—just a brief pause, perhaps, while she peers into the entrance-hall—there is a thud from the flimsy front-door.

"Oh, dear!" says Mrs. Tuke, who must now dress much more slowly, and change her shoes, too, before patrolling the gutter with Lulu and an electric torch. Yet she is used to it all, in a way; and though she will now listen for sirens all the time—almost as keenly as Mrs. Margetson—she is upheld not only by far greater stupidity but by the conviction that another little titbit of scandal has only, as it were, been put safely on the larder shelf. It won't be wasted. She is perfectly sure of that.

"Good dog, Lulu," she says, as she turns off the radio. And Lulu, encouraged again by those kindly words, follows her hopefully through into her bedroom.

We, too, move on; crossing the hall again—which is again deserted now that the Warden has gone forth into the night—and passing towards Nos. 3 and 4. There is no one in the former nest of cells; for some reason, in fact, the morning milk-bottle is still standing on the doormat. But in No. 4— with his tunic loosened and a pipe in his mouth—we come on Major Hurst.

That tobacco smells, in these days, of the very best part of three shillings an ounce, and the pipe, we should judge, though old, cost a good deal, too. Major Hurst would appear to be forty-something, or on the verge of even more. But though there is a slight hiatus in his dark hair, on the crown of his head, he strikes us, even in repose, as an active and vigorous man. His breathing is perhaps a shade plethoric, but his face is the genuine colour at which Miss Tuke, we should imagine, has aimed in vain. His military moustache is firm and bristly; his cheeks and chin, at this stage in the evening, are faintly shadowed with a very virile growth; while the backs of his hands are distinctly hairy, too. He looks clean and well-cared-for, as the saying goes, and though large and heavy could never be called fat. There is suitable display of ribbons over his left breast-pocket. And though he has put on a pair of horn-rimmed spectacles, for the purpose of reading an evening newspaper, these don't seem to age him, either. In fact, they merely add to his air of—well, not exactly distinction, for that's going a bit too far; but of completeness and a kind of personal efficiency as a well-known martial type.

Nevertheless, and although of course he wouldn't be wearing those ribbons if he hadn't earned them once, Major Hurst has not been under fire, in the professional sense, since the close of the last campaign. He wasn't even a Major then, though he was a Captain, and during the years between the two great wars he has had no connection with the Army at all. He spent them in business, with ups and downs and a good deal of to and fro. He also spent part of them as a married man which strictly speaking he still is, though he hasn't written to or heard from his wife for quite a number of years. Yet all the time, one imagines, he possessed that healthy appearance —one can see him indulging in a considerable amount of golf; and in any case, with those crowns on his shoulders, he is unquestionably a Major now.

We can't quite explain it all, for the art of war is a mystical art at the best. Its heroes it often rewards with no more than death. But if you get on the right side of it—and why shouldn't you get on the right side of it when you're forty-something?—it can do a great deal more for you than that. This Major Hurst, for instance, is still—though again only technically—in business; that is to say that a seat is awaiting him in an office, and that though he doesn't go there, he still takes a share in the profits. But of course that isn't all that he does.

He's a soldier, too, now. Consider his rank, and look at his uniform. Moreover, while other soldiers—Colonels and even Major-Generals—who find themselves situated in London have no priority even in bus-queues, a mud-coloured car calls punctually for Major Hurst each morning, and returns him again at night. It is driven, though not very well, by a stoutish young woman in another uniform. Yet even this isn't all that Major Hurst has acquired. Somehow, though in theory this is now impossible for anyone below the rank of Brigadier, he has contrived to secure and to retain a personal batman.

This batman is called Private Bunny; and though it isn't our business to ask—and we should never find out if we did—just how it is that he has found himself relieved from all other duties, so that he even sleeps with his family in Hounslow and often gets week-ends off, the fact remains that he is an admirable valet and almost a first-class cook. Do we want him to be sent abroad and shot, then? No, of course not. One never does, if it is put to one like that. One prefers to think of soldiers as troops—so do the newspapers—and to gloss over mutilation or extinction by speaking of casualties, as though these were only chance mishaps. No, certainly we shouldn't move a finger—again if we could—to put Bunny on a landing-barge. The truth is that we feel much more inclined to congratulate him on his present, comparative safety. Besides, Bunny is obeying orders, and what more can he do than that?

He adds, of course, enormously to the Major's local prestige. So does the mud-coloured car. And so, though his system is different from Mrs. Wardrop's, does the Major's largess to the staff. Mrs. Wardrop, you may recall, provides a steady supply of small silver. But the Major, though he holds them in suspense much longer, is a man who deals in notes. Just as a porter, or Eldritch (if that can really be his name), is wondering if it will ever happen again, it happens; and though they may get no more in the end this way, the system certainly keeps them far more alert. Their unanimous verdict on the occupant of No. 4 is that he is a very nice gentleman—which, as a matter of fact, he is not—and they even carry this loyalty to the pitch of snubbing any tenant who is moved to question either Bunny's importance to the nation or the necessity for the mud-coloured car. The Major probably knows all this, for in certain directions the Major knows a good deal.

He knows, presumably, where he goes in the car, and what he does when he gets there. But he is deep. He doesn't tell people. At Huddleston House he tends to keep himself to himself—though of late there has been one qualification here—while at the office, or barracks, or wherever it is that he is taken, he would never, one feels sure, allude to his private life. No, he's not in the Secret Service; of that we're convinced, for he couldn't keep nearly such regular hours if he were. But he is in something, of course, where he can't be dislodged, and with the ultimate approval of the Secretary of State for War. Let's leave it at that, then, when he leaves the building. For even we can't follow everyone everywhere; and at the moment—though this is the last of the flats that we shall enter to-night—we prefer to remain where we are.

We watch him once more, then, as he sucks and puffs. But though there is a light on his sleeve and a light on his paper—both from the same heavily-shaded lamp—we can't see much of the rest of the room. It is clear, however, that he is on familiar ground, and that if he wants anything he has no need to rise. When he feels for a match-box, it appears, as by magic, in his hand. So, after a few more seconds—when the pipe is going nicely again—does a glass of yellowish fluid. When he has sipped he puts it down on what might or might not be a table; but though he doesn't look at what his hand is doing, the glass is again safe in its place.

He has laid down his paper now. He has removed his spectacles, which makes him look no younger, but rather reveals an experienced crow's-foot or two. He is rubbing his cheek. He looks calculating, doubtful, and then, you would say, dismisses some inner thought. It is for the same reason, perhaps, that he slightly shifts his position, and takes a sudden glance at his watch. Yet when a man says "By Jove!" in a room by himself, and raises his eyebrows like that, one is sure that there's something more complex afoot than mere passing concern with the time.

If it is an act, though, he goes on acting. Again his hand reaches out into the darkness, and there is a click, and in a few more moments here's William Whippenstall again. The Major crosses his legs and relaxes. His whole attitude now is that of one who, after a hard day's work, is entitled to a chair in a cosy room, and to a news-bulletin, too, if he likes.

And yet he is still acting. For one thing one could swear that he's not listening to a word. And for another have you noticed that hand? It starts tapping the chair-arm. It moves. It comes back. The Major shrugs—again, it would seem, for the benefit of some astral observer. He looks tired. His mouth gives a curious twist. And then he seems almost amused, in a consciously world-weary manner, as he lets the hand go forth once more, and a telephone comes into view.

He lays the pipe down. He silences the announcer with another click. He has got the telephone within easy reach now, and he listens, and then dials. His mouth would appear to be whistling at this point, though we can't hear a sound.

Then he leans forward, and his voice, when it comes, is surprisingly soft and low.

"Primrose ?" he says. "Bill here. . . . Yes, me."

That concludes our immediate survey, on this dark, autumnal evening, of Huddleston House. Bricks, concrete, breeze-blocks, and quick-drying plaster all solidify and are opaque again. From outside, in fact, we can see nothing at all now—not even an outline against the sky; for the searchlights stopped practising some time ago; there is no moon as yet; and cloud hides all the stars. That moment of penetrating vision is over. Indeed, shut out like this in the cold, black night, we may even feel that it was a trick of the imagination.

Yet if not, if we did play Asmodeus while the clock struck nine, we are also left with some general impressions as well. First, the complete absence of children, from babes in arms right up to an age at which they no longer wish to be considered children at all. This, we should say, is partly due to the constricted quarters that are available in the twenty-five flats; though there are plenty of children in the humbler Dwellings, only a few blocks away; and plenty of youthful larrikins—in the day-time, at any rate—on the blasted site where Crofton Street once stood. But it is also due to the war, of course. For even the London day-schools have gone into the country now, and have ceased—at some cost to the parents—to be day-schools any more; while still younger children—if there are any—of a nursery age, are staying with grandmamas, aunts, or even their own evacuated mothers, a long way from Huddleston House. This, then, is something that we are now conscious of missing, and whether we happen to like children or not. It adds, insensibly until we pause to think, to the general nightmare quality of the life that has just been revealed. For once, even here, perambulators could be kept in a shed in the exiguous yard at the back, which could be reached through a door at the side. There are none now, though. There isn't even a shed, for the so-called land-mine made short work of that. And right up to sixteen or seventeen—when they are now registering for national slavery or service—the elder children are all away at their schools.

That is one impression, then. Another is that we have only seen one dog; though again this may largely be attributed to the architecture—and, if it comes to that, even Lulu is here by the grace of Mr. Todman, or possibly owing to his fear of Miss Tuke; for it has always been a clause in the Syndicate's leases that dogs are not to be kept. There are plenty of dogs, however—in daylight, again—when Lulu is taken out. There is a woman in Bessingham House, for instance, who has so far got round Mr. Todman as to run a kind of crèche for them, while their owners are out at work. And they come from the smaller streets, though not from The Dwellings, where they are much more rigidly barred. And a few of them—wretched, half-starved, unlovable, pathetic creatures—conduct a kind of gipsy or pariah existence (though it is believed that they have homes, of a sort, at night) amid the rubble and devastation beyond the vanished perambulator-shed. No, London is far from dogless at present, however childless it may have become in this particular class.

That brings us to the third impression, though in fact it is more of a query. What class *is* it—or is it a class, in the old sense, at all—that has assembled beneath the sloping pantiles and big water-tank that are hidden just now in the dark ? How many, in the cross-section that we have so far examined, can be placed in the pre-war social order, or has all that, too, gone by the board ?

Mr. Vardas ? We're beaten at once. That's to say he is certainly not an English gentleman, but what would he have been at home ? We don't know. No war, no Mr. Vardas. That's absolutely as far as we can get.

Miss Kenton-Hinksey ? Oh, of course she's a lady—surely; though it's true that she serves in a shop. Mrs. Amberley ? How far *déclassée*, with all that paint, and living as a bachelor—though that isn't her fault—and working at a bench in a factory most of the day ? The exact answer eludes us. Or already we are adjusting our standards. Once we've done this, we must certainly pass the two girls, called Bugs and Echo, in No. 15, though of course they're not sticking—and they can't—to the pre-war rules. Mr. Everard, half a fossil in any case, remains whatever he was when the war broke out, and he's certainly respectable enough. So is Mrs. Margetson, though she clings much more desperately and consciously to all that is slipping away. Full marks, then, there can be no doubt, for Mrs. Margetson; though when it comes to her daughter June—well, again we can't possibly apply the old standards here. She's a child of change. She's part of the war, too. If it ever stops, she may still be able to find her place, though it can't be the same as her mother's. Poor June; though she has dreadful manners.

The Champions are comparatively easy. Mr. Champion is at once given away by his diphthongs, of which, however, he is so little aware that he has never attempted to cure them; while his wife, though more careful or adaptable herself, calls their sofa a couch and believes that the phrase "ever so" is a qualifying adverb.   As snobs, then, we can cope with the Champions, though this doesn't necessarily mean that on a vote they wouldn't prove to be right.   As snobs, again, we have no doubt about Mrs. Musselberg, or about L. Wilson Barker, as he signs himself, on the floor below.   Neither of them could ever be admitted to the Royal Enclosure; though as there isn't one now, this can hardly affect their grade.   Once more, we *must* remember that it's now that counts.

All right, then.   Mrs. Wardrop gets through on almost any reckoning, or near enough.   There were shades in the grades once, and then even Mrs. Wardrop of Muncaster Mansions was far from the topmost rung.   But though a little inclined to treat herself as the Lady of the Manor here, she isn't a bad old thing.   Her airs are transparent.   Her future haunts us.   And for that alone, in a sudden access of generosity, we shall give her the benefit of the doubt.

As for Major Bertram Hurst—for that is his real style or title, though he has long been known by the more sociable name of "Bill"—he just isn't a gentleman, whether nice or otherwise, at all.   He has many of the stigmata, for he set off all right, and his father—dead now—was a highly-respected Canon in a cathedral town.   Major Hurst, therefore, can still put on another act, and does, most of the time, and gets away with it with the porters, and with Bunny, and perhaps with others as well.   But you know how it is.   Reaction, for one thing.   The last war, for another.   And the kind of vitality that begins by being amused at breaking the rules, and then can't be bothered to stop.   There's plenty of it about.   There has been a positive landslide since Mrs. Margetson, for instance, was a girl.   But whether this was because the rules were too strict, or because people like Major Hurst deliberately picked at the foundations, it would perhaps be a bit hard to say.

He has picked, though.   As a matter of fact, he has had no principles whatsoever since he emerged with those medals at the end of the last war. That, of course, is why his wife has left him, though she won't divorce him—not that he much cares—for some reason best known to herself.   He is as near a crook as you can be and remain at large.   He despises and is lost without women.   We don't care what the porters think, or where he was educated, or what he is doing now.   We'd far sooner trust L. Wilson Barker, who at least has some species of conscience.   Whether snobbish or not, we have no use for Major Hurst at all.

That, then, is the summary.   What is the conclusion ?   Well, of course, that there aren't any classes now; and isn't this—though we weren't told so at first—what we have all been fighting for?   Huddleston House is a melting-pot, with at least as many more ingredients as we have yet had time to observe.   It's symbolic, perhaps.   It's a microcosm.   An epitome.   It is London, at this period, in duodecimo.   Though on the other hand, whether it looks up to its larger and grander neighbour across the street or not, of course it looks down on The Dwellings.

CHAPTER VI

AT THIS PERIOD, ALSO, A CHANGE HAD COME OVER THE ATTITUDE OF A NUMBER of Londoners towards their still almost innumerable pubs. Right up to the outbreak of the second world-war, a whole section of the community—men as well as women—though quite prepared to enter a country inn, and even to affect some technical knowledge of darts, would turn a blind eye, and so far as possible an insensitive nose, on doors that swung at London street-corners and other profitable points. They were content to remain in the darkest ignorance as to what went on within, or as to the subtle distinction between a private and a saloon bar. Occasionally, when barrels were being lowered down a slide into a cellar, they would step into the roadway so as to avoid a very thick bit of rope. But they rather resented even this admission that the London pubs existed. They had only the very vaguest notion about licensing hours. And on the whole, though public intoxication at this epoch had become very rare indeed, they were mildly in favour of such places being entirely abolished. They thought them sordid—which a lot of them were, no doubt, though by no means all. If they should see an acquaintance stepping into one of them, or coming—however steadily—out, they entered an immediate black mark against him as one who wasn't only a prospective drunkard, but was letting the whole side down.

Then came the change. It was due to a variety of causes, though they were all based on the war. There was a general breakdown of much of the old stiffness. It became increasingly difficult to get a drink—or a meal, either, if it comes to that—by the old methods or in your own home. The black-out tended to subdivide the metropolis into a quantity of little villages, as it were, so that perhaps, after all, a pub was no worse than a country inn. And there can be no doubt that people wanted to drink; partly because they believed, whether rightly or not, that this was of assistance in easing the strain, and partly because, if it is difficult to get something, all human nature rises to this challenge at once.

So as prices rose and supplies ran short, a new class of client came in through the swing doors, and, having done so, fumbled their way round the various defences. It was the private or saloon bars that they made for mostly, though some still thought they were unbending; and here, for a while, they both puzzled and annoyed the aborigines. Some of these, indeed, felt so much disturbed at being watched where they had once been secure from observation, that they took their custom elsewhere. But this made no odds, for the newcomers by now were in all but the very meanest dives. So the aborigines returned. But they didn't mingle. Drink, or drink in these days, would appear to be an inadequate solvent. The old hands withdrew to one end of the counter. The newcomers stuck to the other. Yet presently, of course, and allowing always for a few rare spirits—the race of the future, perhaps—who contrived to keep a foot in each camp, this system was acquiring the patina of an established convention. England, in other words, was again showing its genius for compromise. In fact, the only people with any cause for complaint now were the publicans, who just at the moment when they ought to have been making their fortunes, were faced with a shortage of stock. "Sorry, no gin," they kept saying. "Sorry, no whisky." Or: "Sorry, no barley-wine." So then everyone must drink swipes, at one and twopence a pint—where once, or at any rate within a few yards of this spot, good beer had been sold at fourpence a quart. Yet if they weren't exhilarated, they had got the habit. While the State, which might be held to be ultimately responsible for the whole condition of affairs, was quietly absorbing the best part of a bob on each tankard.

To Huddleston House, then, the Royal Oak had become a kind of annexe. It was the nearest licensed establishment—even nearer than the San Remo Restaurant (under Cypriot management), which in any case wasn't licensed at all—and had a so-called dining-room, as well as four categories of bar. Saloon, in other words; public; ladies'—about the size of a bathing-machine; and jug-and-bottle—even smaller still. It was gloriously ugly, both within and without; having been entirely rebuilt, about thirty-five years ago, in place of a quite charming tavern—or charming, at any rate, in a photograph hanging in the saloon—which had gone when the main road was widened, together with its stables and a horse-trough.

Once, also, and much more recently, the so-called dining-room had provided sound and well-cooked meals. Not much variety, but then this wasn't wanted. The regulars, in those days—commercial travellers, bank-clerks, and small tradesmen—could enjoy a three-course lunch for one and sixpence, or a slightly more sumptuous dinner for two shillings. But it was never crowded. The one waiter could attend to them all without any difficulty, even though part of his duties was to keep dashing in and out of the saloon bar to collect the drinks. In those days, also, no one outside its special circle even knew that such a place existed.

Now, however, all this had altered, too. The prices had gone up, the quality and quantity had both come down, the waiter, who was naturally no younger, had lost his nerve and forgotten his manners; for here, again, new patrons had come swarming in. They swarmed, especially in the evenings, because the alternative was to cook their own meals—which some were incapable of doing, while a number had all been too busy to go shopping or had run out of what they had bought. So that though the table-cloths in the Royal Oak dining-room were now stained and had holes in them, though the portions were pitiful, the plates weren't too clean, and if you wanted a drink you would almost certainly have to fetch it yourself, this was still, perhaps, better than starvation; it was a change, at any rate, from the San Remo; and it saved you, if you lived at Huddleston House, from boarding another bus in the dark.

Two residents, to whom we have had a slight clue already, had decided to come here tonight. After waiting a bit, they had snatched two seats at a table for four; so that during the next phase of waiting they were privileged to be very close to a fat man who picked his teeth and a thin man with a nasty cough. Later, some unattractive debris were removed. At subsequent intervals they were each given about three spoonfuls of tepid, brown soup; some cottage pie, consisting of gristle and potato, with some damp, anæmic green vegetable, over all of which a further quantity of the same brown soup would appear to have been poured; and a dollop of pulpy apple, accompanied by an equally pulpy piece of pastry. They were given no bread, though they had frequently asked for it. They knew better, having been here before, than to ask for coffee. About half-way through this protracted and not very nourishing meal, their original companions had been replaced by a lance-corporal whose battle-dress had for one of them a familiar though unappetising smell, and a worn-looking woman, with red spots on her cheeks, who kept sniffing and blowing her nose. The lance-corporal, however, seemed devoted to her, kept plying her with mild-and-bitter, and whenever he returned with a further supply shot a dark and defiant glance at the two residents, as though he suspected them of having made advances to her during his absence.

They hadn't, though. Nor had they succeeded in getting anything to drink themselves, for the bar, at this stage, was blocked—except, apparently, to a lance-corporal—by an irruption of sailors, who were manning it three deep. Eventually, however, they succeeded in catching, paying, and tipping the waiter—whose gratitude took the form of saying that he wished they had his feet; and so, for the sailors had gone by now, they at last made their way into the saloon.

Here one of them—the one whom the waiter's remark had seemed more particularly to perturb—did rather an odd thing. He deliberately avoided, indeed he shrank back from Maisie, the barmaid, though she was disengaged at the moment; and even waited his turn for attention from her consumptive-looking male colleague. But we can explain this, and there is no hint of romance. The truth was that Maisie, some weeks ago now, had suddenly offered him a bottle of whisky for £3 10s.; that though he detested the stuff, he had been too shy or self-conscious to refuse it; that it was now, in fact, in the coat-cupboard in the little lobby of No. 12, Huddleston House; but that the fear which still racked him was that she would make the same offer again.

That's Life, of course. Many people would willingly have paid more, even for so unfamiliar and doubtful a brand as Auld Sandy. Others, again, would have raised an outcry, and have had the premises prosecuted. But not this young man, who hadn't even taken it as a compliment. He had paid through the nose for what he didn't want, but his only thought or hope, as we have said, was that he shouldn't find himself doing it again. So much for a first glance at his character, of which you will almost positively learn more before long. Meanwhile, he had secured a glass of swipes. So had his companion—to whom Maisie, for whatever reason, never dreamt of offering anything more. And now, still clutching their coats and hats as well, they both backed on to a couple of hard, wooden chairs by the wall.

The air was full of smoke and stuffiness, and would remain so, no doubt, until the black-out was taken down in the morning. There were some brilliant lights, which were rather painful to the eyes. There was a good deal of noise, because almost everyone present was talking. And since it was essential that each glass of swipes should be filled to the brim—for the State, once more, insisted on this—there were rings in the room wherever they had been set down; and as the rings slowly evaporated, they added to the general reek.

For decoration—apart from some elaborate carving on the partitions at each end of this section of the counter—there was the afore-mentioned photograph, a mirror—which also advertised a proprietary brandy—a notice about betting slips, another about young persons under eighteen years of age, and a palm, more dead than alive, in a spirally-fluted, pink-and-chocolate pot. For entertainment there was a radio-set, though it was silent just now; and a glass-topped, sloping table, covered with holes, obstacles, little coils of wire, and electric-bulbs, and with a perpendicular picture at its further end of a quantity of airships and speed-boats. If you put a penny into this contrivance, and then pulled and released a plunger—and also, of course, if it didn't happen to be out of order—all sorts of things happened. A ball began hurtling around; lights flickered under the glass, in a totally incomprehensible manner; and among the airships and speed-boats some insane kind of adding-machine sprang suddenly to life. In no circumstances, apparently, did your penny ever return. Nor did it seem clear to the un-enlightened observer if any skill was involved, and again if you were supposed to play by yourself or with an adversary or partner.

For sometimes solitary patrons attacked it, and sometimes two or three in turn. But they all cheated; or at any rate they all rocked the table as the ball bumped round. And they all, invariably, left it as suddenly and arbitrarily as they had approached it. It was as though it fascinated them at first, and then disgusted them. It was temperamental, though, or else was getting old. And tonight—five sailors having fed it with a surfeit of pennies—it had again given up the ghost. It just stood there, with more empty glasses on it—and rings, of course—while a public-spirited character, seated beside it with his own mug of swipes, warned anyone who came near it that it had gone and conked out again. So much, then, for what might be called the mechanical part of the entertainment.

The rest was swipes and talk. A group of newcomers—though in fact they were newcomers no longer—had congregated at one end of the counter, while the old hands had assembled at the other. Further patrons were sprinkled on chairs and benches; sipping, smoking, musing, conversing, and sometimes gesticulating as well. One heard laughter sometimes, but not often. One heard the cash-register. One heard the swish of beer-engines; the flapping, from behind the black-out curtain, of the swing doors; and ever and anon, with the regularity of ritual responses: "Sorry, no whisky," or: "Sorry, no gin."

You could hardly call it, thought Gavin Guernsey—which was the name of the present owner of that bottle of Auld Sandy—an obvious sink of iniquity. It was ugly, and had foul air. There was something faintly objectionable about those partitions, though if you were an old public bar-man (not barman), you might possibly prefer the exclusive society of your equals. Yet the faces in this superior sanctum weren't, honestly, to be admired. The Demon Rum, or some member of that family, had all too clearly marked a number of them in the group to the right; while in the group to the left there was a kind of willingness, he felt, to drink for rather more than thirst. Was he a prig, then? No doubt. In any case, a more self-critical young gentleman can hardly have existed. Yet he was an observer, and even a bit of a thinker, too. Pubs, he was thinking, *were* demoralising. You couldn't get away from it. And this beer was muck; you couldn't get away from that, either. On the other hand, was the human race worth saving? Yes, this was the kind of thought that came to him, though no one—for he had barely tasted the muck in question—could possibly have been less inebriated than this ruminative and rather pale young man.

His companion, of about the same age and also in civilian attire, was sallow rather than pale, wore very thick spectacles—so that if you could see his eyes at all, they appeared enormously magnified—had an almost expressionless face, apart from something in the nature of a faint but perpetual sneer, and could have done with a hair-cut. His name was Moulton. D. P. Moulton. Or Derek to the young man by his side. And the curious thing was that, by the chances of war, it was Gavin who was the authentic tenant of No. 12, Huddleston House, but that he was now staying there as D. P. Moulton's guest.

As his paying guest, to be more precise. Or even as joint tenant, in a way. Or as tenant and sub-sub-tenant at the same time; which seems to need a little explaining.

We must go back to Oxford, then, where they had known each other, and had been members of the same college, but could hardly have been described as friends. Rivals, rather, in those days; though distant rivals at that. They both wanted to write, though neither of them had; or not, that is to say, in the professional sense. And they found this out; and D. P. Moulton certainly looked more like a writer—or so Gavin thought—as well as being the possessor of far more books. Mostly they shied away from each other, having very little else in common; yet sometimes they were drawn together, and had long, windy conversations about other writers, and particularly, of course—for this was the touchstone then—about Proust. But D. P. Moulton was a genuine highbrow, and Gavin—though almost incredibly sensitive and impressionable—was only half one, if that. His three real friends—Jock, Ronald, and Charles—weren't highbrows at all; but then his three real friends were dead now—just before Dunkirk, in Crete, and somewhere in the North Atlantic—and this was one reason, perhaps, why he looked so sad.

As to his further history—though he was still only twenty-eight—it may be added that he had been born and brought up at a private school, of which his father had been founder and owner. That his youth had been darkened by the same father's attempts to drive more into his head than it would hold. That his adolescence had been darkened because he had failed to win a scholarship at his public school. That the next phase had been at least overshadowed because he had only gained an exhibition at what his father regarded as the wrong college. And that through all this period he had been haunted—once more with his father's assistance—by an absolute terror that he could never possibly earn his living.

This doesn't mean that he wasn't frequently as happy at Oxford as to be almost delirious. But there were also all too many moments when he was plunged in despair. In the vacations, when he was at home—or, in other words, back at St. Eustace's—he was almost always plunged in despair. And then—which was so extraordinarily like his father, whose qualities he could faintly appreciate from a safe distance, though he still trembled and almost stammered in his presence—an astonishing thing had occurred. On his twenty-first birthday his father hadn't only offered him a glass of sherry, which was amazing and alarming enough, but after a great deal of scholarly humming and hawing had suddenly announced that his mother—whom he couldn't remember—had left him a sum of money which now amounted to six thousand pounds.

No reason emerged why this news should have been held up for so long; though equally—since the sum had been in trust until now—there was no forcible cause why it shouldn't. Gavin attributed the protracted silence—for his mother had died when he was little more than a year old—to sheer joy in hugging a secret; or alternatively to a belief that no boy would work if he knew he was coming into a fortune. But he was enormously relieved And then he wept—on his twenty-first birthday—because he felt that he hadn't thought nearly enough about his mother; which was true enough, in a way, though this was also virtually the first time that his father had ever mentioned her. This he attributed to his intense and appalling reserve; which, by the way, was immediately resumed.

Yet it was the fortune, undoubtedly, that made him cease to care twopence whether he failed in his finals or not. And because he didn't care, he got a Second in History, though his tutor had certainly been praying for no more than a Third. Now he was going to write, though he still didn't know what. But now, also, he could feel in the air that if he didn't do something, and pretty quickly, his father—who had only grunted at that Second, yet had perhaps been a little gratified, too—would rope him in as an assistant master, and keep him imprisoned for life.

So he acted, almost at once. Books were his passion, but if he couldn't wait to create them—and already, after some frantic efforts, he was wondering if he had postponed this too long—six thousand pounds could at least get him out of that trap. For five thousand, as a matter of fact, he was immediately accepted as a junior partner—this was two or three years before the war—in the publishing firm of Messrs. Dingle and Frisby; who weren't in the first flight, or they would have wanted a lot more, but were perfectly stable and sound. His father had flinched, when this news was broken; but in the end, once more, seemed incapable of expressing what there was little doubt that he felt. He withdrew into his shell, and not long afterwards had withdrawn from the school altogether—selling it, through an agency, for a quite satisfactory price.

Gavin, of course, wouldn't have been Gavin if he hadn't experienced frightful pangs of conscience. But he couldn't back out, when he had signed that deed; and though he had tried to be dutiful all his life, he had not yet had any reward. He couldn't and wouldn't and mustn't say that he disliked his father; but it was useless to pretend that he hadn't achieved an escape.

So he came to London, and learnt the publishing ropes; and received quarterly instalments of the money that he had put into the firm—or this was one way of looking at it; and presently, having suffered enough in furnished rooms, took a flat in Huddleston House. It had a small spare-room, in case anyone wished to stay with him—such as two of his three great friends, for the third lived in London anyhow; or such as his father, once in a while, though they had still found little or nothing to say to each other. R. J.—for it was thus that he thought of this parent, and generally addressed him, having acquired these habits when a pupil at St. Eustace's himself—had seemed suspicious of even such trifling comforts as were afforded by No. 12. But they weren't comfortable visits for Gavin. Nor was he any more at his ease when—duty again—he stayed with R. J. in the little house that he now

C

occupied near Windsor. It was a strain. You couldn't pretend it wasn't a strain. Though possibly if not probably it was a strain for R. J., too.

In those days, Gavin—still shy, as he always would be—was attended at his London residence by a florid and dishonest Mrs. Skinner, who was at the same time indispensable and the bane of his life. Now—for there was no end to what the whirligig could do in war-time—Mrs. Skinner was earning a great deal more in a filling factory (where it was to be hoped that she didn't drop quite so much), while he himself was actually in the partial care of her mother, Mrs. Mudge. But of course this was only one of the surprising changes.

At the beginning of the same war, it is true, the first surprise had been that there was almost no change at all. Having undergone quite a considerable amount of military training at his public school and again, though without much more enthusiasm, as an undergraduate, he had fully expected to be hurled into the fray at once. Not so. For in the first place there was hardly any fray, and in the second it seemed that anyone in his position must be held in reserve and suspense. Though he had no wish to be killed, he champed a good deal for the best part of a year, but went on publishing—for he was now forbidden to do anything else—while his three less, or more, experienced friends were swept into the machine, and one of them ceased to exist.

Then the machine gave a jolt or jerk, and now it appeared that everything he had learnt must be learnt all over again. He was posted as a cadet to an OCTU. He was sent to the north, and to the west, and to the south-west, and to the north-east. The blitz was going on in London, so that no one would take over his flat. But in the following summer—on short leave, though still with an endless vista of courses—he fell in with Derek Moulton, whose eyes and toes had placed him in the Ministry of Propaganda, but who was also doing regular reviewing for a weekly, which was as far as his own literary dreams had come true; and Derek became his sub-tenant on very reasonable terms.

Meanwhile, Gavin went on with those courses, which with the best and occasionally the most suicidal will in the world he seemed quite unable to avoid, and if he came to London, as he did now and then, it was he who naturally occupied the small spare-room. Now he was commissioned, but still, so it appeared, only so as to be sent travelling from one part of this country to another. It got on his nerves. He was ashamed of his own war-effort, though it had often been very exhausting. But it was his fate that if he applied for more active employment—as he did more than once—then either nothing happened, or there was a shake-up in the machine which resulted in his former companions being sent to some front, while he himself received orders to remain more or less where he was. To a sensitive character this was almost as painful as being handed white feathers. And though no one else blamed him, he was continually reproaching himself.

Then came the next phase, which tormented him, perhaps, even more. Once, twice, nay, three times, he was granted embarkation-leave. He braced himself—for he had plenty of imagination, though he still hadn't managed to write; he bade farewell to R. J., which was his duty again, though they were still on the far sides of some gulf; he felt sombre, and devoted, and nervous, and doomed; and there was no embarkation—for the machine had back-fired—and he was again dispatched, though as an instructor now, on still yet another course.

It was enough to drive even a far less war-like young officer almost frantic. He felt now that he was living at the expense of others, and particularly, of course, of those three special friends who were now all gone. But Destiny—though it can switch violently if you once spot its methods—is, when left to itself, a strangely repetitive power. It must have marked Gavin down as one to be saved from the furnace at all costs. And when his fourth embarkation-leave came along, it certainly did a queer and rather callous thing.

Again he had visited his father, but of course he can be excused for remaining only one night, when they still had so little to say to each other, and when this was their fourth farewell. He was left, accordingly, with some days in hand. He didn't know what to do with them. In an access of sentiment, or it might have been boredom, he suddenly decided to take leave of his old nurse as well; though it was several years since he had last seen her, and they had little in common by now. He sent her a telegram, however —which wasn't delivered, as, though he didn't know this, she had recently changed her address. He bought her a hand-bag, with some difficulty, as a parting gift. He took a train to a town in Kent; asked the way; began walking; heard some guns, but no sirens; saw some people scampering; decided, though he wasn't in uniform, that he wouldn't scamper himself; was suddenly conscious of a violent and numbing shock; and came to his senses in a bed in a cottage hospital, where he was presently informed that he now had only one foot.

This partly explains why he didn't smile very broadly when the waiter at the Royal Oak made that ancient crack about feet. It would take a great deal more to explain what the machine does, or did, when a serving officer, not on duty and in civilian attire, has one of his extremities smashed by an almost red-hot fragment of anti-aircraft shell. Portions of the machine seemed just fascinated by the chance which had led this fragment to hit him in so unlikely a place. Others were deeply concerned because he hadn't immediately transported himself, on one leg, to a military hospital. Nobody seemed to believe his story about the old nurse, which indeed lacked some elements of plausibility when it turned out that she had been living with her sister near Hereford for the last six months; and when the hand-bag had been pinched by some Good Samaritan as well; and when Gavin looked so very much—through shame—as though he was lying. Then there was a hint—or he thought so—from other cogs in the machine that he had done the whole thing on purpose, so as to avoid being sent abroad. No charge was laid. It couldn't be. But this sort of thing didn't lighten his spirits or hasten his recovery. Not that he was in unbearable pain—except, occasionally and strangely enough, in the foot that was no longer there. But, oh, what a *fool* he had been !

He needn't have taken that journey. He couldn't imagine why he had, now. If he had dived into even a shop doorway, he would by this time, in all probability, be serving his country in North Africa, or at least on the way there; for that last embarkation-leave had proved to be the real thing. It seemed to him, also, and worried him a good deal, that hundreds of pounds had been spent on his training, and that all he had then done was the equivalent of being knocked down by a private car. Yet it wasn't quite the equivalent. Yards if not miles of paper were now being used by the War Office and other interested parties to determine the personal responsibility and public liability in his very irregular case. Gavin himself just didn't care, which the machine found extremely provoking. A little later it struck him, though he still felt an ass, that if he had arrived in North Africa and had immediately had his foot shot off, he would merely have occupied space on a transport—and also, perhaps, on a hospital-ship—with no more result than considerable extra expense. He didn't put forward this point of view, for he wasn't such an ass as all that. But it comforted him slightly, in the passive attitude that he had now adopted, and which caused such perplexity and annoyance to the whole machine.

For the machine wanted to thwart him, of course. It wanted him to claim something, so that it could put him in the wrong, or so that it could pass his papers eternally from one branch to another. But he didn't collaborate, and made no claim at all. He was rather inclined to cry quits with the machine, for if he had wasted its money, it had also wasted his time; or again, if it wanted him to be wounded, then he *was* wounded—and it could darned well decide for itself whether as a soldier or not. Eventually, in this mood—which derived, no doubt, from a number of rather obvious physical and psychological causes—he handed the whole thing over to his cousin, Claud Kingham—who was R. J.'s nephew, but older than himself, and a solicitor—with little expectation that he would ever hear anything more.

Eventually, also, having been reclaimed by the Army—though chiefly, he imagined, because he would sooner have stayed where he was—and having recovered from a long and exceedingly uncomfortable drive in a military motor-ambulance, he made friends with the Medical Officer in charge, who supplied him—under the counter, as it were—with a very expensive new foot. If he hadn't done this, there was every sign that he might have waited for months, if not years; for though the Army had accepted or seized him as a patient, it was still not convinced that it owed him anything more. Nor was Gavin. His cousin, so far as it was possible to judge, was still locked in slow-motion correspondence about far more elementary aspects of the affair.

So Gavin paid for the foot himself. And presently he was hobbling on it with two crutches; and then with one crutch; and then with no more than a stick. Ultimately he discarded even this—for it was a very ingenious foot indeed—and, except when he used it too much, didn't even limp. In the Air Force, of course—or so he had gathered—he would now have been expected to return to his duties; but in the Army his discharge could only be a matter of time. It would have been quicker, perhaps, without Claud, and in fact had only just taken place. But meanwhile he had been granted indefinite leave; for six months now he had been back with Messrs. Dingle and Frisby; and also—since no other arrangement seemed to have occurred to his present companion—had been occupying the smaller bedroom in what was actually and factually his own flat.

To sum up, he was half-amused and half-tormented—quite a common condition among his contemporaries—by the mess that he had made of his effort to take part in the war. He was extraordinarily self-conscious about not being in uniform, though he would have put up with almost anything sooner than attempt to explain why he wasn't. Owing to the disappearance of the two intermediate partners, on more or less active service, he was occupying a much more important and responsible position than he had held when he had last been a publisher. He still felt no burning affection for his flat-mate, though they were both saving money this way, and shook down all right on the whole. And the loss of his original foot had done nothing to increase any intimacy with his father, who was now seventy-three, as he happened to know, but otherwise quite unchanged. He— R. J., that's to say—had visited him in both his hospitals, and was no more ashamed of him, apparently, than he had been before. It was the son's notion, moreover, that he must be given a good mark for this. But he was remote. He was oppressive. If one felt that one was a failure already, he did nothing to counter this thought. And Gavin Guernsey—though his firm at the moment sold everything that it issued, whether D. P. Moulton slanged it in the *Friday Reflector* or not—had little or no confidence, after that upbringing and a more recent experience, not to mention the obstruction that had made him publish when he wanted to write, that he could ever regard himself without slight distaste.

By the way, there has been no mention of his love-life, because he hadn't got any. His imagination, that is to say, was in perfect order, and was indeed very romantic, though so far it had been quite content with the most misty ideals. But he was shy, in real life. And diffident. And he had been busy. And he had had his foot taken off. Who wanted to marry a cripple? Nobody, of course. And whom did this cripple want to marry? Nobody, either, whom he had as yet even set eyes on; though it was a fact, of late— undetected by Gavin himself—that the form of those misty ideals had been narrowed down. Is this possible, without knowing it? Quite. It is as possible as that in every love-affair there is a point where you can either go forward or turn back. Afterwards, of course, no one can ever believe this. But it's true. Nothing ever happens, in real life, without preparation. Even if your foot is suddenly shattered by a bit of anti-aircraft shell that has been fired by mistake, this is because you have never got on very well with your father and once had a good-natured old nurse.

"What's that?" said Gavin, in the saloon bar at the Royal Oak.

"If you're not listening," said D. P. Moulton, "it doesn't matter."

"Oh," said Gavin, with his mind still some distance away. And then a thing happened that was familiar enough, and told him, moreover, the time. The consumptive-looking barman—who did this, punctually if apathetically, night after night—reached up to a shelf, and switched on the Royal Oak radio. No one paid any attention to this now almost symbolic act. The uproar continued at both ends of the counter—the old hands being rather louder, and the newcomers rather shriller—while the apparatus just added to the din. Perhaps if it had said something really startling, this would have communicated itself to both camps. But it didn't. No one expected it to. And Nature, in pubs at any rate, seemed to have furnished her children with some power of resistance against hearing anything less.

Presently, in due course, the same agency would turn it off again, and there would be a general sense of relief. Meanwhile, by beaming an ear, as it were, you could listen if you really insisted. So Gavin did this for a moment or two—though more as a test for his personal equipment than for anything else—and heard a voice saying something about complacency; and could have supplied the rest of the phrase with the greatest of ease, but preferred, so far as that personal equipment was concerned, to switch off. The noise became a mere hubbub again. No it didn't. Derek was saying something else to him now, and nudging him, too.

"Steady," he protested. "Mind my beer."

"Todman," said Derek.

"What? Where?"

But now Gavin had seen Mr. Todman, too. There were his bat-like ears by the bar; and it was bat-like, too—and characteristic—that he should have placed himself half-way between the two camps. For Mr. Todman, as it took little perspicacity to discover, was plagued partly by the fear of not being identified as an ex-officer and gentleman, and partly by a dread of being thought to presume on these facts. Even this wasn't all. He was scared of becoming too friendly with the tenants, lest they used this for their own advantage in matters of tenancy. And chiefly he was perhaps bewildered even more than alarmed by having at last held the same job for more than three years on end. You could see that, with even the minimum of metaphysical insight.

Gavin, who could remember his predecessor—the bluff and brusque Mr. Kirby, who was now in Persia—felt a certain sympathy for anyone so invariably ill at ease. He knew, too, how Mr. Todman was bullied by some of the tenants, was wheedled by others—but must still try and resist them, because of the Syndicate—and was perpetually receiving either complaints or insults from both residents and staff. If he chose to come in here, after a hard day's work, for a quiet pint, it would have been Gavin's notion to leave him alone. But Derek, with much less sensibility, or even the cold-blooded cruelty that one might expect from a reviewer, appeared to think otherwise. He called out to him.

"Mr. Todman !"

The "Mr." was possibly correct, for there was the best part of a quarter of a century's difference in their ages. To have called out "Todman!" might equally have been taken by that thin-skinned creature as treating him too much as an employee. But there could be no doubt that D. P. Moulton's expression, or spectacles, gave him a slight air of intellectual condescension at the best of times. And Gavin wasn't surprised when the manager looked resentful for a moment, as well as startled, before coughing and coming stiffly towards them.

"Good-evening," he said. "Good-evening," he repeated, oscillating rather than bowing towards Gavin. "Is there—is there anything I can——"

"Nothing," said Derek, in that customarily precise and unemphatic tone. "I was going to say 'Have a drink.' Only I see you have one. Have a cigarette."

"No, thank you, sir." Mr. Todman's ears were becoming that rich red again. "I—I'm afraid I don't smoke."

Gavin knew why he didn't, because he knew that Mr. Todman had been gassed. He knew, also, that Derek had at least been told this; so that he suffered for both parties, though one of them seemed perfectly calm.

"Of course," said Derek. "I'd forgotten. Sorry. Why don't you sit down ?"

"Well——" began Mr. Todman, who certainly seemed taller and thinner than ever as he stood there right over them. He might have added that there was nothing to sit on. But he didn't. He just looked suspicious, and harassed; and Gavin was appallingly sorry for him again, though he didn't see what he could do.

"I don't know," Mr. Todman began again, "that I oughtn't—I mean——"
He tried to look at his watch, and spilt some of his swipes. "Dash!" he

said; and then he spilt still more of it, because a fourth character, having just detached himself from the group of old hands, had come up and slapped him on the back.

"Hullo, old man!" said this fourth character, who seemed full of self-possession and well-being, as the old hands—when not fat or sodden—so frequently were.

"Oh!" said Mr. Todman. "Hullo—er—— Lemme . . ."

He appeared to be preparing a compendious introduction, in the very best traditions of the saloon bar. But he was coughing, too. Gavin, at any rate, caught nobody's name but his own. And there was at least a hint in the manager's somewhat anguished and flustered expression that he was slightly ashamed of his friend. Or perhaps only that he felt he ought to be, for nobody's expressions could be more confusing, or could chase each other more swiftly across so very narrow a face.

The friend, however, seemed quite at home.

" 'Evening," he said. " 'Evening, gen'lemen." And then back to Mr. Todman. "Well, Toddy——" here Mr. Todman blushed and blinked for a second, before recovering himself—"have you heard the big news ?"

Both tenants looked up. Mr. Todman looked blank.

"Combermere Court," said the new arrival; which meant something to Gavin, though not much as yet, for it was the name of a large block of flats that he passed, at about the moment when his bus-fare was being taken, every morning—except Sundays, of course—in his life.

"What about it ?" he asked, since someone was clearly supposed to say this, and Mr. Todman seemed slow on his cue.

"Gone!" said the new arrival, heartily and triumphantly. "Eh ? How's that ?"

"Gone ?" echoed Gavin, as it still seemed his turn; and, besides, he was considerably shaken. "When ?" he asked. "Why, I passed it this morning, and surely—— Why, there hasn't even been a warning for a week!"

"Ha, ha," said his still unidentified acquaintance, though this was also, just possibly, a tribute to his unconscious wit. "Not gone like that, I don't mean. Taken over. Clearing 'em all out. My!" he said, with a good deal of relish. "What a scramble there'll be. Eh ?"

"Requisitioned ?" said Derek, at this point; and inevitably—or so it seemed to Gavin—making use of the longest possible word.

"Eh ? Yes, that's right. That's what they call it. For the Yanks, they tell me. Well!" Here the speaker drove a knowing elbow into Mr. Todman's lean flank. "Just thought you'd like to know, old man. Your turn next, I dessay. What ? Eh ? Well, cheerioh!"

With another merry burst of laughter, and a nod for the two seated customers, he then withdrew once more to his own end of the counter, where he could be heard shouting for something called a Black-and-Tan.

He had undoubtedly, however, left a considerable sensation behind him. Mr. Todman looked anxious and shocked; for this was far the nearest that a very old threat had yet come, and if it came any nearer—as it now easily might—then there was the end of his job. He gulped. He drained his glass, and planked it down on the top of that sporting contrivance.

"Did you hear that ?" he asked—almost as though hoping to be told that he had mis-heard it himself.

"Yes," said Gavin, with a coldness in the pit of his own stomach, too. Not that in many ways he wouldn't be glad enough for this present partnership to be broken up; even though—being Gavin again—he was quite prepared to believe that it was he who was the more mutually-irritating factor. But London was crammed, and would be still more so with all those refugees from Combermere Court. He saw himself flat-hunting again, and ultimately paying a higher rent for something considerably worse. It was true—this was the other angle once more—that Derek could be darned difficult, and didn't always—no, honestly he didn't—pay his own fair share. But then —the first angle again—it was the war, of course, that made everyone get on everyone else's nerves. And at the back of his mind—no, he couldn't put a name to it at the moment—there was some other reason, he *knew*, why he had the strongest objection to being turned out of Huddleston House.

The war . . . Back it came, as the cause of everything. The weight that never lifted. The test under which he had so very conspicuously and ridiculously failed. Now he must go through all that again in his mind. Hell! No, he wouldn't. He was going to clear out of this place.

He began rising. But Derek was rising, too; and was quicker, because he didn't have to take those still only half-automatic precautionary measures to keep his own balance.

"Going ?" said Mr. Todman, who still seemed a good deal disturbed. "Here—I'll start with you. I've got a torch."

So they all left together. First they must negotiate the thick curtain inside the swing door. Then they must accustom their eyes to the pitch blackness, for Mr. Todman's torch gave a very inadequate light; and he kept waving it about, too, so that the pavement itself seemed sometimes to be undulating up and down. They all knew the way, though. They had only to go about fifty yards along the main road, and then turn into their owln street. And the other invisible wayfarers could at least see enough of a gimmer to avoid them.

"Dashed cold," said Derek's voice in the darkness. "When are we going to have some heat, Mr. Todman ?"

"I beg your pardon ? Oh, next week, I hope. Whoa! Here's the corner."

Another part of Gavin's mind had come into action. Perhaps the word "cold" was the clue; or perhaps it was the cold itself. But still and always —though he had as good as given up hope now of being an author himself— he was strangely affected by the printed or even the typewritten word. It coloured his thoughts. It swayed him—though, characteristically, he was rather ashamed of this, too—almost like a reed in the breeze. He was immune, he liked to think, from real tosh; and certainly he believed little or nothing that he read in the newspapers—for no one who had been in the Army could ever do that. But books, whether published or unpublished, could take hold of him again and again. He was absorbed—until the influence wore off. He was particularly, though still secretly, sentimental after reading a love-story. After reading an historical work, he saw everything—until another work drove this out—almost as though the present era was a mere mist between himself and the past. Mr. Bendish, the Senior Partner and Managing Director of Messrs. Dingle and Frisby, had learnt both to value and to mistrust this susceptibility; for though he could withstand it, and did, he knew also that it was a spirit which, in a publisher's office, can all too easily be lost and then badly missed.

The immediate point, though, was that to-day—for one must do anything and everything when a firm is short-handed—the junior partner had been checking the galleys (in which the erudite author had attempted to make far too many alterations) of a book about fossils and rocks. Not that he had known anything whatever about these objects at breakfast. But by lunch-time he was merged in them, too. He had returned from the office, in fact, as virtually a prehistoric man—though perhaps nobody would have guessed this; and now, though otherwise more or less back in the current century, he had just recalled something else. For the erudite author had mentioned, as though it was a well-known fact, that there had been five Ice-Ages already, and that there was no reason to suppose that the fifth was by any means the last.

Well, if so, thought Gavin, as he plunged along in the darkness, what on earth did it matter if a boiler was lighted or not ? What on earth, in fact, did anything matter, if London, within a few short years—taking a broad view, that was to say—was again to be under a glacier? He felt consoled, for some extraordinary reason. He even smiled, though at the next moment he was smiling at himself. But in any case he was far, far away from his present companions, when Mr. Todman suddenly stopped.

He was growling, too, as he directed the rays of his torch into a short *cul-de-sac*.

"What's the trouble ?" asked D. P. Moulton, though speaking, as always, in that flat and dispassionate voice.

"That feller's car again," said the manager, emboldened by rage, or resentment, or possibly by his own invisibility, to allude to another tenant as a feller. "If I've told him once, I've told him a thousand times. He can't leave it there!"

"I say," said Derek; "shall we let the tires down? How does one do it?"

But he was mocking, of course. He was always mocking. Gavin, who had now forgotten about the approaching Ice-Age, gave a tug at his arm.

"What?" said Derek.

"My foot," said Gavin, though in truth he was no more conscious of his disability than before. "Do you mind if we go on?"

"Oh. Your foot. Right. Here—hang on to me, if you like."

The words weren't spoken with undue sympathy, but Gavin did hang on. He also called out "Good-night" to Mr. Todman, who in any case would only be going a few yards further now, to his own quarters—a combined office and miniature ground-floor flat—in Bessingham House. But he was no longer consoled. For though it was right to pull Derek away, when he started behaving like that, it was unforgivable to have mentioned his foot. Why? Sensibility again, of course. Though it *was* hurting now, as it so often did, in response to the state of his nerves.

But he relaxed his grip—in fact, he let go altogether—as they re-entered their own block. The hall was as gloomy as ever. The lift was just nearing the top, for there was the counterweight, dropping to rest through the grille. "Dash!" said Derek, and stood waiting—for no one, at any rate, could have had less sympathy with machinery—with his finger pressing the button. Gavin thought of sitting on one of the fire-watchers' chairs; but then if he did that, he'd only have to get up again. He then suddenly wondered if he was fire-watching himself, and moved over to Party-Leader Popham's typewritten roster, which hung by the deserted niche.

No, it was all right. He needn't even sign the school exercise-book, which had been laid out on the imitation-mahogany shelf, and already bore the signatures of Miss Kenton-Hinksey and a couple of other tenants. Yet he still looked at it. Carefully, until he saw something; and beyond the something—which was only another and earlier autograph on the same page —at a vision far from clear. He wasn't only uncertain if the name—a sprawling "Bryony Bretton"—belonged to the vision or the vision's friend, but had even managed (though he didn't know this) to confuse their appearances as well. Hardly anyone else in the block could have done this; or if they had, and had been conscious of it, they could have asked a porter and settled the whole matter at once.

But Gavin couldn't possibly put questions like that. Nor, if he could avoid it, did he speak to these war-time porters; because they wore medal-ribbons—though they didn't look very soldierly—and if this meant that they despised him, he would much rather they did so behind his back. So he didn't quite know Miss Bretton and Miss Marsham apart—until a few weeks ago, in fact, he hadn't even completely distinguished them from Miss

Margetson; he had now attributed Miss Bretton's decidedly more flamboyant personality to both girls; but at the same time when he thought of this rather composite creature, he frequently found himself thinking of a lifted eyebrow, too.

This state, then, could hardly be described as infatuation, or as warranting any amendment to what has recently been said about his love-life. Yet he had, unquestionably, been drawn towards the exercise-book. He had paused by it, though it added nothing to his knowledge. And he gave a start now—not having heard the lift descend—as D. P. Moulton inquired if he proposed to remain there all night.

"No," he said. "Sorry."

They ascended together; and if Gavin shook his head in the cage or craft, it was only because he was now thinking of his father, and of how he must visit him again soon; because he hadn't been down there since August, and R. J. didn't want to come up. Well, why should he, now that air-raids had started again?

A sigh marked this point in his reflections; but you could have groaned, in the cage, without anyone hearing. Then it stopped, at the second floor. Both passengers got out, and each began feeling for his own latchkey. But the one with two genuine feet was naturally the first to reach the door of No. 12. He fumbled, he turned his key, and the door opened.

"Hullo!" he said. "Look what you've done. You've left the light on."

If there was one thing of which Gavin Guernsey was absolutely positive, even in this extraordinary and fantastic interval between Ice-Ages, it was that he had done nothing of the kind. He even remembered now, in the clearest possible manner, how he had stood by the lift before dinner, and had called out to his companion to hurry up. But he didn't say so. He would rather, it seemed, remain in the wrong than attempt to put himself in the right. He did clench his teeth, though, in that dim-lit passage. And he did wonder how much longer he could stand this sort of life.

CHAPTER VII

THE APPROACHING SOLSTICE HAD COME TO A POINT NOW WHERE IT WAS DARK in London for thirteen and a half hours on end, and though sunset had been postponed, by the State, the same thing had inevitably happened to sunrise. Not that there was much sun. There was a thick grey pall for most of each day, or at best it was pierced by some lurid rays of light. Amateur meteorologists, who had enormously increased in number since the outbreak of hostilities—and not merely owing to the suspension of weather reports—were divided into those who thought that the *Luftwaffe* would be put off by fog or rain (and therefore tended to welcome such conditions), and those who believed, or at least hoped, that even starlight was of assistance to our gunners and night-fighters, and were accordingly encouraged when the pall rolled away at dusk. With a little more observation, for which opportunity, in London at any rate, would be provided as the season wore on, both parties might be driven to qualify their theories, or even to merge into one party with no assurance at all. Others, of course, had actually trained themselves not to think of the thing, or not consciously, until the trouble began. And the trouble, at this period, wasn't really serious yet. That is to say that even five consecutive nights without a warning had now become distinctly unusual, but that these warnings, still as often as not, led to nothing worse than a distant bump or two. Or perhaps merely to the much louder sounds of a Civil Defence worker trying to start up a cold engine, or relieving his feelings by yelling: "Put out that light!"

For those who had been through the first great assault, this was nothing; or in a sense it was nothing. In another sense they secretly and separately found—or a lot of them did—that their nerve hadn't really improved during the lull; and that though in day-time they were fully aware that the odds against being hit were at least many thousands to one, at night, when the wailing had started, these suddenly and unaccountably shrank to an even chance. It was Yes or No now, as one waited either for more bumps or for the hopeful silence that might presage the long-drawn note. But you couldn't just skip in and out of London now, in the way that had once been possible. If you were here, you had got to put up with it.

Something else, too—and we don't mean the comparative peril of the Armed Forces, which was actually of little moral or statistical comfort when a rocket went up and sounded just like a bomb coming down. But in the first assault the populace—still with a certain amount of pre-war composure left—had been told, and had on the whole believed, that this monstrous and murderous business was the act of outlaws, and that by showing such pluck as they could manage to muster they were proving that decency must win. They were exalted as well as scared. They accepted such flattery as came their way—Heaven knows they had earned it—and felt, when the lull arrived at last, that by sticking it out they had saved rather more than themselves.

This was true, in terms of the game into which they had been forced. But the war wasn't over. Bombs now began falling on, or near, enemy objectives, to the accompaniment of frightful threats from characters like Mr. Lionel Haycock as to how their number and size were going to increase. The populace, though mostly consisting of Christians, didn't mind a bit of revenge. They thought it reasonable, so far as anything was reasonable now, that there should at least be tit for tat. But personally they didn't want more. And if the whole competition could have been called off when a balance had been reached, most of them would have been considerably relieved.

But it wasn't. It went on. The Press and the Haycocks worked themselves into a lather of enthusiasm over the first thousand-bomber raid. The much quieter populace wasn't so sure. They had had their vicarious revenge now, and it didn't taste as good as all that. They saw, moreover, though the Press and the Haycocks kept very mum about this, that they were now passing into a position where revenge might be exacted again. Even when Bishops said that this was the way to shorten the conflict, and newspapers printed aerial photographs of craters amid roofless buildings, they still weren't at ease in their hearts. They were slow at expressing their feelings, and in London at any rate, by this time, it was thought rather provincial to mention the conflict—except in its more personal aspects—at all. Yet how was it, even with the aid of unspecified instruments, that only targets of military importance were being hit, when thick cloud, as it was also stated, made observation impossible ? How, some of them wondered, could even an Archbishop get round that ?

We're asking for it, they thought, still kindly indentifying themselves with the State. So that they felt rueful rather than heroic when the hostile assaults were resumed. They shrugged their shoulders, or in some cases were buried alive, with certain doubts in their minds. This was different from last time, and they knew it. If they were kept awake by their own bombers going out, with a sound like a vast, bubbling cauldron, they naturally hoped that as many of them as was possible would return. But in spite of all the rhetoric and leading articles, they didn't really enjoy the sound. Not in London, which had now got to take it again; and would do so, but never in quite the same spirit as before.

It made for more sadness, though still of a silent sort. Yet at dawn on a November morning, in this huge, shabby, battle-scarred city, one would hardly expect to find very much gaiety about. There was a slight fog, and a dampness on the pavements. Overhead, looking foolish, if devoted as ever, those balloons were again just visible in the leaden sky. Presently a few windows would glow here and there, as residents unhooked or drew back their curtains, and at last were enabled to breathe a little fresh air. There was no blaze, though. For the dawn, though half-hearted, was already overtaking the smaller and only apparently more brilliant lights. They began going out again. There was no special glow in the east more than anywhere else. But it was day now; and the outline of Huddleston House was no longer a mere silhouette.

Here came the milkmen, trundling those hand-carts with their clanking loads. Apart from the weekly pool-delivery service from the big shops —for which in practice it seemed that very few people could wait—nothing but milk, newspapers, and letters was now brought to the door. But this didn't mean that one got what one expected—unless, of course, one was Mrs. Musselberg, who had her own methods; and often it was found necessary, though only half-dressed, to rush out on to the landing and argue about the day of the week. In such arguments—again except in the case of Mrs. Musselberg—the milkman invariably came off best. It was always his view that you had had more yesterday, or would have more to-morrow, than he had been able to bring to-day. You yielded, though convinced that he was mistaken, for you were officially wedded to him now for the rest of the war. You even thanked him for bringing nothing, in the end, for it was better and safer this way. No coffee this morning, though. You must waste some more tea.

The milkmen all used the lift, and you couldn't blame them for not walking up twelve flights of stairs—for each stage was divided into three. But they did rather tend to leave the gates open while serving each landing; so that the postman shouted at them, and the boys who brought the newspapers screeched at them, and the Daily Helps, who were arriving too, now, emitted some loud and rather pungent remarks as well. If any tenant wished to leave the premises at this sort of hour, as a number of them were at least forced to do, they had long since learnt to descend, even from the top floor, with no other aid than their legs.

As for the porters this morning, Popham had now retired to his own home, which was beyond The Dwellings; Freeth, who was on day-duty now, was changing, without haste, into his uniform in the basement, and chatting with Eldritch, the stoker, as he did so; while the invaluable though exasperating Truelove, having left the cord of the electric-sweeper trailing across the entrance-hall, so that anyone in a hurry was almost bound to trip over it, was now—attired in his overalls—polishing the brass finger-plates on the inner, main doors. This meant that if you survived the cord, you had to wait while he moved a bucket of dirty water—the exact purpose of which was not wholly clear—and get out of the way as he told you, still without haste, what he thought about the weather. According to Truelove, it wasn't so bad this morning, though something had touched up his back. But you mustn't argue with Truelove, either. He was far too invaluable. You must just simmer, and control yourself, and step sideways, and so burst into the street. Then he replaced the bucket, and was ready for the next encounter.

Nearly all over the block the tenants were hustling through breakfast, or had finished already, so as to emerge—roughly speaking, in an order that was in inverse ratio to their importance—and make for the bus-queues again. Mrs. Amberley was one of the first, for though not due at her bench until noon, she had arranged to have her hair done this morning as soon as the one and only possible establishment opened. She had had time to put all her paint on, though, and looked very vivid as she sped forth. Then came Miss Kenton-Hinksey, the only one who seemed really interested—though she wasn't, and he quite obviously thought the less of her for her sympathy

—in Truelove's back. Next came June Margetson, running and looking angry; and looking angrier still as she all but fell over the cord, and only just saved herself by dropping her hand-bag.

"Not your lucky morning," said Truelove, suspending his labours. He didn't add "Miss," or attempt to retrieve the bag.

"God!" said Miss Margetson, under her breath, as she swept past him. He heard her all right, but he liked them young. He even came out on to the pavement, so as to watch her running again, which she did gracefully enough, towards the end of the street. He approved so much of this spectacle, indeed, that he winked at a postman, and made a vulgar noise with his tongue.

More youth for Truelove, though this time he was too late to obstruct it. Miss Marsham, not quite so pale, perhaps, when seen alone, came hurrying out, and down the two steps. It was less easy to be graceful, with a bundle of washing tied in a sheet, and having to be supported and embraced like an unwieldy baby; while in addition to this Miss Marsham had her own hand-bag, and a shopping-bag as well. The washing, it was to be hoped, she would deposit at the laundry—though it had an awkward habit of locking its door, without previous notice, when surfeited with such bundles. But the shopping-bag must go with her, by omnibus, to the office, for it must be filled—whatever happened to Echo herself—in the lunch-interval.

Or should we call her Jemima? This was still her real name, and particularly her real name at home; or at what she thought of as home, which in other words was where her mother was staying—like so many mothers in these days—with her grandmother in the country, though as anything but an idle guest. Her father got over for week-ends, sometimes, from a town nearly a hundred miles further away, where he was temporarily though indefinitely stationed with a training battalion. One of her brothers was in Palestine, at the moment, and the other in West Africa, which in a way might have been much worse. She even had a considerably younger sister—so that it was quite an unusually large family for the present epoch—at the school where she had met Bugs; now transferred from the South Coast to Shropshire. But too much had happened, and too much time had gone by, for her to think of another damaged and deserted London house as home. Grannie's was home, though it also—or most of it—was the headquarters for some Canadians, and she had spent perhaps as much as five weeks there, altogether, since the first full summer of war. Such, now, was her background; but if you were christened Jemima only a couple of years after the other war, there was something to be deduced from this.

For one sees at once, if one's vision can be cast back, that her parents must have been youngish and rather gay then. That Jemima, for them, would have no connotation with an elastic-sided boot; but on the contrary represented independence of spirit, and even an illusion that they were at the dawn of a new era. It presents a picture of hope, and even of slight impertinence to the world at large. It was calculated to make one's friends say "How amusing!"—just as they used to say it about the striped wall-paper in Mrs. Marsham's drawing-room, which was held to be a very dashing form of revivalism then, and her collection of *papier-mâché* furniture. The Marshams were still enough in the same mood to call their next child Jonathan. But after this it would seem that they were a bit more caught in the toils. For their second son was called Michael, which proved presently to be so widespread that they had clearly either lost or abandoned their claim to be pioneers. And the last child, who appeared after a longer gap, was merely one of an innumerable quantity of Annes.

There's history for you; both domestic and national, if your mind is attuned to such detail. And now Jemima had become Echo in London; so much so that even her mother knew of it, and was a little resentful, but had learnt too much, and was also too busy, to mention this feeling aloud. She knew, in a way, that it was Bryony's doing; but then—for time goes so fast as your children grow up—she still saw Bryony (whom she never dreamt of calling Bugs) as a stoutish, pig-tailed child. Or it was from this point that she must always start, when she thought of her, and indeed she had hardly set eyes on her since that stage. She knew her mother, though, and in spite of having had four children herself of whom not one had turned out to be the least what she expected, still felt that she knew Bryony, too. So she was glad that the two girls were friends, and could, as she put it, look after each other. It was something off her mind, which was rather overladen at this period. For not only was she doing housework for her own mother—which was made no lighter by constantly being told how tired she looked; not only was she separated from her husband, who looked just as tired if she ever saw him; not only was she distracted by the delays in communicating with her sons, and at the same time conscious that other mothers thought she had nothing to complain of, because they weren't in Italy; but she was also in a considerable dither—though she would have laughed it off easily enough a few years ago—because Anne kept writing to her and saying that she wanted to be trained for the ballet.

So the elder daughter had letters, too, but there wasn't much in them, because Mrs. Marsham wasn't nearly as anxious about her; having acquired —even if largely in self-defence—an attitude towards air-raids on London that might briefly be described as out of hearing, out of mind. Well, one couldn't worry about *everything* at once; and her elder daughter didn't worry her, and never referred to them, either. Truelove, still on the pavement, said: "Careful does it!" as Miss Marsham flitted past him; and was rewarded —which was rather more than he deserved—with the eyebrow trick and a faint but patient smile. The postman had gone now, and there was no one to wink at. He returned, rather reluctantly, to his work.

A few minutes later Mr. Everard came down, with his official expression already set for the day, and carrying a black portfolio emblazoned with the Royal Arms.

" 'Morning, sir," said Truelove, with a shade more respect. "Not too bad last night, eh ?"

He was alluding to the sirens, which were all that had sounded, so that only a few people with weak hearts—and none in this block—were any the worse. But Mr. Everard was indisposed to discuss them.

"If you leave that wire across the floor like that," he said, "you'll break somebody's leg. I—I've spoken about it before, you know."

There was a brief clash of wills, and Mr. Everard's won.

"Very good, sir," said Truelove, relapsing for a moment into almost pre-war servility. He even made as if to kick the cord out of the way, as Mr. Everard shot into the street. Then it came over him, though not quite correctly, that had this been Russia, it would be he who would be ordering the tenants about. He relaxed. He muttered menacingly to himself. He went back to the finger-plates.

Two tenants suddenly came in now. Mr. Waterman, of No. 20, whom you haven't met yet, and may well not meet again—for he was employed in a branch of the censorship which kept him at work all night, and in bed nearly all day; and Miss Tuke, off duty now, also, and swaggering briskly home.

Then more emergence. Gavin Guernsey, who was lucky enough to have caught the lift, though he had first had to go up to the third floor, and then to the top, with Mrs. Goosey and a belated milkman. Then, among more figures, in and out of uniform—and some of the uniforms would have seemed startlingly outlandish not so many years ago—came Mr. Barker, who had had no excuse to bring his car back last night, and must therefore make an early start; and Derek Moulton, with another portfolio, but this time with nothing but his initials stamped on it; and Miss Bryony Bretton, high-heeled and hatless, and also with the newspaper that Miss Marsham—who had prepared both their breakfasts—hadn't yet had time to read.

Some of these characters, though they came out one by one, would almost certainly be assembling, in a sense, at the nearest bus-stop. But others would be assembling, also, at this first of the two rush-hours, so that even if they knew each other by more than sight, they might still be kept apart. Each bus, as it approached, appeared to be full to the bung, and hardly any of them stopped so that their step, or rear platform, was opposite the head of the queue. Traces of chivalry also complicated the boarding of these vehicles; and the varying personalities of the conductors and conductresses;

and alighting passengers who fought madly, at the last moment, to get out;
and a widespread divergence of opinion as to the morality of embarking to
the right of the platform when you didn't really mean to go on the top.
Some of the smaller conductresses were nothing but a high, urgent voice,
or an arm like that of a drowning person coming up for the third time as
the congestion of bodies overwhelmed them. Yet gradually the queue
grew shorter, and the buses just slightly less crowded, and the sky perhaps
a shade or two lighter as well.

At Huddleston House the invaluable Truelove had now finished his
polishing, had picked up his bucket and emptied it into the gutter, and had
even coiled up the cord of the electric-sweeper, too. He had vanished, in
fact, in a subterranean direction; but Freeth, fully accoutred by now in a
jacket with embossed buttons—which had first been worn by a porter now
fighting in Burma—and a somewhat shiny pair of trousers which didn't
quite match, and a cap with a grease-mark on the top and a peak in front,
had come up and taken his place. He waited a moment. He looked at his
big watch. He glanced out through the swing doors again; and there—
punctual as ever—was the well-known, mud-coloured car.

"All right!" he shouted, momentarily opening one of the doors with his
foot. "I'll tell 'im!"

For this, each morning at exactly the same hour, was Freeth's contribution
to the war-effort; or every alternate week, that's to say, when Popham wasn't
doing just the same thing. He even managed to look slightly military himself
once more—though there had been something like twenty-five years of odd
jobs and unemployment in his life since the date of his demobilisation—
as he squared his shoulders and gave two sharp pokes at the bell-push of
No. 4.

"All right," said the voice of Major Hurst from within. "I know."

"Your car, sir," bawled Freeth.

"Coming," said Major Hurst, and he came; smoking a cigarette, and
looking very well-shaven, and also a bit of a brute. On the threshold he
paused, and turned round, so that Freeth was left touching his cap, for the
moment, in vain.

"Bunny!" he snapped.

"Yessir?"

"Might be having a guest for dinner to-night. Leave enough for two,
will you?"

"Very good, sir. Would you like me to stay on, sir?"

"No," said Major Hurst. "But see it's all right."

"Very good, sir."

Major Hurst then turned round again, slamming the front door as he
did so, and Freeth renewed his salute.

"Ha!" said Major Hurst. " 'Morning."

"Good-morning, sir. Not very bright, I'm afraid."

"Eh ? Oh."

Not very encouraging, but Freeth wasn't the least damped. He hurried, with his stiff leg, into the hall; he opened one of the swing doors as wide as it would go; he dashed through it after the Major, overtook him on the pavement, and opened the door of the car.

" 'Morning, Miss Gooch."

"Good-morning, Major Hurst," said the fat, female driver.

The Major then ducked, and with quite an agile contortion for a man of his age, twisted himself on to the back seat. Freeth closed the door with a business-like bang, and again was unusually erect.

"Right away, miss," he said, rather, in a sense, as though starting the Flying Scotsman. The fat, female driver gave him the tenth part of a dirty look from her small, pig-like eyes—to show him, perhaps, that she took orders from no one like that. But in the circumstances she couldn't very well stay where she was; so she raced the engine, let in the clutch, and set off with such vigour as to remove possibly the best part of an ounce of rubber from both the back wheels. They were enormously thick tires, though; for though it had never been there, the car always looked ready to go straight to the nearest battlefield—or the furthest, if it comes to that. It set off, accordingly, like a shot from a gun, squealed horribly as it braked to take the corner into the main road, and so disappeared from sight. Yet Freeth, still left saluting again—until suddenly he seemed to come to himself, and was noticeably round-shouldered once more—certainly wouldn't have had it start in any other way. If one re-examines his procedure during the last few minutes, one will see that he had done nothing whatever of any real value, and had neither been thanked nor tipped. But apart from the fact that he undoubtedly would be tipped, and almost positively before the end of the month, he had shared in something. In theory he might be as red and revolutionary as Truelove, and as singularly envious and ignorant of conditions in Russia; but all this went when a man was a Major, and spoke to you like a dog, and drove off in a mud-coloured car like that. Henceforth, though he had undoubtedly many duties to perform, and to a certain extent would even carry them out, there would be no jumping to it on the part of Freeth. He would be slow, obstructive, and deliberately stupid. He would forget messages. He would gossip, he would loiter, he would linger. He would be as insolent as he dared. And—with a watchful eye for Mr. Todman—he would slip more than once in and out of the Royal Oak.

But he had had his great moment for all that Now, for he had no wish to lose its flavour by contact with any other tenant—except possibly Mrs. Wardrop—he returned to the comfortable warmth of the cellar.

This moment also marked, once more, the end of the main morning exodus. Anyone on his or her way to an office—except possibly Mr. Vardas

and Mr. Musselberg, who each in his own way kept very erratic hours—
would have passed through the hall and joined in the general dispersal.
It was the hour, again, when the last Daily Help had arrived; though as many
of them were pluralists, serving more than one flat, it might still be a long time
before all the beds were made. And Huddleston House, always a little
shabbier with each day that dawned, might be imagined to relax just a little,
as its main doors stopped swinging, and there was no longer a perpetual
droning from the lift.

But it was neither empty nor asleep. Mops were being banged against
skirting-boards, crockery was being sluiced and chipped, dusters were being
flapped out of windows, and in a number of cases, where the tenants were
now absent, such labour was being lightened by the use of their radio-sets.
Presently, also, if not already, such tenants as were still on the premises must
leave their more purely domestic duties, and set out once more for the shops.
They couldn't telephone now—or there would be no result if they did—
and of course no one called for orders. They must wrap up, because it was
cold; they must make hopeful lists on the backs of old envelopes; they must
find their ration books; they must pick up the bag or basket that accompanied them nearly everywhere nowadays; and they must again go forth
to take part in the battle of life.

Thus, also, then, Mrs. Geoffrey Margetson, of No. 18, having listened
for as long as she thought necessary to Mrs. Goosey's morning gossip, put
on her coat—and a hat, too, for somehow she still clung to this custom—
and with a swollen hand-bag under one arm, and the other through the
handle of a somewhat battered basket, emerged from her own fastness,
and pushed the button for the lift.

It clanked; it moaned; the cage appeared, and stopped, not exactly at
the landing, but near enough for the gate to open, and for anyone at all
familiar with its habits to avoid tripping over the step. So Mrs. Margetson
embarked, and shut both gates, and pushed another button. After slight
hesitation, and some shuddering, the lift obeyed her, and took her down to
the hall—or, to be precise, about four inches beyond it. She released herself,
she climbed out, she shut the outer gate—without answering the voice that
was shouting impatiently from aloft—and then she, too, passed through
one of the swing doors, and was in the cold, grey street.

To say that she was a little shattered this morning, is to state no unusual
fact. Yet there were reasons, and again she couldn't quite shake them off.
In the first place, she had had a bad night, because of the Alert. In the
second place there had been no letter from her husband or from Robin,
and both were considerably overdue. In the third place—though this
happened nearly always after a warning—Mrs. Goosey had been late. While
this, in turn—which was the fourth weight on her mind now—had led to one
of those scenes with June, in which June had first cursed the name of Goosey

at the top of her voice, and had then indulged in something approaching a fight with her mother while each of them had attempted to get the other's breakfast.

"Stay where you are, can't you, mother! You're only getting in the way."

"But, darling, you must catch your bus."

"I *know* I must. But if you *will* keep—— Oh, lord, what *have* you done with the sugar ?"

"It's on the table, darling. I put it there. Now, do just let me——"

"I won't! You just muddle everything!"

"June!"

"What ?"

A look of absolute defiance. And June had won, too, as she always did. Not only because she was younger and stronger, even though she, too, was tired; but for another reason that only her mother knew. For her mother, though pained and piqued at being addressed like this, could never forget what a much easier time she herself had had during the first world-war. True, she had done something called war-work—as she was again doing now. But it had been nothing. It had even been rather fun. Then, too, there was never going to be another war, and June had been brought up in this belief. And now there was one, and all June's own fun was ended; and she had got this job—for which her mother saluted her—but whether useless or not (and about this Mrs. Margetson could never feel really or comfortably sure), it involved the most appalling hours. At one moment the child had been a butterfly, at Wallington Gardens. At the next, or almost at the next —for no one could now distinguish one phase of this second and endless war from another—she was away for ten hours each day, with no half-holiday, and even on Sundays with no guaranteed break or rest.

I brought her up to get married, thought Mrs. Margetson—though perhaps she was under a common illusion in believing that she had steered or directed her daughter at all—and how can she do that when there aren't any men, and there aren't any houses, and nobody's got any money ?

This was an exaggeration, of course, if least so in the case of the houses. Yet comparatively speaking it wasn't untrue; so that when her daughter became covered with prickles, and spoke to her in the language of a legendary fishwife, and then flung herself out of the flat with a violent slam of the front door, Mrs. Margetson must still make allowances, and still love her—because of course one loved one's daughter—and still keep contrasting the life that she had missed with the life that she was undergoing now.

Poor June, she thought, in fact. And again she blamed herself for not having learnt more about cooking in the days of peace. And she thought that perhaps she *did* muddle everything, though she still tried to feel that she was giving her daughter a home. She *can* be so nice, thought Mrs. Margetson. Well, naturally, she thought, she takes it out of me, because I'm nearest and she sees me oftenest. But she didn't proceed from these premises to the very faintest notion of leaving her child in the lurch. She didn't even consider whether in fact it would be the lurch or not. She was a traditionalist, though all tradition was being battered and blown to pieces. If only, she thought, as she approached the main road, there could be a Man.

But there wasn't; or she had seen no sign of him; and how could there be in a world that had become like this ? It isn't, thought Mrs. Margetson, suddenly defending herself, that I want grandchildren. Who *could*, in a world like this ? But at the same time . . .

The whole web of thoughts became tangled. She did want grandchildren, and so, she was sure, did Geoffrey. After all, that *usedn't* to be such a selfish wish. It was part of the pattern. You wore yourself out over your own children, and were rewarded, about a quarter of a century later, by spoiling your children's children without any fear of the consequences. She thought of her own grandparents. The *solidity* that there had been there, even through the first world-war. They were like gods; though it was true that they were dead now. All those servants. Amazing. Yes, of course they were kind; but what had they got to worry about ? Even her parents had just scraped through in time. But she and Geoffrey hadn't. And now what was happening ? Families were being squeezed and telescoped in this awful world, so that even if you had a grandchild—and one was about as much as you could expect—you couldn't get away from it. It was dumped on you—she knew dozens of cases—though its father and mother weren't even together elsewhere.

How lucky, she thought—though this hardly accorded with what she had been thinking a moment ago—was her sister Daisy, who lived safely in the country with a retired husband (by which she meant a husband who had retired from work), and had no child at all. And then her conscience smote her, so that she looked flushed and uneasy as she entered her bank. Yet there was plenty of time in which to steady herself, so far as this was possible; for, as usual, there was a queue here, too.

As, usual, also, it contained a large proportion of people—from shops, she supposed—who were paying in notes and coins that must be counted, apparently, not less than three times. Further beyond the counter there seemed no urgent activity among the staff, some of whom were quite clearly just chatting. But in war-time a customer must always wait, and there was only the one cashier. He flipped, fingered, started again, made ticks with a blue pencil, and then hurled all the money into a drawer or on to a shelf as though it was as valueless as most of it looked. But only then did the client at the head of the queue explain that he or she wanted three pounds back again; and only later still that five shillings must be in coppers.

You couldn't say that the cashier was impatient. But you couldn't say that he was in a hurry, either. Nor, by some metaphysical alchemy, was anyone, however restless beforehand, who finally claimed his attention. There was further chatting across the counter, in fact, as often as not. And then, again, a secondary queue had developed, edging forward from the other direction; so that even when Mrs. Margetson was at last at the head of her own, she still missed three turns owing to lack, she supposed, of the right kind of personality.

"Yes, madam ?"

She started from another dream. She opened the swollen handbag. She even found her cheque, though not quite as quickly or promptly as she could have wished.

"Could I——" she began.

The cashier had gone. A young woman had come forward from one of the desks at the back, and was holding him in muttered converse. There was a jingling thud, and a youth from the opposing queue had placed a bag absolutely bursting with bullion between Mrs. Margetson and the grille. Her impulse was to step back, though fortunately she couldn't, owing to the ize and personality of the man just behind her. She trod on his foot, though.

"Oh!" she said. "I'm *so* sorry!"

He didn't answer her. She was abased. She was bewildered. Perhaps, she thought, she had dropped something, and had trodden on that instead. She turned round. She looked down. There was nothing there; but as she rose and revolved again, she was just in time to see the youth discharging the contents of his bag in a shower of specie. The cashier, or her own character, had betrayed her. It would take at least five minutes, she calculated, if not ten, to count and re-count such a mass of money as that.

She gave it up. She felt a fool and a weakling, as she so often did in these days, and she was convinced—though perhaps wrongly—that everyone was staring at her as she gave up her place and went out again into the street. But she had had enough. Her spirit couldn't stand any more. Perhaps Gilpin, the grocer, would cash her cheque—well, he would have to, in a way, if he wanted to be paid—though she knew well enough that he would bluster and complain; which was why she had gone to the bank.

But she wasn't going back into the bank now. She couldn't. It was impossible. She was quite late enough already.

A brief pause now; partly in the hope of regaining her poise, or whatever was still left of it, and partly to consult a scrap of paper at the bottom of the basket. Yet actually it was into a shop that wasn't listed at all, and on another uncontrollable impulse, that Mrs. Margetson now made her way. It was a small jeweller's, and like many of the shops which hadn't now been closed altogether, had had its window reduced, by boarding, to about the size of a picture-frame. But it was empty enough. At the moment, in fact, it seemed to be quite unattended. Mrs. Margetson waited.

Hesitated. Moved towards the door again. Thought of her recent irre-solution at the bank, and came back, and tapped on the counter.

A furious-looking man popped out through an inner door.

"Look here," he said, "you can't expect me to do everything at once. What is it?"

Mrs. Margetson blinked, moistened her lips, and looked apologetic.

"I'm sorry," she said. "I—I didn't know you were busy."

"Some people," said the man, in the same injured and exasperated tone, "don't seem to think at all. Do you want something?"

These last words were, comparatively speaking, so gracious that Mrs. Margetson—who had received much rougher treatment than this in many a shop, and for even less cause—looked almost grateful.

"It was about my watch," she said, humbly. "I was just——"

"Watch?" The man seemed provoked almost beyond endurance again. "I keep telling people," he howled. "We don't stock 'em, we don't sell 'em, we don't clean 'em, and we don't repair 'em. If anyone comes in here and says Watch to me again——"

He indicated the probable effect by a frightful rictus and the clenching of both fists. Mrs. Margetson took half a step backwards.

"But——" she began rather desperately.

"That's what they all say!" said the man. "But it makes no difference. I tell 'em—I tell 'em till I'm tired of telling 'em. Think they can get round me. Think it's all under the counter. Think I can make a watch out of——"

Baffled, apparently, for a sufficiently ridiculous noun here, he was reduced to glaring for a moment; and this gave Mrs. Margetson her chance.

"But I don't *want* a watch," she said. "At least," she corrected herself, with some courage, "it's only my own watch I wanted to ask about. You—you've had it since April, you know."

"Eh?" said the man, now looking at her for the first time as though with some attempt to distinguish her features. "Oh," he said. "It's Mrs.—— Mrs.—— Mrs. . . . ?"

"Margetson," said Mrs. Margetson, obligingly, though at this stage without much hope.

"That's right," said the man, but a little grudgingly, and as if he might easily have said that it was wrong. "April?" he repeated.

"Yes."

"That's nothing," He was contemptuous again. "I tell you, people have left watches here *far* longer than that. It's the war, you see." (Oh, dear, thought Mrs. Margetson.) "*I* can't do 'em. I won't even take 'em now." ("There!" he seemed to imply. "You see what a favour you've had.") "They all go away; an' if they don't come back—well, that's why I won't touch 'em now. Got enough trouble," he added, gloomily, "without that."

"Oh, I'm sure you have," said Mrs. Margetson. "But you did say I could look in again this month——"

The man stopped her by shaking his head.

"Not before Christmas," he said. "Not now. Not a chance. Absolutely not a chance."

He seemed a shade happier. And Mrs. Margetson was certainly no worse off.

"I see," she said. "Thank you."

The man was mute. All passion, as you might say, was spent. Indeed, he appeared to have subsided into a form of catalepsy—or was it a present-day shopkeeper's nirvana?—as Mrs. Margetson turned, and left him, and went out into the street. For herself she was hardly soothed by the encounter; yet it was better, in a way, to start off with a row and end with a species of calm than to suffer the far too common alternative. She wondered—she couldn't help wondering—how on earth her recent antagonist made a living; and, being Mrs. Margetson, she was even oppressed by the troubles to which he had referred as well as her own. But it was also the case that in more than six watchless months, and in a city where at least three-quarters of the public clocks were now out of order, she had acquired a considerable gift for guessing the time.

So she guessed now, and was rather shocked by the answer—for there was still nothing but that list in her basket. Yet somehow this reminded her of her daughter, who would be immured—while she herself was in a sense at large—for the best part of eight more hours. And this decided her, despite the basket, to have another shot, on June's behalf, at Hernshaw the Cash Chemist's.

It was easy enough to cross the main road nowadays—but, oh, wha wouldn't one give for the perils and hesitations of the past!—and within matter of minutes she was in another shop, where again, thank Heaven there was no queue. The assistant or manager—but no doubt he was both now—was even waiting behind the counter, in a white overcoat and a state of suspended animation. His face was quite colourless, unlike the jeweller's, and he looked, as was so customary now, just a little mad. But he wasn't in the habit of being particularly rude, and though he gave no sign of recognition as Mrs. Margetson approached him, he could hardly be unaware, she hoped, that it was a long time since she had dealt anywhere else.

"Good-morning," she said; and then she began talking about June's face-cream. Something in his continued silence and immobility made her drag the story out, so that at one point she even heard her own voice, which is always a little embarrassing. But she kept on talking. She explained what the face-cream was called, and how and when it had been ordered, and how she had been in before, and how her daughter had been in before, and how there had been no actual promise that it would be kept for them if it turned up, but that her daughter, who had so little time for shopping herself, just happened to be rather particularly keen on this special brand.

She tried a smile at this point, but as there was no response she re-trod some of the old ground. She was aware that she was repeating herself, and that she was also becoming a bit breathless; but if the man just stared at her like that with those pale eyes, it seemed essential to continue until he at least showed some sign of life. I've done all this before, she was thinking. He's always like this. Does he hate us, or is he ill, or what *is* the matter with him ? But again she thought: At least he's not rude.

And he wasn't; or not in any manner that could possibly be compared with the jeweller. He just waited, looking worn, drawn, and exhausted, until Mrs. Margetson finally ran down. And then, very slowly, he just shook his head.

"Oh," she said. "You mean, it hasn't come in, then ?"

Looking unutterably mournful now, he gave a faint, faint nod.

"I see," said Mrs. Margetson. "Well—thank you. Thank you very much. I—I——"

She gave it up. She was too tired herself to start the whole story again, and there was nothing else to say. Would it please him if she bought a bottle of disinfectant ? She couldn't tell, yet somehow doubted if it would. Of course, as soon as she got outside, she remembered that she hadn't had the month's soap ration, and that this ought to have been on the list. But she couldn't go in again. At the moment, in fact, she wasn't at all sure that she, too, hadn't lost her voice.

She had recovered it, however, by the time that she stood in another rather informal and unprincipled queue at Hacking's—the baker—where she was eventually supplied with a loaf that she wanted and a farthing that she didn't. Hence she proceeded—crossing the road again—to Mudford, the greengrocer, where there was more honour in the queue (but it was much longer), and she was finally furnished with a rather battered-looking collection of Brussels sprouts.

And so at length, with a thoughtful glance at the Britannia Wine Stores— but even if they were open they wouldn't have anything, and even if they had anything she couldn't pay for it until she had cashed that cheque—Mrs. Margetson arrived at Gilpin's. Its windows, as usual, were crammed with piles, pillars, and pyramids of tins and cartons, nearly all of which—as everyone now knew—were dummies. Inside—for after Mrs. Margetson had disentangled herself from a dachshund's lead in the doorway, she entered without further obstruction—there were the remains of the old, pre-war smell of coffee, mingled with a less attractive aroma of customers' mackintoshes. Here, also, there was no shortage of tins, cartons, and bottles, whether there was anything in them or not. Not only were they on shelves on all sides, but they had also been used to form a series of machicolations along the counter itself, which was thus divided into a number of open bays.

At two of them, as was obvious, one could wait for ever without anything happening at all.   At each of the remaining orifices there wasn't so much a queue as a swarm of persons with bags and baskets, who were all more or less forcibly impinging on each other and at the same time making ready to catch the assistant's eye.   Once, though this seemed quite fantastic now, Mrs. Margetson had had a weekly book at Gilpin's, and Gilpin's had a boy with a box-tricycle, and one telephoned, or one's cook—just imagine having a cook!—gave orders on one's behalf, and commodities flowed into Wallington Gardens as fast as, or indeed sometimes faster than, one chose.   In those days Mrs. Margetson had hardly ever come here herself—for already it was a case of either trusting the cook, whether trustworthy or not, or having no cook at all—and in consequence, to her subsequent regret, had established very little personal goodwill.   Yet for a while, as an old customer, she had at least imagined that she would have acquired some standing, and at the beginning of the war had even acted, not altogether unsuccessfully, on this belief.

Then, however, it was gradually borne in on her that though she herself was becoming a little more servile at each visit, the proprietor and his assistants were taking less and less pains to distinguish her from anyone else.   Goodwill, if there had ever been any, seemed to have vanished entirely.   She was just a unit now; another nuisance with a ration book; and again not only had the State decreed that she and Gilpin's must be bound together as firmly as in matrimony, but she was well aware that if, by moving mountains, she obtained a divorce through the Food Office, she would receive exactly the same treatment elsewhere.

The trouble, or part of the trouble, was that she quite saw how if a shop couldn't lose a customer, and if it, too, was incessantly tormented by rules and regulations, and if stocks and staff were both inadequate, then naturally it would behave as it did.   But this knowledge or sympathy was no advantage. It merely weakened her position still further.   Other people, who still fussed and complained, or shouted and threatened, didn't always, it was true, get as much as they seemed to expect.   But their spirit wasn't yet broken; whereas Mrs. Margetson, who had at first only meant to be civil and had now become servile, was incapable, at the first sniff or cold stare from behind the counter, of even demanding her rights.

June wasn't.   Once or twice, on her day's leave, June had come here with her mother, and with a mixture of youth and impatience had burst through Gilpin's defences with most profitable and amazing results.   "There you are, mother," she would say.   "You've only got to stand up to them. You'll never get anything if you're so polite."   True?   Absolutely.   But Mrs. Margetson couldn't help being polite, and, what was more, felt bound to be politer than ever after one of June's incursions; so that next time she got less than ever, and in the long run was no better off. She thought of this now, as she eyed the two knots or bunches—one of which was certainly smaller than the other, but on the other hand was being dealt with by the proprietor, who was distinctly more irritable than the dumpy woman nearer the door—and again she wondered if June wouldn't really manage better without her.

Yet it was an old and unanswerable speculation, and must remain so, for a thousand reasons, while present national, financial, and domestic conditions prevailed. So she thrust it aside. She plumped for the dumpy woman, though it would probably be at least twenty minutes before her own turn came. And she relapsed, so far as possible, into a gently shuffling automaton—with moments of rigidity when even she felt that she might otherwise yield too much ground—and thought of little or nothing, one is bound to admit, as the preliminary process of shopping at a grocer's ate up some more irreplaceable time.

Sometimes there was a quick customer, and she had a flash of hope. Then there was a slow one, and her heart sank. Sometimes, again, the dumpy woman disappeared for so long that one doubted if she would ever return. And there were foreigners, of course—there were always foreigners now, even in this part of London—who weren't only slow but exigent as well. It occurred to Mrs. Margetson, though she tried to down this thought, that a little humility on their part would be more in order, and that if they had behaved like this in their own country they might not be in exile now. But of course this kind of thought had no effect on them; and even the dumpy woman seemed more amused than annoyed when one of them kept on asking for eggs.

Then, quite suddenly, Mrs. Margetson was at the counter at last. The dumpy woman immediately stopped smiling, and looked at her—or this was unquestionably the impression that she gave—with traces of disgust.

"Well?" she said; for Mrs. Margetson had wasted a moment in smiling herself.

"Oh." With some difficulty, owing to pressure from behind, the new customer got her basket on to the counter. "Good-morning," she added. "Could I just have my rations, please? Oh, and——"

"Book," said the assistant.

Here Mrs. Margetson's over-charged hand-bag exploded, but since the two ration books came out as well as much else, she was able to sweep them forward promptly enough. Dumpy picked them up, fluttered their flabby leaves, and did some snipping and scribbling.

"No bacon," she said.

Mrs. Margetson thought this was a question.

"Well, I would *like* some, if——"

"I say there isn't any." Sniff. "It's come in bad."

"It's . . . ? Oh, I see. Thank you. Well, is there any marmalade ?"

This question, also, was put too politely. Several previous shoppers had been given marmalade—which June liked, though Mrs. Margetson didn't much care one way or the other. Moreover, they had been supplied from a shelf that still appeared to have a number of jars. But Dumpy, sliding away sideways so as to collect the other rations, looked scornful again. "No," she said, as she vanished. "Only plum."

So Mrs. Margetson practised more patience and self-control. One could have a sort of row, perhaps, but one was unlikely to come off best. Or, again, perhaps it was just possible that she was being told the truth. And then how awful to stand behind this counter all day ; even worse, of course, than standing in front of it. She decided against argument—though she knew this was betraying June—and re-packed her bag ; with everything, that is to say, but the cheque, which she held for the moment concealed.

Presently Dumpy returned, in the same crab-like manner, and flung what she had brought into the basket—adding, also, a jar of plum jam. She then became a vocal calculating-machine, though not a very audible one, and ultimately announced that Mrs. Margetson owed her six and fourpence-halfpenny. For a fleeting and deceitful instant Mrs. Margetson was once more staggered and even exhilarated by a comparison between this sum and what she used to pay at Wallington Gardens. How *could* things be so cheap in war-time ? But they weren't, of course. Her household was two, instead of six or seven ; she had got hardly any butter ; no bacon—oh, dear, June wouldn't like that at all ; and what she had got wouldn't really keep even two people going on anything remotely resembling the old scale. So that once again she was a little cast down, and troubled with some divisional calculations herself, as she picked up the ration books and rather hesitatingly produced the cheque.

"I'm afraid," she said, "there was such a crowd at the bank that I——Well, *do* you think you could possibly cash this for me ? It's—it's for five pounds, I'm afraid."

Dumpy's expression hardened.

"Is that all you've got ?" she asked.

"Well, I—I've got about three shillings, but——"

"*We're* not the bank," said Dumpy. "You ought to know that."

She drummed with her fingers on the counter. She wanted a row. It was obvious that she wanted a row ; as, also, to Mrs. Margetson's sensitive soul, that the crowd behind her wasn't only restive—as it had been all along —but now looked on her as a deliberately anti-social, plutocratic obstructionist. She could have wept with no effort at all. Her legs were aching. Her back was aching. She knew that what she was asking had for some reason become a favour, but what on earth was she to do if it was refused ? Unpack the basket again? Or leave it—which would be regarded as a favour, too—and go back to the bank? Her voice broke.

"Oh, *please*——" she began, though even now she knew better than to allude to the days that were past. "I—I'm so . . ."

She looked round helplessly. She caught someone's eye. A little man, with a yellowish face between a green hat and a bright-brown overcoat. For a moment she hadn't the faintest idea who he was; but though he neither shifted his hat nor removed the cigarette that he was smoking, his dark eyes were surely registering some kind of recognition.

He spoke, too. He said: "Want any help, Mrs. Margetson?"

She knew him now. She even knew his name, though she couldn't think how, and was surprised that he knew hers.

"Oh, Mr. Musselberg," she said. "Good-morning. No, I don't suppose you can do anything, but——Well, I wanted this cheque cashing, and——"

"Why not?" said Mr. Musselberg, in a crisp and slightly exotic tone. "Why not? Here—give it to me."

The crowd, in some miraculous way, seemed to dissolve. In some equally miraculous or at least unaccountable manner, Mr. Musselberg had got hold of the cheque. Mrs. Margetson thought he was going to cash it himself.

"I can't possibly——" she began, though in anything but a haughty manner.

"That's all right," said Mr. Musselberg. He turned round. "Hi!" he called out. "Mr. Sanders! Just change this cheque for my friend Mrs. Margetson, will you?" He turned back again. "What's he to take?" he asked.

Mrs. Margetson made three efforts to speak. The first came to nothing, because she was equally and overwhelmingly relieved and embarrassed. The second met with the same fate, because ever since Wallington Gardens she had thought—not unnaturally, perhaps—that the head of the establishment was called Mr. Gilpin, and realised, moreover, that she had addressed him in this apparently inaccurate fashion again and again. But at the third shot she succeeded.

"Six and fourpence-halfpenny," she said.

"Six, four and a half," snapped Mr. Musselberg, passing right through the other herd of customers as if they were so many ghosts. And: "Right!" he said. And: "Thanks," he said. He jerked his head in an extremely knowing, competent, and familiar manner; withdrew again; and was handing Mrs. Margetson her change.

She said: "That's terribly kind of you, Mr. Musselberg. I——"

"Not at all. Pleasure. Glad I saw you. Here!"

"I beg your pardon?"

"Basket. I'll take it."

"Oh, but, really——"

Mr. Musselberg, however, had taken the basket—not without a good look at the contents. They were in the street. He had even opened the door for her, though he had gone out first.

"Got everything you want ?" he asked.

"Oh, yes—thank you. Thank you terribly."

"Don't see any bacon," said Mr. Musselberg. "They've got it, you know." He slapped one of his capacious pockets. "Like some ? Shall we go back ?"

"Oh, no, thank you. I—I don't really want any."

Untrue. "What a fool you were, mother," June would say, if she heard this part of the story. And she would say: "That awful little man—how *could* you ?" And, again, wasn't it rather queer that someone called Musselberg should have bacon, while someone called Margetson went without ?

But perhaps he wasn't one. She looked at him again, and there could be no doubt of it. She was also walking along the main road with him, under a very considerable obligation. Aspects of an insoluble enigma teased her. He looked so much too bobbish for one to feel sorry for him. There was no hint of an indication that he was sorry for himself. Very odd. On the other hand, not the least unusual. The extraordinary thing was how, with that sort of spirit, they ever actually managed to get persecuted. But Mr. Musselberg, at any rate, seemed entirely at his ease.

"You know, Mrs. Margetson," he was saying, "I don't often do the shopping. Mrs. Musselberg's maid's supposed to look after that." Here Mrs. Margetson made another very secret note; and then looked particularly interested, while also wondering if she was a snob. "But," said Mr. Musselberg, "just every now and then, you know, it pays to keep 'em up to the mark. The shops, I mean. So then I go round myself."

And very effectively, too. And why couldn't Mrs. Musselberg do it ? And a lot of other questions—not one of which, however, was as important as how Gilpin's would be likely to treat Mrs. Margetson next time. Would she be black-listed now, or favoured as Mr. Musselberg's *protégée ?* Neither alternative was quite what she wanted, or had set out this morning with any notion of having offered to her. If only, she thought, just a little ungratefully, I could get that basket away from him again.

"You see, Mrs. Margetson," Mr. Musselberg was saying, "Mrs. Musselberg's rather funny about crowds."

"Oh ? Is she ?"

"Yes. She doesn't like 'em. So as we have this maid, you see—or if I'm not too busy myself——"

"Quite," said Mrs. Margetson; but as she was about five inches taller than Mr. Musselberg, and was walking beside him, it was unlikely that he could see her face.

"You mustn't think she doesn't like company, though, Mrs. Margetson. Mrs. Musselberg entertains quite a lot."

Mrs. Margetson was half-touched, and half-alarmed. In a very swift vision she saw Mrs. Musselberg asking her to tea, or even lunch; and June's face when she heard of it; and the necessity of returning such an invitation; and the vile character of anyone who didn't return it. Why on earth, she thought again, didn't I wait at the bank?

She drew breath to say something that she hoped wouldn't commit her too deeply or too soon. And Mr. Musselberg suddenly stopped.

"If you don't mind, Mrs. Margetson——" he began. And then: "Well, how are you off for gin?"

What an extraordinary question. It must be admitted that if anyone said "gin" to Mrs. Margetson, she immediately thought of June—though certainly not the other way round. It couldn't even be said that June lived for gin. She didn't. But she was always complaining that she couldn't ask people to the flat because she hadn't got it. So that somehow, and truthfully enough, Mrs. Margetson answered: "We haven't had a bottle for months."

"Well, well!" said Mr. Musselberg. "That's fine, Mrs. Margetson! Come along."

He had still got her basket. She could hardly—even when she thought about it afterwards—have done anything else. About five minutes later, having meanwhile addressed the man at the Britannia Wine Stores as Mr. Gregory and shown an astonishing knowledge of his own private life, Mr. Musselberg had put a bottle of whisky in one pocket and a bottle of gin in the other; while a second bottle of gin was now nestling in the basket. It was true—which was just a faint comfort—that Mrs. Margetson had paid for this last item. It was true, also, that her daughter would quite unquestionably be delighted to see it. Yet again it was true that Mrs. Margetson would have to account for its presence—there was no chance now, as she had almost decided, to keep the whole story to herself—and that when she did this her child would be far from either amiable or pleased.

She knew this, though she loved her child, and felt for her, and sympathised with her, and could guess well enough what it was like to come back in an overcrowded omnibus, night after night, in the black-out. Yet it was this sympathy, partly, which made her so tired herself; and though Mr. Musselberg still chattered as he walked by her side, she knew, also, that some of her answers were almost wildly off the point.

Thus, however and at last, they reached Huddleston House together, just about an hour and half after Mrs. Margetson had set out. There was a slight struggle on the pavement, for it was here that she became determined

D

to recover the basket, and that Mr. Musselberg insisted on carrying it as far as the lift. Mrs. Tuke saw it from behind her lace curtains—in fact, she even saw the gin-bottle—and presently, there could be no doubt, she would make a full report to her own child. But neither Mrs. Margetson nor Mr. Musselberg saw Mrs. Tuke. They ascended together to the second floor—and if Mr. Musselberg still kept his green hat on in the lift, this merely showed, perhaps, that he was technically more an Englishman than an American. And then they parted.

"Cheeri-oh, Mrs. Margetson."

"It *has* been so kind of you."

Again, it was custom, in all probability, rather than anything more personal which caused Mr. Musselberg to wait, while the lift resumed its ascent, for what appeared to be a somewhat close scrutiny of Mrs. Margetson's legs. Then he was out of sight; and she sighed, and shrugged, and had another familiar and compendious thought about her husband, and Robin, and Wallington Gardens.

Now she must write letters—in her bedroom, if Mrs. Goosey was still banging about in the sitting-room, or in the sitting-room, if Mrs. Goosey was still banging about in the bedroom. Afterwards she would lunch off the two sausage-rolls which June had rejected for supper last night. Or so she thought. But unfortunately, in her haste to get out to the bank this morning, she had left them in a place where Mrs. Goosey had, for once, quite justifiably assumed that they were part of her perquisites. So by one o'clock there weren't any sausage-rolls. Nor was there any Mrs. Goosey. And though of course she needn't have done anything of the sort—for she could easily, in a way, have gone round to the San Remo—Mrs. Margetson kept body and soul together with two slices of bread and margarine, and a cup of slightly chlorinated cocoa.

Refreshed by this, she set off, about ten minutes later, for her unpaid, part-time job.

CHAPTER VIII

ON THE FIRST OF DECEMBER, PARTY-LEADER POPHAM PUT UP ANOTHER NOTICE in the entrance-hall at Huddleston House. It wasn't typewritten this time; not that he had done more than sign the previous notice about Fire-Watching, which had been typed by Mr. Todman; while at the foot of this new announcement there was no signature at all. The Party-Leader's name appeared in the text, though. In his still rather childish handwriting it was stated, not altogether accurately, that in response to inquiries and in order to avoid inconvenience, and again so that the tenants might be enabled to show their appreciation of the services which they had received, he was now prepared to accept donations to the Staff Christmas Fund, with best wishes—though it didn't explain in which direction these were being wafted—for a Merry Christmas. All this he wrote out—after a certain amount of trial and error —on a sheet torn from the back of the afore-mentioned exercise-book, and then stuck it on the wall with some fragments of an economy label. It wasn't quite straight, but it was visible enough, and within twenty-four hours nearly all the tenants had read it.

Some of them were just startled to find that Christmas—which, in accordance with annual custom, had as recently as October been widely accepted as marking the probable end of hostilities—had crept so near, and with so little sign now of any end at all. Others, though they had tipped in the past and knew that they must tip again, were provoked by this open and early appeal to their purses. For last year, and indeed as far back as any of them could remember, there had been no such public announcement; the whole thing having been left to seasonable good-feeling, together with an abrupt and most noticeable change in the porters' manners. Some of them rather suspected Mr. Todman of being behind the innovation, and they confabulated, and arrived at pretty general agreement on what they were all going to give. The announcement, in other words, did more to close the ranks of the tenants—which one might take it had been anything but the Party-Leader's intention—than to quell competition among the staff. It was a sign of the times, though. Everything must be done by proclamation now—generally before the proclaimants had come to any real accord (for in this case they were still wrangling like anything in the cellar as to how the spoils were to be divided), and almost invariably with unexpected results. But of course, as has been hinted already, Mr. Todman knew nothing about it. Or not for two days and nights.

On the third morning, though, he spotted the notice, and became inflamed, as was at once apparent from the colour of his ears. He strode towards the stairs, and shouted sharply down them. He waited, looking almost as fierce. And presently up came Party-Leader Popham himself, buttoning the jacket of his uniform and exhibiting nothing in his expression that could be described as either peace or goodwill.

"What," asked Mr. Todman, pointing to the announcement, "is the meaning of this ?"

Popham just squinted, and said nothing.

"Did *you* put it up ?" asked Mr. Todman, though he had no doubt of this, for an obvious reason.

"Yessir."

"Then take it down," said Mr. Todman, as authoritatively as he dared. "You know perfectly well——" He began to cough.

"Beg pardon," said Popham, "but I can't 'ardly do that."

"What do you mean ?" asked Mr. Todman.

The Party-Leader's ill-attuned eyes gave the only answer, but it was clear enough. "If I walk out," they said, "you won't get anyone else in a hurry. There's plenty of jobs for me," they said, "but there isn't for blokes like you. Or do you think I'd go," they inquired, "without raising the hell of a stink with the Syndicate ? How'd you like that—eh ?"

"Look here," said Mr. Todman, though his Adam's apple wasn't quite under control; "anything of this sort, you know—well, we can't have it. Christmas is Christmas, I know," said Mr. Todman, which was perhaps rather an exaggeration in war-time, "but this sort of thing—without consulting me—— Well, *that's* the point, Popham. These walls——" yes, he was doing better now—"aren't meant for *anyone* to—— Oh, good-morning, sir."

And there you were. Or, rather, there Mr. Todman was. Just as he was risking a good deal, and knew it, in the cause of decency and discipline, a tenant must appear beside him and hover; and because he was only the manager he must break off and be humble—and in front of Popham, too. "Is there anything," he was in fact bound to say, and now said, "that I can do for you, sir ?"

Mr. Vardas nodded.

"If you please," he said. "I t'ink possibly, in ze dost-pin last night, I put my leetle book. For ze Russians."

"For the Russians, sir ? Popham!" Never mind about the notice now; it must wait. "Have the bins been cleared ?"

"Yessir. That was Freeth last night, sir." Slightly injured rectitude.

"Well, did he find a book ?"

"Couldn't say, sir."

No, of course not. No porter either could or would say anything about any other porter; except, of course, for the purpose of passing, as Popham had just passed, the buck.

"Oh," said Mr. Todman. "Would it be in the salvage, do you think ?" As it was quite clear that Popham had no intention of hunting through the salvage himself, he turned back to Mr. Vardas. "That's your best chance, sir," he said. "I'll—I'll come through with you to the yard." Popham was now contriving to look completely deaf. "Was the book *printed* in Russian, sir ?"

"No, no," said Mr. Vardas. "Not Roossian. My Russians-book. For my food I eat."

"Oh!" said Mr. Todman. "You mean your ration book. I beg your pardon, sir. Of course. Of course."

The Party-Leader gave an unmannerly snort, and turned away. So far as he might have done this to disguise the snort, Mr. Todman could hardly blame him. But having turned away, he then went away— right back to the cellar, where it was now almost certain that he would be repeating this story at Mr. Todman's rather than at Mr. Vardas's expense. As for the ration book, it wasn't in the salvage-bin, though Mr. Todman got very dirty as he scrabbled among the contents, and as Mr. Vardas stood and watched him. By this time—but it was always happening—the manager must also vex his own spirit by wondering if he would ever learn when to be firm with a tenant, when to be impassive, and when (as it seemed that he was again doing now) to let himself be treated as a slave. Why, having originally come here to discover if it was true that the ball-cock in Mr. Everard's bathroom was out of order—for he had long since learnt that Mr. Everard had a higher standard in these matters than almost anyone else—should he now, nearly half an hour later, find himself routing in a battered receptacle on behalf of a tenant who, in his own view, ought to be in the Isle of Man?

Again there was only the one answer. He was incompetent. The porters laughed at him. The tenants despised him; just look at the way that fellow Barker still left his car standing about. The Syndicate saw through him, or would obviously do so at any moment. As fast as he tried to get any system into his work, he was defeated by one thing after another—interference, interruptions, impertinence, his own confounded——

"Woof!" said Mr. Todman, for the dust here was making him cough again. He straightened his long, thin back. "Woof!" he repeated. "I'm afraid it's not here, sir."

"Bot," said Mr. Vardas, "wizzout 'im I cannot nozzing. I get anozzer Russians-book—yes?"

"Well, sir, if you're quite sure you've lost it——"

"Am I kvite zure?" How excitable these foreigners were. "Look —zere iss only two place I keep 'im. Wizz my papers, vhere 'e is not. And wizz my ozzer papers—like zis."

Here Mr. Vardas dipped into an inner pocket, and fetched out such a quantity of letters, envelopes, press-cuttings, printer's proofs, and other literary matter that it was hardly surprising that some of them began blowing away. And who picked them up? Mr. Todman, of course; while Mr. Vardas merely tried to stamp on them, and once all but succeeded in stamping on Mr. Todman's hand.

"That's the lot, sir," said Mr. Todman, as he rose, crimson-faced to his feet. "Woof!" he said again. And then: "What's that you've got there, sir?"

"Vhere? Ach, zat iss vair' fonny! I 'ave 'im, zen, all of ze time."

"Looks like it," said Mr. Todman, eyeing the well-known booklet. And now, he thought, he was at least going to be thanked for his pains. But he was wrong. Either, it would seem, Mr. Vardas had been trained in a different school of manners, or else—but perhaps this was also the case—he could conceive no circumstances in which, as an exile, he owed anything to anyone at all. He just stuffed the whole bundle into his pocket again, and turned away with a faint, preoccupied shrug. Mr. Todman looked towards Heaven for a moment—though all he saw was a barrage-balloon—and then just shook his head. He had also now forgotten about Mr. Everard's ball-cock —of which, however, he would be pretty sharply reminded, on the telephone, when Mr. Everard came home—and as he passed through the hall again, on his way back to Bessingham House, he had even forgotten about Popham's Yule-tide announcement.

Later, when he remembered it, he preferred, on the whole, to leave the matter alone. Sometimes he thought of tearing it down, when Popham was off duty; but he knew that if it disappeared he would be suspected, and after all he had made his point—or liked to think he had—about its being put up without his permission. So it stayed there. Presently its border became decorated with telephone numbers, and other memoranda, and even a profile or two, for which various hands were responsible. Then one of the top corners came loose; and then another, so that it flapped, upside-down, with its face to the wall. In this condition it attracted even more attention, if not from the tenants, than before; for almost any transient outsider who caught sight of it felt compelled to turn it up and read it. This was its final undoing. The remaining gummed strips couldn't stand the strain, and well before Christmas itself an outsider, finding himself with the whole thing in his hand, had crumpled it up and tossed it through the grille of the lift—the cage being aloft at the time—where it joined a number of old matches and cigarette-ends in that dark and greasy pit.

Yet it served its purpose. The tenants, or nearly all of them, paid up much more promptly this year, while the porters were relieved of a good deal of civility and suspense. They had discovered, or Popham had, that a notice—at any rate in war-time—is far more effective, and much less trouble, than any amount of hints. It is quite true that the Party-Leader's method of distribution gave no satisfaction to anyone but himself at first. But those card-games that went on down in the cellar did a good deal to rectify this. The money was soon in circulation again, what with Nap, and the Royal Oak, and Eldritch's connection with a bookmaker specialising in dogs. By quite early in the new year, in fact, it had as good as vanished. But we mustn't go leaping ahead.

For it was quite early in December, still, when the State suddenly sent everyone postcards telling them that, for the furtherance of the war-effort, their milk could no longer be delivered in the present manner, but must come from a single and much larger organisation considerably further off. It added—did the State—that there could be no possible appeal from this decision, and this surprised no one, for they had all learnt something about the State by now. But it didn't much surprise them, either, of course, when the larger organisation sent round just as many milkmen (only rather later) as the combined strength of their predecessors; nor that some of the new milkmen should actually prove to be the old ones, though the bottles that they now brought were a slightly different shape; nor that, in spite of this, there was a period of confusion during which some people received an embarrassing glut—so that they were quite ashamed of all the bottles on their doormats —while others, whatever floor they were on, remained high and dry.

It was early in December, again, that the ever-watchful occupants of No. 2, Huddleston House, took note of some further facts. For if Mr. L. Wilson Barker thought that he could bring his secretary back with him— but only, since as soon as he had done this he became terribly nervous, for the reason he had given her, which was to dictate a confidential report— then he was mistaken in supposing that neither her arrival nor departure need necessarily be seen. It is true that he provided her with a simple supper, in which he naturally shared. But he then became far more business-like than at the factory. He never once even approached her shoulder. He walked to and fro, with the table between them, dictating until he was almost hoarse. And then he as good as pitched her out into the street again, though still without touching her, notwithstanding some very different intentions that he had once had, and a look on her face which might possibly have been interpreted as something between disappointment and annoyance.

But they were spotted, both coming and going. Miss Tuke saw them coming, and knew at once, by some Tuke-ish gift, that neither was entirely at ease. While Mrs. Tuke, oddly enough, made three separate sorties that evening—which was rather puzzling for Lulu—and was rewarded on the third occasion by seeing them, as she lingered in that lower passage, stepping out of the lift. Mr. Barker then said: "Well, good-night, Ethel. Thanks a lot." His visitor said: "Not at all, I'm sure," in a slightly stifled and stilted manner. While Mrs. Tuke, of course, said nothing whatsoever. But when she made her report, she was convinced, as she said, that there was something in it. "Mind you," she said, "it *may* be all right; but they both looked very self-conscious."

"That's what *I* thought," said her daughter. "Not that she struck me as the least like the ordinary type. But there's not much in that, now."

Mrs. Tuke didn't ask how her heavyweight child knew this, but it was clear that she quite agreed.

"Not," she admitted, "that I'd have thought he was that sort of man himself. He's always seemed quiet enough—so far."

"My dear mater," said Tuke, "if you heard a quarter of the things that *I* hear . . . But I don't know that I blame him," she added.

"Why not, dear—when his wife's away?"

"P'ff!" said Tuke. "That's just it, mater. If you ask me, she's *asking* for it."

"Mrs. Barker, you mean? Oh, I don't think you ought to say that."

"Well, just wait and see," said Tuke. Her mother looked greedy and gratified, though she had just done a good deal of waiting and had seen very little. How the Tukes knew that there was a Mrs. Barker at all, and that she was away, and even that she was in North Wales, should need little or no explanation. They had learnt it, simply and straightforwardly enough, through Mrs. Vowles.

And now they knew that Mr. Barker had had a young woman in his flat from about seven until half-past nine. If she came again, they would almost certainly know this, too. But at the moment he didn't want her to come again. A project, which wasn't really a project, had come to nothing, and he was thankful and immensely relieved. Alternatively, and at the same time, he had been a fool not to do what the young woman must almost obviously have been expecting. Alternatively, again, could anything conceivably be more caddish than to take advantage of someone whose *fiancé* was in the Armed Forces? Ugh! Yet this outlook faltered at the factory, where he felt that he had been stiff and clumsy during that un-adventurous evening, and that though at first he must be stand-offish—so as to show that there had never even been the ghost of a project at all—he must then, as his secretary seemed silent and offended, reverse the process if only so as to indicate exactly the same thing. So he did this, perhaps rather more than he had intended, and their relationship became much easier again in one way, though not in another. But of course he was going to be darned careful. And of course, having come to this conclusion, he *would* get a letter from Doris with a lot more stuff about Captain Tubbs. Well?

Unanswerable. He detested the whole situation, but he was far too busy for another visit to Rhyl. Honestly. And, besides, there was nothing whatever in it—or at least not at this end. Or if there was, how on earth could he help it? Unanswerable again. Yet of course he had gone further than he thought; because as soon as you're being watched and discussed —if only by an old lady and her somewhat masculine daughter—it has ceased to be what you *do* that counts. Already it is what they choose to pretend or believe that you do. In fact, this is one of the most interesting illustrations of how we are all part of one another's dream. It wasn't a very nice dream, though, at No. 2, Huddleston House.

But it moved from point to point, as dreams do. The responsibility for minding other people's business was too great to waste on only one object. And now, or just about now, the team was extremely watchful of Mr. Musselberg's comings and goings; and though defeated in its hopes of further associating him with Mrs. Margetson—for the truth was that he had no ulterior motive here, but had just been showing off—had much magnified the memory of that gin-bottle. It became mingled—and quite correctly, though the team was in fact still guessing—with a vision of hoarding and other objectionable practices at No. 14; and though Mr. Musselberg was as careful as ever to bring nothing else home except in his pockets or a suit-case, he had already made one mistake in the matter of gin. The team was hardly in a position to report him to the authorities, and if it had been might well have preferred to hug the knowledge to itself. For secret knowledge, so far as it thought the thing out, was secret power. Yet Tuke did say something at the Wardens' Post—oh, quite confidentially, of course— to a member of the Special War-Time Constabulary who looked in from time to time. Plop, as you might put it, went her pebble into the pool. And the rings on its surface widened.

In the case of another pebble, neither Tuke nor her mother dropped it, and by the time the ring reached them, it was so faint that they could merely resolve to be even more on the alert. It came to them from the customary source, who had absorbed it from Mrs. Garrison ("Smashums"), who in turn had been advised of it by the elderly but still acutely observant Mrs. Mudge. For Mrs. Mudge, looking down from the kitchenette window of No. 15, which she found more soothing and restful than doing her work, had seen Mr. Todman and that Mr. Vardas at the salvage-bin. Whether it was Mrs. Garrison or Mrs. Vowles who switched the *dramatis personæ* must remain unknown. But by the time Mrs. Tuke heard the story from the latter, there was no mention of Mr. Todman—perhaps because he was the manager, or perhaps because his presence would have spoilt it—and it was Mr. Vardas who was piecing old letters together and trying to read them. So he was a spy; though perhaps it was odd even for a spy to work quite so openly. The team wasn't fully satisfied, though of course it had suspected him from the first moment. It didn't snub Mrs. Vowles, because she was much too valuable a part of its intelligence service. But this again was a case where it might be better to wait—and to watch, of course—before swallowing the story whole.

Besides, there was a much clearer affair at the moment, which was really far more in their line. One party to it, in fact, was only just across the hall, and though the other was up on the top floor, if they went out in taxis together they could scarcely expect to be unseen. For if anyone wanted a taxi in these days, it was quite useless to telephone. You either set out on foot until you found one, and then—provided that you weren't going to Putney or Hampstead—got into it or alternatively persuaded it to come back for your luggage; or else you made interest with a porter, who would then, if the interest was sufficient, disappear for a very long time and possibly return, in a rather dangerous and daring manner, suspended from the side of the vehicle. A further feature of this second method was that if you attempted to allow for the long disappearance, it tended—by the war-time law which governed so much—to be miraculously short; and the driver became angry at being asked to wait, and the porter became angry because you weren't ready, and someone turned up before you could start, and bribed the taxi away. In any event it was a public performance, often involving a good deal of uproar, at which the Tukes, or at least one of them, occupied front-row seats.

When, however, Major Hurst wanted a taxi—which could only be in the black-out now, and after he had come back in the mud-coloured car—he created no uproar himself. But the staff did. Two at least of them—for even Eldritch would take part in this ritual if necessary—would go dashing into the main road, would flash torches in the eyes of every conceivable kind of driver, would shout and yell, would down all rivals in the most arbitrary and piratical manner, and would return, within an average period of not more than five minutes, in complete triumph. But this wasn't nearly all. Now they must knock as well as ring at the Major's door. They must bawl out: "Your taxi's here, sir!" And they must attend his egress and embarkation with more noise, more torch-flashing, and a final slam of the taxi door which could be heard as far away as the end of the street.

So of course the Tukes heard it, too, and much that preceded it, and though they couldn't look out of their window now, they naturally kept abreast of the affair from the door. Not both at once; that wouldn't look well. But what could be simpler than for Tuke to go out, and then fumble with her latchkey—indeed, she could hardly help fumbling, as she wasn't looking at the lock—and to watch, and to come in when she had seen what she wanted to see, and to furnish her first-hand statement ?

"Mrs. Amberley and the Major again, mater. They don't seem to care *who* knows."

"Well, dear, they're hardly the kind that would."

"*He* isn't," said Tuke, with a touch of venom. "I know *that* sort, thank you," she added, almost—though this was preposterous—as if she had been assailed by the species herself. Then came a struggle between the forces within her. "As for the girl," she said, "well!"

That wasn't quite clear. It was Tuke simultaneously sticking up for women, especially for those who were compelled to listen to "Music While You Work;" and jeering at them—especially those who still managed to look fashionably emaciated instead of merely haggard. At the same time it was of course essential to disagree with her mother whenever she could. So she summed all this up with the word "well!", and Mrs. Tuke was rebuffed by this; and yet was so used to rebuffs that she at once bounced back.

"Let me see," she said; "wasn't it last Thursday they went out ?"

"Don't ask *me*," said Tuke, though her memory was quite as accurate as her mother's. "All I say is that if *I* made up like that——" here she eyed the reflection of her brick-coloured countenance with complete approval— "I shouldn't be surprised if people talked."

"That's what I say," said her mother. "And you'd think, in these days— well, I mean, *even* in these days—that a girl in that position——"

" 'Girl' !" snorted Tuke, though she had just used the expression herself. "I bet she's at least twenty-nine."

"Oh, Sylvia—do you really think so ?"

"Oh, dry up, mater. What's it all got to do with us ?"

Nothing, of course; though one shouldn't imagine, because Tuke was momentarily exasperated again, that the subject was now going to be dropped. There would be a pause, while Mrs. Tuke bridled, and looked hurt, and received no apology for being told to dry up. But the team hadn't finished, even though it could add little or nothing that hadn't been said before. As the taxi rolled off through the blackness towards a West-End restaurant with a French name, the discussion in No. 2 was very thoroughly and repetitively resumed. And as the driver picked his way with quite extraordinary skill—yet it was true, also, that he had had plenty of time to learn how to see in the dark—Mrs. Archie Amberley leant back in her corner, and relaxed just a little, and closed her eyes. It faintly amused her that her companion should have just given her a cocktail, at No. 4, of immense size and strength, and should be under the illusion that she had drunk it. She hadn't. She had tipped it away, into the bowl of ice, when he wasn't looking. Why ? For fun, of course. Because it was so damned funny that men should be such damned fools. What a pity she was too tired to laugh.

"I say—Primrose."

"What ? Oh—hullo."

"I've been looking forward to this, you know."

"Have you ?" How odd, when you must have done it thousands of times before; and when *I'm* not going on to the Monkey House, even if you think I am.

"By Jove, yes. It'll do you good, too. What you need, my dear. All right, then; what we both need."

Now he's going to hold my hand, thought Primrose. And he did.

"I'm sorry it's so rough," she said.

"Eh ? What is ?"

"My hand. Comes of working, I'm afraid. But you can't have everything, can you ?"

"By Jove, don't say that!"

Mrs. Amberley said nothing, and seldom if ever can a hand have shown less response. Thinking of that mammoth cocktail, her companion admired her more than ever. He wouldn't even be surprised if he wasn't serious in a way—whatever he may have meant by that. He decided to let go suddenly, and see if anything happened. He did. And it didn't. By Jove, perhaps he'd got his work cut out here. Or perhaps he hadn't. Rather sport, not knowing. And if there was anyone else in the wind, she was dashed discreet. Quite right. He breathed deeply, and just a shade stertorously, in his own corner.

"Don't snore," said Mrs. Amberley. If there had been any light, he might have seen her shuddering with a kind of frantic disgust. But there was no light, and he was highly amused. What a crack! And what a voice to say it in. Worth taming—what?

It was also at the beginning of December that Gavin Guernsey kept an appointment to lunch with R.J., and his cousin Claud, at the latter's Club. This wasn't quite what had originally been planned. The thing had started by R.J. writing ("My dear Gavin . . . Yrs. R.J.G.") to announce that he was coming up to see the dentist; by his adding, as was usual now, that he couldn't stop the night—though he could if he had wished to, since there was still an emergency method of putting him up; and concluding with the almost Delphic statement that he would be returning by an early afternoon train.

For this was a catch, and an old one. It meant that Gavin must ask his father to lunch, which he was more than prepared to do, however little they might have to say to each other. But it also meant that R.J. would write a second letter, taking slight offence at this suggestion, and explaining that when he asked someone to lunch himself (which he hadn't done), he meant precisely what he had (or hadn't) said. He now announced that he would be in the hall of the Great Western Hotel at Paddington at 12.45 p.m. on the date in question, and that if Gavin chose to join him there, he would be glad to see him. Tortuously as it had been arrived at, this was, of course, the equivalent of a Royal Command, and Gavin made haste to accept it. Yet already he was plunged in uneasiness, the best part of a week in advance. He could almost feel himself back in a little grey flannel jacket and knicker-bockers at St. Eustace's Preparatory School; such was either the power of R.J.'s personality or the miserable weakness of his own. Moreover, if he took a taxi to Paddington, his father would almost certainly be looking out of a window, and would see it, and would address him on the subject of extravagance. Whereas if he adopted any other form of transport, he would have to leave his office—very likely to the annoyance of Mr. Bendish—by at least a quarter past twelve. So that even by the end of November there was a cloud—accompanied, inevitably, by every kind of self-criticism and reproach—on this sensitive young gentleman's soul.

But the war-time Law of the Unexpected still held. For now it was that his cousin Claud rang up—or, rather, that his clerk rang up, so as to keep Gavin waiting as long as possible until Claud was ready—to say that he would like to ask him a few more questions, though he must have asked him several hundred already, and that Gavin must lunch with him on Wednesday at his Club.

Very kind, of course, whether it eventually went down in the bill or not. But it was on Wednesday that R.J. was coming up to the dentist's. Gavin said so, and explained about the Great Western Hotel. Claud, who seemed somehow to have become far more overbearing since accepting his cousin as a client, was at first huffy and then said that of course R.J. must come along, too. One o'clock sharp, he said, and rang off. Gavin wrote a long letter to him, tore it up, and telephoned to his father. This, also, proved anything but straightforward. R.J.—without really listening, as one could tell—immediately formed the fixed impression that Claud wanted to lunch with *him*. He said why couldn't Claud write, and what was it all about? Gavin again tried to tell him. R.J.—always an adept at delayed action of the brain-cells, which in this case appeared invariably to put himself rather than anyone else at an advantage—suddenly got on to the truth of the matter, or part of it, and wanted to know if Gavin would be there, too. "Where?" asked Gavin. "At Claud's Club," said R.J., impatiently. "Didn't you say so?" "Oh, yes," said Gavin; "only I thought——" "I can't hear you," said R.J. "Speak up, my boy!"

Oh, it was quite a toll-call. But it was fixed in the end, though Gavin was exhausted, and R.J., for some reason, seemed almost as huffy as Claud. It would have been rather funny, thought Gavin, a little later, if they hadn't all been relations. But that was the trouble. Fathers oughtn't to have been schoolmasters; or schoolmasters oughtn't to be fathers. If they were, one could never hope to be on reasonable, adult terms with them. One must always start with a note of apology in one's voice, and end with a feeling of guilt. And if one's cousin was a solicitor, one must always—there was no getting away from this—be a little afraid of him, too. Why? And why was Claud still being a solicitor at all, and sleeping comfortably at Woking, when thousands of far unhealthier men of his age——

No. That thought was barred. In the first place it stamped anyone who thought it as a meddling, bloodthirsty pest. While in the second place what had he, himself, ever done? Nothing; except lose his left foot in the most ridiculous manner that one could imagine. Again—it was like tumbling back into a trap that was always waiting—he must go through the whole chain of horrors once more, and curse his own folly and fate.

Yet he was soothed that evening by a typescript—which he read right through a rather noisier Alert than of late—in which a Countess, or a Countess with the confidentially admitted help of a literary ghost, had written an account of her life. Partly he was soothed because it was all so gloriously remote—or escapist, as everyone said now. And partly because, despite the best efforts of the ghost—whom he had met, and pitied, and rather admired —such a portrait of selfishness and snobbery had emerged that almost anyone else's conceit must be slightly restored. Was this a good reason for publishing it? He wondered. He corrected a little more of the Countess's grammar; for the ghost, he was convinced, could never (like Shakespeare) have written "between you and I." He had also noted, as he was bound to note, the dog-eared corners—particularly at the beginning—which showed how it had already been the rounds. Poor old girl, he thought; I suppose she's hard up now. It's muck, of course. It's drivel. It's been done again and again, too. But it's a *story ;* she can't kill that. And I must say I rather wish *I'd* been an Edwardian.

There was a resounding bang from without, and he glanced across the sitting-room at D. P. Moulton. Derek, in a cloud of pipe-smoke, was simultaneously scowling and grinning over a review copy which he had only opened ten minutes ago, though now he was nearing the end. Someone's going to get it in the neck, thought Gavin; but he might *read* them, you know. Well, a bit more than that, I mean. And then he was soothed no longer; for Derek had closed the book abruptly, and as he spotted the wrapper he saw that it was one of his own firm's.

It was going to sell, too—not that anything didn't sell at the moment, if you could only get the paper to print it. Nothing could stop that, in a crazy world; but this wasn't the point. Why should Derek, who could write nothing himself—("Nor can you," said a familiar voice, though it was partly drowned by a salvo of guns)—why should Derek, who didn't even need the money, because he'd got another job and a private income as well, just sneer, week after week, at what, after all, was the source of those extra guineas? Oh, he did it amusingly and bitingly enough, but, gosh, people didn't want to be told what *not* to read. Why couldn't he *praise* something? Yes, and why on earth couldn't he stop gassing about M. de Charlus in every review that he wrote? Look here, thought Gavin, shall I have a row with him?

It was the right time, in a way. That noise got on everyone's nerves, and one could shout now, even in this blasted block, without anyone hearing a sound. Though why blasted? It was all right, thought Gavin—rather forgetting the war for a moment, in spite of the noise—before *he* came in. Why can't he clear out? Oh, I know it's as much his own flat as mine now. All right; more, if you like. But dash it—— I mean, dammit—— Oh, help, what *is* it I want?

D. P. Moulton looked up from the notes that he was making, and peered through his thick glasses.

"A trifle plangent to-night," he said.

There you are, thought Gavin. Wouldn't that sort of stuff drive *anyone* mad in the end? But look at his cheek twitching. He's scared. Who wouldn't be? And why on earth do we all pretend we aren't? Besides, one just doesn't have rows. It's only that we're both half-suffocated by this infernal black-out. And—to do the old boy justice—by that stinking, poisonous pipe.

He opened his mouth to say something inoffensive; but D. P. Moulton got off the mark first.

"How's the dear duchess?" he asked.

"What duchess?"

"The one you find so absorbing."

"Oh." My God, he doesn't only knock our books when they're published. He goes peeping at 'em when they're in typescript. He *must* have. *I* never told him—— Oh, this is becoming impossible!

The junior partner in Messrs. Dingle and Frisby twitched rather violently himself.

"She's not a duchess," he said. "But there's something—well, there's something about her, you know."

"Snob appeal?"

"Very likely," said Gavin. "I think it's stopping."

Derek's pipe gave a repulsive, bubbling sound.

"Did you say," he asked, "that the raid was stopping, or that those memoirs were topping?"

"Both," said Gavin. There was another thump. "But I might be wrong," he added. "Shall we put the lights out, and look out of the window?"

"No," said Derek. "Don't let's be morbid. Besides, I'm working."

"Well, if it comes to that," said Gavin, "so am I."

Silence; and silence outside now, too. A disinterested observer or thought-reader might have been hard put to it to say which of these two young men had more justice or justification on his side. It was really a most complicated case. They were linked, and yet they had to bicker. They felt compelled to provoke each other, and yet each, it would seem, had some sort of self-control. One—the one in spectacles—wasn't nearly such a high-brow as he pretended to be, and perhaps only wrote his reviews in that style for the very simplest psychological reason. The other—the one with an artificial foot—was as certainly far better-read than he chose to admit, but was much more impressionable, too. And in too many ways, perhaps; for even at this moment he was wondering how far he had been influenced in his reactions to the Countess by the knowledge that his companion would have shuddered at almost every line.

What it boiled down to, in publishing terms, was whether her ladyship should have the paper or whether it should be switched, with sanction from the Controller, to yet another edition of *Little Betsy and the Brownies*; a juvenile work which he had come to regard with some nausea, though Mr. Bendish didn't, because the type was standing and it could still be sold, for some reason, as fast as it came on the market. But what it boiled down to in the other sense was that a publisher and a reviewer ought never to do their work in the same, stuffy sitting-room, whether there was an air-raid going on or not. One of us, thought Gavin, had got to shift, or there *will* be a row. I suppose it'll be me, too; in fact, I never ought to have come back here. Only, dash it, why shouldn't I ? And, besides . . .

He lowered the typescript, which indeed had been putting rather a strain on his left thumb, and again he was momentarily haunted by an eyebrow —or perhaps one should say by the unusual and curious manner in which it was able to behave. And again, as so often of late, he wondered how on earth he could ever have associated it with the wrong face; though of course he hadn't really known one girl from the other then, and now—thanks, oddly enough, to another Alert and a session in the hall downstairs—he knew both in a way. Well, then, could one or should one be attracted by two girls at once ? Obviously not. Yet one was a beauty and sort of kept things going (not, he assured himself, that I'm the least serious about either, of course), whereas the other, apart from that eyebrow . . .

Yes, but it was very definitely *her* eyebrow now. The first one, the gay one, was prettier, of course. Or so he had thought. And as she did all the talking, she made one feel less of a lout. But she didn't *listen*. Whereas the other one . . .

Dash it, thought Gavin, why on earth did I bring old Derek into it, too? We could easily have dodged them that time. I wonder if *he* thinks—— Well, I wonder if *he's* up to anything now. Well, would he have *said* he'd met them on the bus again, if he was ? Or am I just going mad ? Why the devil *shouldn't* he know them ?

A word eluded him. He was convinced that it began with a "C"; so of course it didn't—for that's another Law—and when it came to him, in bed that night, it was "Propinquity," and he didn't like it. It was a cheapening, mean, ungenerous word. It might possibly apply to less honourable chaps, or to weak-minded puppets in fiction. But personally, now he had found it, he was disgusted with it. It had nothing to do with *his* case. Even, that's to say, assuming that it was a case at all.

Having reached this decision, he slept, for there were no more sirens that night. Yet again the disinterested observer might form the view that at this phase in his life he was unlikely to be soothed, when awake, for very long at a time.

He certainly wasn't soothed, on the following Wednesday, as he entered his cousin Claud's Club. Not that it was physically his cousin Claud's Club, which was now represented by some jagged walls, some charred beams, and a mass of debris. But spiritually Clubland was still standing four-square to all threats of dissolution, and the members had at once been offered the hospitality of another monastery. This meant congestion; for though a lot of members were now either overseas or lurking in the backwoods, a lot more of them required feeding, between one and two—far more than in peace-time—and came crowding together like anything, day after day. In the evenings the place was still calm and cloistral, or so far as this was possible with waitresses in attendance. But then Gavin wasn't concerned with the evenings, either here or elsewhere. He had no Club himself, or no Club had him. The war had interrupted some rather vague speculations as to their possible value, and he had taken no steps since then. So that as he passed through a vast swing-door at about five minutes to one, he wasn't only a bit nervous but even, one might say, a bit awed as well.

As two sets of members were now occupying the establishment, there were also two porters in the hall. The original porter was in a glass box, while the porter of the Club which had been destroyed was doing the best he could at a desk in a dark corner. So Gavin went to the glass box first, of course, for it was all he could see; and was rebuffed—though not until he had accounted for his presence at some length; and then had to tell the same story to the porter behind the desk. He was now, in fact, rather expecting to be thrown out altogether. But he wasn't. His cousin, it appeared, hadn't yet arrived; there was no sign of his father; but he was handed over to a lanky page, who watched him suspiciously while he hung up his hat and coat, and then ushered him into a room of a desolate description, which was about twice as high as either its length or breadth.

Not that it was deserted. There were several solitary figures, each trying, it would seem, to keep as far from the others as he could, or to pretend that they weren't there. There were some small tables. There were some rather hard, black arm-chairs. There were bookshelves, ascending until they were yards out of anyone's reach. There was a fireplace, with no fire in it. And there was a huge window, the surface of which, however, was covered with some protective preparation which made it impossible to look out. Yet naturally it was a shade lighter by this window, and it was here—since it was also furthest from the other occupants, whom he, too, so it seemed, must now do everything to avoid—that Gavin stood. A little later, and rather daringly—but he had hurried through the streets so as to be punctual, and his non-existent foot knew it—he sat down.

There was a dark, round, polished table in front of him, and someone—even more daring, for they must have taken it from a shelf—had left a book on it. Gavin glanced at the back; or at the spine, as they said in his profession. It was a bound volume of *Punch*, dated 1927. He was tempted. He didn't really see why he shouldn't open it. He didn't pick it up, but he raised the front cover. On the first page there was a picture of a hairy and villainous-looking Russian, dangling a small but equally villainous-looking Chinese marionette. The marionette was brandishing a sword in one hand.

With the other it was waving a flag, on which was written "Down with the British." Good heavens! January, 1927, when Gavin himself had been—wait a moment—yes, eleven. One might say, then, that this had been part of his upbringing; for though he had entirely forgotten the picture, his father had always taken in *Punch*, and he—Gavin—had at least always looked at the illustrations. Or certainly and quite positively during the Christmas holidays.

There was no other legend, for it was a kind of title-page. But this was what the backbone of the country had accepted in 1927, and the awful thing was that it would still accept either this or anything else that was put before it like that. It would go much further. It would fight anyone that it was told to. It had no memory; no logic. When Father—that's to say the Press and the Government—said "Turn," it all turned. He had turned himself, though with singularly little effect. Back came the old feeling of frustration and failure, doubled and confused, because he *ought* to be fighting now, while at the same time there was no reason on earth for any fighting at all.

He closed the book. He had had quite enough of it for to-day, thank you. More than enough. The waiting-room vanished, as he stared at the appalling lot of the human race. He found himself thinking of archbishops again, and scowled. And then of that fruitless, bootless, stupid, blithering notion of calling—what an ass he had been!—on Hannah, his old nurse. Indeed he was in a pretty frightful condition all round, when the door suddenly opened, and somebody called out his name.

He jumped up; nearly fell down again, because he was so much in the past that he had forgotten the new kind of balance; and clutched at the table as Claud addressed him once more.

"Been hunting all over the place for you," he said—looking rather old-fashioned himself in his black jacket, bow tie, and stiff collar. "Why did they put you in here?"

"I don't know," said Gavin, truthfully enough. "I—I'm sorry. Is it late?"

"Ten past," said Claud. "But it's all right. Your father's holding the fort. Do you want a wash?"

"Oh. No, thanks." Clean enough, anyhow. And, besides, to a tone like that there was only one possible answer.

"I mean, do if you want to. Only we've got to look sharp."

"I don't want to," said Gavin. He was on the point of saying that he never washed. But Claud didn't give him time.

"Come on, then," he said. "This way."

Off they went, through a corridor thickly lined with coats, hats, and service-caps. Through an inner hall, where, owing to the congestion of members, they had to do a good deal of swerving and dodging. Through another corridor, similarly and copiously adorned. And so into the enormous dining-room, where approximately a million members were munching and shouting, while a further cohort were arguing with the steward, and others, between the serried ranks of the tables, were getting in the waitresses' way. For the days were gone—not that Gavin remembered them—when each table stood by itself. They had multiplied. They had joined together in long rows. And the chairs, though no longer of one pattern, had multiplied, too. Few school-treats or banquets of Oddfellows could have rivalled the remarkable scene.

"Ah!" said Claud, over his shoulder, and with a sound of relief. "It's all right, I think. Better look sharp, though. Oh, sorry—how's your foot?"

"All right, thanks," said Gavin, as a Colonel all but felled him to the earth; and then gave him—yes, he knew that look—another suspicious glance. He was distinctly breathless, in fact, quite apart from any other discomfort, as he approached the spot where R.J. was sitting on one chair, and valiantly guarding two others.

"Splendid!" said Claud. "Well done, Uncle Bob. Now, then, Gavin—you go over there."

He then sat down next R.J., while Gavin, having exchanged an inexplicable look with his father—but it was just as inexplicable to himself as to anyone else—edged round the end of the table, and took the remaining seat. In other words, he was between two strangers and separated by about a yard from the only two persons in the vast chamber whom he knew. If he spoke, it would be the strangers who would be far the more likely to hear him. This thought, among others, rather added, on the whole, to his reserve.

He had a good view of R.J. and Claud, though, and he looked at both. R.J. never changed, of course. Well, he was greyer, perhaps, than ten years ago, and perhaps just a shade smaller. But his expression was precisely the same. It announced his calling as clearly as if he had been labelled. He couldn't possibly be anything but a schoolmaster—even though he wasn't one now. What did he *do*, his son wondered? He had a house full of books, and a cook-housekeeper whom he had swiped from St. Eustace's, though she was getting a bit old, too. He did the *Times* cross-word puzzle. He still occasionally drank sherry—which argued a good deal of foresight in this particular line—but nothing else, whether he had got it or not. He still wore, or appeared to wear, the same clothes that he had always worn, and the same spectacles, too. He pottered about. He seemed comfortably off. There was no sign that he regretted his retirement or found the days long. He was, one might say, inhuman—as he had always been, so far as Gavin was aware. There was no question, in fact, that he was a bit of basilisk, even when one had escaped, in a way, from his thrall. He was amazingly dull, too. It might be breaking a Commandment to admit this;

but what else, now that one looked at him again—and whether he had transmitted this quality to his only child or not—could one possibly admit ?

Yet he had married. You couldn't, thought Gavin, do a thing like that without just a trace of emotion. Or could you, if you were R.J. ? Some memories came to him as he sat, looking as intelligent as he could, and waiting to be either fed or addressed; for so far he had merely been provided with a quarter of a small roll, and had still hesitated to shout across the table until more obviously expected to do so. So he was thinking of his late Uncle George now—Claud's father—which was encouraging, not only because he had worshipped his Uncle George, in a youthful and humble fashion, but because if Claud was so unlike him, then perhaps there was less reason why he himself should be like R.J.

He remembered his Uncle George giving him a pound on that last visit —he couldn't have been more than about eight or nine at the time—and how he had then rather audaciously asked him about his mother. Not much. And he hadn't been told much, except that she was fond of flowers. But this had started something. Not only had it momentarily breathed something like life into a fading photograph in his father's study, but—he didn't blush, but he still felt uneasy—had set him to reading his father's old diaries, too. R.J. didn't know this, of course. It had all had to be done when he was out. But they weren't locked up; they were all there on a shelf; and there was dashed little in them, as a matter of fact, except the briefest and driest record, interspersed with financial entries which to a child on a hearth-rug meant nothing at all. Indeed, they were dull diaries, too.

Yet he had learnt just a little. He had seen his mother appear in them, as he had hoped. First as Miss Archdale, and either living or staying, it would seem, somewhere in the neighbourhood. Then as Miss A. Then as E.A., and translated—but he had been faintly aware of this already— into a mistress who had taken the place of a master at the beginning of the last war. Then she had become Elspeth. Then, with no warning at all in the diary, his father had married her. Then he himself had been born. And then, about fifteen months later, in the winter of 1916, she had been taken ill and had died.

That was all, and he had never re-read it, for once had been quite enough. He had been moved and shattered. He had felt horribly guilty, not only because he knew he had been prying, but because at that age—and even now, at times—he had been tormented by doubts that her death had in some way been due to his own birth. It had been too late, though, even to hope that his Uncle George might relieve this anxiety, for his Uncle George was now dead, too. He couldn't possibly question his father, any more than he could have asked his Aunt Evelyn, with whom he had been almost as uneasy, until her more recent decease.

If his mother had had any relations, he had never heard of them; so it was to be presumed, which was conceivable, that she hadn't. But she had had money; far more than the diaries seemed to suggest, though of course there was no reason why they should refer to it at all. And she had left it to him; not to R.J. And R.J. had said nothing about it until the day when he had no more choice. That, in fact, was the whole story; but if one saw him, at a slight distance like this, it was inevitably bound to come back. Had he loved her? What an impious and impertinent thought. Yes, but *had* he? And could she have loved *him*, when surely—quite apart from anything else—he must have been at least twenty if not something much more like thirty years older?

These questions came, and were unanswered, and would go again—until they came back. The whole business, in fact, was dashed puzzling even in far clearer cases. Look at Claud, for instance. Not a trace of Uncle George in him. But, except to look at, not much of Aunt Evelyn, either. I'm taking all this too seriously, thought Gavin. I haven't been asked here to think things like that. I shall now pull myself together.

So he did, to the best of his ability. R.J. was now telling quite a different story, which he had heard already, about the waste that was going on at a near-by camp. Claud—but he would!—was trying to interpolate another story on a similar subject. Gavin, who had been furnished at last with a small, reconstituted omelette, leant forward as if to show considerably more interest than he felt. He had thought of another question, too; not only one that it was possible to ask, but that he ought to ask, as soon as he got a chance.

The chance came. Both narrators had been supplied with omelettes, too. There was a moment when neither could talk with his mouth full. So Gavin leant forward once more, and said: "I say, father, how did you get on at the dentist?"

His two neighbours gave sudden starts, and stared at him. Claud, who had swallowed first, said: "Dentist? Oh, yes, of course. Eh?" In other words, he had adopted the question as his own; but it was at Gavin that R.J. looked grim.

"I was attended to quite satisfactorily, thank you," he said. And if he had added: "A gentleman doesn't discuss another gentleman's teeth at a third gentleman's Club," he could hardly have made his opinion of the inquiry clearer.

"Oh," said Gavin. He subsided completely; now even less than a schoolboy again. It was Claud who kept his head and changed the subject. Hypocrite, thought Gavin. Shut up, said the old inner voice; who's paying for the lunch? Yes, but why? Only because he can't bear being thwarted. And when is he going to get on to *my* business? Not now, I hope—in front of R.J. and with all these members listening.

But of course solicitors don't conduct their affairs like that. They're much too secretive. If they can't put you in a lower chair than their own, with a strong light in your eyes; if, that's to say, they don't haul you round to their office, they like to have you at their complete mercy elsewhere. There was no chance of this just yet; so Gavin's cousin Claud talked about the war to R.J., in a windy and omniscient manner, while R.J. lapped it up —though still with some doubtful grunts, for Claud had once been his pupil, too. In Gavin's opinion his cousin was now merely throwing his weight about, while his father, he judged, was bluffing a good deal as well. Was the war being fought, then, he asked himself, so that people should sit and talk nonsense about it? The inner voice said: Can't you stop criticising for a second? What are *you* contributing?

Nothing, thought Gavin. That's true enough. And then he thought that it would be worse, of course, if he was alone with R.J. at the Great Western Hotel at Paddington, where there could have been little or nothing but awkward pauses. Worse, too, if he were now lunching alone with Claud, and being cross-examined about publishing, and being caught up and contradicted and put in his place all the time. Presently he was given a portion of extremely sour apple-tart, though it would be wrong, of course, to blame Claud for that. He would have liked some water, having declined anything else. But though there was a large carafe in front of him, he had been given no glass. It seemed stupid to ask for one, even though it might have furnished him with a little more occupation. But he couldn't say that he craved for it; or for anything—except a breath of fresh air.

The uproar was slightly abating. One neighbour had left. And then the other got up and left, too. Though Gavin had spoken to neither of them—well, of course not—and neither had spoken to him, he rather missed them now. He felt more exposed. He found, as his father and host went on talking, that he was moving his head from side to side, like someone at a lawn-tennis match. But he wasn't listening. He was just watching their faces, in a detached and, it is to be feared, a rather critical manner again. He thought: This has all happened before—and became lost in a fog of speculation about this curious and recurrent illusion. He wondered if it would be permissible, or rude, to smoke one of his own cigarettes.

He was being addressed. He almost leapt in the air.

"Coffee?" his cousin was saying.

"Oh. Well—yes. Thanks awfully. I mean if you're quite sure——"

"I'll just pay the bill, then," said Claud, rather mysteriously. "We'll try and find a corner outside—eh?"

That made it less mysterious; but it was hardly for the two Guernseys to find the corner, while Claud queued up at the cashier's. They stood side by side—one of them rather towering over the other. Claud seemed to be writing a cheque now. I *must* say *something*, thought Gavin.

He said: "Will you be up again soon, father?"

"I don't know," said R.J., in a guarded manner. "Perhaps you'll be coming down some time."

"Oh, yes. Of course."

"Christmas?" It seemed torn out of him. Why should one accept what was hardly an invitation, when Christmas itself would be dreary enough without that? The inner voice said: Even if he doesn't want you—and perhaps he does, though he'll never show it—remember he's getting old and you're his son. I wish, thought another brain-cell, he didn't always make me feel such a selfish fool. He made a great struggle to infuse some geniality into an acceptance, though still he didn't know if he would be really welcome or not.

"That's very kind of you, R.J. I'd——"

"Ah! There's Claud. I must go."

Gavin was on the outskirts again. He followed the others into a passage. He watched and endeavoured to assist in a search for his father's coat and hat. They were found—by R.J. himself, who after all should have known where they were. Claud was hoisting the coat on to his back; not very successfully, for the collar of his jacket still stuck out. It always had, thought Gavin, standing by with the umbrella. He was touched, exasperated, baffled, and in an extremity of irritation and distress. R.J. turned round, with the deliberation of a tortoise, and put out his hand. Gavin thrust the umbrella into it; and was then agonised because he was almost certain that he had been meant to shake it.

They were in the outer hall, and if only Claud hadn't been here . . . But he was, with more justification than anyone, and what word could possibly have been spoken to set right what had been wrong, so far as Gavin was concerned, from the beginning of time? None. An uprush of sentiment which he knew to be false made him wonder if his father would be dead before he saw him again. Supposing he had a heart-attack in the train, and——

"Gavin!"

"I beg your pardon, father."

A scholastic and contemptuous snort. "Didn't you hear me saying Good-bye?"

"I'm sorry, father. I—ah—— Oh, good-bye."

The lanky page-boy had opened the door, and R.J.—who had naturally refused a taxi, though it would have been a job to get him one—passed out. He descended the steps with no air of pathos at all, but rather—so far as could be judged from a back view—as if the Club belonged to him. He walked away springily, though at the same time—a lost profile just showed this—with a familiar expression of authority, even on a London pavement. Yes, and even the maladjustment of those two collars couldn't hide the implication that the world, for R. J. Guernsey, M.A. (Oxon), was still but an extension of St. Eustace's Preparatory School.

"Wonderful old boy," said Claud. "What is he? Seventy?"

"Seventy-three," said Gavin, in only a slightly sulky tone. Nor did he advise his cousin—though there was a strong temptation—to be less damned condescending.

"Amazing," said Claud; and seemed to dismiss the whole thing. "Well," he resumed, taking Gavin by the arm and turning him round, "now what about—— Ah, excuse me just a moment. Sir Arthur! Sir *Arthur!*"

Gavin was dropped. His cousin Claud had shot off after a pursy gentleman—oh, a genuine monk, undoubtedly—and had more or less pinned him against a pillar. He had now, in fact, got hold of the pursy gentleman's arm. He was working him round the pillar to some spot where, whatever this urgent business was, it could be conducted without both parties being in everyone else's way. As they moved, he just had time to telegraph, as it were, a message to his remaining guest. But it was hardly an apology. Its purport seemed rather an instruction to stay where he was, because Sir Arthur must in no circumstances either escape or be interrupted. They both withdrew into a sombre and gigantic nook, and Gavin was left alone.

For a while he was occupied in eluding still more monks on their way out of the building. Then, not unskilfully, he reached the tape-machine, which at once stopped clicking, as if to show that it had identified him as a stranger, and had no more to tell him, when he peered at it, than that the quick brown fox was still jumping over the lazy dog. "Testing," it suddenly added, testily; and relapsed into silence again.

By fetching a cautious circuit he could now see that his cousin Claud and Sir Arthur were still hard at it; or that Claud was hard at it—for he was gesticulating a good deal—and that Sir Arthur was at least still hemmed in. For two pins, thought Gavin, I'd leave him. You know, he thought a little later, if I don't leave him I shall miss that trunk call from the printers. After all, he thought, if he's really got anything to tell me, he can always write or ring up. Well, how rude would it be if I beat it?

It was a problem in horology. The longer he was kept hanging about like this, the less any question of civility came into it. So presently he found his own hat and coat, and put them on. And glanced into the nook again, where his cousin and Sir Arthur were now seated on a small sofa, with the latter so far resigned to his fate that it was he who now appeared to be telling the story of his life. And then Gavin spoke to the second or supplementary porter to whom he had originally been referred, and asked him to let Mr. Kingham know that Mr. Guernsey was very sorry but he had been called away. And with these slightly inaccurate tidings as a farewell, he, too, slipped out by the main entrance, and walked down the steps, and turned in the direction of his office.

He was far from feeling that he had scored off anyone. He was just galled and exhausted by the whole business. The unexpected, in this case, had certainly played its part; for though it was true that he hadn't hoped to enjoy himself, it was really astonishing how he had spent more than an hour in the Club—nearly an hour and a half, in fact, altogether—without any real contact with either of the relations whom he had been specifically invited to meet.

To what, then, should one attribute this ? To lack of character, of course. And to moral cowardice ? By all means. For one of the relations still paralysed him, and though he wasn't exactly afraid of the other, he had singularly failed to stand up to him as even a client. Twenty-eight, he thought —which was his own age, of course. He was ashamed of himself.

He thought of his Oxford friends—Jock, Ronald, and Charles—whom he didn't often or for long forget; and wondered, supposing they were still alive, if they would be ashamed of him, too. He concluded that they would be, for indeed this young man with a very slight limp was an adept at darkening his own sky.

At about four o'clock, a wave of conscience rather than curiosity caused him to ring up his cousin's office. A woman's voice answered him. Then the Clerk came on the line. Yes, Mr. Kingham had looked in, but he'd gone again. No, he certainly wouldn't be back to-night. (That's loyal, thought Gavin, at this time of day. I suppose he wants a seat in his train before the black-out.) And no, added the Clerk, he wasn't aware of any special development in Mr. Guernsey's business. There had been a letter last week, but it had only been what you might call another acknowledgment.

"I see," said Gavin. "Thank you."

He rang off. Why the blazes, then, couldn't someone have said so at the time ? He stared mistily through his dirty window at the grey sky, and, of course, at a barrage-balloon. He wasn't at all sure that he liked this world. Though naturally—here came the familiar and inescapable corollary —if he felt like that, it was probably his own fault.

CHAPTER IX

ON THE SECOND SUNDAY IN DECEMBER A CONSIDERABLE NUMBER OF THE HOME Guard, assisted and occasionally impeded by other auxiliary forces, held some exercises in the immediate neighbourhood of Huddleston House. Just behind it, of course, where Crofton Street and its gardens had once stood, there was an area so much like a battlefield already, that you might have imagined, if ignorant enough, that they would exercise here. But they didn't. It remained, though of course not at the moment—for the members of this junior and unofficial battalion were all watching the Home Guard—the exercise-ground for a gang of somewhat savage boys, ranging in age from about eight to fifteen, whose fathers were away and therefore unable to control them, whose queue-weary mothers had mostly abandoned the attempt, and who assembled, from The Dwellings and other streets in that direction, to shout, scream, indulge in mock-battles, unite for the purpose of doing any further damage to the property that was still possible, and to alarm all the passers-by.

Ginger's Gang, they were called; or so one would gather from an ill-written slogan chalked on a shattered wall. But if you had dared to go further, you would have found similar references to other heroes—to Pickles, to Nobby, and (evidence of the educational influence of films) to Butch. Some of them, perhaps, were ex-leaders, who had retired or fallen from power. It was hard to say. But a great deal of bawling went on—even boys only a few yards from each other would always yell—and a great deal of ambushing, and hurling of missiles; while so far as it was possible to understand any words that were used, they were very coarse and objectionable words indeed. Little girls sometimes stood on the edge of this devastated area, and seemed to admire what was going on. But it cannot have done them much good. The police, both regular and reserve, rather tended to keep away from the spot; especially towards dusk, when the yells were more blood-curdling than ever, and the missiles weren't always discharged with respect or care. In fact, it was all rather like the Balkans; except, of course, at such moments as the Balkans happen to be on our side.

At one epoch the authorities had made an effort to enclose it with a rough kind of fence. But either the materials had run out, or had been taken —under cover of night and faster than they could be replaced—for firewood. The effort had accordingly languished and lapsed. There were only a few yards of fencing now; though at one point an ancient legend was still visible on a splintered board. It must have come from one of the little shops in the side-street, that had been destroyed at the same time. "Families," it said, "Waited On Daily." What an extraordinary, fantastic, and almost mediæval idea. . . .

It wasn't, however, so much because the Home Guard were afraid of these boys—though they well might have been—that they left this region alone. The point was that in their own mock-battles they were supposed to be engaged in street-fighting, and that you could hardly even pretend to do that on an open space where there were no houses at all. So despite the fact that it was now admirably adapted for a whole series of machine-gun nests —as they are so charmingly called—and that its roofless cellars might almost have been regarded as ready-made tank-traps, they paid no attention to the devastated area, but assembled, in the first place, outside Bessingham House.

They stood there for a while, looking rather self-conscious and not very happy, while a small crowd collected, and belated units kept stumbling, as surreptitiously as they could, into the rearmost ranks. Then they received their last, confidential instructions. And then you might have thought the whole thing was over—as some of the crowd did—for they broke up, and became dissipated (in the more literal sense), and more or less vanished from sight.

They were still there, though, or in the offing. Indeed, if you looked more carefully, you would have seen that there were now a number of sentries or patrols at a quantity of doorways and corners. They stood there, except when they had to move so as to get out of a civilian's way, eyeing each other in an expectant and anxious manner, and obviously aware of the weight of their equipment and boots. The porters came out of both blocks of flats, and chatted with them, to the complete neglect of their other duties; and children formed rings round some of them, and asked them when it was going to begin.

If they knew, they were of course pledged not to tell. In fact, they didn't answer, though they still looked anxious. Nor did they hand over their rifles for examination, as they were also invited to do. "Get away, you boys," they said, though this term might also be taken to include quite an equal number of girls. Sometimes, when they said this, the ring would momentarily recede for as much as a yard. But not always; never further; and it was soon back again. It was in self-defence now that they merely glared at each other. Yet the first phase of the battle, though long and slow, and so far extremely disappointing to the younger spectators, was nearly over.

Suddenly a boy gave a shriek, and pointed aloft. Ah, this was more like it! A sinister figure—or sinister, perhaps one should say, from this distance —had appeared on the roof of Bessingham House. He had a Sten gun. He looked over the edge, and immediately retreated. One couldn't blame him, even if one couldn't imagine what he was supposed to be doing there, for there was no parapet and a sheer drop of about eighty feet. But he wasn't alone now. There were more heads or helmets beside him. And there were other figures on other roofs. There was even a group on the top of Huddleston House; which would account, no doubt—though it wasn't heard in the street—for a panic-stricken cry from Miss Kenton-Hinksey, who was having a rather belated Sunday-morning bath, and had just seen a man in uniform, only a few yards away, through the window. She was no exhibitionist. She snatched at the bath-towel, and contrived to envelop herself in it even before emerging—rather more like a porpoise than Venus— from the watery element. The result of this was that she had to dry herself, in the passage, with a duster and dish-cloth—for as usual the laundry had got everything else. And this was yet another thing that the National Government had failed to foresee when it wobbled its way into war.

Meanwhile, though, the tempo of battle was quickening without. The first blank cartridge or fire-cracker—followed at once by a wild yelp from Lulu in No. 2—unquestionably exploded in error. In fact, as would appear at the subsequent inquiry, it was this that led to the invaders rushing forward before they were all quite ready. But of course this is just the kind of thing that happens in a real battle; and of course, again, as soon as some of them began rushing, the remainder felt more or less bound to take action, too. It was rather a mob, though, that came hurtling into the street, and order was scarcely restored by the conduct of the men with the smoke-bombs. Here, too, they would say afterwards, and with some justification, that though they hadn't exactly been told to let them off, they were afraid of being too late. So they did let them off. The children shrieked, with almost pure pleasure. The elder spectators—of whom there was a large body, for a quantity of them had accompanied the invaders—coughed, and brought out their handkerchiefs, and as they ran to and fro added very considerably to the confusion. Huddleston House, and even the lower half of Bessingham House, disappeared in a thick fog. And you could hardly even hear Lulu barking now, for the entire Home Guard seemed animated by but one impulse; which was to discharge all their ammunition as fast as they could before anyone told them to stop.

Now, also—though again a little sooner than had been planned—the vehicles began arriving, too. A mobile canteen; though this was only for show, as it were, and had nothing in it, as the warriors would presently find out. A trailer-pump, with some devoted adherents, who in less than no time were tripping up dozens of warriors and half-blinded spectators with lengths of hose-pipe. A small and recklessly-driven car, with an officer standing up in it—that's to say, until it braked too abruptly—and cursing his troops in an almost professional way. And a loud-speaker van.

This parked itself in the thick of the smoke-screen, on top of a hose-pipe, and began broadcasting. In alarmingly magnified accents it announced a number of wholly imaginary news-items. The enemy, it said, had captured the Town Hall. They were advancing from various points of the compass. They had destroyed a railway bridge. They had blown up the water-main. And so on. The children again took all this in very good part. The Home Guard appeared to consider it none of their business, or were perhaps too much preoccupied to indulge in any further, simulated action. But the deafening intelligence, immediately following on all those explosions, disturbed some more sensitive adults; such as Mr. and Mrs. Champion, for example, who decided to go down to the Shelter.

As the fog cleared slightly, and some of the noise died down, little groups of Home Guard Officers could be observed quarrelling and arguing with each other; for some it would seem, wished to start the whole thing afresh, while others were bent on justifying their own share in the fray. It was about now, too, that Mrs. Wardrop—very smartly dressed, though in a pre-war outfit —came home from church, and began seeking someone in authority to whom she could complain of this treatment of a Sunday morning. Fortunately, perhaps, she failed, and was reduced in the end to shaking her head at Freeth—who, in hopes of a tip, was prepared to agree with anything.

Tuke, however, had been more successful. Tuke had come out in a frenzy, and had actually got hold of an officer by one of his buttons.

"My dear man," she was booming, as she shook him to and fro; "I know all that. I've been a Warden since the whole thing started. But if you understand anything at all about dogs—well, you'd know this isn't *their* war. What's that?"

"I said, I'm very sorry, madam, if——"

"Sorry! That's a fat lot of use when the poor bitch is shivering and hiding under my bed. Why couldn't you go somewhere else?"

The officer, who invariably said "lady dog" himself, became speechless and pink in the face.

"I shall report this," said Tuke, grandiloquently and fiercely. "No one can say I'm not keen on Defence. But when it comes to going out of your way to frighten a poor harmless—— Good God! What's that?"

She let go of the button, and the officer vanished. There was a sound of martial music. It was also extremely discordant. Bugles were being blown with far more vigour than skill. Drums were being rattled and thumped with no thought, one would say, but to make the maximum din. Tuke dashed towards her flat again—presumably so as to assist her mother in comforting Lulu—and a platoon of little boys, in belts and forage-caps but no other uniform, led by a low-category young man in a similar outfit, came marching along from another divine service. It seems clear that if the young man had thought of making a detour, there was nothing to stop him doing it. But he hadn't. Or he was carried away by the music. Or as he had always come this way, after attending that particular church, he was coming this way again.

So he did; and neither smoke nor hose-pipes, neither Home Guard nor anything else, could stop him. The remaining combatants, in fact, were swept aside. Most of the children decided that it would be more fun now to follow the bugles and drums than to wait on the off-chance of further hostilities. And this, in fact, was virtually the end of the proceedings. The men came down from the roofs. The loud-speaker van dried up and drove off. The men with the trailer-pump got their gear together, and vanished, too. So, after it had beaten off a rather eager assault, did the mobile canteen. The troops were collected, inspected, cursed, and eventually dismissed. The last head came in from the last upper window, and again it was a grey, cold Sunday, with nothing to show for how it had just been employed but the remains of the crackers and smoke-bombs, which were soon kicked into the gutters.

Any comment? Not much. It was all perfectly logical, granted the first premise of a so-called total war. Just as Sunday, if business wasn't to be completely disrupted during the rest of the week, was the only and obvious day for the thing to happen. It wasn't quite in accordance, perhaps, with some of the prayers in which Mrs. Wardrop and the boys' brigade had joined, or with a lesson to which they had listened. But in England there has been no question, for four hundred years, that the Church must obey the State. And anyhow, by not later than about a quarter to one, the whole affair was at an end.

Now, if it had been peace-time, which it wasn't, a great pall of a different kind of smoke would have hung heavy in the air, while innumerable Sunday joints were being cooked; and from the higher floors of Bessingham House —whence there was a very good view of it—you could almost have watched that big gasometer sinking towards the ground. Its descent to-day, though, was considerably slower—if still not quite slow enough for the Ministry of Fuel and Power—for so many kitchens were empty now, and even in kitchenettes there were no great joints any more. Another Ministry had seen to that—correctly, no doubt, under the above-mentioned premise; and then, again, there was still some notion that this was the day of rest, and if it was also interpreted as such by your Daily Help, then a snack might be better than wearing yourself out; or a meal, if you couldn't face that, at some restaurant.

Not at the San Remo, though, which was closed—as was also the Dining-Room at the Royal Oak—on Sundays at lunch-time. You must go further. You must also start much earlier than a quarter to one—which in spite of the battle a number of tenants had succeeded in doing—for it was a feature of this epoch that all public meals must be set further and further forward (just as the bus-stops were being moved further and further from the places named on the fare-boards), and particularly on Sundays you must either lunch at twelve-thirty sharp, or be offered a scored-through menu, after waiting in yet another queue, if you arrived at what had once been a more conventional hour.

So some had already gone forth; some were preparing to have the kind of lunch that Mrs. Margetson had given herself after that morning's shopping; and only a few were now at all seriously at work in the kitchenettes. Of these, one was Miss Jemima Marsham; in whom there was at least some slight or passing resemblance to Cinderella.

Not that she was in rags; though she would have been if she had been wearing any of her present store of stockings. Not that she had two ugly sisters; for she hadn't, and her one, decidedly good-looking sister was younger than herself and at a boarding-school. Nor, so far as she was aware, was any prince giving a ball to-night. On the other hand, she was alone in the flat, even though the exigencies of the temporary Civil Service had released both herself and Miss Bretton to-day. Miss Bretton, however, had gone out, before the battle, and had not yet returned. In no circumstances whatsoever was any help to be expected from Mrs. Garrison, or Smashums, on a Sunday. So that Echo, once more, was alone.

This wasn't necessarily a cause for pity in itself. It might even be pointed out that in a kitchenette of that size it was at least convenient and almost essential. But then it also happened to be her birthday. Yes, Fate, which in quite a number of ways had not yet notably blessed her, had arranged that she should be born within a fortnight of Christmas; which, as everyone knows, is a grave disadvantage in childhood. And now that she had just become twenty-three, it had also arranged that this date should fall on a Sunday; so that there had been no letters, no parcels, and even Bugs, as it happened, had gone off without wishing her well.

Not really worth sniffing about. No genuine cause for even a single tear. To-morrow, almost undoubtedly, there should at least be a letter from her mother, and if it came it would almost unquestionably contain an enclosure. But, for all this, there was a flatness to-day. Impossible not to think of other birthdays, not really so very long ago. And then twenty-three. It was an age. One couldn't pretend that it was still practically the same as twenty, or even twenty-one. It meant, as you might say, that one was getting on now. But the war was getting on, too; and if one regarded it as an interruption—which was still the way that millions of people must take it—then it was hard not to feel, and especially on a birthday, that one was being robbed. Also, that one could never conceivably be paid back; for who wanted extra years at the wrong time? It was Miss Marsham's soul, perhaps, more than her very gentle and long-suffering mind, which made this protest. It was, in fact, a feeling rather than a thought. But it was there in the kitchenette with her; and just once or twice, it must be admitted, she shook her head.

She performed plenty of other actions, too, though. The equipment of this cell was of a rather primitive nature; partly because Bugs's Aunt Babs had removed all she could, partly because it couldn't then be replaced, and partly because of what Smashums had broken. But there were plates, if they didn't match, on the little dresser. There were cartons with various contents—or at any rate with the remains of them. There were certain implements, though of necessity they must be put to uses for which they hadn't exactly been designed. There were even bottles, though the one labelled *Fine Champagne* (an American sailor had given it to Bugs nearly two years ago) now merely contained a little war-time vinegar; and another—less actually misleading, and one had to use *something* for salad-oil—described itself as Highly Refined Liquid Paraffin, for Medicinal Use Only. There was a badly-scorched oven-cloth that must still last for the duration. There were some rags that had once been dish-cloths. Overhead, if it comes to that—disposed on and still gently dripping from a contrivance known as a Scotch Airer—there were some feminine undergarments, the property of both inmates, which Echo had been washing this morning, instead—like Mrs. Wardrop—of going to church.

These last items must just wait there, and perhaps absorb a slight scent from the curious substance now sold as cooking-fat. But among the rest Miss Marsham's fingers were constantly flitting. And she stood on tiptoe. And she crouched down. And she tossed her hair out of her eyes. And sometimes, though not often, she glanced at a cookery-book on the top of the little refrigerator. For as it was her birthday, and as Bugs had the day off, too, she was trying to cook a rather special lunch—so far as this could be done with three cutlets (consisting mostly of bone and gristle), some potatoes, some Brussels sprouts (which she hated, but Bugs didn't—particularly if she had more than her share of margarine), some rice (on Points), and some tinned fruit (ditto), every one of which items she had somehow procured herself. There was also, if necessary, some virtually tasteless cheese wrapped up in a torn table-napkin in the refrigerator. While further provision had been made for some adulterated coffee.

Quite a banquet, in fact, and it had been quite hard work already—in addition to making both beds (because Bugs had gone out without doing anything to her own) and catching up on a good deal of sweeping and dusting that Smashums had as usual overlooked. And then there had been all that noise suddenly, and the smoke and the shouting, which had been enough of an interruption to put the rest of the time-schedule back. So that Echo's movements must be quicker than ever now; for Bugs had promised to be back by one, and had held out some hopes of free tickets for a concert this afternoon. A birthday treat, after all, then? Well, yes, if it came off, and it almost certainly would. For anything that Bugs really wanted, she generally got. She was really rather wonderful, you know.

One difficulty about cooking even a two-course meal for two persons, when tackled entirely by yourself, lies largely in the fact that nothing ever takes the same time (notwithstanding cookery-books) as it did when you tried it before. The object, naturally, is that everything for the first course should be ready at the same moment, while everything for the second course should be just about ten minutes behind. Yet experience, and even bitter experience, seems little help. No wonder good cooks have bad tempers, when not only can the gas-pressure vary from hour to hour, but the very ingredients would appear to be endowed with unpredictable characteristics of their own. One potato, or even cutlet, looks very much like another. And surely, you would imagine, nothing could be less high-strung or neurotic than a Brussels sprout.

But wait till you cook them. Yesterday the potatoes were stubborn, so they must obviously be allowed longer to-day. Or last time the cutlets were ready too soon, so that now they must have different treatment. Even the same lot of Brussels sprouts will have become pulpy on one occasion and remain raw at the next, if you assume for a moment that they will react twice running in the same manner. So that although Miss Jemima Marsham had so little temper, in the worse sense, as sometimes to be falsely suspected of having no character either, as zero-hour approached she was kept more than ever on the *qui-vive*. Her eyes, in fact—one of them under that celebrated eyebrow—were dashing all over the place, lest something should flare up or boil over, or something else should be backward, or some fresh implement, which might urgently be needed at any moment, should prove to have been hidden by Smashums. Also, her hair kept getting in those eyes again, particularly when both hands were occupied, so that on such occasions she must contrive to blow upwards, very hard indeed, while simultaneously (it might be) moving some obstacle (such as the old but almost priceless biscuit-tin in which the bread was kept) out of the way with one foot.

And then the telephone-bell rang. It would, of course. She must also answer it, though first she must eye the whole set-out once more, and hurriedly dry one hand, we're afraid, on the oven-cloth. Then she dashed. As she did this—so swift is the human brain—she thought of at least six people, including two friends of Bugs's, her mother (with birthday greetings), and perhaps, just possibly, someone else, whose identity might be about to be revealed. But it was none of them. It was Bugs herself.

"Oh!" said Echo. "Hullo, darling."

"I say—can you hear me?"

"Yes. What is it?"

"Well," said Miss Bretton's voice, "have you started lunch yet?"

"No, of course not. Oh, cooking it, you mean! Yes, of course. It's nearly ready. Why, where are you?"

"I'm awfully sorry, darling, but—— Well, they want me to stay on."

"Who do?"

One could ask that, surely, without appearing inquisitive. Indeed, and though Bugs sounded in an awful hurry, one was probably meant to ask it.

"Well, darling," said the voice, again, "I don't think you know them. But you see, I found Claire was working to-day when I got there—I'd made a muddle—so I rang up Avis, but she was out. So I was just coming back, when I suddenly met Nigel—yes, he's on leave; isn't that good?—and then he gave me a drink, and there's a sort of party going on, and, well, I couldn't very well say No, and I think some of us are going on to a picture afterwards.

E

I'm awfully sorry, darling. You see, I didn't really *know* until just now. Can you manage ? Will you be all right ?"

Such a kind voice at the end of it all. Hardly the least impatient. It might have seemed to some, of course, though it didn't to Echo, that the story would perhaps scarcely stand the test of cross-examination. That the muddle was probably authentic, but that it was rather unlike Bugs to ring up a girl after that if she could ring up a man. That a chance meeting with Nigel was really rather unlikely, seeing that his family had a flat in Westminster while Claire lived near the Marble Arch. But Echo, though she had cooked largely in vain and realised that the concert was now off, took special pains to say that of *course* she would be all right.

"I'm *so* glad," said Bugs. "I do feel a *bit* of a swine, darling."

"Oh, but of *course* not!"

"Well, what'll *you* do ?" Somehow it seemed that the immediate urgency was over; unless it was that one must always telephone as long as one possibly could.

"Oh, something," said Echo. "Don't worry, darling—*please*."

"You're *sure* you're all right ?"

"Yes; absolutely. I——"

"Has anything been happening since I left ?"

"No, nothing. Well, 's a matter of fact, there was one of those Home Guard things again. Just outside here. They made an awful noise and smell."

"Oh, I'm glad I missed that. But no one rang up ?"

"No, nobody."

"I see. Well, all right, darling. I'll be back some time, I expect, and if anything's left over we can have it cold. But don't worry if I'm late. I'll be somewhere."

"I see."

"And take care of yourself, sweetie," said Bugs, more affectionately and dictatorially than ever. "All right. Just coming," she added, though this was clearly to someone else. Then she hung up; and the resemblance of her deserted companion to Cinderella had become even more marked than before.

Not that she wept, though she did say "Oh, bother." And yet, having said this, she could still reproach herself. She shouldn't have begun cooking so soon. And of course it was a bore for Bugs to be saddled with someone who never seemed to get herself asked out. It's my fault, thought Echo. I'm dull, you see. I just haven't got—well, whatever it is. Not that I *mind*. I don't really *want* to go out—except that I suppose it's waste if one doesn't. And if I *do* go out, I always seem to start thinking of things, instead of trying to talk. I wish——

She was on the point of wishing that she was more like the girl who had just let her down, but whom she still felt compelled to admire, when another bell suddenly rang. Front door, this time. Oh, dear, she thought, what a mess I'm in! I do hope it isn't—— But it can't be. I wish it was, though.

There was another flash in her mind. Perhaps the lunch wouldn't be wasted, after all. Of course, nobody—or no one like that—would ever come calling by chance at an hour like this. Nothing, she was convinced, could be less in his line. Or if she was wrong—right?—of course it would be Bugs who had drawn him.

And yet it *was* her birthday. Surely *something* must happen.

She skipped into the little lobby. She wasn't so simple—being a woman of twenty-three—that she hadn't a selection of expressions ready, nor that all of them weren't planned to conceal what had passed through her thoughts. But in fact she used none of them. She just looked astonished. For it was Mr. Everard, her neighbour from No. 17, who was disclosed as she opened the door.

"Oh!" she said. "Hullo."

"I—I—I say——" said Mr. Everard.

"Do come in," said Echo, hospitably.

"Oh, no, no, no," said Mr. Everard, looking ridiculously scared. "I mean, it's very good of you, but—well, the point is——"

He seemed to choke slightly. Though he had never attempted to do so before—indeed, the sum of their conversation so far had been a few good-mornings in the lift—Echo was now under the illusion that he wanted to borrow something. All right, then. By all means. She smiled, and the eyebrow went up.

"Yes?" she said, soothingly and encouragingly.

No permanent Civil Servant—and that's saying a good deal—could possibly have blinked with more vigour.

"Perhaps not my business," said Mr. Everard. "No wish to—oop!—intrude. Just happened to look out, though. Window." He jerked his head to indicate Heaven knew what. "Certain amount of—beep!—smoke."

Echo was rather fascinated. He said "oop" and "beep" so extra-ordinarily distinctly; and though she had met a number of permanent Civil Servants since becoming a temporary one herself, and had an overlord who was in the habit of interjecting "erp" about three times in each sentence, she was particularly charmed by "beep." But of course she must also answer him, for she was a very polite girl.

"Oh," she said. "Yes. It was only the Home Guard."

"No, no, no," said Mr. Everard, again—but it sounded like "Noo, noo, noo." "I—oop—observed that, too. I—I quite realise what you mean. But this—oomps—quite different. Much blacker." He suddenly smiled himself now, or at any rate showed a lot of teeth. "And apparently proceeding," he added, "from one of *your* windows. In fact—ur-urm . . ."

He sniffed. Echo didn't need to sniff. She had really been aware of it all the time; only, although the human brain can work very quickly, it can't always deal with as many as three things at once. But there was no doubt what was happening now.

"Oh, hell!" she said—for you can't have a total war, and conscript young women, and then expect them never to say more than "Bother!" "Oh, hell's bells!" she said, now dashing into the kitchenette. "It's the lunch!"

And so it was; or had been. Thick, black smoke was pouring from the gas-cooker, and out of the window. The smell was as powerful as it was unmistakable. The cutlets and the so-called cooking-fat were obviously on the verge of incandescence.

"It's *too* bad!" she said; and she turned the tap off. "Oh, dear!" she said, pushing the window still wider open. "And the washing!" she wailed, looking up at the Scotch airer.

"I—I—I do hope," said Mr. Everard, who appeared to have joined her, "you didn't mind my—oop—drawing your attention——"

"No, of course not." Though I might just have stopped it in time if you hadn't. "I mean—— Oh, *blast!*"

She opened the oven door, and they were both nearly asphyxiated. She slammed it hastily.

"What a *fool* I've been!" she said. "I mean, it was *awfully* kind of you."

Sometimes—just occasionally—Mr. Everard came so far in contact with real life as actually to see a fellow-creature, instead of regarding them either as mechanism for carrying on his duties or as indistinguishable and almost purely statistical units. One of these moments came now. It perplexed him. He realised, for instance, that he had come here expecting to find two young women, and that he was now alone in a kitchenette with only one of them. This brought her, as it were, into comparatively sharp focus. She was looking at him. He didn't notice the eyebrow, for he wasn't nearly as observant as that. But buried bits of him even went so far as to detect a touch of pathos—stupid as it might be to set fire to one's own lunch—while others, perhaps nearer the surface, advised him that it was about time he left. There was a slight inward struggle. He opened his mouth. He said: "Er, possibly—that's to say—beep——"

And this was where Echo began to laugh. She didn't mean to be rude. She felt in anything but high spirtits. But when everything goes wrong at once, and on one's birthday, and when a curious, pompous little man comes into one's flat and says "Beep"—well, of course it was inexcusable in a way, but it was also completely unavoidable. She could see Mr. Everard stiffening and looking shocked, but now this could only make her laugh the more.

"Oh, please!" she was trying to say. And: "You don't understand; it's just one of those things." But at each attempt the laughter interrupted her, and not a word, or certainly not more than a word, could Mr. Everard hear. He was then terrified and affronted, because—as he backed away— she put out an arm as if to stop him; and though this, too, was but a further and fruitless motion of apology, he was now the complete Civil Servant again. His little eyes became glazed. He puffed out his chest, with what he took to be dignity and authority. He gave a brief, cold, formal bow. And he was gone.

"Oh!" cried the nymph Echo, for at the same moment it seemed absolutely incredible that she could ever have laughed in her life. "But I *am* grateful, Mr. Everard! You *mustn't* think I'm——"

The front door closed with a thud. Mr. Everard had heard, right enough, this time; but can one imagine him coming off a perch which he had just mounted, merely because he was invited to descend? No, no. He had performed a very neighbourly action, and had quite possibly saved the whole place from catching fire; but the young woman, like all young women—not that he knew any, though unfortunately he was compelled to speak to some of them nowadays at his Office—was a flibbertigibbet. If he met her, or her companion, again, he proposed not to allude to the matter. He had very nearly unbent—or so he believed—but the only result was that he had been treated without courtesy or respect. He took note of this, though he was really in no need of a warning. If that girl was on *his* staff, he thought, he would call for a report on her work the very first thing to-morrow morning. He was only sorry—and again, of course, this had nothing to do with the eyebrow—that she wasn't. In fact, he looked very fierce and efficient indeed.

He also thought for a moment, and with fresh approval, of Mrs. Everard, who was not only of a much more responsible age but had hardly ever laughed since he had known her. Laughter? he thought, and then scratched one of his ears, which was suddenly tickling. Then he dismissed the whole thing; collected the sandwiches which he had been on the point of collecting when he had suddenly seen that swirl of smoke from the other kitchenette; and returned to his chair in the sitting-room. For though he wasn't at the Office to-day, for once, he had brought back plenty of papers. He was, in fact, very deeply engaged on a memorandum which was headed "Post-War Reconstruction." It was true that he didn't know when this epoch would begin, or what conditions would be like by then. It might be true, also, that if an outsider had seen that memorandum—but of course that is a fantastic supposition—he might have found far more about the permanent enlargement and despotism of Mr. Everard's Department than anything that might have appealed to him, as an outsider, with more allure. But Mr. Everard wasn't worrying about outsiders. It wouldn't have been in the tradition if he had. He read, munched, chewed, frowned, and made notes with a propelling pencil. And presently, on the cover of an official file, and in this case with a fountain-pen, he wrote "B.F.", and then added a date and his initials. To the Registry this would mean that the file must be Brought Forward again on the date in question. In fact, this was absolutely all that it really meant.

As for Miss Marsham, she sighed, and shook her head, and made an attempt to shrug her shoulders—though this hardly represented her true frame of mind, for to have hurt someone's feelings was for her the worst crime in the world. Then she opened the oven again, decided that if she scraped and then minced the cutlets—which she would have to do with a pair of scissors, for the flat had no mincing-machine—then it might perhaps just be possible to make something of them for supper. But she had no lunch, because she had no appetite. Very foolish, of course. Far, far too thin-skinned; and on her birthday, of all days, too.

But if you can't eat, you can't; and particularly if there is no one to make you. She put everything away, and lay down on the divan, which was also her bed, with a Sunday paper. Her eyes swam a bit, we're afraid, when she tried to read it. As she kept assuring herself, however, she would be all right presently. And presently—subject to a number of inevitable qualifications during a total or global war—this forecast was more or less fulfilled.

She went out for a walk, without too many thoughts as an accompaniment. She didn't exactly forgive her friend Bugs, for at no moment—and we should try to control any wish to shake her—had she regarded her friend Bugs's conduct as requiring forgiveness. She thought she had behaved naturally—as was indeed the case—in snatching at a better opportunity of lunching and filling the afternoon. In fact, she didn't even use the word "snatch" in her mind. She just saw her friend Bugs as one to whom opportunities were always coming, and herself as one to whom, for some reason or other, they didn't. But there was still far less jealousy or pique than admiration. It was so lucky, she thought, to *have* a friend like that, when she was always dreaming, and missing things, and forgetting things herself.

In a quiet street, though, or perhaps one should say an especially quiet street, through which her steps chanced to lead her—a street, like all streets now, with fading paint, and stumps of old railings, and a certain amount of patched roofs and windows—she observed an old lady, of a shabby and distinctly insane appearance, dart suddenly forth, from an area, into the road. With a furtive look she felt under an ancient cape that she was wearing, pulled out a scrap of old paper, showered some crumbs on to the ground, and darted back into the house. There was little or no question, in fact, that the old lady had just committed a pretty serious Offence. But the sparrows, and then the pigeons, that came rushing towards the fragments didn't seem to think so. Nor did Miss Marsham think so. In fact, as her eyes began swimming slightly again, she was thankful that on this occasion, too, she had apparently been invisible. Poor old thing, she thought. And poor birds—what *could* they think of the air-raids? She tiptoed away, so as not to disturb them; and she wasn't unhappy now—a queer creature—for in this sort of way she rather enjoyed feeling sad.

Despite what the State had done to the clocks, it was still December, and dark very soon after five. Furthermore, there was still an increase—even if, as was to be hoped, only seasonal—in the number of Alerts, and most decidedly in the noise of the barrage, compared with only a very few months ago. If you believed in the newspapers, but it must be confessed that this wasn't always too easy, then you might have gathered that Londoners liked this additional din, and slept the more soundly on nights when it shook the whole sky. A High Authority had also informed them that the present series of falling bombs was of no strategic value; which of course was the greatest comfort to anyone in a building that was hit, even if still, after all these years, they were unable to distinguish between strategy and tactics.

Nevertheless, if they weren't at work when dusk returned, or weren't up in London on leave, of which not a second must be wasted, most citizens were now already ensconced in their own fastnesses, and would probably stay there. Again, there is a saying that the better the day, the better the deed. So that at about five o'clock on this Sunday afternoon—or evening, as you might call it now—having had her own light tea in No. 7, Huddleston House, and having also washed up the tea-things, Mrs. Wardrop prepared to set forth on her charitable and predatory rounds.

She was in arrears, of course. That goes without saying. She was still, as a matter of fact, trying to clear up her accounts for November. And the accounts were in a muddle, as they always were; and always, it seemed, in some manner that required her to make up the balance herself. Yet even this brings a feeling of virtue, if you happen to be as innocent and improvident as Mrs. Wardrop. She was a nuisance, too, if it comes to that. But she didn't know this, any more than she was aware of those other qualities. And again it seemed right that she should dress rather carefully for the occasion. While again, in some curious manner, the fact that she was now going out begging—for shorn of sentiment and flapdoodle this was all that it was—animated her with the old and powerful sensation that she was the Lady of the Manor at Huddleston House, and that everyone else was a cottager, as you might say, or even a retainer. As economists, we must still be rather sorry for her, because she was living so well beyond her means. But as annalists we cannot deny that she seemed pretty well pleased with herself.

She had several note-books—all of which had started as something else; so that one, for instance, set off with an attempted and obsolete inventory of her furniture, while another had originally been supplied by the butcher (and still bore his name on the cover, and a number of his own entries inside) who had served her in the days of her glory at Muncaster Mansions. And she had a pencil, though its point would almost certainly snap before she finished the round. And a small, lady-like shopping-bag, for fumbling in. And a tin with a slot in the lid, slung over one wrist. And some savings-stamps, in an old envelope at the bottom of the bag. And a pair of spectacles, without which she could neither read nor write, but which she would constantly mislay, in one flat after another, so that she was always returning and ringing again, just as the inmates had hoped she was gone for good.

She began at the bottom of the building, but with little success. It is true, that is to say, that Truelove, who was hanging about and doing nothing in particular, said: "Good-evening, mum." But when she asked him for his penny-a-week—which had recently and rather confusingly become twopence, but which in any case he had last actually provided (in exchange for a shilling, because he had picked up her spectacles at the same time) as long ago as September—he became galvanised into violent activity; said: "Excuse me, mum; that's for me, I think:" and shot like a stoat into the cellar. Mrs. Wardrop, who had already managed to get the right book open at the right page, was so startled that she put a pencil tick in it. This meant that when she next checked up, she would find herself responsible for three-and-eight-pence. But not net. For though no one could be more honourable or honest, and she always came out a bit on the wrong side at the end, one must also admit that she sometimes put the tick among the butcher's saddles and loins.

With the rest of the ground floor she drew blank. No. 1 didn't answer, and was perhaps away, for its newspaper was still stuck in the letter-slot. A ring and a rat-tat at No. 2—the rat-tat seemed more official, and it had never occurred to Mrs. Wardrop that it was also, by now, an unmistakable warning—produced Mrs. Tuke (also Lulu, quite recovered, and yapping instead of howling), who said that Sylvia did everything of that sort, but that she was over at the Control now; and that she (Mrs. Tuke) would certainly remind her when she came back, but that she might not see her till the morning, and that in any case she herself, she was afraid, was down to a threepenny bit. Even Mrs. Wardrop could hardly deprive her of that. Besides, Lulu was trying to ladder her stockings. So she withdrew, with as bright, kindly, and patronising a smile as she could manage. Lulu was caught. The door closed behind her. And, having re-crossed the hall, she rang and rat-tatted at No. 3.

At first there was no answer here, either; and to-night there were even a couple of milk-bottles waiting. But as she could distinctly hear voices inside, she repeated the summons. This time the door was plucked suddenly open, and a gigantic, swaying, beaming, and, so far as Mrs. Wardrop was concerned, completely unknown United States officer seemed to fill the whole gap.

"Oh!" said Mrs. Wardrop, rather caught off her little high horse. "I mustn't disturb them, but——" she exhibited some of her equipment— "if you *could* just ask Mr.—or Mrs.——"

"C'me awn in!" said the officer, in the most sociable manner, and a voice which appeared to ascend from the depths of some echoing mine-shaft. "All welcome. Have lil drink!"

In an excess of semi-saturated *bonhomie*, he waved a small, thick, empty glass, and incautiously let go of the door-handle. His balance was obviously affected, and he looked pitifully surprised. "Pardon, ma'am," said that booming, muffled voice again. As he lurched forward, Mrs. Wardrop took a step back.

"Ah!" he said, in a profound, wheedling tone. "Doan leave us, lady. All friends here." A doubt appeared to flit across his noble features and almost olive-coloured eyes; but he dismissed it. "*All* frens," he repeated. "Come right in!"

This time he lurched backwards, and at the same moment there was a crash from behind him—suggesting that a tray and at least half-a-dozen glasses had hit the floor—followed at once by a burst of merriment.

"There you are!" said the giant, triumphantly. "An' how many miles 've I come? Three thousan'. Four thousan'. Twunny thousan'! Fine buncha fellers, too. Here!" Now he was tilting forward once more. "Show you picture. Wife. Lil girl. Dawg." He hurled his own glass away, and began wrenching at buttons.

"Oh," said Mrs. Wardrop, "please don't trouble. Some other time, perhaps. In fact, I really think——"

"Ah, jes' *one* lil drink!"

"No, really not, thank you."

The giant gave up. Shook his head. Looked indescribably mournful. And sat so heavily and abruptly on a small dark-oak chest that it gave a splintering sound. It was Mrs. Wardrop, in fact, who shut the door, pulling it firmly by the outer knob, for indeed there seemed little chance of collecting anything here. "Disgusting!" she muttered. "Really!" she said, as she turned towards No. 4. And yet the poor giant had said nothing offensive, and was unhappy now, and had only—one feels almost certain—tossed spirits down his throat in the hope of forgetting his wife, and his child and his dog. He had also come at least three thousand miles, as stated in that original estimate, in order, very likely, to be mutilated or killed. He was a hero, in fact. But he had obstructed Mrs. Wardrop in the execution of her duty, and she was not only very angry with him, but meant to have a word with Mr. Todman about his host and hostess, too. For even in a war we must each and all see things from our own point of view.

Meanwhile, she was baffled in her approach to No. 4 as well. That is to say that, even before she could ring and knock, she heard the telephone pealing away inside; and as no one answered it, though it continued pealing in the most persistent manner, it seemed clear that Major Hurst was out. Well, she was rather relieved, really. For one thing she didn't much like him, for even at her age she was convinced that he didn't really respect her sex. And for another thing he had a habit of treating her recurrent visits and applications in a much too offhand way. "Here you are," he would say. "Here's ten bob. Sort it out yourself, and keep the change." Oh, generous, if you like; and of course she didn't keep the change, or never intentionally. But it wasn't polite. It gave her no opportunity to *explain* about the various good causes. It made her feel—and there may have been some reason for this—that he just wanted to get her out of the way. She would have spoken to him fairly sharply, once or twice, if he hadn't practically forced her out of the flat.

So she didn't ring, and she didn't knock. She just entered some symbols —which she would subsequently be unable to interpret—and went up to the first, or her own, floor. And here, though undoubtedly there was an undercurrent of annoyance still, she did very much better than below.

Mr. Barker, for instance, opened his door so quickly—though he stayed in the opening, instead, as he should at least have done, of asking her into the lobby—that he might almost have been waiting on the mat. But he was prompt and business-like. It would appear, in fact, that he, also, kept a record of his payments, for he pulled out a little diary, and consulted it— while Mrs. Wardrop was still fumbling with her own records—and then dipped into a trouser-pocket and brought up a handful of coins. "There you are," he said, making practised use of a thumb. "That's right, you'll find."

"Oh, thank you *so* much." Here was the Lady of the Manor again. "Most kind of you to be so regular." A display of gums. "But of course it *is* so important——"

"Could I have my stamp, please?"

"Your stamp?" Mrs. Wardrop, cut short in her lecture on public service and philanthropy, looked a little flustered.

"For the Savings Group."

"Oh. Yes. Of course. How stupid of me!"

Down went two books and the old envelope on to the floor. But Mr. Barker had them up again in no time.

"Just coming!" he called over his shoulder.

"I beg your pardon?"

"Perhaps I'd better take it," said Mr. Barker; and he took his stamp, and returned everything else. "Thanks," he said.

"Oh, not at all," said Mrs. Wardrop. "And how is *Mrs.* Barker?"

"Excuse me," said Mr. Barker. "I—I'm rather busy at the moment. I——"

"Oh, quite," said Mrs. Wardrop, graciously. "More war-work?" she added, archly; though why archly, she had no very clear idea.

"Yes," said Mr. Barker, after only the slightest hesitation. "Well," he said, "much obliged." And then he shut the door. Not a gentleman, of course. Quite a different class from some of the old tenants here, and unimaginable at Muncaster Mansions. Yet his brusquerie had translated itself, in Mrs. Wardrop's mind, into a feeling—indeed, an assurance—that she, too, was engaged on war-work. A highly successful and efficient little interview, she thought; and quite forgot to make any entries at all.

That was No. 5.   No. 6 had paid up during the week, having been caught in the lift, and could now be passed over.   No. 7 was her own flat, so that naturally it was passed over, too.   No. 8 didn't answer, it is true, but couldn't hope to escape when it showed signs of life, for she could hear every sound through the wall.   No. 9 was a French naval officer, whom she hardly expected to be in; but he was, and though he opened the door looking any-thing but breezy, his sad monkey-face and long eyelashes had quite an effect on Mrs. Wardrop; and though she couldn't quite understand what he said—because she had been carried away into saying "Bong jour," from which moment he had spoken nothing but his own language at a perfectly appalling speed—she had then discovered, after a good deal of page-turning, that he didn't owe her anything, either.   Or so the books seemed to say.   He then said: "*Enchanté, madame,*" and vanished; and Mrs. Wardrop was left not only with a further though perhaps illusory feeling of achievement, but with the belief that she had done a good deal to overcome any difficulties at Algiers.

Second floor now.   Endless delay at the Champions'—but no one could have behaved more as if they were keeping Mrs. Wardrop's lodge—while they insisted on her coming in and sitting down, and then wouldn't sit down themselves; and contrived, also, that the subject of the fourpence—which was the total extent of this virtuous couple's arrears—should be approached gradually, and by a roundabout route; and that, when reached, it should be left in the same way.   Mrs. Champion did the talking, but with an obvious and continuous effort, while Mr. Champion kept nodding, as if to say "This is worth listening to," and also provided the cash.   Quite a little session at No. 11, notwithstanding the fact that two members remained on their hind legs.   But Mrs. Wardrop had no doubt that her presence was a favour, and continued to be exceedingly gracious throughout.   Particularly when she returned for her spectacles.

Slight set-back at No. 12.   The summons was answered by the owlish young man in the much thicker glasses, who immediately withdrew and could be heard calling for the other young man; the one who, in Mrs. Wardrop's opinion, had no right—for she didn't know how he had escaped from the Army—to be here at all.   He was very polite, as indeed he had better be. And she was rather stiff, just to show that—whatever he was doing—she was aware where his real duty lay.   Then they went through the accounts together, for she could hardly stop him when he seemed to think he was helping; and, lo and behold, it turned out that he had already paid up, for himself and the poor short-sighted young man, to the end of the year.

"Oh," said Mrs. Wardrop, indicating that in these circumstances—of which she still didn't seem quite convinced—he could be let off with a caution. She then dropped the shopping-bag, and he picked it up for her—but he needn't have grunted like that—and waited, again civilly enough, until she had moved away.   Oh, yes, he was nice-looking; but he had better be careful. Not that *she* was going to make mischief—and, indeed, she very seldom did

—but the war-time antipathy between age and youth had somehow been roused again. Besides, nobody else ever paid in advance, and it only, as he ought to have seen, led to waste of her time.

No. 13, like No. 10, she *knew*—though she happened to be mistaken—had also paid up. What about No. 14 ? She hesitated. It was her own duty, of *course*, to tackle the Musselbergs. Nor was she exactly afraid of them, because naturally she despised them. But the truth was that neither of them had ever given her anything—except once, when Mr. Musselberg had offered her a tip for a greyhound race, and had then afterwards told her (most offensively, she thought, but apparently with no sense of shame) that if she had taken it she would have been on at twenty to one. As if she was a gambler. Really! Or as if, even if one knew how to, one could possibly use charitable funds as a stake. She still quivered with indignation as she thought of it; and since, furthermore, someone was now playing *The Rustle of Spring* very loudly on the Musselbergs' piano—either of the Tukes could have told her that it was Mrs. Musselberg's cousin Connie, for somehow they knew even that—Mrs. Wardrop succumbed to discretion, and turned away.

She told herself, in this one case, that it wasn't the moment to interrupt them. She was so innocent, too, that it never occurred to her that Charities themselves, if they don't publish accounts, and pay their more sophisticated collectors, and arrange auctions at which dealers buy goods that can only be sold back to persons enriched by the war, and get listeners to the radio to bet on which of three indistinguishable noises is a real man blowing his nose, are less concerned with the source of their income than with constantly whooping it up. But in any event she had now left the Musselbergs and *The Rustle of Spring*, and was climbing, still full of virtue, to the third floor.

She began, for no particular reason, at the other end this time. That's to say, she woke up Mr. Waterman, at No. 20, quite an hour before he was due to rise, and have his curiously-timed breakfast, and go off to that branch of the Censorship; so that he appeared, half asleep, in a dressing-gown, and blinked, and said nothing, and retreated, and came back with two shillings, and shut the door in her face. She was a little shocked by his costume—for he wasn't even wearing slippers—and affronted by his manner. According to the books, moreover, he should have given her at least two-and-six. Yet even Mrs. Wardrop could sometimes tell when one assault was enough. She decided, all things being considered—and particularly, perhaps, Mr. Waterman's torso—to pass on her way.

She missed out No. 19, where again there were no dues. And she missed out No. 18, for the same reason, though she always enjoyed a chat with Mrs. Margetson—whether, it might be added, Mrs. Margetson enjoyed it or not. At No. 17 she caught Mr. Everard, who looked darkly suspicious, as he always did; who eyed her, in fact, as if he would like to ask for her identity-card; but paid, though he rather flustered her by watching her with the same sort of air as she entered his gifts in the books. But again he would have nothing to do with the Savings Group, though he still wouldn't trouble to explain why. He just sneered when it was mentioned, and waved the very thought aside. One was left to guess whether he was satiated with savings, belonged to a Group at his Office, realised the inherent economic duplicity of the whole system, or felt, as a Civil Servant, that it was for the rest of the community to fork out. Nor would he chat. He wouldn't even rise to a singularly blunt question about the prospects of a Second Front. He closed his mouth like a trap, and glared. So Mrs. Wardrop left him.

She passed No. 16, for here, too, the inmates had earned a temporary and rather qualified peace, and knocked and rang at No. 15. "Coming!" called a young voice from within. And the door was snatched open.

"Oh!" said the same voice. "I beg your pardon, Mrs. Wardrop. I thought you were Bryony. She—she loses her latchkey sometimes. It's the Red Cross—isn't it ?—and the other things. Do please come in. I—I'll just get my bag."

So Miss Marsham—still alone, it would seem, though it was now almost time for the six o'clock news-bulletin—made the requisite offerings on her own and her friend's behalf. And Mrs. Wardrop was again gracious, and almost queenly—the invariable effect when anyone was polite to her now— and told Miss Marsham that she should take a good holiday this Christmas.

"I'd love to," said Echo, without explaining that she would be in bondage even on Christmas Day. "Thank you, Mrs. Wardrop," she said. And this business being transacted, Mrs. Wardrop made one more ascent, feeling a little tired but still full of efficiency and merit, to the top floor.

Here, as it happened, the lift arrived at the same moment; and Mrs. Archie Amberley got out. She was smoking, of course. Her face was still brilliantly coloured, and she was wearing a shabby fur-coat, and a scarf tied over her head. Undoubtedly she would have dodged Mrs. Wardrop if she could have. But she couldn't.

"How lucky," said Mrs. Wardrop. "I was just coming to you. You've been working ?"

"Hullo!" said Mrs. Amberley. "Yes."

And she was home early because two other girls had fainted, and the charge-hand—knowing, perhaps, how contagious this was—had risked letting the rest of them go. In this, thought Mrs. Amberley, he had been both right and wrong. Yet it had slightly affected her own morale, and she was longing for a drink.

"Well," said Mrs. Wardrop, accompanying her along the faintly illuminated passage towards No. 25, "I mustn't keep you, in that case—though of course this is *my* work, too. But if I might just trouble you——"

"Yes ?" Mrs. Amberley unlocked her own outer door, and—having assured herself that the inner doors were shut—switched on a bright light in the little lobby. "Yes?" she repeated. "What's it for this time?"

She really looked like an actress or something, with all that paint on her face, and that exceedingly gaudy scarf. And Mrs. Wardrop didn't quite like her tone.

"You know," she said—but the fate of Ananias and Sapphira will always remain an exception—"I'm not doing this because I like it. It's got to be *done*, you know, Mrs. Amberley."

"Oh, absolutely. I'm ready."

Mrs. Wardrop either controlled herself, or was a little afraid of this intransigent tenant.

"Well," she said, "I know you were very generous last time——"

"That's right."

"——when you bought all those stamps. So I won't bother you about *them*." Another smile, or glimpse of the gums. "But there's the Red Cross——"

"Oh, God!" said Mrs. Archie Amberley, under her breath; but Mrs. Wardrop missed this.

"——and the P.O.W., and——"

"What's that?"

"My dear! What a question from you, of *all* people! But you're pulling my leg—aren't you?"

The smile looked slightly forced for a moment, and then switched to what was clearly intended to represent an air of solicitude. The voice became much lower. "Prisoners of War, I mean. So useful." The head tilted a little. "Have you—have you heard from your husband lately?"

A brief and perhaps menacing silence.

"No," said Mrs. Amberley—a bit thickly, but then she had just swallowed quite a number of oaths. "Will five bob cover it?" she asked. "Well, it'll have to, I'm afraid. I'm a bit short. Here you are!"

She had opened her bag, and was proffering two half-crowns.

"And I'm awfully sorry," she said, "but I—I—— Oh, do please take it, and leave me alone! Thank you. Thank you! *Wonderful* work! Good-night."

Really! As good as pushed out into the passage like that, when all one had done was to show a little kindness and sympathy to a young woman who ought—well, who ought to be *ashamed* of her appearance. If people only *realised*, thought Mrs. Wardrop, what it meant to go tramping round like this. Wearing herself out. Being insulted. Keeping all these complicated accounts. Though of course if one lived in a block like this, with all these extraordinary people that the war seemed to have thrown up ...

Leave me alone, indeed! How *dared* she—to someone old enough to be her mother! Or grandmother, if it comes to that.

I shall write, in future, Mrs. Wardrop decided. I'm not going through *that* again. Still rattled and ruffled, she turned to attack No. 24. It can't be denied that she rang rather longer than she need, and knocked in an equally unnecessarily authoritative manner. But of course she didn't know what had happened to Miss Kenton-Hinksey in her bath this morning, nor how this was still affecting her nerves; nor how that inadequate drying had now given her more than the suspicion of a sore throat; nor even what it meant to her, on top of all that, to be interrupted just as she was preparing to have another bath, as it were, in the six o'clock news.

Miss Kenton-Hinksey turned off her instrument, but she was simmering as she went to the front door. She was slow to wrath, poor woman, despite all her troubles; but there was just one thing that she couldn't stand, after a day like this, and when she was trying to get a few minutes' rest with the radio before she went off to the canteen. And that was being suddenly startled.

But Mrs. Wardrop was simmering, too. The two tenants met—one can only say—like angry cats on a wall.

"Well ?" said Miss Kenton-Hinksey. "What on earth's all this noise about ?"

"Are you by any chance speaking to *me* ?" asked Mrs. Wardrop.

"Yes," said Miss Kenton-Hinksey. "Do you think I'm deaf ?"

"I think you're very ill-mannered," said Mrs. Wardrop, "but——"

"Well, if that's all you've come to say——"

"Now, please don't imagine——"

"Is that meant for an apology ?"

"No, certainly not," said Mrs. Wardrop. "If *anyone* should apologise——"

"Thank you. We all know *your* views by this time."

"Miss Kenton-Hinksey! Never, in all my——"

"And never in mine, either," said Miss Kenton-Hinksey, with tremendous vigour, though she could now see at least three Mrs. Wardrops, and was almost choking with what appeared to be a small incendiary bomb just under the top of her skull. "Can't you even," she demanded, in spite of these symptoms, "stop plaguing us all on Sundays ?"

"Plaguing!" said Mrs. Wardrop, to whom Miss Kenton-Hinksey was now flickering in a reddish mist. "Do you realise that I give up my time —that I'm authorised—that I spend hours and hours——"

"Go on!" said her adversary. A phrase came back to her from Miss Smallwood's rather downright vocabulary. "Put a jerk in it!" she said.

"I shall not stay here——"

"All right. Don't, then!"

Bang! Yet another door had been closed—indeed, slammed, this time —in Mrs. Wardrop's face. Behind it, Miss Kenton-Hinksey's incendiary bomb had gone down to the region of the pharynx and larynx, and she was reeling and moaning—so very unlike her—and there was a pain in her eyes; and she wanted to be angrier than ever, but couldn't be, though she was still some way from being ashamed of herself yet. "It was that *man!*" she gulped, alluding doubtless to the man on the roof. "It's just *everything!*" she groaned. "It's this bub-bloody war!" she summed up.

As for Mrs. Wardrop, she was almost unrecognisable as she tottered blindly towards the lift. Her face, that is to say, seemed to have fallen in, though at the same time it was suffused with strange patches of pink. Luckily the cage was still there, and she could stumble into it. She was also just capable of pushing the right button—for the last three flats must remain undisturbed to-night—but as she descended, her mouth was working (so much so, indeed, as to imperil the security of her teeth), and she, too, kept muttering terrible words.

Presently, of course, both ladies would calm down a little; and later, though it is doubtful whether either of them would actually apologise, they would possibly each choose to pretend that an exchange of nervous smiles had—if chiefly because of their own great powers of forgiveness—washed the unfortunate episode out. It was just, in fact—as Miss Kenton-Hinksey had perhaps been the first to surmise—another of the things that are bound to happen in war-time. It hadn't been mentioned in the original ultimatum, nor was it at all likely that it would be referred to at the Peace Conference, if any. It would be scrupulously omitted from all official and even unofficial histories of the great conflict. But it had happened, inevitably. And it was just as inevitable, while the war still lasted, that the same sort of thing would happen, all over the wide, wide world, not once, but again and again.

CHAPTER X

IN AN ORDINARY YEAR—BUT THERE WERE FEW, BY THIS TIME, WHO REALLY remembered an ordinary year—it would now have been Christmas-week. But though the strangest collection of auxiliary postmen had appeared in the streets—for strange they must indeed be if they were able or free to take on any more work than they were doing already—and kept stopping other people to inquire where they were, and after all this merely delivered a quantity of irrelevant cards (with pictures, for instance, of plough-horses, women in crinolines, and pirate-ships), there were few other signs of the festival as it had once been known. Gluttony and generosity were both in compulsory abeyance; and so were family gatherings, when nine out of ten families, or more, were scattered over the face of the earth. Besides, though the shops would shut and the omnibus-service would be punctiliously reduced on the day itself, this didn't imply that work elsewhere could stop. In all too many cases, and though some would be solaced by overtime rates, it simply implied that you missed your lunch and had to walk home in the dark.

There had been one flash from the old world. At Huddleston House—though to a much smaller extent than at Bessingham House, for it was less than a quarter the size—once more, while what was left of the festival was still approaching, there was the sound of juvenile voices. For another school-term had ended, and though those who had been released were almost all on their way through to grandparents or aunts in the country —partly as a precaution which again seemed advisable, and partly because there was no room for them here—they quite changed the air of both blocks for a day or two.

They clattered and chattered. They bounced and skipped. They went out and came in a great deal. It was a higher note that now penetrated the breeze-block partitions; while at no other season—except, of course, during similar periods of migration, about four weeks from now, and at Easter, and in July and September—was there quite such a constant and reckless use of the radio. The luckier arrivals were rushed off to plays or films—for their benefit some of the former were now starting as early as ten o'clock in the morning—while others were taken to dentists instead or as well. They also played with the lifts a great deal, showing absolutely no fear of the porters; and at Huddleston House, as it happened, a child of about eleven succeeded in putting the entire mechanism out of order within an hour of his arrival and for the whole of his brief stay. More worry—for he could do nothing himself, and there was hardly a tenant who didn't ring up and tell him—for poor Mr. Todman.

Then the brief flash was over; and Christmas, such as it was, must go on and be somehow surmounted by adults only. In the last war, thought Mrs. Margetson—but she didn't say it, because June always jeered at her now when she mentioned the last war—there had certainly, so far as she could recall, been ration books, and a mild kind of black-out, and casualty lists, if it came to that, of (touch wood!) far greater length; but she couldn't remember that Christmas had been a casualty, too. There had still been big family lunches, whatever they had all eaten, and genuine presents, whatever they had all cost. Or was I too young? she wondered. Was it much more like this, for those who weren't young, than one thinks? And then: Twice, she thought again, in a lifetime. I know I've missed it, in a way, at both ends—not old enough last time, and too old now—but even if poor June has to work on the Day itself—well, she's still got *something* before her, perhaps; and there *can't* be a third one.

But she didn't quite believe this. How could she, when she had seen the first one exposed for the muddle and waste that it was, but must be swept into another as though there had never been any exposure at all? Besides —and this was the awful thing now—June herself didn't think this was the last one. None of them did, this time. They looked at you as if it was all your fault. They were perpetually girding and gibing at what they called "The Old"—which apparently meant anyone over the age of about thirty-seven or eight. But though of course they would grow older themselves some day (if spared, added Mrs. Margetson, crossing her fingers for a change), they never seemed to take this inevitable fact into account. Well, *I* didn't, perhaps, thought Mrs. Margetson. And perhaps I did feel that people like Mother and Father ought to have *done* something. But I know I wasn't as hard on them. And I did belong to the League of Nations Union as long as one possibly could. But June, she thought, just doesn't believe in anything. And then she sighed, and she thought: Why should she?

Two days before Christmas she had a cable from her husband of a seasonable nature, and asking her if she had received his Number 223. As he had been back, for a few weeks, during the summer before last, this didn't really mean—for they always numbered their weekly letters—that she hadn't seen him for more than four years. But it felt like it. And then she *hadn't* received No. 223, so that though she was touched by the brief message— but it again sent her into the vicious circle of wondering whether she shouldn't have moved Heaven and Earth to join him in America after all—she was also tormented by its implied importance. What had he written? Why couldn't he say? Could it possibly mean that he was coming over again— for good, perhaps, this time—and that she ought to be hunting for a larger flat? She telegraphed back: "All Christmas love darling 223 not arrived please cable if urgent." and was left feeling that she had probably fussed him. Also there was no answer, or none by Western Union; though again one didn't really know if it, or her own message, had been stopped. We're all prisoners, she thought, as she sped round the circle again. June said: "Don't *worry* so, mother. You ought to be jolly glad you hear from him at all." Was this mere natural barbarism, or did it mean that there was someone from whom June herself didn't hear? One longed to ask her. One knew just how one would be snubbed if one did. And meanwhile —not even to be mentioned to June, though of course she knew it—no card, no letter, no cable, nothing at all from Robin.

Extraordinary, what a lot one could stand and still keep just this side of insanity. For even if Robin came through the war in one hemisphere, it had already been announced that he would have to go on with it in another. Or perhaps he was in that other hemisphere already. Or perhaps . . .

On Christmas Day itself there was a kind of eerie celebration, behind drawn curtains, at breakfast; which was still timed by the clock, as there was still no further news of Mrs. Margetson's watch. Her presents for her daughter were numerous, but only costly in the sense that they weren't, by any ordinary standards, worth the money. They were just little things that she had thought or hoped that June would find useful, though many a pilgrimage had been involved in making the collection. It included, however, the special face-cream, which the silent man at Hernshaw's had at last produced. There was also, on behalf of her husband, and in accordance with instructions in No. 221, a cheque.

"But," said Mrs. Margetson, "I'm afraid it's not very like Christmas."

June said that she couldn't agree with her mother more, which was a phrase much in use at the time. She also told her that she oughtn't to have bothered, which might possibly be interpreted as thanks. But she did, in a shame-faced, offhand sort of way, produce a gift herself. "There!" she said, slamming a carton of face-tissues down on the table. "But I didn't pay for them, I'm afraid. They came over from New York in a bomber."

"Oh, but darling——" (Did this mean that there was still another friend about whom Mrs. Margetson knew nothing?)—"are you sure you can spare them?"

"They weren't brought for *me*," said June. "I got 'em from a girl at the office."

"Oh—I see." (Exit the gallant, enamoured airman, as abruptly as he had appeared.)

"But if you don't *want* them——" said June.

"Well, darling, of course I think it's a wonderful present. But shall we share them?"

"You're a bit hard to please," said June. "All right. But I must go now—damn everything!"

So Mrs. Margetson opened the carton, and took a few tissues, and put it on her daughter's dressing-table. Not, of course, that she wanted any present from poor June at all; who, besides, or at least for poor June, had performed a good deal of a gesture. No, thought Mrs. Margetson, I know she despises me, but I don't think she really hates me. Thus a war-time or twentieth-century mother consoled herself; and was further consoled by the impossibility of shopping to-day. So she wrote some letters—still using the Wallington Gardens notepaper, and painstakingly correcting it, as was another widespread war-time custom—and for once she was rather less anxious about the chances of a raid to-night. One never *knew*, of course. Yet still, perhaps, there was just this much left of Christmas; that men in machines might momentarily interrupt that particular form of murder. And as it happened, they did. Or were allowed to.

On the floor below, Gavin Guernsey spent the day alone—but reading typescripts—for D. P. Moulton had also gone off, to sign on at the Ministry of Propaganda. He felt a little guilty—when *didn't* he feel a little guilty?—at not being down with R.J. in the country. For though he had been invited and had accepted, or believed that he had been invited and had accepted, on that day at Claud's Club, of course he must then check this impression. One could never just merely turn up. And of course—it had happened before—when he tried to discover on which day he would be welcome, R.J. had been vague and obstructive; seemed offended about something; and had then shielded himself behind Mrs. Woolley, the cook-housekeeper, who had made other arrangements, he said. Yet at the same time he had rather more than hinted that he was old and neglected. It now looked as if the New Year week-end must be offered; which was done, in the humblest and most obsequious manner. "I'll have to see," said R.J.—for they had now reached the stage of toll-calls again. "I might be busy. I'll have to let you know."

By all this he had put Gavin in the wrong, had virtually ensured that he, too, should have a lonely Christmas, and had also left him in considerable suspense. Typical, thought Gavin. Couldn't be more characteristic. And that stuff about his being busy was just the wildest tosh. But of course he still felt guilty. The filial relationship, so far as he was personally aware, consisted entirely of doing things one didn't want to do, with no reward, but on the contrary even more than one expected, very often, to justify this reluctance; and getting out of or being released from what one didn't want to do, and then suffering pangs of conscience. What a life, in fact. And even the typescript to-day was a war-book which must remind him at every turn of his own experiences, and of how they had all led to nothing. It was true that the lucky author seemed somehow to have got out of the whole business himself—he didn't explain this; he just wrote sadly and nostalgically about the comradeship of arms, so perhaps he was now in the War Office— but he was either a great liar or most certainly had once been with the Eighth Army in Cyrenaica. While the present reader, whose absent foot began throbbing abominably as he once more came round to this thought, had. never been nearer the Front than a town in Kent.

So he was oppressed; though in another and not altogether useless character he was beginning to feel pretty sure that the book would do. Also that Derek and his literary colleagues would have rather a job to sneer at it; for they always allowed five marks, as it were, out of ten for anything containing enough genuine guns and corpses. Odd? No; their private defence-mechanism, of course. Minerva, who never did any fighting in spite of her armour, giving a pat on the back to Mars. What a cad I am, thought Gavin, with rather more satisfaction suddenly. But even Derek, he thought, wouldn't find it too easy—(yes, I'm going to *force* it on old Bendish, whatever he says about too many war-books)—to link this sort of stuff on to M. de Charlus.

Ha, ha! in fact. And then the feeling of frustration and irritation, because really it was absurd to be so pleased at having the flat to oneself when, dammit, it was one's own flat. And another thing. Derek and those. two girls. Going on like a dried-up old satyr—oh, very likely because he didn't know any better and got it all out of the wrong books. But—dammit, again—he'd taken to something almost like leering. And asking them questions—well, honestly some of them were going a bit far, even if they weren't a bit off. "Do you find that you are frequently assaulted when you leave your office?" In that dead sort of voice. Honestly, one ought to stop him somehow; though of course one couldn't. Nor, if it came to that, did the girl Bugs seem to mind much—(Bugs? Yes, of course, and already, and in fact long ago; for the very shyest of young gentlemen would only draw attention to themselves now if they followed the old convention) —but it was different, it was altogether different, with the girl Echo. . . .

Down went the typescript; and if anyone else had been in the long sitting-room at No. 12 now, they would have seen rather a strange sight. The occupant, that is to say, trying to lift one of his own eyebrows without wrinkling his forehead. He couldn't do it, of course. He knew this, by a test with his fingers, for it hardly occurred to him to employ a mirror. Interesting. Most interesting. *Must* get on with this book, though. And thus Gavin became a publisher again.

Not much else to record on Christmas Day. For most of the tenants it was scarcely more than a kind of unwanted Sunday which had strayed into the week. It also reminded nearly all of them of contrasts between past and present, which most of them would have been quite glad—had this been possible—to forget. Mrs. Wardrop went to church, of course, and mustn't be mocked at for doing so, though she was still some way from having forgiven Miss Kenton-Hinksey. The Daily Help was unanimous in claiming the day off, and couldn't be blamed, either; or if it was, would only fail to return altogether. The porters, who had divided their spoils some time ago, just quietly decided to do as little as possible for anyone. Otherwise, it was a case of harder work for those who went forth—for though the fact was that precious little was being done, even at the Ministries, there was at least ten times as much reluctance to be overcome; and of harder work for those left behind, because of the same persistent if obsolete feeling that it was a day intended for putting one's feet up, and because one couldn't if one was compelled to brush, dust, cook, and make beds.

As for entertaining, how could one do it? It was off. It was out. It was finished; whether this was an anniversary or not. No one expected it any longer, either. It had become, to all intents and purposes, impossible. A virtually Barmecide tea-party was about as much as could be managed in these days; and even this, at the moment, must be confined to one's very near neighbours, because of the black-out. Such, then, was Christmas, so far as it was worth mentioning or noticing at all; or so far as it still couldn't entirely or completely be overlooked. Yet of course there is always the exception.

It wasn't a very appropriate one, perhaps; to the extent, that is to say, that the date has ever been a purely Christian festival. A little research, however, is almost bound to raise doubts here. It appears, for instance, that the date was observed by the Ancient Romans in honour of Phœbus; and though neither Mr. nor Mrs. Musselberg could possibly be regarded as an Ancient Roman—Mr. Musselberg's nose being alone quite enough to dismiss such a fanciful theory—the fact remains that it was at No. 14, Huddleston House that the only real or old-fashioned celebrations were being held.

They began with an exchange of lavish gifts—quite unobtainable by anyone with an ordinary nose. And they worked up to a large lunch-party, at which there wasn't only a turkey and plum-pudding, but brandy-butter and mince-pies as well. Believe it or not, there was even crystallised fruit. And Mrs. Musselberg's sister Addy came, and her cousin Connie; and Mr. Musselberg's brother Ben—a few rungs behind on the ladder, but climbing fast—and his wife, and their exceedingly intelligent and luminous-eyed little boy. And Mr. Jack Jonas, who was Mr. Musselberg's friend and legal advisor—though he couldn't have looked less like Gavin Guernsey's cousin Claud; and in some mysterious way was a kind of partner, too—off and on, and very much off so far as the Inland Revenue was concerned. The one-eyed and slightly hump-backed maidservant was in attendance, also, though distinctly against her own wishes; and the guests arrived at one o'clock sharp, and remained until after four.

As it was a dullish, darkish day outside, and on account of all the curtains and pelmets in the sitting-room, there was a considerable display of electric lighting. And as it was a coldish day, too, the windows were kept tight shut, and the radiators were reinforced by the big electric fire. In addition to this, Mr. Musselberg and his brother Ben and his friend Mr. Jonas smoked a number of admirable cigars. And there were a lot of sweets for the ladies and the little boy. No one complained of being hot, however, or of suffering from lack of air, though if a stranger had entered the room he would hardly have been able to breathe. During the course of the afternoon there was a great deal of conversation about money, to which the intelligent, luminous-eyed boy appeared to listen with the closest attention. And when the radio-gram wasn't giving a performance of what might perhaps be described as background music, Mrs. Musselberg's cousin Connie obliged with some rich renderings on the piano. She played Liszt, and Chaminade, and the *Valse Triste ;* despite which last item, no one—except possibly the one-eyed maid in the kitchenette—seemed the least cast down. In fact, as has been said before, it was a real, old-fashioned, family Christmas.

When the last guest left—with much laughter on the landing—Mr. Musselberg embraced his wife, and unbuttoned his waistcoat, and the one-eyed maid brought in a very good tea. His eyeballs were a bit yellow, but then they always were; and of course it was too late now—even if such a notion had occurred to either of the Musselbergs—to go out for a brisk walk. So presently they had a very good cold supper—after which Mr. Musselberg undid the top button of his trousers—and then at last the one-eyed maid with drew, and they both sat up talking until nearly everyone else in the block was asleep. They talked of the future, of which they seemed to have no fear, and of the superior flat—which they, if anyone, would surely find if they looked for it—in which they would be perhaps spending next Christmas. They had no idea that Tuke had seen the guests departing, had immediately identified them—or at least the flat that they had come from—and had positively seethed with the desire to see them all, not to mention their host and hostess, in a concentration camp. To this end—to which she had been stimulated by a recent rebuff from the Britannia Wine Stores (for she had never forgotten that blatant gin-bottle)—she even proposed to get in touch with the Police again. True that she had been snubbed there, too, on a recent visit, to which she had been urged by the spectacle of Mr. Musselberg driving up in a big hired car, and skipping out with what she was convinced, from the shape of a package imperfectly concealed by his ox-blood overcoat, was a large and illicit ham. But now she had seen the turkey as well—ridiculous, whether sanctioned or not, for a family of two—and her sword wasn't going to rest in its scabbard.

Was this the right Christmas feeling ? One would say not. But one may say, also, that even if the Musselbergs had known all about it, in the first place they would have felt very little concern, and in the second they would have borne no grudge. For in the first place, again, they were both pretty sure that they knew how to take care of themselves ; while in the second place, once more, they had been born and brought up with the knowledge that anyone resembling Miss Tuke would always dislike them. But they didn't return this feeling. They were far too familiar with it, alas, to take such unnecessary trouble.

So much for Christmas, then, which passed into Boxing-Day without any air-raid. And in a trice, as it seemed, the old year had passed away, too, and another had begun. It wasn't saluted, as had once been the custom, with hooters, whistles, and motor-horns. It was only to be hoped—and again this hope was fulfilled, if possibly on meteorological rather than benevolent grounds—that it wouldn't be saluted with sirens. At the hub of the Universe—represented by a protective pyramid on the site of a now almost legendary statue—a congregation of citizens, and warriors of both sexes and most Allied Nations, gathered together; howled popular songs in the dark; and then found considerable difficulty in dispersing. But elsewhere the occasion passed off very quietly indeed. And most people were anything but enlivened.

Another new year had started. Already civilisation's second great effort to destroy itself had lasted nearly a month longer than the first one. What next, then ? And when, if ever, would this further attempt break off ? This year ? Again there was a strange temptation to believe it, if on no very settled grounds. But first—for the oligarchs in all countries had promised this—there must be a climax of slaughter and destruction; and since few ordinary people were really at all keen on the idea, there was a tendency, also, to avoid looking ahead. Very wrong, of course. Mr. William Whippenstall and others were perpetually introducing unseen voices to explain how wrong it was; and at the same time to hold out flickering and fantastic hopes of the paradise that was being prepared. Yet ordinary people were perhaps less credulous here. In a dumb, dogged sort of manner the thought had come to them that oligarchs capable of planning such a future— and to tell the truth they weren't so dashed keen on a lot of its aspects, either—should have been capable of keeping them out of the present mess. No microphone was available, in any case, for this point of view; though there was a faint hint of it just now and then at, for example, the Royal Oak. But it existed. Indeed, it was almost bound to exist. And it was a poor accompaniment to what one would have liked to be thinking at the outset of any new year.

Time, however, could soon deal, to a certain extent, with that. There was a monotony in the horror, despite occasional and illusive high spots, which —even for the young—made one week remarkably like the next. They say, also, that there is nothing like occupation for making the hours slip by; and never had there been more occupation, whether productive or not, or more fatigue in the brief intervals, to dull the sense of time. At one moment, for instance, Miss Tuke was standing in a queue at the post-office—well, strictly speaking, she was pushing a bit, though she also looked so alarming that there was very little resistance—for the purpose of purchasing Lulu's new dog-licence; and at the next, as it seemed, the month was half over; so that she, and almost everyone else, had forgotten about the new year now, or had accepted it and recovered from it, and could worry about other things. Yes, that, with a war still going strong, was what time could do. It was merciful, perhaps. Or perhaps it just didn't care twopence. Or perhaps, as they say again, it didn't really exist.

Days came and went, though; and all were still much too short. One hadn't noticed this once; or once, even in January, it had been cosy to come in from the lighted streets—perhaps, if in the right mood, with a little bag of roasted chestnuts—and to have a good tea, and to draw up by the fire. But now—quite apart from the absence of the good tea and the chestnuts— it had been generally observed that January was a month in which the days hardly lengthened at all. And torch-batteries were running out in the shops again; if, indeed, they hadn't already done so. And the moon, of which scarcely a Londoner had been conscious once, had become singularly suggestive and important. It was a tricky orb, too. At the beginning of wars—or of wars with the additional advantage of aerial bombardment— you had hated its great, fat face, because it left you the more exposed in spite of the black-out. But then, so it seemed, the face was your friend, and it was a silvery crescent, or no moon at all, that you must specially learn to dread. A logical deduction might be that the black-out was now serving no purpose at all, or no purpose that need trouble the enemy. It was no more protection—according to some people—than the balloon-barrage; though here again there was a constant and perhaps useful reminder that death might be pouring down in a few hours or so.

Unfortunately, however—if such an adverb is allowed—there had been no definite statement, from either one side or the other, that raids and full moons could be regarded as permanently incompatible. Somebody knew, perhaps; but if they did, they wouldn't say so. Or conditions might change —without warning, of course. So that if the subject was at all on your mind, as it was rather apt to be—for no one becomes fonder of air-raids as time goes by—then still you must rather mistrust that face; whose calm, in any event, was distinctly provocative to anyone more obviously affected by the Law of Gravity.

If we searched the hearts in Huddleston House, there would be few—from Mr. and Mrs. Champion to Tuke herself—that were really immune from speculation, at least, when another night closed down. Mrs. Margetson certainly wasn't. She still had to control a start, if not a pounding beneath the ribs, when a bus or lorry emitted that rising note; or whenever—which was often enough, if you once began hearing them—there was a distant and unaccountable explosion. But she didn't tell June, because she was her mother and was here to look after her; and must do nothing, therefore, that could either add to her fears, if she had any, or that might possibly ease her own mind. She sat on the safety-valve, though knowing also that if she once got off she could never get back. Yet this isn't a position that improves with time, for of course you can still feel the pressure as long as it's there. And June teased her, incessantly, because she couldn't help it. The best, in fact, that one could hope for from June was an occasional "Poor old mother!", and a rough, brief, bear-like hug. And yet once June had adored her. She knew it. What had happened? Was it the war, was it Geoffrey being away, was it all this endless work? But the first of these possible answers included the others; as it also explained why, night after night, they must sit in the same stuffy little room, where one of them, at least, kept getting on the other's nerves.

Then they ought to separate? How could they? Why should they? She would never forgive herself if——

She gave another start, for these thoughts had come to her—about the middle of January and in the same little room—when they shouldn't have come. Not that she was with June; but she wasn't alone. Her sister Daisy —Mrs. Holton in a wider world—had come up for the day from her house in a Home County, and had invited herself to a very early tea. Because, she had said—which wasn't really so very unreasonable—she must catch her train back. But she said other things, too. She always did. Or she seemed to hint at them.

She said, for instance, that Henry, her husband, was working too hard; which Mrs. Margetson knew to be a preposterous statement, for he had never worked hard, even before his retirement, and it was inconceivable that he should have altered as much as all that. She complained about her servants —fancy having two servants, whatever their age, and then daring to complain about them! She said it was so awkward only having a daily gardener now, and appeared to expect sympathy. She spoke of the expense of things, and the difficulty of getting them, as if this was some special and exceptional handicap from which she alone suffered. She moaned because she wasn't allowed more petrol. She said it was so tiresome not being able to buy enough clothes; and again as if Providence had singled her out from the rest of the human race.

Not once did she thank Heaven, on bended knees, for such blessings as that she was still in her own home, that no one was billeted on her, that Henry was still very well off, that no bomb had yet fallen within seven miles of them, and—though at this thought Mrs. Margetson was again a little ashamed of herself—that they had no children. On the contrary, she pretended that she envied the flat, though it was quite obvious that she thought it poky and mean; and she said what fun it must be to do all one's own cooking, which was insolent as well as untrue. And she said how odd that Geoffrey didn't come back, as if he was staying out there for fun, too, and on purpose. And how interesting it must be for Robin to be in such interesting places, though of course she had no more idea where he was than Mrs. Margetson herself. Moreover, at a given and inevitable point, she said wouldn't June really have done better to have gone into uniform—as if constant long hours cooped up in an office were just a method of dodging her duty.

But Mrs. Margetson didn't growl, or even answer back. She had expected to be irritated, for all this had happened, at irregular intervals, whenever her sister appeared. And she *was* her sister, though it seemed hard to believe sometimes, and of course one couldn't have a quarrel. Yet there was a certain regrettable antipathy here, too; if only, once again, on account of the war. She didn't *want* poor Daisy to be ruined, or blown up, or even— though of course this was out of the question—to have a son of her own at sea. But there was a gulf between even the Home Counties—or at any rate that particular part of them—and London. It couldn't be bridged. The people outside just didn't understand, and if one tried to explain——But one couldn't. One wasn't brave, Heaven knew. One had got, for some extraordinary reason, to adopt the exact attitude that was expected; or in other words to pretend that there was no gulf at all. But there was. And one couldn't forget it.

At about a quarter past four Mrs. Holton, who had recently been glancing at the clock a good deal, and had twice asked if it was right, got up and announced that she must go.

"Must you really?" said Mrs. Margetson. "Are you sure you won't have another cup of tea?"

"No, thank you, dear. You see, I don't know *what* I should do if I missed my train. Well, Henry would be so anxious, you see."

"I see," said Mrs. Margetson. "Well, if you *must* . . ."

She would have kissed her sister—for, after all, it was an old custom, and they had known each other for more than forty-five years—but her sister had moved to the window.

"I'm a bit worried about this fog," she was saying. "I do hope it won't make me late."

And there you were. A fog, though not raid-proof in these days—or not unless it was much worse than this—was still a kind of comfort, about sunset, to Mrs. Margetson. Subconsciously, in fact, she had been hoping the whole time that it was getting worse. But it wasn't. There was distinctly less of it. Even Nature, it seemed, was taking the Home Counties' side; though the Home Counties could still think of nothing but their own trains.

"Your gloves, Daisy. Oh—and here's your bag."

"Thank you, dear. Well, it's been lovely seeing you. I'll let you know, if I can, when I'm up next time."

"Yes, do," said Mrs. Margetson. "Please."

Mrs. Holton almost ran towards the lift, and then exhibited the most violent impatience because it, or perhaps one should say the cage, wasn't there. When it came up, she dashed into it, and pushed the button so quickly that she could only wave a final farewell. What a beast I am! thought Mrs. Margetson, for some reason or other. It's not *her* fault, she thought. Why *should* anyone spend a night in London, if they happen to live outside?

This was philosophy, and there was something in it. Yet it was never easier to shut oneself in again, and to start wondering if it was time for the black-out, when someone had just beaten it for safety like that. She felt lonely and on edge. But presently she did do the black-out—always with that other unbidden speculation as to whether this was the last time she would do it; and then she washed up the tea-things, carefully preserving an almost inedible cake. And then, as she was in the kitchenette anyhow, she began preparing the supper. And then she looked for the evening paper on the lobby floor, but either it was late to-night or the porters—though of course they must still be paid double—had forgotten it again.

At a few moments before six—having meanwhile done a little more darning—she was drawn, by something stronger, it would seem, than concomitant reluctance, to the radio-set. She switched it on. It warmed up, and first hummed and then pipped at her. Another very familiar voice emerged from the machine.

". . . and this," it was saying, "is Reginald Rampart reading it." It then took on a slightly jaunty note. "This morning," it said, "a strong force of Wallabies, Wastrels, and Waterspouts, escorted by Windmills and Wagtails, carried out another wide sweep over enemy-occupied territory. Last night——"

But as this was just what it had said at one o'clock, and as if anything new had happened since then, this would presumably have come first, Mrs. Margetson switched it off. What names! she was thinking; for though she had heard them often enough, something in her mood had suddenly made them strike her afresh. What *would* I have thought, she was wondering, if I'd turned on that set five years ago, and someone had started like that? It was indeed quite a question. Before she could stop it, it had brought up such a lot of subsidiary points that she must have remained in a muse for quite ten minutes; and might easily have stayed there even longer, if the telephone-bell hadn't pealed.

June! she thought, leaping up. She's going to be late, I suppose. In fact, as she picked up the thing that one holds, she very nearly answered with the words: "Yes, darling?"

Not quite, though. And lucky, she was now thinking, that she hadn't. For there was a man's voice vibrating against her ear. It wasn't too clear, but it was asking if that was 18, Huddleston House. "Yes," said Mrs. Margetson. She had another and extraordinary idea that it was Geoffrey, though she knew well enough that High-Ups and Panjandrums had hogged the trans-Atlantic telephone for years. Or had he come back—suddenly— by air? For a second she felt almost as giddy as though she had just done this herself. And then the voice was saying: "Which of you is it? Is that Mother?"

She gasped. "*Robin!*"

"That's right. I say——"

"Darling—where *are* you?"

"Well——" said the voice. "Oh, by the way," it said, "that *is* Mother, isn't it?"

"Yes, darling; but——"

"In that case," said the voice, "it can now be revealed that I'm at King's Cross."

"*Here*, you mean? In London?"

"Smells like it," said the voice. "Shall I come along?"

"Yes, of *course!* Do you mean you've got leave?"

"That's the general idea," said the voice. "Just a morsel, that is. I say, can you manage a bed?"

"Of *course!*" said Mrs. Margetson again, and a little ahead of the facts of the case. "Robin—are you——"

"What's that ?   I say, this is a rotten line."

"Yes, I know, darling.   Perhaps——" It was awful to let him go when he had suddenly been given back to her; yet the longer she talked now, the longer it would be before she could see him.   "I'll arrange it *all*," she was saying.   "Just hurry, darling.   You remember where it is—don't you ?"

She wanted to dive through the telephone, and help him to find a taxi— though even if she had achieved the first feat, she would have been little or no use at the second.   But he only laughed at her.

"I'll be round," he said.   "Oh, by the way!"

"Yes, darling ?"

"I—I'm afraid I've got a beard.   Thought I'd just warn you.   Right ? Carry on."

Lieutenant R. G. Margetson, R.N., then rang off; and his mother felt giddier than ever.   Certainly there was deep joy and gratitude in her giddiness, but apart from two urgent problems of food and a bed—which must be settled somehow at this decidedly unpromising hour—she had also, for some mystical and maternal reason, been picturing her son Robin, despite his resounding tones, as a child, or as a little boy, or at the utmost as a cadet. So that this news about the beard made her mind's eye see more than double.

Despite the urgency, again—or perhaps this was part of it—she knew that she must tell June before she did anything else.   For one must hold the scales.   One mustn't earn a reproach for delay here, or for selfishness, either.   Besides, on Robin's last leave—good Heavens, more than eighteen months ago, too, now!—June had given up her room and slept, more or less, on the sofa with the end that let down, at the foot of Mrs. Margetson's bed.   It was true that she had then sworn never to do anything so uncomfortable again, and that it had been in the summer when perhaps one needed less sleep; but still, if she *did* offer—just for one night—or if Mrs. Margetson went on the sofa herself, or if everything else failed . . .

However—though she was nervous not only because of this, but because June had told her again and again not to ring her up at the office—Mrs. Margetson did have a shot.   And she said : "Extension 504"—now trembling a good deal—and there was no answer.   June, then, was presumably on the way home, or at any rate one could waste no more time.   So her mother, still very much doubting that sofa plan, thought madly of all the other tenants whom she slightly knew; and decided that even if they had room, which they probably hadn't, she had left it too late, and in any case didn't know them nearly well enough.   Then she thought of an hotel, not far away, of which she had heard good reports—though she couldn't remember from whom or when—and rang it up, and was almost felled to the earth by an offensive and unqualified rebuff.

"Oh," she said.   "Thank you."   And then she had another idea.   At Bessingham House there had once been guest-rooms, and though it seemed inconceivable that they shouldn't all be full—even if they hadn't been turned into still more flats—she could at least speak to Mr. Todman, if he hadn't yet left, without having her head snapped off.

So she dialled again. And Mr. Todman answered. And she apologised for ringing up so late; and he wasn't only quite nice about this—perhaps because it was such a relief not to be told that another ball-cock had stuck —but actually said that there was a room which her son could have. "It's the raids," he explained, elliptically but quite adequately. And he would see about it now—"Not at all, Mrs. Margetson"—and would leave the key with the night porter.

Thank Heaven! ("It's the raids," came an echo, accompanied by a chill round the heart.)

"Thank you *so* much," said Mrs. Margetson, with a little extra intensity, because her ears—if no more—had warned her that she was about to be interrupted. "It's *most* kind of you," she said. "I can't *tell* you what a help that is."

She hung up. June was in the room.

"What *is* the matter?" she was asking. "Who on earth are you talking to?"

"Oh, darling!" said Mrs. Margetson. "What *do* you think!"

"*I* dunno," said June, flinging her bag on to the table, from which it immediately slid to the floor. "Damn!" she added, stooping for it.

"Robin's here!" said Mrs. Margetson.

"Is he?" said June, straightening up and looking round the sitting-room. "Where?"

"I mean, he's just rung up. He's on his way from the station, and——'

"Have I got to sleep on that thing?"

"No, darling. I'm just telling you. I've just arranged——"

"Oh, lord, have we got enough to eat?"

"We can go out," said Mrs. Margetson. "We can go to the San Remo," she added, hastily; for after all—though the raids, as she knew, were behind this suggestion—of course poor Robin would be tired.

"Muck," said her daughter, looking anything but thrilled. "Well, in that case," she went on, "I'd better have my bath while there's a chance and before he takes all the hot water."

"But, June——"

"What?"

Mrs. Margetson almost hesitated. If June were in the bathroom, she could welcome Robin alone. She was terribly tempted. But she mustn't be selfish—even if June thought this was exactly what she was being. Besides, after a year and a half. A brother and sister . . .

"Just tonight, darling," she said. "*Do* put it off."

"Why? I'm filthy!"

"Yes, but——"

"Don't you realise there's been a fog? I tell you, if I don't have my——
Oh, lord! There he is."

There had been a ring at the front door. Both female Margetsons
made a dash towards it, but there could be no question which of them was
more agile, or which, if there was any danger of colliding in a doorway, would
be the one to draw back. Yet in a flat of this size, of course, no one could
be very far away from anyone or anything. So June opened the front door,
while her mother tried to peer round her. There was a thud, as of a suit-case
striking the woodwork a heavy though glancing blow. And then June said:
"My God, what *have* you done to your face?" And then she said: "*Don't*
do that!"—for Robin, though he kissed her, too, had just given her a fraternal
slap on the behind. And such was the sailor's return.

Mrs. Margetson couldn't help rather wishing that June *would* have a
bath now, as they filed into the sitting-room. But she didn't. She sat on
the arm of a chair—which creaked and wobbled, as a result of the same
treatment on a number of previous occasions—and she didn't exactly join
in, and she didn't exactly stay out. But when she did come in, it was always
with an interruption, and it was always her mother whom she interrupted.
Mrs. Margetson knew that she mustn't ask her son where he had been—
though possibly, perhaps, he would tell her; so she had asked him if he was
hungry, and he had said Yes, and it was she who must then go off in search
of a snack. That beard doesn't suit him, she thought, but I mustn't say so.
The rest of his face looked pale, too—for it is a fact that when sailors aren't
on their decks or bridges, they have very little fresh air. And he looked
tired. And he ate wolfishly and untidily ("I must sweep up those crumbs,"
thought Mrs. Margetson, "before Mrs. Goosey comes in"), and of course
he was disappointed that there was nothing to drink.

"If only I'd known——" said Mrs. Margetson.

"Well, mother, I'd have missed the train if I'd told you any sooner.
Never mind; I'll nip into a pub. And I say!"

"Yes, darling?"

"About arrangements. How long have you taken this room for me?"

"I didn't say," said Mrs. Margetson. And faced it. "How long have
you got?"

He looked guarded.

"I dunno," he said, "quite."

"Rot!" said June. "Of course you know."

"I don't! I—I've got to see some people. Well, I've got to go to
Admiralty."

"Is she pretty?" asked June, swinging a leg. "Is she married?"

"Now, see here, Juggins——" (Mrs. Margetson was trying hard not
to look disgusted and shocked)—"you'd better behave yourself, if you want
a drink. I haven't come here to be ragged. Have *you* got off, by any wild
chance?"

"Oh, Robin——" said Mrs. Margetson.

"Shut up!" said her son and daughter, simultaneously; united, it would seem, in some sudden and passionate confederacy. So Mrs. Margetson did shut up. What else could she do? It was a curious and fitful confederacy, however, for all that.

Sometimes—indeed, far too often—they seemed banded together against her. But, good heavens, how they bickered, too. Presently, that first evening, they had gone off to the Royal Oak—with Mrs. Margetson now trying to look as if nothing could be more natural; but then, of course, they had been late at the San Remo, and the San Remo had been rude to Mrs. Margetson for keeping the table—which she had succeeded in doing, nevertheless—and when at last they arrived, the food had been horrible, and they both seemed to think this her fault. But even in the dark street on the way back, afterwards, they were teasing each other again.

War-nerves, of course, she thought. Perhaps it was a relaxation. Yet they didn't seem to *like* it; though they were as one again when Mrs. Margetson —innocently enough, she felt—began trying to make a few plans.

"Oh, mother!" said June. "Can't you leave him alone? He doesn't *want* to have everything arranged for him."

"That's right," said Robin. "You might give a chap a chance."

So again their mother subsided, and was puzzled, and tried not to feel hurt. To-morrow, she thought, she'd get Robin alone, and they'd have lunch somewhere together—never mind about her unpaid work for once— and perhaps go on to a film. This, she thought, would be different, and she would forget this evening, and they could really have a good, quiet talk. But she mustn't be unfair. She mustn't show favouritism; for even though that beard suggested Arctic Convoys, and she hadn't seen her son for eighteen, anxious months, she knew that poor June had had a deadly time, too—in the other sense of the word. Yes, this was what she told herself. But they did seem to delight in annoying each other; they seemed, in fact, to have stepped right back into a schoolroom era which she had also done her best to forget. Sometimes she could almost weep as their shafts went home. And then, again, she could almost weep for pity.

She did *hope* there would be something better than this to tell Geoffrey in her next letter; not, of course, that she was going to tell him anything about the shafts at all.

Or ought she to take June aside, and remind her of just a few things— though as a matter of fact she could only imagine them—that poor Robin must have been through? Perhaps she ought. But she didn't do it. For one thing, June was a great deal too wary to be caught like that; for another the merest hint of criticism was enough to produce a storm of fury—and Mrs. Margetson had got to go on living with her; while for a third thing, and though mother-love, in some extraordinary way, could still remain quite untouched, there was no doubt that her son, for whatever intelligible or unintelligible reason, was being very wearing indeed.

For instance, he accepted that invitation to lunch, and then didn't turn up; though he did telephone to the restaurant—in fact, he had even done so before Mrs. Margetson got there, so that she was spared a repetition of the awkwardness at the San Remo. Then she was expecting him for dinner at the flat, and he blew in, when it was half-cooked, to say—but with no further explanation—that he couldn't make it. His beard had been trimmed now, and he was almost recognisable—or perhaps it was that his mother was getting used to it—so that again her heart went out to him (poor boy, she mustn't spoil his fun); until again he slapped his sister's behind so hard that she turned and slapped his face.

"*June!*"

"Well, mother, I can't stand it! How would *you* like it if you were always being thumped and banged?"

"Temper!" said Robin.

"Oh, Robin—please——"

"Shut up!" said both offspring, together. Mrs. Margetson flushed, and was silent. She was now also in, as she well knew, for an evening of June's sulks. Oh, dear!

At the next phase—though in the midst of it there was one dreadful night at a theatre, where, quite apart from the now customary sense of strain and failure, an illuminated panel announced an Alert, so that Mrs. Margetson could think of nothing else (though it proved to be a quiet one) for the rest of the play; at the next phase, we were saying, the Lieutenant was even more elusive, and preferred to appear, it would seem, when he did so at all, merely as a voice through a couple of wires once more.

What have I done? thought Mrs. Margetson, after one of these brief conversations. And what's *he* doing?

She had dark, maternal suspicions, for she could never forget what June had said the first night. "Is she pretty? Is she married?" She was disgusted at harbouring, as they say, such a thought. At the same time she was longing for Robin himself to get married. At the same time she was convinced that sailors were always trapped. But if June knew the truth —and somehow Mrs. Margetson thought she looked as if she did—it would be no use asking her. The confederacy, she knew, would rise up in full force again.

On the following day—and really she was ashamed of not having done it before—she went round to Mr. Todman's little office; partly to thank him again for helping her out, and partly so as to discover what she owed him, and to discharge the account. It was surprisingly small. For war-time, indeed, it was almost fantastically cheap.

"Are you sure this is all right?" she asked.

Mr. Todman's ears turned red. "Oh, yes, Mrs. Margetson," he said.

"I made it up myself." Well, naturally, for he had no one to help him. "Four nights," he went on, "at——"

"Four nights! But——"

"Yes, that was all, Mrs. Margetson. Lieutenant Margetson offered to pay when he left; but as you'd told me——"

"Oh. Yes. Quite right. How stupid of me! Thanks very much."

With supreme self-control, Mrs. Margetson actually sat down and wrote out a cheque. She even waited for the receipt. But where had her son gone, then? Where had he been since Tuesday? Why hadn't he told her? Or had he, by any chance, told June?

No, she couldn't, and wouldn't, and mustn't ring up her office. It might possibly even be better to keep silent when June returned. But where was he? Why on earth couldn't he have said something? It—it was almost underhand. No, it wasn't. How *could* it be, when he was Robin, and had just had eighteen months in unspeakable danger? But, to say the very least, Mrs. Margetson was perplexed.

Something else perplexed her. That very evening, returning a little later than she liked from a very rare call (but friends who came up to London and stayed at hotels with deep dug-outs weren't always either punctual or considerate), she found herself ascending to the third floor of Huddleston House with one of those two girls at the other end of the passage. With the really very pretty one, in fact. The one who still somehow managed to look so sparkling; though sometimes, perhaps, just a little improper, too. She wasn't quite sure of her name, but of course she knew her well by sight, and June knew her, though she didn't seem to like her very much (but whom *did* she like?); so Mrs. Margetson gave her the usual sort of Huddleston smile.

Whereupon the girl said: "Oh, I say, Mrs. Margetson—*could* you possibly tell me? Is Robin still here?"

At which Mrs. Margetson was doubly bewildered; since for one thing she had no notion, until this moment, that her son even knew of this girl's existence; while for another it was, in any case, a remarkably hard question to answer.

However, of course she must answer it somehow. So she said: "Well, he's not been staying with me, you know. But—well, yes; he's still on leave."

"Oh," said the girl. "I suppose you don't know his telephone number?"

As this was just what Mrs. Margetson didn't know, but as such ignorance was just what she didn't want to admit, she was now more confused than ever. She said: "Well, I *don't*, I'm afraid; not just for tonight. You see, he's just moving." That sounded pretty stupid, she thought. She tried to leap the hurdle, no matter where she landed. "Can I give him a message?" she asked.

The girl drew back. "Oh, no, thank you," she said. "It—it doesn't matter at all." She was really amazingly pretty. "I—I'm afraid I must rush," she said.

As they were now on the landing, she did rush. Mrs. Margetson was a trifle baffled. Yet this incident, surely, she could mention to June; and she did—though with a natural suppression or omission—almost as soon as June herself came in.

"Oh," said this other war-worker, brightening a little. "Yes—Bryony Bretton. I suppose he got sick of her, then."

"But," said Mrs. Margetson, "I'd no idea——"

"Oh, yes!" said June. "Well, 's a matter of fact, it was I who introduced them—just outside here. She's like that, you know."

"Like what, darling?"

June shrugged her shoulders.

"Well, she just wants to be taken out all the time. So Robin took her —I suppose he'd got nothing else on. But of course he got sick of her, then. I bet they all do."

"Oh," said Mrs. Margetson. Her child didn't seem to think she had said anything surprising. It was an understood thing, apparently, that you met a completely strange girl on a landing, and that she then either asked to be taken out or looked as if she wanted to be taken out, and that you then did this. Out? What did it mean? Well, to start with, it hardly looked as though Robin was very deeply entangled elsewhere—which was a relief, if true; to go on with, it seemed clear enough that he had already shaken himself free of this particular girl; but as to the remaining facts and implications —as to where they had gone, what he had spent, and when they had come in again——

"June."

"What's the matter?"

"I suppose——"

But no; one just *couldn't* ask her. One couldn't ask her what they did, any more than one could ask her if she knew where he was. One was beaten; flummoxed; anxious beyond words. But one mustn't go on like an old hen —yes, and probably be told of the resemblance.

So Mrs. Margetson broke off, and dropped it; though she still thought Miss Bretton unusually pretty, as indeed she was. On the other hand, she was perhaps again just a little disloyal to her own sex; for she was undoubtedly pleased that Miss Bretton had been dropped as well. She knew why, what's more; though indeed almost everyone knew why, except Bugs herself, and the still faithful and mesmerised Echo. In *my* day, thought Mrs. Margetson—and for one brief, unexpected moment she even felt a faint trace of complacency—we broke *some* of the rules, I know; but at least we'd the sense to keep *that* one. And one is afraid she wasn't sorry for Miss Bretton, for all her great kindness of heart.

But as the moment passed she was again fairly sorry for herself. And still more so as the evening went on, for to-night, as it happened, her son didn't even ring up.

On the following morning, though she had managed to sleep and there had been no Alert, there was a pang from another source. A cable from Geoffrey. "Very sorry cancel 223 writing all love." She read it again and again. She managed to put at least a dozen different meanings into it, though not one of them contained any comfort. The twelfth shot—more ingenious, perhaps, but no more consolatory than the others—was that 223 had announced a successful operation for appendicitis (though from sensibility about censors it hadn't been mentioned in three later letters), and that now there had been a relapse. She was still trying to fight off more guesses, and to draft some answer—which must still be unfussing, of course—at the same time, when there was another rattle from the letter-slot, and a ring at the door-bell, too.

Mrs. Wardrop? I can't face her. Oh, all right. Here goes.

She was in the lobby. There was another envelope on the floor that she identified at once. She snatched it up. She looked at the post-mark. She cursed the Examiner who had stuck on that label, and the very hard-tried postal authorities, too; but this, after all, was unquestionably No. 223 itself. So she tore it open. And the bell rang again.

"Hullo, hullo!" said a voice outside. "Anyone there?"

Robin! She let him in. He kissed her. She was being scratched by the beard.

"Oh, darling," she said—though perhaps for the first time in the last week this wasn't quite true—"I was just thinking about you. Come in here." They were in the sitting-room. "Oh, Robin——"

"I know, mother. Haven't I been a ——?"

It seems better to print the word like that, though it must be admitted that Mrs. Margetson had heard it—and from both her children—before. But, oh, how it warmed her soul now, and seemed to tickle the backs of her eyes.

"Oh, no, darling," she said. "I quite understood."

"I couldn't help it," said Robin, beginning to march about the floor—though, as you may remember, there were a good deal of obstructions. "It was getting to London again. I—I felt sort of half cooped-up, and half —well, sort of *mad* to go on the loose. Not that I have been, particularly. But I met a fellow—oh, *you* wouldn't remember him; same year at Dartmouth, though—and he's got six months ashore, and a flat with a spare bed. So I—I sneaked off there. Well, you don't know what it's like, mother. You *can't!*"

"No, darling. I mean, yes, darling. It's quite all right."

"I felt a ——," said Robin, using another word now from the same branch of his vocabulary. "But there it was. And then *I* didn't want to keep having rows with Juggins. By the way, will you tell her? And give her my love?"

"Tell her what, Robin?" But already Mrs. Margetson was afraid that this time she had guessed right.

"Leave over," said the Lieutenant, glancing at his watch. "Catching train in under an hour. I mean, if I'd known for certain—even last night——"

"I'll come with you," said Mrs. Margetson.

"No, you won't. Much better not. Can't stand scenes at stations."

"But, darling, I wouldn't——"

"Yes, you would. So you're not coming. It's—it's just bloody well barred. Here!"

He dropped on to the sofa from Wallington Gardens, and patted his lap. Mrs. Margetson sat there for six minutes—until both of them, in fact, were aware of incipient cramp. Yet she was rewarded for something. She was more than rewarded. And even when he had gone—but still having told her nothing of where he was going—though she almost choked as the lift-cage disappeared, there was still an astonishing glow.

She tried not to think of anything at all, so as to keep it as long as she could. But this was asking the impossible, of course. It was fading already. Already it was slipping, treacherously, into the past tense. She knew, too, that there must be worse pain than this, before she was back in the half-numbed condition where he had found her. The kind of condition which she had gradually reached, though with frequent relapses, in the case of——

Geoffrey's letter! She'd opened it. She'd put it down somewhere. And then, of course——

It was still on the little table just inside the front door, though. So that now, after nearly three months, she could learn (in strict confidence) how her husband had heard (though she wasn't to tell anyone) that John (which was a key-word for his Chief, whose name wasn't John at all) might be bringing him over in January; and that if this happened they must at all costs have at least a week together at an hotel somewhere; and he had better not mention this again, but could she and would she take steps to arrange it?

In Washington, in other words, even Geoffrey seemed to have forgotten what English hotels had become like. But it was sweet of him. Only he wasn't coming. He had just sent that cable instead.

And Robin was just Care of the General Post Office again; an absurd and even offensive address—or so Mrs. Margetson suddenly felt—for someone who was now in constant peril of being bombed from above, shot at from the same level, or blown up from below. And she, and June, must now—though they were both worn out by it all—go on as before.

When she told June that evening, she answered: "Well, that's what happens, mother." And presently: "Yes, I knew he was staying with David Andover. Somebody told me." And a little later, which might possibly be taken as sorrow or sympathy from June: "It's not much catch having brothers these days, I must say."

Later still—at any rate for a short while—it came over Mrs. Margetson that, despite the alleged nausea with which the girl at the far end of the passage had afflicted her son, one should smile at her with rather an additional air of friendliness when one met her; though the exact reasons for this impulse were decidedly involved and obscure. Perhaps she wanted to show that she understood what she certainly didn't understand. Or, perhaps, with Robin at sea again and in no danger any longer, it would appear, from this particular source, she wanted to practise the kind of look which one day— as she was now dreaming again—she might give to a daughter-in-law.

But the girl wasn't very co-operative. She looked guarded, and even slightly resentful. Once more, an invisible spectator—if he could momentarily have disregarded her figure and features, not to mention her colouring and clothes—might have thought that she didn't care to be reminded of yet another affair which had again been too like the lightning. How long would it be before Echo observed this, too ? Or had she, by any chance, already observed it ? Wasn't it true, since Robin Margetson had flickered and fled, that something—though she was still trying to be as loyal as ever, and to resist it—was clearing her own vision in a slightly disturbing way ?

CHAPTER XI

AS THE MOON WANED, AND ALSO ROSE LATER AND LATER, THERE WERE A NUMBER of people who could at least say: "I told you so." The sirens were now sounding for three, four, or even five nights in succession, and slight enemy activity—as Messrs. Whippenstall and Rampart called it—was again part of London life. Sometimes, indeed, it was no more than an Alert, and within an hour or so one could make another attempt to sleep. But sometimes, again, there was a complete if still mercifully abbreviated rendering of the whole performance; from the wailing and the hoarse shouts of "Put out that light!", through the crashes and reverberations, the shuddering of buildings and the pattering on their roof-tops, to the final, distant rumble of the retreating storm. In the morning even the bravest felt irritable, and even the calmest were a little annoyed to be told—when they had seen the ring of fires for themselves—that their own comparatively central district was no more than "the London area."

In the morning, also there were rumours; and it was astonishing how they were communicated and spread. In Darkest Africa, one is told, it is done by tribal drums; or again there is a reputed system known as the Grape-Vine. But there are no tribal drums in London, or at any rate none that are used. No plant, you would have thought, could have sent a tendril down into a deep, inner cellar. Yet somehow, for example, when Eldritch came up from the boiler-room—where the stock of coke was becoming alarmingly low—he could already tell anyone who happened to meet him precisely what kind of missile had fallen where. And what damage had been done; how many people were still underneath it; and even the street where an unexploded shell had come in through a window and put paid to an old lady in bed.

He wasn't always completely wrong, either, though it was seldom that he was completely right. He seemed to pick up transmissions on a secret wave-length, but either they were sent out before the facts had been fully ascertained, or else he never waited for the end of a message. And then other cross-rumours were filling the ether, too. If they were irreconcilable, you added them together; struck an average, in accordance with your own taste for the gruesome; and passed on the result at once. For speed was important. Not only did you increase your score if you got in first, but it was also understood that you could exaggerate to almost any extent before —shall we say ?—nine o'clock in the morning. While from then onwards you must be much more careful, until by the afternoon—supposing, that is, you could still find anyone to listen—you were virtually confined to the truth.

Was it Eldritch, then, who started the rumour about The Dwellings ? Very likely. Almost positively, in fact, for he was an extremely early bird; whereas Freeth, though on duty that night, was notoriously slow off the mark. At any rate it began spreading, with the help of the milkmen, and even seemed to be confirmed when flat after flat began waiting in vain for its Help. Quite a number of tenants set off for their work in the firm persuasion that The Dwellings had been rased to the ground. Others, peering hopefully or a bit desperately from their doorways, soon learnt of the rumour, too, and were doubly distressed. It was true that there had been no particularly deafening bang in the night—or none judged by the standards which all had been forced to adopt—but then perhaps this was some new kind of bomb, and in any case where were Mrs. Vowles, and Mrs. Trudgeon, and Mr. Everard's Mrs. Grimes ?

A little later in the morning the rumour changed. One hardly knew how; for, as always, it seemed to be plucked from the ambient air. But it was now generally known or believed that though The Dwellings themselves were intact, a delayed-action bomb had fallen among them, and that all Dwellers had been told to clear out. This was a relief—except, of course, to that secret and shocking part of the human mind which must always be disappointed when catastrophe, for others, isn't horribly complete; but it was still some way from the truth.

For the objective truth—whether it would ultimately prevail or not—was that a small high-explosive bomb had crashed through a man-hole cover in Pilsbury Place (which was separated from The Dwellings by a whole block); that it hadn't gone off; that only a few families in that street had been ordered to move; that even before daylight a hero had been lowered on a rope by other heroes, and had calmly and competently extracted the fuse; but that the sewer had been cracked—which was all that the first hero complained about—so that the hole was still fenced off, and there was an extremely unpleasant smell. As to why this should have attracted the Dwellers so much, there might be various views. But it did. As soon as they were allowed to, they thronged into Pilsbury Place, and gloated over the hole, and gossiped, and sniffed. Their children came and played there, or as near as they could, so that the devastated area behind Huddleston House was for once completely deserted—except for the dogs. The hero, who had now long since vanished, aroused, one is sorry to say, but little concern. He was rather taken for granted, one is afraid; though again it is true that if bombs are going to fall like this, then the State is almost pledged to provide heroes. To us, it may well be, he was far the most interesting character, as we find ourselves speculating on his birth, upbringing, and ultimate selection of this extraordinarily dangerous job; or as we suddenly recall another and similar hero, who was first praised to the skies for saving a national monument, and then placed in the dock on a charge of looting.

But the smell was the point for the Dwellers; and the narrowness of their own escape; and the crowd, though they were forming most of it themselves; and the opportunity, for all, at any rate, who were in no fear of being fined or punished, of taking the morning off. On the whole, in fact, this was one of the most popular bombs—it was Mrs. Mudge, by the way, who described it as a Descendiary—that had ever come down in the district; since it had provided not only free entertainment, and that appalling though apparently fascinating stink, but a holiday—and a holiday with pay, what is more—as well. For Huddleston House must again, for the most part, do its own brushing, sweeping, and bed-making as best it could, at least until its vassals' return. And when they did return, they must still palpitate and be restored with tea, before attending to anything else. But of course no one suggested —they didn't dare—that their wage should be docked. No, however exhausted, they weren't quite as reckless as that.

For Major Hurst, on the other hand, at No. 4, Huddleston House, all, on this particular morning, seemed just the same as before. He had heard the barrage—which, indeed, it would have been hard not to hear— but so far he had missed the rumour, for so far he hadn't got up. It would also appear, though he had certainly heard some bombs as well, that Hounslow, or part of it, was still on the face of the earth; for Bunny, his well-trained batman, was as punctual as ever with the Major's first cup of tea.

"Quarter to eight, sir," he said, as he placed it by the Major's bedside.

The Major grunted, without opening his eyes—so that he couldn't see Bunny's rather dogged and harassed expression. But he was no sluggard. After exactly the right number of seconds he drank the tea. After exactly the right number of minutes he rose, went into the bathroom, returned completed his toilet, passed into the sitting-room, and found breakfast ready, with a couple of bills and a newspaper neatly arranged by his plate.

All, so far, in other words, was precisely in accord with his expectations. The breakfast was excellent. The bills needn't be opened; but he could pay them as soon as he chose. The newspaper, though still regrettably brief, was quite good company; indeed, at this hour of the day he had no wish for any other. He read, he ate, he swigged; and presently he lighted a cigarette.

Then he said: "Bunny!"—though not at all at the top of his voice— and his henchman almost immediately reappeared.

"Listen," said the Major, without looking at him, and speaking always with that rather noticeable reverberation in the nose. "No dinner to-night. But might want something left. Might have a guest. Don't lay the table. Get it ready on the tray. And for God's sake put a damp cloth over it or something."

"For two, sir ?"

"You heard," said the Major, still without turning his head. He exhaled rather violently. And then suddenly he did turn his head. "What the devil's the matter ?" he asked.

Bunny—who should of course have withdrawn, but hadn't—said: "Could I have a word with you, sir, please ?" He seemed quite respectful, but a little hoarse. He was standing stiffly at attention; but he gave three blinks.

"Eh ?" said the Major, now looking him up and down. His next words were kinder than the tone in which they were spoken. "What's the trouble ?" he asked. "Anything wrong at home ?"

"No, sir. Thank you, sir." Gulp. "But I wished to say, sir——"

"Well ? Come on!" But the Major stubbed his cigarette out, though it wasn't nearly finished. "Buck up!" he added.

"If you could see your way, sir, to find someone else, sir—p'r'aps, sir—so I could——"

"Look here," said Major Hurst; "are you trying to give notice ?"

Bunny just stiffened still further.

"You can't!" said the Major. "Don't you understand your position ? Don't you realise you're under military discipline, and—and there's a war on ?"

"Yes, sir. But if you could make a rec'mendation, sir——"

"Rubbish!" said the Major. "Why should I ? Do you want to lose a perfectly good job ? Do you want to be Boarded again ? Do you want to go off and fight ?"

Odd question, perhaps, from a Major during a total war. And it evoked rather an odd answer.

"I don't so much mind, sir," said Bunny, "if I do."

His liege-lord took out another cigarette, and stared at him.

"You're not," he suggested, "trying to be insolent, I suppose ?"

"No, sir."

"Well, but—— Well, but look here—what *is* it, then ?"

But Bunny didn't look there. His eyes dropped. And so did his voice. "I'd rather not say, sir," he said.

Major Hurst clicked his lighter, and swore—just possibly because there was no flame. "Here!" he said, holding it out. "Fill this."

"Very good, sir."

"No—wait a moment." The Major drew back his hand. He knew just what that schoolboy phrase had meant. He'd been careless, he supposed. In fact, he knew he'd been just a little careless. There was nothing, of course, that Bunny could do. If Bunny imagined for one moment that he could, then he'd never been more mistaken. But if all this was genuine; if the idiot was shocked; if he thought he could drop a hint of that size and expect it to have the slightest effect——

At this point the Major's blood began boiling, which was at once a relief and—suddenly—a still further incentive to passion.

"No!" he snapped—and he pocketed the lighter, so as to show, whether it would light or not, that he had had enough of this blasted impertinence. "You'd better clear out," he said. "You'll clean up first, of course, and——" some rather cooler emphasis here—"I want that tray, if you don't mind. But you needn't come back. In fact, you'd much better not, if you don't like it. You can report for duty; don't worry—I'll see that they're expecting you all right. *They'll* take care of you, Bunny, if that's what you want. Or," added the Major, "whether you want it or not. I think you'll find," said the Major, at the very top of his form now, "that there's plenty of work for a healthy young fellow like you. D'you hear me ?"

"Yes, sir."

"All right," said the Major. "Get out, then."

"Very good, sir," said Bunny, without a trace of anything that could conceivably be described as insolence, though the Major glared after him, and favoured him with a snort as well. This wasn't actually their last meeting, for within a few moments—which had been employed by the Major in some further and privnte sorting—Party-Leader Popham announced the arrival of the mud-coloured car, and Bunny must return so as to pass on this item of news. He also helped his liege-lord into his great-coat, and handed him his cap and gloves. But Major Hurst didn't address him; and presently, having completed the house-work, gone out for a little final shopping, and prepared the supper-tray—with scrupulous attention to the damp cloth— he placed his latchkey on the exact centre of the Major's blotting-pad, and so passed from this scene of his labours for the very last time.

He said nothing to the porters. Nor had he said anything to them pre- viously, whatever they now might either suspect or guess. He wondered, inevitably, how much of a fool he had been. He knew that he hadn't the very slightest wish to leave Hounslow, and still less was he eager to find himself drafted abroad. But if he'd got to, he'd got to; and he had very little doubt what—in the absence of the protection that he had hitherto been granted—any Medical Board would say. Nor was he upheld by his conscience, for he didn't even know that he had one. He had just spoken like that because the moment had come when he couldn't keep quiet any longer. It puzzled him; for, as a matter of fact, he had very few moral standards, either. But it had happened, and he was glad it was over. The Major, ran his thoughts as he trundled along in a train, don't ought to have done it—not with a young lady as is in a position like that. Well, not, anyhow, he kept repeating, so as the bloke what looks after him can't help not finding out.

A mixture of sentiments ? Certainly. He was a human being. Farewell, Private Bunny. . . .

As Major Hurst bowled along, with an eye, but no more, on Miss Gooch's distinctly broad back, he, too, was compelled for a while to commingle his meditations. Nuisance, he reflected. Ass, he thought—but this didn't refer to himself. Damn the lower orders, he mused. He didn't doubt for an instant that he could fix the thing up; that's to say that he could take care of Bunny—or this was his phrase—and find a successor at once; or almost at once. The new man would have to be trained to his ways, though. And even that wasn't all. Not that Major Hurst was the least worried in one sense; for he had outfaced many and much worse threats in the past. But then—dammit—the damned thing was, you see, that he'd lost a good servant this time, just when the affair was (again in his own phrase) on the turn. Even a month ago he might have thought it worth it. But then a month ago he hadn't only himself been protected (or it was thus that he saw things) by his wife, but Primrose was also protected (in the same rather strange use of this word) by a husband in a prisoners' camp. The husband couldn't get at her, or make trouble, but he was there all right. Only then he'd stopped writing, or that was the effect at this end, and—well, one wasn't a cad, of course, but if she *wanted* consoling . . .

His mouth twitched. Now he was thinking only of Primrose, yet from two points of view at once. He was annoyed with her, as he was annoyed with all women, because either they were putting on a pretence of virtue or else they wouldn't let go. She'd lost him his servant. And she'd no business to be under the same roof, when of course this would be the obvious result. It was all her fault, in fact; and yet—the second point of view was like a wave overwhelming the first—there was still something about her; you couldn't get away from it; and—with a sudden rush of memories—he didn't want to. No, honestly it was different this time. And *she* was different. He'd been crazy to imagine that the thing was finished, or even nearly finished. He thought of that supper-tray. He felt reckless and enchanted again. Never mind about Bunny; he was well out of the way.

In fact—though he hardly looked it at such an early hour in the morning
—Major Hurst was now under the curious illusion that he was also feeling
young.

So the mud-coloured car rolled along. Pedestrians saw it; and some of
them were envious, some were indignant, while a few, for some remarkable
reason, were even impressed. But the great point for the passenger was that
he had just thought of asking Miss Gooch if she had a box of matches, and
she had, and he had borrowed it, so that now he was smoking again. That,
he was now thinking, had been the real trouble. It was hell not having a
light.

This particular drive—and Bunny's journey on the District Railway,
of course—took place at the tail-end of January; and by the tail-end of
January, though somehow we haven't found space for this topic before, there
was again a distinct recrudescence of coughs and colds. In ordinary years
—or again so far as this standard could still be recalled—the race, roughly
speaking, had a bad cold in the autumn, which in those days generally
seemed to inoculate them until the following February; in which month they
of course went down with the same thing again. If it was accompanied
by a slight rise in temperature, they called it influenza. So did their doctors,
in those days, if they had any tact. And so did their kinder and less refractory
friends.

Or they all called it Flu, in a more familiar manner, though they treated
it with anything but contempt. They stayed in bed—we are speaking,
of course, of the middle classes and their betters now; they were punctilious
about remaining there for twenty-four hours after the temperature had
abated; they were plied with slops, oranges, and other delicacies; and they
emerged in a state of readiness to describe their symptoms to anyone who
could be induced to listen, or even to those who quite clearly weren't listening
at all.

Happy Times—though presently, of course, they must be spurned
and assailed as ignoble. And of course, again, we are not thinking of serious
diseases, on which no one would wish to look back. Yet in any event the
whole business had altered now. With regard to serious diseases, the Press
was constantly announcing the most miraculous new cures; which weren't
yet, however, available for the ordinary public, so that they must just put up
with the present shortage of doctors, medicaments, and nurses as best they
could. While with regard to influenza, or Flu, there was a double change.
For to start with, the old system of self-inoculation seemed somehow, in
war-time, to have failed; and to go on with, quite four out of five victims must
rise, whether they wished to or not, because there was no one to look after
them if they didn't, and they would just starve if they stayed in bed. Perhaps
these aspects were related. Yet even they weren't all. There were intricacies

of certificates and sick-leave which almost forced some patients to conceal their sufferings, because if they didn't they would find that they had exceeded some technical limit, and would lose their full pay, if not their next ordinary leave as well. Or even where there was someone to provide food, there were certainly no delicacies. There was no time to soothe brows now, or to say: "Mind you stay where you are." And there was far greater fear of infection, for no longer could one hope to believe that illness meant rest.

The Executive made two contributions—apart from what has just been described. In the first place it was repeatedly informing the public that they had never been healthier in their lives; even hinting that it had declared war for this beneficent purpose. And in the second place it issued millions of posters advising them that if they coughed and sneezed into their handkerchiefs, their troubles would all be over. It didn't furnish the handkerchiefs, of course. Indeed, it had taken great pains to make it almost impossible to obtain them, or to have them washed if you did. But it certainly used up a lot of paper, for which everyone had to pay.

So much, then, for the Executive. Nevertheless, people did have coughs and colds, and they did transmit them, and at the tail-end of January there was again something like an epidemic all over Huddleston House. Inmates appeared with watery eyes, and vanished, and reappeared looking flushed at one moment and horribly pale at the next. The long, crooked nose of Freeth, the porter, was scarlet, and constantly dripped. A similar pestilence in The Dwellings caused handmaiden after handmaiden to fail to turn up; and just—though this wasn't their fault—when they were needed most. In many cases—though of course some were much worse than others— this was the fifth or even sixth assault since the beginning of autumn, and all were at least secretly aware that February still lay ahead. But they still did their best. They struggled into their clothes and to their work. They even laughed at the epidemic when they met, and coughed, in the lift. But for a while the Fire-Guard parties consisted almost entirely of invalids, substitutes, and even persons who were only there in theory, or in the exercise-book, because in fact they were tossing feverishly on a bed.

Luckily, chance still spared the building. Luckily, also, for some people, it was impossible to feel as ill as that and to be alarmed by the uproar at the same time. Yet in the midst of it all—and much else, also, that still strained the system—there was one case which should perhaps have special mention. The moral, if any, can follow a brief account of it. But this was what happened.

Mr. E. A. Everard, of No. 17, had a visit, at about this time, not only from his wife—which was a quite frequent event, though she seldom stayed more than a night—but from his son, Cyril, as well. The child was to see an oculist, for there was a myopic tradition among all Everards—though no one is saying that this is why their lives were dedicated to the State—and the plan, on this occasion, was that there should be an early start from the country, a consultation in Wimpole Street, a family lunch at a Regent-street restaurant, and a return by the afternoon train. In other words, there had been no prospect at the outset that either Cyril or his mother should go to Huddleston House at all. Or at the most Mrs. Everard had hoped, if there was time, to look in there for a few minutes, and collect a few things, on her way back to the station.

But in the middle of the lunch-party Cyril said he felt sick. His father advised him to eat more slowly; but from this moment, as a matter of fact, he ate nothing at all. He was also looking a bit green now; but when his mother suggested that this was due to the drops that had been put in his eys, he did his best to agree with her. By the end of the meal, however, he was looking red. Even his father observed this. He said: "Are you feeling all right now, Cyril?" And Cyril, who was rather afraid of him, said: "Yes." But then Mrs. Everard said: "Say 'Yes, thank you, father.'" And this was the point at which, with no further warning whatever——

Well, it was all very embarrassing in such a crowded and public place, and no help to the appetite of anyone else within sight or hearing. Civilisation, however, didn't quite collapse; or no more so than it had done already. The crisis was dealt with, and the child—looking ashen now, for a change—was whipped into a taxi and hustled to Huddleston House. His father, of course, went back to his Office; but on his return that evening he discovered that Mrs. Everard and Cyril were still there; for there had been further upheavals, and indeed, as he was bound to admit, this had been the only course to pursue.

So Cyril passed the night, in one of his father's flannel shirts, in the smaller of the two bedrooms—the one, that is to say, which his mother was accustomed to use—while his parents kept colliding, and apologising, and then colliding again, in Mr. Everard's bed next door. Why, you may ask, had no doctor been summoned? But he had been. Mrs. Everard had telephoned six times during the afternoon and evening; once to the doctor who had brought Cyril into the world, but it appeared that he was now in the Army; once to the doctor who had taken over his practice, but it appeared that he had been stricken himself; and four times to a third doctor (recommended by the second doctor's secretary), who on the first three occasions was out. On the fourth occasion he answered Mrs. Everard himself, but said that it was impossible to come round that night. He did, however, listen to a description of the symptoms—which he could hardly avoid without ringing off—and prescribed one tablet of aspirin (which the child had been given already), rather as though mentioning some very rare drug of which no one else could have thought.

So all three Everards had rather bad nights, with another Alert in the middle, and in the morning the youngest seemed much the same—a temperature of about a hundred and one, that's to say, but with an obvious cold in place of the sickness—while his parents were still rather anxious. As, however, the hitherto unknown Dr. McGregor had promised to come early, and as Mr. Everard was more than entitled—if you count what he hadn't had since the outbreak of war—to at least six months' absence from duty, he rang up his Office to say that he would be a little late. Well, he was a bit fussy, you know. And he hadn't had at all a good night.

He didn't have at all a good breakfast, either, for naturally there was very little food in the flat, and Cyril must have the dregs of the milk. Furthermore, Dr. McGregor wasn't early. They waited until eleven, and then rang up his house. He'd gone out, of course. There was nothing to do but wait again. Sometimes Mr. Everard looked out of the window, and sometimes he walked up and down. Occasionally he said: "This is monstrous!", and Mrs. Everard entirely agreed with him. She, for her part, kept tiptoeing in and out of that smaller bedroom, where the patient was now stertorous and scarlet, and saying—though this was little help, either—that she couldn't think what to do.

At ten minutes past twelve there was a false alarm. A car drove up with the word DOCTOR inside the wind-screen—but most people were so used to this now that they had left off wondering why—and a man leapt out, and dived into the building; but nobody rang the bell. The wrong doctor, in other words. More monstrous than ever. Mr. Everard, suffering a good deal from reaction, called up his Office again and said that he wouldn't be in before lunch.

This wasn't quite accurate. There could be no lunch if neither he nor Mrs. Everard could leave the flat, for on ordinary days there was never any lunch here, and though Mrs. Grimes had come in as usual before breakfast, she had long since withdrawn by now. The Everards, in fact, were completely cut off, unless one of them risked missing the doctor. And neither was prepared to do this; not that they didn't trust each other, but of course the more you wait, in such circumstances as these, the more you've got to go on waiting. Luckily some more milk had arrived, though, and there was still the heel of a loaf; so that Cyril could have his slops.

It was nearly two o'clock when the bell at last rang. There was another collision—but in an upright position this time—between Mr. and Mrs. Everard; and Mr. Everard opened the door. Dr. McGregor looked gaunt and exhausted. "Now, then," he said, which of course wasn't at all the right way to apologise. "Let's have a look at your little girl."

"Boy," said Mr. Everard, taking an even greater dislike to him. "Now, if you'll just—oop—come in here, doctor, so that I can explain——"

"Tell me afterwards," said Dr. McGregor. "Or tell me while I'm looking at him. I oughtn't really to be here, you know."

"Why not ?" said Mr. Everard.

"Because," said Dr. McGregor, "I've got about sixteen more cases than I can handle, anyhow. Now, then. Which way ?"

He even tried to burst into the wrong bedroom, but both Everards defended it, and he was deflected. Then, however, he shut the door of the right bedroom in Mr. Everard's face, which registered extreme hoity-toitiness and baffled pomposity. Yet he was quick, kind, and gentle with the actual patient. "Feeling rotten ?" he said. "That's right." Pulse, tongue, chest, temperature; a few sharp questions to Mrs. Everard, following each other so swiftly that she was quite unable to answer except in the same way. And then back with the bed-clothes, and he was scribbling a prescription.

"There!" he said, tearing it from a pad and handing it over. "Soon be all right, I hope."

"But—but what *is* it, Doctor Mc——"

"Eh ? Oh, call it what you like. Everyone's got it. Just a bug."

"A bug, Doctor McGregor!" When one considers Mrs. Everard's very high level of education—which was so lofty that she persistently pronounced Margarine with a hard "g"—one realises or remembers, also, that education can be rather like a blanket; if you pull it up too high, it will no longer cover your feet. So that for a moment, at any rate, "bug" only meant one thing to her; and she, too, not only took on the hue of a turkey now, but made certain sounds as if about to gobble like one as well. Dr. McGregor, on the other hand, had re-packed his attaché-case, and was already out in the little passage again.

"Well, doctor ?" said Mr. Everard, who had been waiting there, but was still far more accustomed to making other people wait. And he indicated the sitting-room, with an awkward wave of the hand. His idea, it is to be imagined, was that there should now be a Conference, with himself, no doubt, in the Chair. He may even have contemplated a few off-the-record remarks—yet naturally of an authoritative nature—about the future relationship of Medicine and the State. But all Dr. McGregor said was: "Hullo! Yes, keep him warm. Ring up if you want me." And then Dr. McGregor had gone.

"Look here!" said Mr. Everard, making an attempt to dash after him. But now Mrs. Everard was clinging to him, for she wanted comfort. And by the time her husband had shaken her off ("Do please be sensible, Gertrude"), the harassed but elusive physician had gone down in the lift.

"If you would have allowed me——" said Mr. Everard.

"Ernest—I've never *met* such a man!"

"Quite, my dear. And I—I shall take steps about it. Did he do nothing for the poor child at all ?"

"He gave me this prescription," said Mrs. Everard.

"Ha!" said Mr. Everard, who perhaps thought he might still catch the doctor on the pavement. "I'll deal with that. Give it to me, dear."

His wife obeyed him. He hustled himself into a coat and hat. He ran down the stairs—for the lift was now, of course, at the bottom—and arrived somewhat breathlessly in the entrance-hall. There was no car to be seen through the glass doors, though. His protests must still be postponed. But there was something else, wasn't there? Ah, yes; the prescription. It was still in his hand. He glanced at it. He couldn't make head or tail of it. But it was all he had. It was important, whether the doctor was an insufferable jackanapes or not. He set smartly off, still panting a little, towards the main road.

A few minutes later, and not yet having recovered his normal breathing, he burst into Messrs. Hernshaw's shop. There was no one there. He coughed. He coughed more loudly. He rapped on the glass counter. He tried to look over it, so as to peer into the penetralia, and his shoulder impinged on an erection of toilet-paper, from which it hastily drew back. Unlike the wall at Aphek or the great tower at Fonthill Abbey, the erection merely tottered and returned to equilibrium. But Mr. Everard's attention was certainly distracted for a moment; so that he was surprised to discover that the pale chemist in the white coat had entered noiselessly, and was now gazing at him in silence.

"Oh!" said Mr. Everard. "I—ah—sorry—I—beep—want this made up. Quickly," he added, as the chemist, having taken the prescription, appeared to fall into a kind of trance over it.

But then—though Mr. Everard had no idea how unusual this was— the chemist spoke. His voice was slow and hollow. He sounded rather like a man in a particularly resonant tomb, vault, or charnel-house.

"Whom," he inquired, "is it for?"

"Eh?" said Mr. Everard, who again was much more accustomed to interrogating others than to being questioned himself. "It's for my—oop— my son."

"Is he in the Services?" asked the chemist, after another slight pause.

"Of course not," said Mr. Everard. "He's a little boy."

The chemist raised his eyebrows to an enormous height, and brought them slowly down again.

"In that case," he said, offering the prescription back again, "I am afraid I am unable to supply you. This drug——"

"What!" said Mr. Everard. "Nonsense!"

"——is reserved at present," said the chemist, now closing his eyes, "for Members of the Forces."

"But," said Mr. Everard, "that's—oop—that's ridiculous! I tell you, the doctor has—beep—only just seen the child. What on earth—ug—do you mean?"

The chemist opened his eyes just enough, it would seem, to assure himself that Mr. Everard was still there; and then immediately closed them again.

"The drug," he said, "is in short supply. You won't get it anywhere. Except, of course, for a Member of the——"

"Rubbish!" said Mr. Everard. "Do you know who I am?"

"No, sir," said the chemist, letting the slip of paper fall on to the counter. "But it makes not the slightest difference. Unless, as I say——"

He began turning away. He was a bit mad, of course. He had again been up all night, with an ambulance section. For several years he had been conducting this business under an increasing number of threats and regulations, and for the last five weeks he had been conducting it single-handed. He may or may not have known what he was saying. He may even have been quoting a genuine regulation, for they reached him not only from more than one department of the Executive, but from wholesalers and the head-office as well. Or, again, it may just have been that solitude and fatigue, and the incessant difficulty of complying with the inscrutable Law, had brought him to a pitch where he would have refused, at this moment, to sell even a tin of tooth-powder. One doesn't know. One can't say. But one does know and can say that for once, and perhaps the first time, Mr. Everard found himself in almost the precise position of tax-payers who wrote to him at his Ministry. He was on the wrong side of the barrier of obstruction this time. And he didn't like it.

"Wait a second!" he blustered. "Are you—gug—the manager here?"

"Yes, sir," said the pale chemist, pausing about a couple of yards away.

"I see," said Mr. Everard, picking up the prescription. "Well, do you want me to—oop—to make a complaint about you? Am I to write—officially, mind you—to the head of your firm?"

The chemist looked a shade less pale. He appeared, for a moment, to be retreating still further. But suddenly he swung round the end of the counter, and was only a foot away.

"'Officially'!" he said. "Look here—I've had enough of 'officially.' Get out of my shop!"

He was about eight inches taller than Mr. Everard, who, as has been said, was on the smallish side. It was Mr. Everard who now retreated, but in the wrong direction. He backed, that is to say, rather heavily against the counter. "Look out!" said the chemist. His arm shot forth—purely and simply, though it was too late already, so as to save that pyramid of toilet-rolls; and Mr. Everard, under a complete misconception, grabbed hold of the front of his white coat.

"Don't you hit me!" said both characters, simultaneously, as the rolls went rolling on the floor. But then they did hit each other, or they tried to hit each other. That's to say, they pushed and panted, and the rolls got under their feet; and they lurched, and waved their arms like windmills. And the chemist said: "I'll teach you!" And Mr. Everard said: "I'll have you summoned for this." And then, though no actual blow had yet been exchanged, the chemist danced sideways on to a cylinder—a faithless cylinder—and away went his foot, and he fell smack on the floor.

"There!" he said, almost triumphantly, and as yet without attempting to rise. "*Now* I'll have your name and address!"

But he didn't. For in that epic instant, though still far from calm, Mr. Everard had seen a sudden vision of a Magistrate's court, of himself being cross-examined, of the very pertinent question "Did you knock him down ?" (to which he still wasn't sure of the answer): and, even worse, of his own name in the papers, and of the Permanent Secretary's face when he saw it. For all its conceivable faults or shortcomings, the genuine Civil Service has been trained to a horror of even favourable personal publicity; and it should be remembered that Mr. Everard had been as good as born in the tradition, for his father had adorned the authentic ranks as well.

So he beat it. He didn't wait for the chemist to get up or to repeat that statement. He just plunged out into the street, still panting and still grasping the crumpled prescription, and praying to Heaven that his adversary would have forgotten the names on it. Moreover—though in a state of alarm now which in turn produced a most unusual effect of humility—he slid into another chemist's, where he was supplied with the requisite tablets almost at once. His son was persuaded to swallow a couple, and though they again made him feel frightfully sick—for they were very up-to-date—and sicker still when he was given a couple more, either they or Nature restored his health, and within three days Mrs. Everard had taken him back to the country.

On the whole, and on this occasion, Mr. Everard was rather glad that they had gone. For not only could he now sleep at night—subject always to the barrage—without constant collisions, but his last fear was removed for the present that his wife would go into Hernshaw's and somehow reveal his identity. A less cautious man might have asked her not to. But secrecy is another marked habit of the true Civil Servant. So Mr. Everard had said nothing; and presently—for of course he was now scrupulous in avoiding the shop himself—he became reasonably convinced that the sword hanging over him was suspended by a good deal more than a hair. At the Office it was noted that he was his own rather grim and testy old self again. His minutes resumed their acid quality, and members of the public, caught up in the toils, received the very minimum of help or solace from their Obedient Servant, E. A. Everard. For he had learnt no lasting lesson at the tail-end of January. That's the moral perhaps. Unless there's no moral at all.

And yet who does learn lessons ? Here we are—but it is early February now—in Mr. Todman's little office, round a couple of corners on the ground floor of Bessingham House. One sees why, as a flat—which was its first incarnation—it was hard to let. Its windows look smack into the face of a stucco wall, where a house was sheared and sealed off when this block was built. It is only a few yards from the assembly and collection point for dustbins. The main flue of the heating-apparatus, though concealed behind quick-drying plaster, forms a far larger and more obstructive bulge than any steel girder. It also, by some well-known thermal process, attracts all the smuts within a considerable radius and distributes them, with a graduated effect, on the upper walls and ceiling. It blows off like a whale, too, when Eldritch—or whoever is in charge of it—performs some recurrent function. You simply can't hear yourself speak then.

Once, when Bessingham House was rather touting for custom—that is to say, when the Syndicate was going bankrupt—and Mr. Kirby was manager, the Letting Office was also a Specimen Flat, or part of it; and Mr. Kirby hung out amid Jacobean chairs, and plush, and brocade, and old warming-pans. But that's all over; long ago. As the block filled up, these furnishings were returned to the shop that had lent them, and as a matter of fact it is the former Specimen Flat that is now occupied by the woman who keeps a crèche for dogs. The Letting Office was, as it were, chased along the corridor, —for at this stage it was continually letting even itself—until at length it reached that point by the emergency exit where, as this was virtually un-inhabitable, it was allowed to remain.

Such, then, are Mr. Todman's quarters. It is here that he works, and next door—with the other half of the bulge—that he sleeps. In his office he has been provided with a table and two chairs (but the comfortable one is, of course, for clients), a telephone, a second-hand filing-cabinet, and a typewriter which seldom completes even half a page without jamming or having to be turned upside-down while a hooked wire is put back in a hole. It might also be noted that though he has been here for the best part of four years now, the table is still too low for him, or the uneasy chair too high. He seldom sits down without bumping his knees, which for this reason— it can perhaps be revealed—are almost permanently black and blue. But if he complained, he might lose the job. If he jacked up the table on old telephone-directories, which he has occasionally dreamt of doing, then again, he fears, he would at the very best be cautioned for not keeping this pitiful office in a manner consonant with the dignity of a syndicate in liquidation. So he suffers and controls himself, and sometimes looks like a backward, overgrown schoolboy at too small a desk in a kindergarten. And this, once again, is what he is doing now.

"I see, Miss Pattinson," he says, as he inscribes another meaningless symbol on his blotting-pad. "Yes, I quite see that."

"Well, then," says Miss Pattinson—who, as you may remember, is the actual tenant of No. 22, Huddleston House, and was moved with her branch of the unarmed forces to the sea-coast of Lancashire, but now appears to be back; "well, then," she says, "what am I to do?"

"Rather awkward," says Mr. Todman.

"Oh, Mr. Todman, it's really worse than that. I mean, I suppose I *should* have had a written agreement. And perhaps I *should* have done something when he didn't pay me. But then—well, he had nowhere to go, you know, poor man. And—well, of course, he isn't exactly an ally, but he's a refugee, and—well, one wanted to do what one could."

"Quite," says Mr. Todman, with the utmost politeness, and deleting the last symbol.

"And then, you see, he's really doing quite important work. I mean, there's this paper that he writes for. And if they wanted him to broadcast —well, they might, you know—in the European Service, I suppose he's got to be—well, in touch."

Miss Pattinson then looks hopefully and trustfully across the table. It is just faintly borne in on Mr. Todman that this is about the fourth time that she has made these points; as it may also be borne in on him that she is remarkably good at representing the other side. But she's kind-hearted, you see, as well as plain. She's trying to be fair; or perhaps one should say just. And she does occasionally slip in a word for herself.

"Naturally," she says, "it's inconvenient for Mr. Vardas. But then *I* didn't know we were going to come back; and as a matter of fact—well, last night, you know; it doesn't seem a *very* good time to be in London. Is it often as bad as that, Mr. Todman?"

"Oh, you mustn't worry," says Mr. Todman, heroically. "It's mostly noise, you know."

But not entirely. He has been trying, in fact, to forget one particular thud; for he has since learnt—and it is no rumour this time—that there has been a power of damage at Combermere Court. No lives were lost, for it was still being redecorated for the Americans, and even largely rebuilt, so that no one was sleeping there. But if there was enough destruction, they may move on. Here? It is this that haunts him. He wouldn't trust them not to. His fitful security flickers again. He jerks himself together.

"I beg your pardon, Miss Pattinson?"

"Well, I was only saying—well, of course there's no *permanent* damage ——" (Here Mr. Todman barks one of his knees again)—"but it *was* rather tiresome of him to paste things up on my walls."

"Mr. Vardas, you mean?" There's a memory, too, of a search through a salvage-bin, and of Popham grinning. Not soothing or pleasant. In fact, if one *could* help Miss Pattinson—— But how *can* one? Enough troubles and rows here, God knows, without taking on somebody else's.

"——I mean," she is saying, with that earnest and equine expression, "that I *know* I've got an actual *bed* at the moment. A friend of mine—in the office—*most* kind; but then she's at Harrow—I mean, her people live there—and anyhow it can't go on." Perhaps this isn't quite clear. "I mean, of *course* one's a bother."

Clarity, however, it would appear, hasn't even yet been achieved. Or perhaps Mr. Todman was thinking of that bomb again.

"Not at all, Miss Pattinson," he says. "Not at all."

She looks puzzled; and his ears start glowing slightly.

"Have I said the wrong thing?" he asks, anxiously.

"No, no, Mr. Todman. You've been *most* kind. But you see—well, the whole point is, Mr. Vardas just says he won't go. I mean, the arrears are nothing. I mean, I know that's my own fault—in a way. But—well, couldn't *you* turn him out ?"

This isn't exactly Beauty appealing to Chivalry. It's just a very plain woman of about forty-four asking a much-harassed man with weak lungs for help. In a way (as Miss Pattinson has just said) he would like to give it, too. He is not such a slave—though he *is* a slave—but that the thought, at least, of kicking Mr. Vardas in the seat of the pants has a certain attraction. Yet apart from the fact that Mr. Vardas looks a wiry little fellow—particularly when he hasn't shaved within the last few hours—and that Mr. Todman is all length and no breadth, there is the point that a manager mustn't assault even a sub-tenant; for that is another route by which a manager goes out on his ear. So he merely stabs at the blotting-pad.

"We haven't the power," he says, regretfully—though he is not displeased with that "we." "Unless, of course, he makes a nuisance of himself in some way; and even then——"

Even then, he was about to add, it would be Miss Pattinson on whom the Syndicate would drop. But he is interrupted. He has reckoned without another element in his visitor's personality.

"Oh, Mr. Vardas would *never* do that!" she declares. "He's a foreigner, I know, but he's got wonderful manners. I'm not sure he wasn't a *professor* at home—in his own country, I mean. At any rate, he's a most cultured, a most *interesting* man. Oh, no, he'd never do anything like that!"

Even Mr. Todman suddenly wonders if Miss Pattinson is in love with her incubus. He decides that she can't be; that such a passion is impossible. Yet love, ladies and gentlemen, has more than one aspect; and certainly —or almost certainly—if a rival appeared and attempted to rob Miss Pattinson of her protégé, it would take a lot to make her let go. After all, she found him. She has been boasting about him, up in Lancashire, for quite a considerable time. As a political exile—for it is thus that she likes to think of him—he hasn't only made her feel more important, but has been a link with romance. Mazzini, you know. Kosciusko. Kropotkin. Not to mention Mrs. Annie Besant. She blinks as some of these thoughts now return to her; though of course he has no *right* to refuse to move out.

"But what am I to *do*, Mr. Todman ?"

"Well, Miss Pattinson——" another stab—"have you tried your solicitor?"

"Oh, yes, but he's *hopeless*. You see, he's been annoyed with me all along, because I wouldn't let him draw up a lease. And now, as there isn't one, he says he can't do anything. But as it turns out, you see—— Well, I—I suppose you haven't got *another* flat. Just a *small* one ?"

"What, for Mr. Vardas ?"

"Oh, no! For me. I mean, I could move some of my things, and——"

Mr. Todman is shaking his head, and Miss Pattinson's voice dies away.

"Not a chance, I'm afraid," he is saying. "Besides, we've got a waiting-list that long."

"Oh, dear. I see." Another blink. "Well, I couldn't really afford it, anyhow. Well, perhaps I could, I mean, but of course——"

At this point Mr. Todman's telephone-bell suddenly rings.

"Excuse me," he says; though really, he is thinking, there is no reason for prolonging this interview. And then: "Hullo?"

Worried as she is, even Miss Pattinson observes the deepening tint of his ears. His sentences, also, appear to be both broken and meaningless—not that it is her nature, good soul, to poke her nose into other people's affairs. She waits, perhaps, mainly because she can't think what else to do; or partly because she mustn't leave without thanking him and saying Good-bye. But her mind is elsewhere when he says Good-bye himself, through the telephone, and lays it down with a sigh.

"Too bad," he murmurs; and Miss Pattinson is recalled from her dreams.

"I—I beg your pardon, Mr. Todman?"

"Oh, nothing. At least . . ." He hesitates. And then, though not seriously affected by the news that he has just heard, he is compelled—for, after all, it is a little dramatic and quite red-hot—to pass it on.

"You knew Miss Kenton-Hinksey?" he asks.

"Oh, yes. Well, just to speak to." And then the tense goes off, with only slightly delayed action. "'Knew'? You don't mean——"

"Oh, no. I hope not. But she's been pretty ill just lately. One cold after another. Pneumonia. I—I heard of it because of the Fire-Watching, of course. Then she went away—she didn't want to, I gather, but the doctor insisted; and now—well, it's her heart, they say; that was *her* lawyer on the line just now. They've got her in a hospital somewhere—lucky, I dare say, to find room; but they don't know how long it'll be, and meanwhile—well, she wants to let her flat. Furnished, of course."

"Oh, *poor* thing! How *dreadful!*"

"Yes," says Mr. Todman, making a note on an old envelope now. "Been a lot of illness, though. Oh, a shocking amount. All over this block, too." He pulls himself together; for undoubtedly it would have been worse—much worse—if that telephone-call had been from the Syndicate again, with another threat or complaint. It is even better, in a sense, than a ball-cock. For a moment he looks quite cheery. "Well——" he begins, half-rising.

"Oh, Mr. Todman—I know it's an awful thing to say—just now, I mean—but do you think—— Well, couldn't *I* have it?"

"Have what?" says Mr. Todman, subsiding and knocking one of his knees again.

"Her flat. How much is it? What does she want?"

Quick thinking here for Mr. Todman. Of course there is a waiting-list for furnished flats, too. But as against this, Miss Pattinson is an old and reliable tenant.   And even if he isn't particularly sorry for her for being so weak-minded, a bird in the hand is far less trouble than any amount on the very nearest bush.   He can settle it now, perhaps, without even writing a letter.

"Well, Miss Pattinson, I don't know that I——   Well, you know what the rush is like.   She's asking six guineas."

"A week ?   I could take it by the week, you mean ?"

"Well—well, yes."   Why not, and get it over ?   "If you decide now, of course."

"Oh, but of course I do."   The bank can lend it me, she thinks rapidly, until I sell something.   "Is that all right, Mr. Todman ?"   It's got to be; I can't *stand* being so far from the office.   "How soon can I go in ?"

It's settled, by the intervention of Providence—which as usual, perhaps, must give with one hand and take away with the other.   For Miss Kenton-Hinksey, flat on her back in a public ward on the outskirts of Bristol—which was where she was taken when she collapsed, in lodgings, near her old seaside home, and where, also, there is again quite a sprinkling of bombs—we of course have nothing but sympathy.   We might even spare a little for Mrs. Wardrop, too, who in spite of the truce that followed that rumpus, must henceforth—or at any rate as soon as she hears of it from her Mrs. Trudgeon—keep wondering if she shouldn't have been more patient with a prospective heart-case.

But for Miss Cicely Pattinson we can actually see rather more than a break in the clouds.   It is true that she must now find herself paying for two flats, that one of them—and the cheaper—comes to almost as much as her salary, and that already, owing to expenses and generosity while away, she has plunged deep into her by no means extensive securities.   Yet apart from the fact that almost everyone with securities has for a long time been doing the same thing, there is a further point to be considered.   Not, as yet, by herself. Indeed, she may never fully appreciate it.   But it is *our* view that when Mr. Vardas finds his benefactress installed on the same floor of Huddleston House, and almost certainly dropping in whenever she wishes to discuss Central Europe, or to get at one of her locked cupboards or drawers, he, too, will begin to wonder how long he can stand this.   It won't, we should say, be his conscience that troubles him.   But he will be irritated, and indignant, and the persecution mania which he has so carefully nursed will be likely to flare up again.   Moreover, we should be extremely surprised if, with his peculiar talents and during Miss Pattinson's long absence, he has not discovered at least one equally benevolent dupe or victim elsewhere.   For they still exist, and if you are like Mr. Vardas you will generally contrive to get in touch with them.   We should say, therefore, that though Miss Pattinson may well weep when he turns on her and leaves her, she won't have to pay that six guineas a week for more than a month or two.   And then, of course whether poor Miss Kenton-Hinksey is better again or not, there is always the waiting-list.

Two more attacks of Whatever-it-was should perhaps also be placed on record. Miss Bryony Bretton, though she escaped pneumonia, had a short, sharp, feverish cold which kept her away from her work of national importance for the best part of a week. She wouldn't, as a matter of fact, even have had a doctor, but for the situation which had arisen by which, though you didn't need one, and they were all overdriven, you must still have a medical certificate. But he only came once—for this, on the other hand, was the advantage of the situation—and scrawled it hastily, and vanished. Otherwise, Miss Bretton was attended by Smashums, who provided her lunch, and Echo, who provided her breakfast and supper. She took over Echo's bed, or divan, in the day-time, so that she could telephone and listen to the radio, but somehow this rather infectious procedure led to no spread of the plague. Echo bore up, did the shopping more rapidly than ever, and except for this purpose, and her own work of national importance, was never out of the flat. So for that week she saw no one, or no friend, except Bugs; and Bugs didn't exactly spare her. For she was bored as well as suffering from symptoms; and as there was no one else available now, she saved it all up for Echo. A little temper was also permissible, surely, if she was ill, and Echo wasn't.

"I *told* you to bring in an evening paper," she said, when Echo came hurrying back with her arms full of other requirements. "No, *don't* rush off like that! You've left it too late now." And then she said: "I don't know *what* your night-gowns are made of, but I just split them as fast as I wear them." And then: "But you don't *know* how awful I feel, or how maddening it is when I could have been going out to-night. Such waste! It's *infuriating!*" And then: "I say—did Mr. Haggerston-Hawksworth ask after me to-day?"

"I'm afraid I never saw him," said Echo; for with the Ministry of Redirection now expanding like the Universe, she had been moved into another block.

"Oh," said Bugs, who had overlooked this point. "Well, I should have thought one of you might have taken the trouble—— There! What did I tell you? There's the kettle boiling over. *Run*, can't you!"

So Echo ran; and it wasn't so much being slanged and cursed that she minded, for she knew well enough, as the eldest of four, what happened when people were ill; and particularly what happened when you and they were sharing the same quarters. No, what she minded—being Echo—was that though she could show patience, she couldn't feel it. She knew that even six months ago—or less, if you like—she would have been flattered, however tired she was, by any evidence that she was indispensable. It was

what she had been always wanting. And how grateful, too, she would have
been to do anything for Bugs, so long as they could be alone together.
So she was ashamed (being Echo) that something—well, herself, of course—
had changed. When, she wondered? And why? How long had she
really known it, and pretended that she didn't know it? She was a little
humbled, as she well might be, when so strong a habit had been so subtly
and yet swiftly undermined. But she knew that Bugs was selfish now.
She knew—well, that sailor had clinched it—that she *wasn't* such a success
with men, though she was always trying to be, and always managed to set
off as if she was going to be; and, what was more, if she would only admit
it, could have had all the pity, and sympathy, and help, and comfort in the
world.

But girls like that, thought Echo, *won't* admit it. Then she was horrified
because she had even secretly alluded to poor Bugs as a Girl Like That.
And then she thought, I needn't talk as if I was such a roaring success myself.
I'm not. I never have been. But then the glow came again, though it was
a glow (because she was Echo) with a thousand doubts in it; and somehow—
for it is all very mysterious, even when you are analysing it in a kitchenette
—she was thankful that she had been so busy this week, and had seen no
one except Bugs, and the people in the buses, and the people at the office.
And she was more patient than ever with Bugs that evening; though Bugs—
despite far less sensibility at any time—suspected something that she could
put no name to, and in consequence can seldom have been more imperious
and exacting in her demands.

She couldn't touch Echo, or Jemima, though. You can only hurt girls
like this when they love you. And the plain truth of the matter was that
Jemima, or Echo, was just waiting now, in a mist that wasn't all fatigue, for
the long and on her own part once almost passionate association to come to
a natural end. *That* wasn't selfish. Or if it was, even in the faintest degree,
then it couldn't be helped. Because I *know* now, thought the temporary
sick-nurse and supplier of spare night-gowns; and once one knows, so much
seems suddenly to be taken out of one's hands.

"Do I *look* awful?" the invalid was asking, though as she was also
examining herself in a hand-mirror, she might have been thought to have
some rough idea.

"No, darling," said Echo, which was the truth again, for nothing, it
seemed, could affect her companion's looks. She heard the enclitic endearment, but had no wish to withdraw it. For after all, she was thinking,
if I hadn't come to live here . . . Well, of course, however I've changed,
I shall *never* forget that. So that she was even grateful to Bugs's Aunt Babs.

The remaining case, which evoked yet another of the rare and fleeting
doctors, was that of Miss June Margetson. She was to have a fortnight

of it altogether, though no one was aware of this yet. But the family of germs, or bugs, which had invaded her were a persistent lot—though not unduly violent—and refused to be hustled out. "Well," said Dr. Franklin, the physician in this instance, "I'm afraid these new drugs aren't *always* efficacious, and if they're not, we must just start again. In my opinion," he said—though naturally he wouldn't have said this if the cure had come off the first time—"some of the older methods are just as valuable."

Mrs. Margetson, to whom he made this confession, didn't ask him why on earth, in that event, he hadn't begun with the older methods. She was too polite, for one thing. He looked too tired, for another. And again, though there were moments when it wasn't all pleasure, even to a mother, to have a daughter tucked more or less safely up in bed, there was the strangest magic about his visits. For he had been the Margetsons' family doctor for fifteen years at Wallington Gardens; ever since, in fact, he had succeeded old Dr. Winslow, whose retirement had once appeared almost to presage the end of the world.

But it hadn't, of course. Or at any rate it had been a rather long-term omen. And meanwhile Dr. Franklin, so dull, so humourless, so monotonous with his infallibly-repeated anecdotes, had grown into a very solid bit of background. Not exactly for nothing, of course, as Geoffrey had sometimes complained. But when so much else had been swept or blasted away; when even a shop like Gilpin's had altered almost beyond recognition— for naturally, again, there had been no lasting improvement there since Mr. Musselberg's odd intervention; when all this had happened, how wonderful it was to find someone—whether he, too, was getting old now or not—who still behaved, when he turned up at all, precisely as he had behaved in the past.

One mustn't be pleased, and of course one wasn't, that poor June should be so ill. Yet if a doctor, by his mere presence and manner, could practically turn this little sitting-room into the drawing-room at Wallington Gardens —well, in any case, Mrs. Margetson certainly looked forward to his visits, and when he told her some of those old anecdotes again, she was far more touched than bored. She would have liked, in return, to explain that the only reason why she had neglected him for so long was that she had been too busy to bother about her own health, and that June, until now, had never had a cold for more than the permitted two days. But as against this, why put ideas into his head? Or why—which was even more important— —say anything that would make Wallington Gardens seem further away than it was? One is afraid that she did rather waste some of Dr. Franklin's time. It is true, also, that towards the end of his visits even she had had enough of some of the anecdotes, and that when she drew him into the sitting-room it was with a curious mixture of apprehension and sentiment, in which the latter didn't always prevail.

But she rather clung to him. She had to, it seemed. And she was as bitterly disappointed when he failed to appear—for even Dr. Franklin, in this present epoch, could hardly be in three or four places at once—as she almost, in a sense, regretted her daughter's recovery.

Well, there was another reason for that; or perhaps more than one other reason. Admittedly it had been hard work nursing as well as shopping, and cooking, and washing-up, and even putting in such time as could be spared at her unpaid war-work; and of course she didn't want poor June to become a permanent invalid. But Heaven knew, thought Mrs. Margetson, that it was the rest that she needed far more than anything else. And, then when she had been at her illest—as some, but perhaps not all, may be surprised to learn—she had also been at her gentlest and kindest, and so much more like the June of those distant days. And then, once more—never to be forgotten henceforth, but never, of course, to be mentioned between them again—there had been the night when Mrs. Margetson's daughter had turned her face to the wall and wept.

"I know," she suddenly said through her sobs—but we can't print them; "I know," she said, "I've been a beast to you here. I know it's all awful for you, too. I know how you miss Daddy. I know I oughtn't to have had those rows with Robin. I know I'm a pest and a nuisance——"

"No, no, darling. You're not!"

"I *am*, I tell you," said June, with a flash of her more normal manner. "But—oh, mother—oh, mummie—you see, I've never told you, but—but you remember Peter?"

"Yes, darling," said Mrs. Margetson. This wasn't the truth—or not at the moment—for in the last phase at Wallington Gardens her child had been as secretive as she herself had been utterly baffled in the matter of catching up with or distinguishing her friends. Besides, weren't they *all* called Peter? Yet what else could she have said?

"Well," sobbed June, "that's the real reason. You see, since he was killed——"

She broke off. She appeared to be trying to force her head under the pillow.

"Oh, go away!" said her muffled voice. "Go away! Leave me! Oh, *please* go away!"

So Mrs. Margetson did go away. Sometimes she thought that she did vaguely remember one Peter more than the others; and presently, perhaps, she would even dig up what might or might not be his surname. Yet though her own heart was far from unscathed now—and indeed one could scarcely have called it unscathed before—there had to be a pang of joy in the midst of her sorrow. For she had been told something. Even if it was exaggerated, and perhaps it was; even if it meant that her child would now never marry at all, which was another possibility; even if the confession had only been dragged from her by influenza—still Mrs. Margetson had been told something,

without asking to be told it.   And still, like rain in the desert, her child—
if only by accident, perhaps—had once more addressed her as Mummie.

Of course, she thought, I mustn't ever say anything more to her about it,
unless she says something to me; for she wasn't so sunk in the past as to forget
what one might call her place.   And if she didn't expect anything more
to be said, then that shows, in turn, that Mrs. Margetson, for all her dreams,
was a good deal of a realist.   For no further confession was made; Mrs.
Margetson must again be told that she didn't know how to make coffee,
by a daughter who glared at her in a decidedly menacing manner.   June,
in fact, was on the mend, and was taking up the reins again.   She was quite
abominably rude and short-tempered during the rest of her convalescence.

Yet still Mrs. Margetson recalled that "Mummie," and scrupulously
forgot, or overlooked, that "Go away!"   Somehow, and for some time,
she still couldn't help feeling a little happier; though the queer thing was,
as you will have observed, that all this feeling had come from her daughter's
grief.   As has been pointed out, it is rather a strange world, and isn't likely
to be any less complex when engaged in a global war.

But that is all about June's illness now, and all the other illnesses.   Except
that when it came to Dr. Franklin's last visit, and his still unalterable tonic,
and when Mrs. Margetson hurried round to Hernshaw's in the main road,
she wasn't only met with a locked door, but with a notice gummed up behind
it.   "This Branch," she read, "is Closed owing to Present Conditions.
All Services may be had at our Branch in Westbourne Grove."   However,
as that was miles away, Mrs. Margetson didn't attempt to go there.   So
that neither she nor anyone else could tell what had happened to the pale
chemist.

CHAPTER XII

IT WAS EARLY IN FEBRUARY, ALSO—PERHAPS PARTLY BECAUSE THE MOON WAS
propitious—that a summons went forth, on some rather blurred scraps of
paper, to the local Fire Guard.   Again it would appear that Authority,
still trying to treat the whole shocking business as something that could be
reduced to rules and reason, was about to amend, cancel, qualify, or elaborate
some of its previous instructions, and wanted a quorum for this purpose.
So it chose eight o'clock on a Tuesday evening, at a trysting-place known
as the Methodist Hall; and if any Watcher from Huddleston House should
be unable to read a fifth or sixth carbon-copy, then Party-Leader Popham
had seen to it that a much clearer announcement was pinned to the February
rota.   They couldn't, as he put it to one of his colleagues, very well get away
from that.

Not that he was proposing to attend himself; for there must be discipline
and decency in all things, and of course he mustn't take lessons at the same

time as the rest of the class. He had, indeed, already received and even partially understood the new directions, at a more private and exclusive meeting. Now he was in process of forgetting them, but his followers must of course take their turn. Do them good, he thought, as he pinned up the notice. Make 'em realise a bit more, perhaps, what things were like in Russia. So he also leapt out at them from time to time, to remind them of this appointment. And since they were all well aware that if they failed to keep it, they would be subject to the most terrible reprisals, it seemed —whether eight o'clock on a Tuesday evening happened to suit them or not— that at least his own troop would be there.

Gavin Guernsey, as you have been informed, was one of them; and though, as it happened, he had a power of reading to get through to-night, he supposed that he must also attend. He supped alone, on scraps from the refrigerator, for to-night, as it also happened, Derek was on duty at his Ministry; and it can't be said that his landlord and tenant had any great objection to that. When he had supped, he cleared the table. Then, as there still appeared to be about a quarter of an hour in hand, he picked up a typescript. And then, for though it was a puzzler he must do it justice, the next thing he knew was that it was three minutes to eight, and that he must run—so far as this had now become physically possible—unless he was to miss the fun.

That was his own rather sardonic term, as he marked the place. Then he put on his hat and overcoat again, descended, emerged, and started hurrying—torchless, because of the waning moon—towards the main road, and across it. and round another corner or two. But though he was late, it was all right, for the proceedings hadn't begun. The Methodist—or ex-Methodist—Hall was perhaps rather a poor advertisement for the kind of occasion that had brought him here, since the big windows at one end had been sucked out by blast and replaced with what looked like tarpaulin, while most of the porch had been destroyed by an incendiary bomb. It was also very, very cold—even colder, it seemed, than the streets outside—and extremely patriotically, or at any rate inadequately, lit. But the class had assembled, and were sitting muttering together—rather, thought Gavin (but perhaps the Gothic arches had something to do with this), as though awaiting a memorial service—and having given his name he slipped into a seat at the back. He noted, as he had noted last time, some already curiously-antiquated war-posters on the walls; placed there, perhaps, to dispel the spirit of Wesley. And again he observed—so far as it was possible to see them—that the congregation, of both sexes, was for the most part middle-aged, grey-faced, ugly, and (but of course he was only judging by appearances, and no doubt he would look the same to them) almost preternaturally stupid. But having formed these opinions, and having privately apologised if by any chance he was misjudging his fellow-creatures, he then, we are afraid, rather let his mind drift away.

Having no typescript now to distract it, either, it immediately passed to

some very familiar ideas. The first was that he was in love, of which he was
as positive as he was convinced that he didn't—again in his own terminology
—stand even a dog's chance. In fact, this was a kind of double idea, in which
the love-concept might often have a start of a few yards, but was invariably
overtaken before he could even begin to enjoy it. He knew both moments
so well. This-is-It, one might call them, and But-it's-hopeless. As to why
it was so hopeless, one might bring forth a number of reasons—such as
lack of experience in such matters, and a certain shock that he had been
through; but Gavin himself was far more ingenious than that. He became
maddened with rage, though there was no sign on the surface, if Love tried
to hold up its head. She wouldn't look at me, he told it angrily. Why
should she, he asked it? Yes, I know, he was good enough to admit, that
I've seen quite a lot of her lately, but that's only because she's so kind. She'd
be disgusted, she'd be horrified, she'd be *appalled*, if she knew what I was
thinking. Of course if I even hinted at it, it would all be over at once. A
man with one foot? A dull, dreary, tongue-tied, boring, uninteresting
blot on the earth? Good God, he groaned silently and crazily as if I
didn't *know* all that! And as if——

Here he fell heavily into the second of the familiar ideas. It centred
round two initials. R.J. For not only, with such blood in his veins, was
he bound to get duller and duller himself as time went on; but could you
see—though of course it had nothing to do with the owner of the initials—
the ghastly reception that *any* engagement would get? For despite the
above-mentioned conviction, he had worked it all out. The heavy, automatic
disapproval. The unbearable questions. The reminders, though never had
they been more unnecessary, of all his past failures. The constant and
watchful readiness for yet another disappointment. The critical eye. The
headmaster's grip on his very soul. And on top of all this—again it came
to him in his sensitive agony—how *could* you expect a girl like that even to
dream of putting up with a father-in-law like R.J.? It was a deadlock—
or as such this perhaps rather exceptional character saw it. And again,
once more, he must torture himself by thinking, as deliberately and desperately
as possible, of that frightful week-end near Windsor at the beginning of the
year.

He thought of the pressure that had brought him there. Of the inevitable
pretence on the part of R.J. that he had come without being asked. Of his
own, almost prodigious efforts to make this a *different* kind of visit; and of
their complete and almost immediate frustration. Of the weather—not
that this, in itself, was anyone's fault—which had kept him indoors, where
he and R.J. must yet seek, though in vain, to avoid each other. Of the mis-
placed sense of honour or duty which had compelled him to stick it out to
the bitter end. Of all the silences. Of all the odious moments when both
parties had tried to speak at the same time, and one of them—himself,
of course—had felt, in consequence, a dreadful load of discourtesy and even

sin. Of R.J.'s generosity with that last bottle of sherry—still an awful memory; because of course one had only shared in it from sheer nervousness, and in complete ignorance—that's to say, until after the final dose—that one was finishing off the cellar. Yes, of *course* it would only have lasted another few days; but how *like* R.J. to force it on one, and then—or so it seemed to Gavin—to create yet another grudge. Some time having elapsed since the New Year, he could see now that this incident had perhaps been no more than a molehill. But there had been further molehills. One or other of the two kinsmen had been perpetually stumbling over them. The effect had been decidedly cumulative, though they had never quarrelled—for this was as unimaginable as that they should have felt for one moment at ease; and indeed, if it came to that, they were already involved in a series of fresh and protracted misunderstandings about their next meeting.

R.J.—and Derek had got to lump this if he didn't like it—seemed to be veering, though guardedly, towards a return-visit. As often as Gavin had written or telephoned to say Yes, of course, and that he himself could easily spend a night in the sitting-room, the prospective guest had at once begun hedging again. But as he had also made it clear that he was only doing this as a reproach—"After all, it's a long time since I've asked you to do anything, so far as *I* can remember"—it had then become necessary, amid pangs of contorted conscience, to urge him more warmly than ever. This, for the moment, got him to the stage of treating the visit as a favour, and perhaps, if one could have kept him there, he would have dropped the idea. But a chance word, even a chance inflexion, would apparently rouse his suspicions. He didn't exactly *say* now that he was coming because he wasn't wanted, but one could feel it—or Gavin could—as a leading motive. So that Gavin, though as firmly hospitable as he was allowed to be, was again and already beginning to be worn out by it all.

"Look here, father——" this was an imaginary conversation, and shouldn't even have been that, for the official lecturer on pyrotechnics was now well away with his address; "look here, father, if only you'd just *once* say what you really mean, and stick to it, then I do assure you—honestly—truthfully——"

Hullo! There she was; after all. Naturally, though we haven't said so, the inattentive young gentleman in the back row had been looking out for her, hopefully, from the moment of his arrival, and even as he had hastened through the moonlit streets before that. He hadn't—because, one supposes of that dog's chance—adopted the more practical procedure of ringing up before starting, or of attempting to call for her as an escort. But there she was. And alone, so far as he could make out. So that if only he *had* run up or called for her——

He became violently excited. Far more so, you would have said, than the rest of the congregation, though they were listening to the most bloodcurdling description of a new kind of double-action bomb. It appeared according to the curiously academic-looking lecturer with the neck like a plucked fowl, that you couldn't positively identify it until it went off. You must therefore approach it from behind a low brick wall—he didn't explain how you were to find or construct this in the middle of an attack—and if it did this, you were to do that. If it did the other thing, it was presumably the end of you; but he didn't harp on the macabre. Far from it. His whole thesis, in fact, was based on the hitherto unproved theory that H.E., as it was known in the profession, could be almost totally disregarded. Or at any rate that a class being instructed in fire-watching had better leave such a subject alone. And no one—though it did cross Gavin's mind for a moment—showed the slightest sign of questioning this rather queer point of view. In fact, they showed no reaction at all. Though perhaps it was all seeping in.

"D'ye see?" the lecturer kept saying. And as quite a different lecturer had once employed this expression, it must now be confessed that Gavin had gone back to Oxford. And that he wasted some time there—with Jock, and Ronald, and Charles, of course—though he was still also looking at the back of a girl's head. On the other hand, he wasn't a complete fool, and as the lecture was adjusted, whether deliberately or not, to the very meanest intelligence, and involved an almost unexampled amount of repetition and recapitulation, he could probably have scraped through a test-paper afterwards—if there had been one.

But there wasn't. There wasn't even a *viva voce* to-night. At a given moment the expert, after the very briefest peroration about all doing our best, suddenly stepped from the low dais with an air—but this was possibly an illusion—of being ashamed of the whole thing; and though a few female Fire-Guards seemed to be drawn towards him, as if in this case they were going to ask for his autograph, the rest of the meeting broke up.

Gavin thought that if he had any sense he would now dash for the doorway. He even reflected that Providence had probably put him in the back row for this purpose. After which, he advanced slightly, and said: "Hullo."

"Oh," said Echo. "Hullo!"

What an absolutely enchanting voice she had.

"Bugs not here?" said Gavin; and cared less for the sound of this rather absurd inquiry.

"No," said Echo. "It's so cold, you see. So they let her off. I mean, because she's been ill."

"But she's all right really, isn't she?"

Not that I care; so why on earth did I turn on that *tremolo*?

"Oh, yes. Practically."

"Well," said Gavin, but not even troubling now to appear relieved; "perhaps we could walk back together."

"Yes, of course," said Echo. And then neither of them could think what to say.

G

Yet in the first, short street they again said how cold it was, and fully concurred with each other. In the second and rather longer street Gavin asked if his companion had noticed the lecturer's neck, and they talked about that for a bit. And in the third and longest street, which led into the main road, Echo suddenly said that what she really disliked was when people, whoever they were, started talking about Man-Power.

"It's so *rude*," she said. "It's such an *awful* sort of thing to say. Or even think!"

In theory, her fellow-pedestrian could have embraced her. For he couldn't, as the moderns put it, have agreed with her more. It was an expression which couldn't fail to nauseate and affront him—and millions of others, one would imagine, too. But he didn't say this. He didn't even explain that the discovery of this fresh point in common had caused him to become more infatuated than ever. He just said: "By Jove, yes." And then he was astonished to hear himself add: "I say—would you care to have a drink ?"

Mark you, he wasn't so lacking in knowledge of the world as to think it the least strange, in these days, to take a girl into a saloon bar—even though this didn't happen to be one of his own habits. No, the astonishing part was that he had issued the invitation at least two seconds, he was convinced, before the notion had entered his head. For if the notion had come first, it was inconceivable that he should have been so daring. However, it hadn't; and as he was still trying to account for this very unusual form of internal telepathy, behold, another audible voice was saying: "Oh, Gavin—well, I wish *you'd* have a drink. Because you see—well, I don't really want one."

Nor did Gavin, if it comes to that. He was, in fact, no keener on drinking at this moment, in the ordinary sense of the word, than was Ben Jonson when he addressed those well-known lines to Celia. Or perhaps even less; for, on second thoughts, there may well have been a very practicable mug on the poet's table; while Celia, if she existed, was almost certainly elsewhere at the time. But Echo wasn't. Nor did it occur to her companion that she was telling him to go and drink by himself. In fact, they were now crossing the main road with the clear, if undeclared, intention of entering the Royal Oak together. Which in one if not both of their opinions was a great deal better than returning to Huddleston House.

They edged round the black-out defences. They blinked as they came into the light. The saloon bar was fairly full—again with divided groups at each end of the counter, but with further clients between them and on the chairs and benches as well. But there were a couple of unoccupied chairs quite near the door; so that Gavin said: "Sit there—I'll be back in a second." Then he said: "Are you *quite* sure you won't have something ?" And then, as the girl shook her head, he sped off in search of swipes.

He still didn't want any. He was also afflicted with the recurrent fear that Maisie would engage him in conversation, or even try to sell him another bottle of Auld Sandy, so that Echo would then think that it was his custom to be matey with barmaids. However, one couldn't very well sit here and spend nothing. Furthermore, thank Heaven, he was served by the consumptive-looking man. So that he was back, as he had promised, in almost no time. He sat down. He put his glass on a table. He said: "Sorry"—which was meant to refer to his very brief absence. And then: "I say —will you have a cigarette?"

But Miss Marsham didn't think she would. She was quite happy, she said; and this was true, subject to the trifling qualification that she would now have liked to be offered marriage. Yet she was scarcely expecting this, perhaps; and anyhow it was wonderful not to have gone straight back. Alone at last, she thought; though they weren't alone, and had been alone more than once before. But only for odd moments, for she remembered them all. So did Gavin. But he was thinking exactly the same thing.

This implied a short silence, which Echo rather liked, though her squire —after a few more seconds—began racking his brains for words. She would think him a fool, of course, if he said nothing, He couldn't very well say "This is marvellous!"—though it was, even in the saloon bar at the Royal Oak. Yet just as he was becoming desperate, he was calmed; by Echo, of course.

"Do you know," she suddenly observed, "I've forgotten all that man said already. But he was awfully dull, wasn't he?"

"Amazingly," said Gavin. "Have you heard from your brothers again?"

He didn't really want her to have any relations at all; but this wasn't a bad question, he thought, from a man with his head spinning round. He even looked eager as he put it, though not entirely from interest in the subject.

"No," said his guest. She seemed a little cast down, and he cursed himself. Then she smiled, and the eyebrow went up, and he was enraptured. "I had an awfully funny letter, though," she was saying, "from Anne."

"Your sister," said Gavin, just to show now—for his condition is seldom marked by complete consistency—how well he knew them all. "At school, you mean," he added, with the same intention.

"Yes. I——"

"Is she pretty?" asked Gavin's voice, in what certainly seemed to be rather an urgent and threatening manner. At the next instant he was visited with a violent desire to kick himself. Why on earth had he said that?

"Well, yes," said his guest; "as a matter of fact, she is. And she's terribly amusing."

"Is she really?"

That's a bit more like it. But I bet she hasn't got an eyebrow like yours.

"Yes—only rather naughty, I'm afraid, too." The guest began to gurgle. "In fact," she said, "she's really just like—Oh, bother! I've forgotten the name." Gavin appeared to be lacerated with rather fruitless sympathy.

"Oh, no! I remember. The naughty schoolgirl in—— But I don't suppose you've ever read it."

"Never read what ?" Just a faint hint of the publisher here.

"*Little Betsy and the Brownies*," said Echo. "But——"

"But of *course* I've read it! Why, don't you realise——"

"Well, don't you *adore* it! *I* do!"

Gavin's voice then so very nearly said what he did adore, that he was forced, in self-defence, to take a sip at the swipes. Then he nearly choked, but not quite. And then :—

"It's ours!" he said, proudly. "Dingle and Frisby's. My firm. Didn't you know that ?"

"Oh, I say! Not really!" Just look at her whole face now. "Do you mean, you know the woman who wrote it ?"

"Well," said Gavin, suffering a slight fall ; "no, I haven't exactly met her. Well, she's getting on, you know, and she lives in Cornwall, I think, and——"

"Oh, how thrilling!"

Just look at those eyes—which were beginning to swim a little. And those parted lips. To-morrow, thought Gavin—who only this morning had been doing his utmost to resist old Bendish on this precise project—we'll order another impression. Of course we will! I only wish we could call it the Echo Edition, and print it on hand-made paper, and then I'd give her a copy, and——

"I say," said his voice again, before he could stop it, for it seemed good enough at these somewhat extraneous remarks; "why *did* they call you 'Echo' ?"

The girl's expression changed.

"They didn't," she said, fingering her hand-bag. "I—I thought you knew. No, I didn't," she added. "That was a lie. Why should you ? It was Bugs that started it. I mean, she thought of it, and then everyone seemed to sort of take it up, and——"

"Bugs ?" Astonishing. Because it was a most exquisite name.

"Yes ; and I rather liked it then, I suppose. Well, you see——" she wasn't quite so pale, and in Gavin's opinion looked lovelier than ever—"you see, I've got the most *ridiculous* name—really."

"Oh," said Gavin. "What ?" asked his voice.

"Jemima," said Miss Marsham, and looked away. Now he'll hate me, she thought, for in her own condition one never believes but that at any moment one is going to be hated. She was quite wrong, though. For another instant, perhaps, it did seem to Gavin that both she and those delicious syllables had dissolved, as it were, before his eyes. But at the next he had more than recovered himself. For in the first place he was now sickened by the thought that Bugs—not that he hated her, either, but she was still, so he imagined, a rival—had had the power to do a thing like that. While in the second place it is probably true that if she had said she was called Mildred or Muriel, he would immediately—or as fast as he could take in the news—have thought this name exquisite, too. Jemima. It *was* exquisite, because he loved her. No, it was exquisite, anyhow. Besides, it was as though she had opened a secret door to him, and though still shy enough, he went rushing in.

"Jemima!" he said. "But it *isn't* ridiculous! It—it suits you *far* better."

"Do you think so?" She seemed enormously encouraged; though he was appalled to think that it could ever have given her the very least distress.

"Of course!" he said—so loudly that one or two of the other clients looked round. But he didn't notice them, and they could hear no more. "In fact," he was saying, "if you don't mind awfully—well, do you think *I* could call you that?"

"If you like," she said. The eyebrow lifted. The forehead remained perfectly smooth. "It's what I used to be called. At home, I mean."

She withdrew—though naturally not physically—into a world of which Gavin knew nothing. How shocking it was to think of the years when he might have known her, and hadn't. It was almost unbearable. Two parents, two brothers, and a sister—all with this advantage over him. On the other hand, she was here now. And the next time he spoke to her—if he had the nerve—he was going to call her what *they* called her. For it wasn't only a singularly beautiful, but a most touching and affecting name. Besides —he didn't know that he had already passed through another doorway here—it seemed to get her away from Bugs.

So what should he say now? He couldn't imagine. Yet that rather untrustworthy voice spoke up again. And so did Miss Marsham.

"About books——" they were both saying.

"Go on," said Gavin. This wasn't the least like the same sort of thing when it happened with R.J.

"Well," said his guest, "I was only going to say that that isn't the *only* book I like. I mean, just in case you thought it was."

The point hadn't occurred to him. But it was the right topic, for it seemed that they agreed about books as well. Or that if they didn't entirely, then wherever they differed he felt a particular appreciation of Miss Marsham's taste. For now he saw how prejudiced he had been, and how invaluable it was to have encountered her point of view. By Jove, in fact, he had been quite wrong in one or two cases. He said so, very earnestly indeed. Miss Marsham looked pleased, though a little puzzled. "Oh, no," she said. "You mustn't *pretend* to agree."

"I'm not," said Gavin, which was the truth by now. "I mean, I just hadn't thought of it that way. Well, you see——" now, this was very important— "I've never had a chance——"

Whoa! Steady. Don't go and frighten her by talking about men and women. Keep away from all that, or of *course* she'll get up and leave you.

"A chance of what?" asked Jemima.

"I've forgotten what I was going to say. Look here——" he knew what he was going to say now, though, stubbornly as he was trying to avoid it —"do you think I'm keeping you here too long? Do you think Bugs——"

"Oh. Yes. Well, perhaps I ought to get back."

It was now inexplicable that he should have had his impulse; that again— for he was vaguely aware of having done it before—it should be *he* (whose sole wish was to stay here for ever) who had so stupidly and unnecessarily broken the spell. Why? What harm would it do Bugs to be alone for once? But he had done it. He had tumbled, though too inexpert to see it this way, into a very old psychological snare. The more you want something to last, and the more conscious you are of this, the more you yourself must struggle to hasten the end. So Miss Marsham got up, and of course, though reviling himself, he must get up, too. The glass of swipes remained where it was; still almost untasted. He was hurrying ahead of her—and also hobbling just a little, as he was apt to after sitting still for a while—so as to guide her through the screens and black curtains.

"There's a step here," he said; for the moon had gone now, or clouds must have covered it, and it was as dark and almost as silent outside as on the Great Gromboolian Plain. The only sound, indeed, was the faint, far-off whine from a lathe, where the closed garage on the other side of the road was still making engines of death. "Wait a second," he said. "Shut your eyes, and then open them. Now. Are you all right?"

She said she was. She didn't add that she was even more accustomed to the London black-out than he was. And neither of them attempted to take the other's arm.

Soon—far too soon for both of them—they were at the corner. "Are you all right?" asked Gavin again.

"Yes, of course. Oh! Am I going too quickly? Gavin—are *you* all right?"

"Of course." It's only that I can't bear leaving you. "Why shouldn't I be?"

"Well, I—I meant your leg."

"My leg?" He stopped dead. "My *foot?*" He was shaken to the very core. "Why—why, who told you?"

"Oh, please——" but there was no chance of anyone seeing her eyes swimming now—"I didn't mean to remind you—to upset you—to—— Well, it was one of the porters, I think."

"Which?" He sounded terrifying.

"Oh, Gavin, I can't remember. But *please* don't be angry——"

"I'm not. Not the least. Only——"

"I couldn't tell him *not* to tell me—could I? I mean, I know you never talk about it, and it must be *awful* for you, but after all if it was in a—in a battle——"

"It wasn't," said Gavin, still standing fast. "Damn those porters," he said. "Look here—Jemima——" this was the first time that he had actually used the name, though as he did it without thinking, you can deduce what you like; "look here," he was saying; "I've got to get this straight. I've never *been* in a battle. I've never been *near* one. It was simply . . ."

The story came pouring out. So far as it was possible to do so, he made it an even more disgraceful story than his worst detractor could have done. And at the end he was fairly breathless as he gasped: "So now you know."

What did he expect her to do then? Spurn him in the darkness? Leave him without a word? She did neither.

She said: "Oh, *poor* Gavin! Were you—were you so fond of her, then?"

"My old nurse? Hannah? No, I *told* you I wasn't. That's what makes it so utterly and hoplessly——"

"Oh, Gavin, it doesn't! And I'm so thankful—I can't help it—I'm so *thankful* you weren't trying to kill anyone."

"Oh," said Gavin. "No, I wasn't doing that. Well, I never got so far as that."

"I know. It's such a relief."

Gavin bit his lip very hard. Not that he had the least wish to laugh at this angel in human form. On the contrary, he was abased by her gentleness. It did occur to him that if nobody tried to kill anybody—— But then they had, and they still were, and they weren't making such a bad job of it, either. And yet she had spoken those words. And all he could do, it seemed, was to bite his lip.

"Do you mean, I oughtn't to feel like that?" she asked.

"No," said Gavin. "But not on account of me," he said, brusquely. "Shall we—shall we go on?"

They went on, past Bessingham House. I've hurt her feelings now, I suppose, thought Gavin. Why on earth did I snap at her like that? But if I hadn't, you see, I should have gone much too far; and then that would have been the end of it all.

Two simultaneous thoughts crashed into each other. She's not put off by my blasted foot. She probably is, only she's too kind to say so. A third and extremely unwanted thought swamped everything else. Of *course* she's engaged to someone or other; she couldn't possibly not be. So of course she'd be *absolutely* disgusted, even if I had the nerve and the impertinence and the selfishness——

"Gavin—is it hurting you now? Why are you growling?"

"Was I? I'm sorry. Oh, no; I'm quite used to it, thanks. Here we are."

Old Mrs. Tuke, returning from the last outing with Lulu, saw them coming into the entrance-hall; but in a Tuke-ish sense the vision was wasted on her.

Little permutations or combinations among the young people in the block weren't the kind of stuff on which she fed. She preferred her specimens to be older and less innocent, for somehow that nourished her more; though she could have been mischievous about the young, too, no doubt—if only the old could ever really see the young at all. That doesn't mean that she didn't stare, from her customary ambush, at this particular couple, as they passed her and entered the lift. But as there was clearly nothing to report to her daughter—for they just looked quiet and tired—her thoughts returned to other cases; and she, and Lulu, slipped into No. 2.

Well, thought Gavin, I've made a nice mess of that. Oh, dear, thought Miss Marsham, it's all over, and I think he just wishes now that he'd never spoken to me at all. But she wasn't going to have asked him in, anyhow —from pride, and because Bugs would be there. And though he came up to her floor, he didn't—because of humility and misery—get out of the lift.

"Good-night," they said to each other; and Jemima looked over her shoulder with an almost supplicatory smile, at this last moment; while Gavin, already descending again, gave her a quite unnecessarily piercing glance. But then he had gone, and that was all. They would meet again, almost certainly, for they would both wish it, and then, sometimes, even a block of flats is not unkind. Yet one at least of them must now be expected to be even shyer than tonight. It was his curse, of course. He quite saw that. But of course he didn't want to make himself, nor to be made, still more unhappy. And he didn't quite see—for in such matters he was distinctly blind—that he had the power to make somebody else unhappy, too.

It was on the Thursday in the same week—still very cold, but with a bigger moon now, and more general confidence, on the whole, in its protective powers—that Mr. L. Wilson Barker drove up in his six-year-old car once more, and once more parked it where it would exasperate Mr. Todman so much. Still, however, the police had no objection, for not only was it definitely on private ground here, but Mr. Barker had quite recently distributed some constabulary Christmas tips. They had been received without emotion, and still less had any terms been struck. But unless Mr. Todman was prepared to offer more—which he wasn't—the present position of the car (subject always to the chance of man-made meteorites) seemed satisfactory enough.

Nevertheless, it might have been noted, with the aid of the moon, that as Mr. Barker alighted this evening, he did so with a certain air of caution. That he didn't slam the door from which he emerged. And that, after locking it, he glanced up and down the alley before coming round in front of his extinguished lamps, and opening its near-side counterpart.

"Thank you," said his secretary, as she sidled out.

"Just a jiffy," said Mr. Barker, adjusting a little handle so that this door

should also be proof against pilferers.   And then this time he did slam it.
"There!" he said.

His tone was final.   He had now, in fact, quite made up his mind that he
was going to say Good-night to his secretary, and leave her—which, if
unchivalrous, was required by the conditions of his petrol allowance—to
complete the journey by bus.   Yet it would seem that it is one thing to make
up one's mind, and another to control an impulse.   Besides, she was still
standing there.

Well, he wasn't going to kiss her.   He had quite decided to cut all that
out.   But of course he mustn't be rude to her; and, gosh, how lonely he
was going to be, in another five minutes, if he didn't—well, if he didn't
say what he now said.

"Care for a little bite, Ethel ?"

"Oo, that's awfully kind of you, Mr. Barker.   Are you *sure*——"

" 'Les'," he corrected her—though against all his better judgment.
But then, though he still didn't want to go forward, he was dashed—still
shaken by that dread of solitude—if he wanted to go back.   And though
the correction was rather a muttered correction, it seemed that she had heard
it.

"All right," she said.   "Les, then.   Only you've got to be good."

He muttered again.   She had changed far too quickly from the grateful
dependant to the equal with a will and whims of her own.   Of *course* he
was going to be good, as she put it.   But it wasn't for her to give orders.

"Let's try the resterong, then," he said, just to show her how little he had
been contemplating anything funny.   "Not sure there's enough in the flat."

She seemed pleased, to his further annoyance.   Perhaps, though this
didn't occur to him, she was hungry.   Or perhaps, again, she, too, had made
a resolution—or yet another resolution—in the car just now.

"Oo," she said.   "That'll be lovely.   Yes, I'd love to."

"Come on, then," said Mr. Barker; and set off, and then paused—for
of *course* he mustn't be rude—and then somehow had taken her arm.   Well,
naturally, in the black-out.   It meant nothing.   Or, again, if he hadn't
done it—well, naturally he didn't want her to sulk.   It was rather a stiff
arm at first, so that in a way he was tempted to shake it.   Then, however,
it relaxed; and he rather wished it hadn't.   But he didn't let go—in fact,
once he did a little work with his shoulder, at which there was no further
stiffening—until they had reached the threshold of the San Remo.

Here, too, there was a rather complicated entrance, round ply-wood
screens, but it was warm, bright, and smelly inside.   Originally erected
as a shop, it was long and narrow, with tables down either side, and another
row in the middle.   The middle row always filled up last—this was partly
due, no doubt, to agoraphobia, and partly to the much greater risk here
of an impact from one of the waiters—and for a moment, though it was
still quite early, Mr. Barker was afraid that all the side-tables had gone.

He paused, looking annoyed again. But the exceedingly greasy and swarthy proprietor saw him. He made a Mediterranean signal—not altogether unlike the V-sign—and indicated another couple who were now on the point of rising. He also leered at Mr. Barker's secretary, but only because this was how he smiled. And then there was some shuffling and edging in the narrow gangway—during which the proprietor, whose eye missed nothing, gave several urgent winks to his minions elsewhere; and then, still leering, he had done the trick, and vanished.

The male half of the departing couple, that's to say, was now having a frightful struggle with his overcoat, while the female half kept dropping her umbrella as she tried to help him, and a customer just beside them had a sleeve flicked in his face, and the bent-wood hat-and-coat stand tottered in the most terrifying fashion. But Mr. Barker and his secretary were unquestionably seated at a table covered with crumbs and coffee-stains, not to mention a still smouldering ash-tray. And it wasn't more than another five minutes before some of the crumbs were removed, and Mr. Barker was offered a thumb-marked card, with some purplish writing on it that didn't seem to be quite in focus, and a number of deletions by a hasty pencil as well.

Nevertheless, he was here, and by the wall, and hungry, too. Nor had Mr. Barker ever patronised the kind of restaurant to which Major Hurst, for example, had formed the habit, in recent months, of taking Mrs. Archie Amberley. He had good reason, also, to know that there was a war on; and though if anyone dined at the San Remo for three nights running, their œsophagus would almost certainly rebel, it could—despite those pencilled deletions—serve up quite a fair amount of more or less human forage. So Mr. Barker and his secretary had some glutinous, greenish soup, some reconstructed steak named after the locality, and chunks of steam pudding flavoured with National flour. Mr. Barker also sent a waiter round to the Royal Oak for two Guinnesses; and, perhaps inspired by the table-cloth, ordered coffee as well. And he said: "Have one"—holding out his cigarette-case to his secretary; and they each had one. He was now considerably assuaged, for the indigestion would come much later, and was gracious to his secretary; while she, in turn, put up with a good deal of boasting. Yet at the back of his mind, as always when the strain was eased, he was also thinking of Doris at Rhyl, and of Maureen, of course, and of the days when they had all lived at *Charlcote*.

This even made him a little sentimental on the surface, but his secretary didn't seem to care for this particular development. She leant forward, with her elbows on the table, but he could tell somehow that she wasn't really listening, and for a moment this made him dry up.

"What's the matter?" he asked.

"Oh, Les," she said. "I was only thinking how I didn't know you then."

Quite true. He was annoyed again. No, he wasn't; he was touched.

Poor girl (but she must have been quite thirty), she wasn't really pretty, of course, but she was—yes, that was the word—feminine. He patted one of her hands, very lightly and quickly. He cleared his throat, to show, apparently, that a pat meant nothing. But at least part of the reason for this was that the proprietor was now looming over him again.

Mr. Barker knew why—for there was quite a knot of famished customers by the doorway—and in a sense, once more, he was rather relieved.

"Want us to move—eh?" he asked.

"Oh, no, sair. Not unless . . ." A significant, Mediterranean shrug.

"Right you are," said Mr. Barker, cheerfully, yet with a trace of the hectoring manner. "Just let me have the bill, then."

It was produced at once. He paid it. What harm had he done in seeking a little company, just for once in a way, in these very public surroundings? None. His conscience was as clear as crystal, and delighted to be so. Now he would just say Good-night to her, and put her on the bus, and then——

And then he would be alone again. Dammit, why *should* he be alone?

They were in the street now. He knew what he was going to say. He said it.

"Coming in for a little, Ethel?"

"Oo, Les—isn't it awfully late?"

"Nonsense." And you know it's nonsense. "I'll give you a little drink."

"Well—well, just a tiny one; perhaps."

But they had passed the bus-stop, which was where he now wished to goodness that he had been a bit more firm. And outside Bessingham House he again took her arm.

"I mustn't be late myself," he was saying, for some reason or other.

She shook him off.

"Les! If you don't want me; if you're going to start all that again——"

"I'm not!" I just *can't* be alone. "Don't be absurd, Ethel. Why do you think I asked you?"

"I don't know," said his secretary. Nor did he, once more. But he had mastered her. As he always could, of course. To prove this, perhaps, he gave her arm quite a sudden squeeze.

"Oo, Les! Not out here. You're hurting me!"

"Rubbish," said Mr. Barker, recklessly. "Come inside, then."

It was Tuke who saw this couple in the entrance-hall. She was on day-duty this week, and had just come in herself; but of course, if ever she heard the main doors flap, she must pause in the usual way. She recognised them both, and would have another little titbit for her mother, or mater, though there was no arm-in-arm as they hurried towards the lift. Someone, thought Tuke, ought to write to his wife. Not that *I* believe in interfering. She pursed her rather thick lips, and shook her head. Well, she was thinking, of course it's different with those dreadful Musselbergs, though it looks to me as if they'd squared the Police. Then she plunged into No. 2, and Mr. Barker and his secretary went up into No. 5, just overhead.

"There!" he said, hospitably, as soon as he had drawn enough curtains. "Take your coat off," he said, dropping his own. "And your hat," he said, turning on a side-light. "That's better," he said, extinguishing the light in the lobby, and closing the door as he returned. "Now, what'll you have?" He opened a cupboard. "Dash!" he said. "There's nothing but beer left. My mistake. But you'll have some?"

"Oo, well—if you're going to, Les."

"Of course I am. Only sorry—— Whoops! Well that's got a head on it, anyway. Now for the—here she comes!—other one. That's it." There was a sound of pouring, and he approached with a glass in each hand. "Here you are," he said, and his secretary accepted one. "Cheers," he said, and took quite a good pull, while she absorbed rather less. "Ah!" he said, and dropped into the biggest chair. "Sit down," he added. "No, not there, Ethel. Come on!"

"Oo, Les, you promised—— Well, just let me put this down first."

So she set down her glass within reach, and sat rather heavily on Mr. Barker's knees. Even before he felt this weight, he was again bewildered as to why he had done just exactly what he hadn't meant to do. But here she was, so he supposed he must put his arm round her. "Comfy?" he suggested.

"Oo, Les—you are awful!"

Yes, and you're sitting on my key-ring, but I can't very well mention it.

"Not so stiff, Ethel," he said. "Please!"

She relaxed. Somehow this made her about twice as heavy, though no one could call her fat. Now I've got to kiss her, he thought. So he did, and with an immense effort of the imagination he rather enjoyed it. Sooner or later, of course, this was going to lead to something, and he hoped not tonight—because the nearer she got to him, as a matter of fact, the less he wanted it; and there was little or no doubt that he had already gone quite far enough. Yet tradition, instinct, films, and fiction, all combined to advise him that it wasn't very manly to stop at this stage. He'd blotted his copy-book, anyhow—ugh! he gave a wriggle and got the key-ring away—and then what if *she* wanted it? Well, what the deuce was she doing on his lap if she didn't?

He put a quite extraordinary question.

"Heard from Frank lately?" he asked.

"Oo, Les—you are cruel!"

Am I, by Jove? He gave her another kiss.

"I don't know what," she was saying, "he'd think of me. I mean, I know he's only in Iceland, but I—— Oh, Les, I can't help it when I'm with you. Somehow, I mean. You're—you're so strong." Aha! "But then I fuf-feel such a *beast* when——"

Oh, lord, she's going to cry now! Why the devil did I bring up Frank? I've never seen him; and I bet he's having no end of a time without her. Oh, help, I'm going to get pins-and-needles next! Yet, clearly and inevitably, it was a case for both arms. He hugged her. She clung to him. He said: "There, there," so far as this was possible with his mouth jammed against hers. And all the time he was thinking: You asked for this, Doris. Why on earth couldn't you stay with me? Can't you *see* the whole thing's your fault?

"Oo!" his secretary was moaning. "Oo, Les! Oo, *why* is it one can't——"

The front-door bell gave a little trill.

"Damn!" said Mr. Barker, and tried to get up. He couldn't, of course. He wasn't nearly as strong as all that. However, his secretary seemed actuated, almost at once, by much the same impulse. She scrambled, and stood. "Who is it?" she asked.

"How should *I* know?" said Mr. Barker.

"Oo, look at my hair," said his secretary, making a dash for her hand-bag.

"For Pete's sake!" said Mr. Barker. "It's prob'ly only someone else's lights, you know. They *always* come to the wrong flat." He glanced at his own curtains again, and they seemed all right. But what *was* his secretary doing?

"Look here, Ethel—just in case, you know—— Oh, my gosh, if you want to make up and all that—— Here! Come in here!"

He snatched up her hat and coat, made a grab for her gloves—why could women *never* put them in their pockets?—and began bustling her towards his bedroom. On the threshold he had to rush ahead, of course, so as to tackle more curtains. But he was back in a jiffy, and had snapped the light on. "There!" he said, in a stage-whisper. "Get yourself tidy. Shan't be a second. Prob'ly nothing. Can't be anyone I know. That dashed woman who comes round collecting, perhaps—you remember, eh? But I—— Well, just you stay there."

His secretary appeared quite ready to do this, or at any rate was still too much startled to argue. He gave her a rather ferocious grin; shut the door; dashed across into the bathroom so as to draw the curtain there, too —also so as to smoothe his own hair and rub violently at his mouth with his handkerchief. And then the bell rang again.

"All right!" he called out. Passed into a brief panic lest his secretary should take this as an invitation to come forth. Recovered from it, more or less, as she neither answered nor emerged. And opened the front door.

A khaki-clad officer was standing there, rather imperfectly illuminated, since Mr. Barker had omitted to switch on the lobby light again. A stranger? Mr. Barker thought so, and prepared to redirect him as calmly as he could. He didn't, at any rate, even attempt to invite him in.

But the officer stepped in. He said: "Good-evening. Can you spare me a minute or two?"

Mr. Barker hadn't quite recognised him yet, but suddenly felt pretty certain that he had seen him somewhere.

"Er——" he said. "I—ah . . ."

"Tubbs," said the officer.

Mr. Barker's stomach—judging, that is to say, by sensory evidence—seemed to drop about six inches. Though virtually an agnostic, he now saw that Fate, at least, had been very prompt, this time, with its punishment. Something awful must have happened to his wife or child, if not to both, to bring Captain Tubbs round here without warning, and to make him look like that. For he looked grim and determined. He'd got bad news. Obviously he'd got bad news. And there was Ethel in the bedroom still, and—— Oh, lord, it would all happen to-night.

"Come in," he said, faintly. He shut the front door, and Captain Tubbs stalked into the sitting-room. Mr. Barker hesitated; saw that it was quite impossible to communicate with his secretary now; and followed him. He then also closed the sitting-room door, very carefully indeed.

"Er," he said, "will you sit down?"

"No, thanks," said Captain Tubbs. Nor did he remove his military cap. He just stood there, ominously, on the hearth-rug.

"Er," said Mr. Barker, "will you have a drink?" And Help! he thought. Look at that other tumbler. He couldn't take his eyes off it now, though he did just hear Captain Tubbs saying "No, thanks" again.

"Well," said Mr. Barker, with what he took to be extreme cunning, "I'll just—ah——" He whipped up his own, much emptier glass, and shoved it away out of sight. He turned round again. "Get things a bit all over the shop," he said, "living here by myself." He even indicated his own hat and coat on the end of the settee. "Only just come in," he took pains to explain.

"Quite," said Captain Tubbs. "I—ah—actually I phoned you first. Or tried to. But then, seeing this is all rather urgent——"

He suddenly seemed a little uneasy himself. He even took off his cap. But Mr. Barker's stomach had dropped about eight inches this time, and he was in no state to observe anyone else's nerves.

"You've been sent here?" he suggested. "Something—something's happened?"

"Well, yerss," said Captain Tubbs. And then: "I say—do you mind if I smoke?"

"Go on!" said Mr. Barker, impatiently. "I mean, of course you can smoke. Here——" He began fumbling for his cigarette-case, but the Captain was already snapping at his own lighter.

"Ah!" he said. He exhaled. "Well, Barker," he said, "this is all rather awkward, of course, and I dare say it may be a bit of a shock to you at first, but——"

He seemed to be in a little trouble now with a shred of tobacco on his tongue.

"Shock ?" said Mr. Barker, after at least three attempts to find his voice. "Which—which of them is it ?"

"Eh ?"

"Don't stand there keeping me on—on what's-its-names!" said Mr. Barker. "For God's sake——"

"Now, now, old man. Take it easy. You know, you can't be so very surprised."

"What the devil," asked Mr. Barker, "do you mean ?"

"Well, put it this way," said the Captain. "When did you last write to—to Mrs. Barker ?"

"Yesterday," said her husband. "What the blazes——"

"Steady!" said Captain Tubbs, though for a moment he had looked a little disappointed. "Give us a chance, old man." He took another puff, and seemed more his old self again. "Very well," he said. "You wrote to her yesterday. All right. But that's neither here nor there. When were you last down at Rhyl ?"

"When was I—— Look here, what in the name of——"

"Ah!" said Captain Tubbs again. "That's just it, you see. Why weren't you there for Christmas ?"

"Because," said Mr. Barker, almost choking with baffled frenzy, "I don't get leave the way you do in the Army. Because I was working, if you want to know. Though what in hell it's all got to do with you——"

"I'm coming to that," said the Captain, in such a manner that Mr. Barker's stomach took a third and almost sensational dive. "You can't expect," he said, "a woman like Doris to swallow all that kind of stuff. She's had enough of it. In fact, if you ask me, she'd had enough of it long before *I* came on the scene."

Mr. Barker just stared at him. The fellow was obviously mad.

But the fellow went on.

"Well," he said, "that's the position in a nutshell, Barker. Naturally I've been very discreet. No hanky-panky up there, I assure you. I've a very great respect and admiration for your—well, for Doris. In fact, I'll go so far as to say I'm very sorry, in many ways, that it should have happened. But it's not my fault, old man, if you leave her to mope by herself. Now, is it ?"

Mr. Barker still couldn't speak. He was now wondering if he had gone mad himself.

"Right-ho," said the Captain. "I quite understand your feelings. But there it is. These things happen, you know, and it's no use blinking 'em. Maybe it's not my job to point out that you've as good as brought it on yourself. But it's no good your saying anything against Doris. Well, we're both gentlemen, if it comes to that, but we're both men of the world,

I take it, too. So to put it in a nutshell," said Captain Tubbs, "she wants you to give her her freedom."

"Her *what?*" croaked Mr. Barker, with his eyes popping out of his head.

"Her freedom, old man. Well, naturally she doesn't want to give up the child. And that's quite okay with me. In fact," said Captain Tubbs, in the most generous spirit, "I don't mind telling you I'm jolly fond of the little monkey. Not," he added, hurling his cigarette into the fender, "that Doris wouldn't always come first. Well, naturally. I'd make that my business."

Mr. Barker stared again, and sank suddenly on to the arm of the big chair.

"Are you trying to tell me——" he began. But somehow, owing to an occlusion of the glottis, his voice had come out in a kind of squeak, and he had to start again. "Are you trying to tell me," he repeated, in a slightly more normal tone, "that you—and my wife—when I was away——"

"No, no, old man. I keep telling you. Dash it, I've got my C.O. to think of as well as myself. I—I give you my word the whole thing's as clean as a whistle." He even smiled. "Well, would I be here if it wasn't?"

Yes, he even smiled, and that last question had certainly been put with an air of the most friendly frankness. He had quite ceased to be grim, in fact. The impression he gave now was that he was over the worst snag. that he felt he had surmounted it with some adroitness, and that it wouldn't be altogether out of order if he had a round of applause. Well, who, if it comes to that, can encounter a crisis without a touch of histrionics? Some of us overact, some of us underact, and those who appear most natural are very likely the most skilful actors of the lot. One would scarcely say this for Captain Tubbs, of the Royal Army Service Corps, though one can give him credit for coming pretty promptly to the point. But that business with the cigarette hadn't really been natural. Neither had some of his language. Are we right in suspecting, then, that he had rather rushed into this affair, that it somehow seemed different in London from what it had looked like at Rhyl, and that the touch of overacting in this case was due—or due partly—to the consequent necessity of forcing some of his lines? That might be so. For who, once more, is a single, unblended character at any time? Or who can rehearse an interview, however thoroughly, and still be the same man, or even mixture, when the curtain goes up?

These are mysteries; and again—for such is life—they can never be wholly dissociated, in the present epoch, from the powerful influence of the films. I know one thing, Mr. Barker was thinking at one moment; this fellow's been a traveller (by which he meant a commercial traveller), or I'll eat my hat. And as a matter of fact he was quite correct, whether this affected the situation or not. Yet at the next moment he was again the prey of far deeper emotion, and must therefore—or so it seemed—begin acting himself.

"Clean as a what?" he said, thickly; and was on his feet again. Or rose, as you might say, Left Centre.

"A whistle, old man," said the Captain. "You must know the meaning of that."

Mr. Barker made a gesture which would have disgraced a member of a third-rate touring company. Yet you couldn't have called it natural, either.

"I know," he said, through his teeth, for a change, "what you're trying to say. But it's a lie!"

"Here—steady!" said Captain Tubbs.

"A lie!" repeated Mr. Barker, raising his voice, and at the same time, for some rather obscure reason, looking pleased with himself. "You come here, and you think you can pull the wool over my eyes with a lot of—of poppycock and all that——" he looked less pleased now, for he had been seeking some much better word—"but let me tell you, Tubbs——" ah, this was more like it again—"I'm not a complete fool. I wasn't born yesterday, you know."

Though this statement was perfectly true, he didn't really quite know what he meant by it. He was distinctly exhilarated, however, to see Captain Tubbs turn red.

"Now, look here," he was saying; "I've come all the way here—ghastly journey, too—for one reason only. I've put all my cards on the table; and if you don't like the look of 'em—well, that's that. But if you're hinting now—if you're trying to suggest—that Doris—well, that Doris and I——"

"Get out!" yelled Mr. Barker, as his scalp suddenly contracted and flames of passion seemed almost to explode in his skull. "Just you mention my wife's name again, and I'll—I'll——"

Action proved swifter than speech, though it took even him by surprise. He had launched himself across the hearth-rug, he had impinged on his adversary with such ardour that the very ornaments on the mantelshelf rattled. He had, in fact, almost every advantage for a moment, and if there had been no mantelshelf, or wall behind it, would almost certainly have borne his foe to the ground. As it was, he was now trying both to cling to him and to hit him—two feats which it is almost impossible to perform effectively at the same time. However, he did shout: "Take that!"—though, as it happened, this was almost at the precise moment that he took something himself.

For the Captain had rallied. He had done something with his elbow to Mr. Barker's chin, and not only was the first clinch at an end, but Mr. Barker, tottering backwards, went crashing into the little table on which his secretary had put her glass of beer. It overturned; the glass was shattered; the beer was splashed far and wide. But somehow it had just saved Mr. Barker from losing the remains of his balance; and now it was he who was coming forward again, with a roar like a baited bull.

"Stop it!" bawled the Captain; but he couldn't stop Mr. Barker. Again he was banged against the mantelshelf, this time with such force that a particularly ugly china statuette of a bulldog covered with shamrocks—the property of the original tenant—first leapt into the air and was then smashed to pieces on the tiled hearth. For a second, in fact, this so far distracted both combatants that they could only glare at each other. But having done this, and drawn fresh breaths, they immediately caught hold of each other's arms, and went struggling destructively round the room, stamping, panting, and lurching from side to side. Their personal injuries, so far, were almost negligible, and though it was a painful sight, there was a good deal of the defensive in these tactics. For though each kept threatening and growling at the other, each was also aware that if he broke loose, so as to strike with his fist, he would also be exposing himself to a similar blow.

So they held on tight as they banged against tables and chairs. Until a point when, either from exhaustion or some strange form of sympathy, they both let go at the same instant; and both gave a parting push; and both staggered back; and both side-stepped, so that the settee was between them.

"Have you had enough?" asked Captain Tubbs, just beating his antagonist to exactly the same question. "Because in that case," he added, quickly, "I'm going."

"And about time," said Mr. Barker, making an almost equally swift dialectic come-back. "Damn you!" he said. "I—I could sue you for this, you know."

Here Captain Tubbs bent forward to pick up his cap; and Mr. Barker took a quick step backwards. Fortunately, however, Captain Tubbs didn't appear to notice.

"I could sue you myself," he said—but he was quite near the door now. "Only," he said, opening it, "*I'm* not going to make this a scandal. I can tell you *one* thing, though—now you've had a lesson in manners."

"Eh?" said Mr. Barker, disregarding the end of the sentence. "What's that?"

"Any further communications from me," said Captain Tubbs, grandiloquently, "will come to you through my solicitors. That's final," he said. "And let me tell you," he added, as a Parthian shot, "you're darned lucky it is!"

With these words he slammed the door; but as there was no light in the lobby, he walked smack into the original tenant's aneroid barometer, which was hanging on the wall there; and from this, at last, he received such a severe contusion that there could only be one name for it in the morning, which was a black eye. His actual departure, in fact, was preceded by a howl that for a moment caused Mr. Barker to fear that he was coming back. But he didn't come back. And when Mr. Barker first knocked nervously on his bedroom door, and then cautiously opened it, he was rather relieved to find that his secretary had departed, too.

What an evening! he thought. What a gosh-awful mess. Doris,

he thought; but he still couldn't really believe it. And Ethel—ugh!—dashed nearly mixed up in it, too. What an escape! But just look at the sitting-room. And that swine calling Maureen a monkey, and thinking —thinking he could take her——

Mr. Barker sank down, and began sobbing. Mr. Barker rose up, after a while, and began tidying. Suddenly, again, Mr. Barker stopped tidying, and tore to the telephone. He couldn't speak to his wife, for it was one of her complaints that the bungalow in which she was living lacked this particular service. Nor could he send her a Night Telegraph Letter, because these had been entirely suspended. But he could dictate an ordinary telegram, to go off first thing in the morning. And this Mr. Barker did.

"Have seen Tubbs," he said, slowly and distinctly, and being careful to spell the last word. "Beg you do nothing till I see you. Trust you utterly." This wasn't quite true, but why shouldn't he say it if he wished to ? "Coming down Saturday without fail. Love to you both." Afterwards, as he tossed and turned—for of course he was suffering from indigestion now as well—he couldn't help hoping that he had made that last clause quite clear. "Les."

He did go down, what's more, on the Saturday—the intervening Friday having been spent in doing two days' work, during which there was neither time nor opportunity to treat his secretary as anything but a machine. It was thus, also—though he hadn't thought of this—that he avoided travelling on the same train as Tubbs. Yet if Tubbs got there first, he arrived with a black eye, and of course not so fast as the telegram. These were two disadvantages; for whether Mrs. Barker was a cave-woman or not, or whether or not, again, she had drifted as far as she had—very much like her husband —through boredom, in the first place she had been much moved by his expression of confidence, while in the second her local admirer had quite obviously, whatever he said, been fighting.

Oh, yes, Mrs. Barker had seen black eyes before, and she had heard about alleged lamp-posts—though perhaps not aneroid barometers—in the black-out. But the Captain protested too much. It may even have been that he was too truthful. Mrs. Barker was thrilled, horrified, and intensely interested; but when her husband stepped off the 3.58 on the following afternoon, clearly and completely unwounded, was he or was he not her hero ?

He was. He didn't, it seemed, wish to speak of his prowess. But perhaps the more remarkable thing—except that women are very remarkable—was that Mrs. Barker never once even referred to her freedom. She just seemed to believe, and ran rings round her husband in doing so, that he had simply come down so as to enjoy a quiet week-end. There was no mention of Tubbs. There was no sign of Tubbs. Maureen, who once spoke of him as Uncle Sid, was silenced so promptly that her father never even caught the phrase. He had vanished, in fact, with his black eye and perhaps a certain resentment against the whole Barker family; and until the 3.15 on Monday afternoon the whole Barker family was reunited.

Even this wasn't all. For on the Monday morning—having received a rather cold, curt note from Captain Tubbs, in which he didn't even express his desire to serve her, unrewarded, for the rest of his life—Mrs. Barker announced that she had taken a loathing to Rhyl, and that though it was impossible, because of her nerves and Maureen, that she should return to London, she had, as it happened, heard of a little house at Llandudno; and if she paid a deposit at once . . .

So Mr. Barker gave her a cheque, and caught the 3.15. The double knot in their lives would now appear, in fact, to have been unravelled; for he had even developed a kind of superstitious horror of his secretary, because he couldn't think of her any longer without immediately thinking of Tubbs. He swapped her—since the Executive had forbidden him to sack her—for an older and even plainer woman, and without any scene, because the whole thing was arranged before she had a chance to make one. She could now, in other words, remain perfectly faithful to her Frank once more. Indeed, this would seem to be the last phase in a quite wonderful, all-round solution.

Was it? Well, Frank was still in Iceland. Mrs. Barker was still in North Wales. Mr. Barker, when he wasn't working himself silly, must now be lonelier than ever. Do you think the Devil had lost interest in any of these characters, or in the gallant Captain, either? One doubts it. For it is unquestionable, in spite of archbishops, that the Devil finds everything considerably easier in war-time; and he is never tired of playing the same or practically the same tricks, again and again.

We should say that he was still at least in the offing. And meanwhile, if not too busy himself, he had something else to amuse him. For if you imagine that you can be spotted by Tuke, as Mr. Barker and his secretary were spotted, or that Tuke and Mrs. Tuke can hear thumps and shouts through their ceiling, or that they can learn through their Mrs. Vowles of smashed ornaments and beer-stains, and that they will then keep all this knowledge to themselves, then, if you will allow us to say so, you are counting on rather more than is likely to take place. Oh, no, they didn't broadcast the information. They regarded it as much too valuable for that. But they would begin oozing hints and suspicions now about orgies in No. 5. And Mrs. Vowles would help. And the porters would help. And even perfectly innocent tenants would find, before long, that they, too, were regarding Mr. Barker if not exactly as Jack the Ripper or Bluebeard then as someone whom they preferred to avoid. We should say he would feel this, for he was far from insensitive, and that it would scarcely tend either to soothe or strengthen his personal morale. We shouldn't be surprised, in fact, if it had almost precisely the opposite effect; or if presently, also, with Huddleston House cold-shouldering him like this, he should suddenly decide that he had had enough of Huddleston House.

If so, of course, No. 5 wouldn't be empty for long, and it would be a fresh exercise in ingenuity and curiosity for the Tukes to discover as much as they could, and in the shortest possible time, about his successor. They could be trusted to do that, without any doubt. And yet, even for the Tukes——

Well, it was very galling for them both. There can be no doubt of that, either. In fact, they came as near to an open rupture—when the news reached them from Popham, and they gathered what they had themselves managed to miss—as they had been for many a long month, or even year. There it is, though. If you're concentrating on one thing, you can perhaps hardly hope to concentrate on another. So it happened that Tuke and Mrs. Tuke were still discussing Mr. Barker—when, but for this, one of them would almost certainly have been on her way to the Post (for which she was already a little late), and the other might just as probably, so she said, have been out in the hall with Lulu—on the evening of Shrove Tuesday, or February 22nd. And, as it also happened, it was on this same evening, and at this precise hour, that a couple of plain-clothes police-officers called on Mr. J. A. Musselberg at his flat on the second floor, and, after a very brief interview led him quietly but firmly away.

CHAPTER XIII

POPHAM HAD LEARNT OF THIS BECAUSE OF A NATURAL LINK OR AFFINITY between all who at any time have had to polish their own buttons. They may let the old neatness and smartness go, as Popham certainly had; or they may temporarily, if not permanently, have discarded the buttons, as in the case of those two guardians of the law. Yet the guardians had known in a flash that the porter whom they passed on their way in had once been a soldier; while Popham, in the same moment of time, had spotted them both as policemen. This was why he changed his mind about going down to the boiler-room, and continued to hang about with that extremely practised air of being just about to do something rather important. This was how he saw Mr. Musselberg—in the green hat, the ox-blood overcoat, and with a small suit-case—descending, not exactly with gyves upon his wrist, but quite clearly under close surveillance. And this was how he was able to spread the news, or rather, perhaps, to release it so that it instantly began spreading itself; until by the morning almost everyone in the block had heard some version of it, to which they would respond, according to their own characters or feelings about Mr. Musselberg, with satisfaction or pity, with compassion or glee.

For the most part, we are afraid, both the tenants and their ephemeral retainers took the line that it was a good thing, and that a blot was now

about to be expunged from the fair name of Huddleston House. Not that
they knew what the charge was, nor, indeed, if there was any charge at all.
But they called on their imaginations, which at once assured them that it
was a pretty serious matter. Black Market, said some, if not most of them;
for they were nearly all aware, or had gathered, or guessed, that supplies
had been reaching No. 14 which no ordinary or honourable member of the
public (such as themselves) could ever hope to secure. Yes, this was the
favourite story; and indeed it is even our own view that, perhaps in its less
exaggerated forms, there was something in it. But others, also flitting
about, spoke of false returns to the income-tax authorities, of breaches of
Orders and Regulations, of attempts to evade the censorship, and even of
still more direct dealings with enemy agents. Many-tongued rumour,
in fact, was as merciless and preposterous as it had ever been in its life;
and only a very few inmates—such as Mrs. Margetson, for instance, who still
couldn't help feeling grateful for Mr. Musselberg's assistance at Gilpin's
and the Britannia Wine Stores—preferred to suspend judgment until just a
little more should be known.

Again it was galling for the Tukes that even they must rely on flights
of fancy; for though Tuke was convinced that she had set the ball rolling—
and this, too, may have been the case—the Police hadn't only acted without
telling her first, or even calling her, as it now appeared, as a witness, but had
been stiffer and less communicative than ever—"insolent" was her own word
for it—when she had gone round there in a purely public-spirited effort to
pump them. Moreover, her original acquaintance, the member of the
War-Time Reserve, was no longer, it seemed, attached to this particular
branch, for it was now weeks since he had last looked in at the post. Or
perhaps he was ill; but if so, this was just as tiresome. Altogether, said
Tuke to her old mother, it was enough to annoy a saint.

Naturally she examined and cross-examined Popham; but though he
was the fount of all knowledge in this case, there was nothing, of course,
that he could add. He had remained, he said virtuously, in the entrance-
hall, where he was on duty, and had seen merely the arrival and departure.
No, he said, no one had said nothing, not neither time. And this was true,
though it was no comfort to Tuke. If *she* had been there, she thought,
of *course* she would have followed the detectives upstairs. Yet it is the truth,
again, that she would have learnt very little if she had. Some low, guarded
tones through a closed door. A silence, while Mr. Musselberg was packing
the small suit-case. A kiss, perhaps, for remarkably sharp ears, as he bade
farewell to his wife. And then, as the door opened again, just the words:
"Mind you get on to Jack."

That was all—quite literally all—until the taxi, with its three passengers,
drove off. And as even Tuke wouldn't have had the faintest idea who Jack
was, what could she have gained from that? Nothing, once more. So she
could only blame her old mother, which she certainly did—though, as

has been stated, her old mother was spirited enough, for once, to blame her, too; and then wait for the newspapers—but without much hope, owing to their present size—and prepare an expression for the next time that she should encounter the culprit's unfortunate wife.

Others prepared such expressions, too. Some, whether they had ever spoken to her before or not, were going to cut her. Some, prompted, perhaps, more by their own brand of curiosity than pure benevolence, were going to approach her with enough qualified sympathy to elicit, as they hoped, illumination if not a full confession. Mrs. Margetson, representing a much smaller class, kept wondering if she could provide any genuine aid; was discouraged by June, who said: "Don't be absurd, mother;" was further discouraged by the knowledge that it was now more than three months since Mr. Musselberg had been so good-natured, and that to start being neighbourly now would only look forced and queer; and was again and still more discouraged by the complete impossibility of offering any kind of assistance to a younger and obviously far more competent woman with a whole-time, one-eyed, and slightly hump-backed maid.

So Mrs. Margetson, in fact, did nothing; though if she had met Mrs. Musselberg—which she didn't—she would have tried to smile. And Mrs. Wardrop, though she still regarded even the Musselbergs as in a sense her parishioners, and was, moreover, a kind sort of busybody at heart, did nothing, either. She made one attempt, that's to say. For she rang the bell at No. 14, with the full intention of being charitable and broad-minded, if naturally a little condescending, too. But the one-eyed maid mistook her purpose; or assumed, in other words, that she had come round collecting again; and more or less shooed her away. So that was why Mrs. Wardrop did nothing, and why she wasn't going to try again. She was now definitely huffy, in fact, poor old thing. Though somehow one doubts, even if she had passed the portals, whether she would have left in a much milder mood.

For the plain though exasperating truth seemed to be either that Mrs. Musselberg had no sense of shame, or else, as was also suggested, that she had the hide of a rhinoceros. She didn't conceal herself. She went out and came in exactly, and exactly as often, as she had done before. She didn't hesitate to use the lift when others were aboard, and if any of them were either cutting her now or attempting to pump her, she seemed quite unaware of this, too. On the very day following her husband's detention or arrest, her piano was again being played, with all the old penetrating brilliance and inaccuracy, by her cousin Connie. While even those who eyed her most closely, as she passed to and fro, were unable to descry the very faintest sign of strain. They were baffled. If this was faith, or heroism, they couldn't and wouldn't accept it as such. They decided that she was heartless. They knew, somehow, that this was no real answer at all. They didn't consider, perhaps, that centuries of persecution—or of conduct, if you prefer, almost bound to invite reprisals—must inevitably toughen the breed. Nor, if it comes to that, did they know anything about Mr. Jack Jonas. Yet they were annoyed with Mrs. Musselberg because she didn't break down in public, or bolt from the block. And particularly they were annoyed with her because still, so it appeared, she had a complete and utter hold over Maggie, the one-eyed maid. For they had at least hoped, if in a deep and private manner, that Maggie would now leave the dishonoured flat; and even, perhaps, that they might snap her up for themselves.

But she didn't leave. Or she hadn't, at any rate, according to the latest reports. And then, though still less than forty-eight hours had elapsed since the first excitement, even the absorbing and fascinating case of Mr. Musselberg lost some of its outstanding importance. This was partly due, no doubt, to a couple of sharp and ear-splitting air-raids on Tuesday and Wednesday nights, which, in conjunction with the state of the moon, rather tended to distract people's thoughts. But quite as much, if not more, was it due to another form of attack. There was no noise this time—that's to say, until Mr. Todman's telephone-bell began ringing; but everyone still on the premises knew all about it by lunch-time. For though the weather was still pitilessly cold and bleak, not a radiator in the whole of Huddleston House was now even warm to the hand.

On the top floor this was at first attributed to an air-lock—a scientific phenomenon to which it was particularly prone. But for once the deduction was false. When the tenant of No. 23 descended in search of assistance, a much worse discovery was made. "It's off, I tell you," said Freeth, with a mixture of joy and impatience; for though of course it was a pleasure to spread bad news, he had already said just the same thing to quite half a dozen inquirers.

"Do you mean something's broken?" asked No. 23, thinking desperately of priority and the notorious difficulty of getting anything mended.

"Naow," said Freeth, contemptuously. "The stuff's run out. That's all."

"Do you mean the water——"

"Naow. The coke. Finished. Can't get no more. Except," added Freeth, a little grudgingly, "for the baths and that. 'Tain't no use blaming *us*," said Freeth.

"Oh," said No. 23; and withdrew; and telephoned—not with the notion of blaming anyone, though the ultimate or original responsibility was clear enough, but in the hope, perhaps, of finding that yet another alarming report was only a rumour. No. 23 telephoned, therefore, to Mr. Todman in his office at Bessingham House; though of course Mr. Todman could only answer as he, too, had answered before. Without going into the question of why the oligarchs had removed the miners from the mines and were now proposing to drive non-miners into them, he could only say that neither Bessingham nor Huddleston House had now got enough fuel left for radiators as well as baths; that there didn't appear to be the faintest prospect of their getting any more before the summer; and that in these circumstances it had been decided that baths must come first. He sounded weary. He didn't attempt to explain why the decision, not to mention the need for it, had been kept a secret. Yet No. 23, like the previous voices, showed no disposition to argue. For one was trained by this time, however valiantly one might have reacted in bygone days, to be suddenly told that one must do without almost anything. One might, as in this case, still have to pay for it—for no one expected there to be any corresponding adjustment in the rent; and as a matter of fact one would now be paying twice over—for naturally, in weather like this, one would make more use of gas or electric fires. But if the oligarchs had landed one in this position, there was nothing whatever to be done. On the whole, also, it was perhaps better to have an occasional, shallow bath, and some warmish water for washing up, than for all taps to run cold while only the radiators still radiated.

Henceforth, accordingly, the constant and confusing announcements about bans on heating being lifted or extended, or cancelled or reimposed, frequently as they would appear in the Daily Press and the news-bulletins, could only have a distant and academic interest for the tenants in these two blocks of flats. All they could hope, if they had the time or spirit for this, was that somehow, for at least part of the next winter, some traces of heat would return. Meanwhile, towards the end of February, they must just shiver in their hall-ways and corridors, and—except in so far as they risked breaking the law—in their private apartments, too. They weren't intentional grasshoppers, for it wasn't they who had either stoked the boilers or attempted to order the fuel. The theory was that they had contracted out of these particular troubles; but they hadn't, it seemed, because there was a war on; and all they could do now, as they wrapped themselves up, or stamped, or blew on their hands, was to pray for a mildish spring.

This, then, explains how the focus of attention rather wobbled away from Mr. Musselberg to more personal matters. But the porters were all right. We needn't be too much concerned about them. For in each block one boiler was still going strong; so that if ever they felt at all cold upstairs, they had only to retire underground.

It could hardly be described as spring just yet, though, and certainly it wasn't mild. "Brrh!" said Major Hurst, as he returned on that first Spartan evening; and then touched one of his own radiators, and swore. And he, too, tried to telephone to Mr. Todman; but as there was rather a rush on the line now, owing to the number of other toilers who had just come back and were engaged in the same attempt, he was forced to abandon this project after two or three shots, and passed out again into the hall.

"Porter!" he shouted, at the head of the descending stairs. "Oy!"

This fetched up the Party-Leader, who arrived swallowing, and buttoning the jacket of his uniform. "Sir?" he replied, after a final ingurgitation.

"What the devil," asked Major Hurst, "have they been doing with the furnace? It's like ice in my place."

"Yessir," said Popham. "Orders, sir."

"Orders?" said the Major. "What the devil do you mean?"

"Manager's orders, sir," said Popham. Then he became more confidential. "Fact is, Major," he said, "you'll find your bathwater all right; an' the sink an' all that. But about the pipes—well, there's been a bit of a disappointment, you see. Nearly 'appened last year, too, as I dessay you'll remember. But it's 'appened proper this time, sir. In fack, there's what you might call no choice."

This was allusive, and contained a good deal of ellipsis; but the Major was more or less there.

"That's a nice state of affairs," he said. "Good God! Can't they *do* anything?"

"It's 'appening all over," said Popham, agreeably. "Stands to reason, I mean, if the stuff ain't there—well, they can't deliver it, you see. It's the shortage, Major; that's what it is. I've said all along if we can't get no coke, we'll just 'ave to make do without. Well," said the Party-Leader, as he concluded this little lecture on economics, "you can call it the war, if you like."

He even had an air of expectancy now; and it was true enough that Mrs. Wardrop had tipped him, about a couple of hours ago, for a much less painstaking version. But Major Hurst just glared, and said: "Bah!" And then he said: "Hell, what a muddle!" And then he just swivelled round and went back into his flat, where he slammed the door with a thud. He also kicked on the electric heater in his sitting-room, but without any very immediate thermal effect. He was still wearing his great-coat, in fact, as he marched up and down. It was an irritating hour of the day. He was now sorry that he had come back here, instead of stopping off somewhere for a drink. This room was clean enough and tidy enough, though still damned cold, but the fact was (he was preparing to smoke now) that this new fellow, whom he had had such a devil of a lot of trouble to get, wasn't really a patch on Bunny. He was slow, and he was stupid, and he seemed to be taking the devil of a time to learn the Major's ways. So that the Major regretted Bunny, though Bunny was far beyond recall. Fate, it seemed to him, had played a pretty dirty trick there—though he wasn't thinking of what it had done to Bunny—and it was a bit hard now that the radiators should go off as well. This damned flat, he thought—visiting on it a kind of cumulative disgust for all the other flats and chambers where of course he had only been trying to escape from himself. Should he leave it, then? Why not? He was sick of it. Dead sick of it. Only, of course——

He inhaled and puffed. He unbuttoned his great-coat. The new man—whose name was Justice—had at least and at last learnt to put the drinks and glasses on the right side of the fire place, so that the Major's next automatic movements were simple enough. He poured, and eyed, and mixed, and sipped. His frame responded. He felt less critical, suddenly, about Justice. And though still annoyed about the central heating—which, dammit, was about the limit, even in these days—felt less inclined to curse anyone just now. The telephone, in fact, which ten minutes ago, or so, had been a prospective method of venting his wrath on Mr. Todman, was now suggesting quite another course. It hadn't changed in appearance, for telephones don't; but somehow it, too, might help to soothe him. He frowned. For of course he was now disentangling himself, or so he thought. But on the other hand if he was bored, and if he was going to leave this place anyhow —for now, whether permanently or not, this thought had become as good as a decision—why, or why, to put it in his own language, in God's name, should he sit here and drink by himself?

So he dialled, as he had so often dialled before. Why not, after all, he was thinking, make another regular evening of it, if he happened to be in the mood? If a thing was over, one could still be good friends, couldn't one? Especially with a girl who never threw fits, as such lots of them did, but just took it as—well, as a thing. This unspoken compliment to Mrs. Amberley made him nod with approval, as he finished dialling. Yet almost at the same moment he was comparing her unfavourably with women who *had* thrown fits. That damned self-possession, he was thinking. Oh, of course it saved bags of trouble, in the long run. But at the same time it was a bit cold-blooded, you know. Made you feel you'd missed something, however sensible it might be. For though scenes were hell, of course, and infernally monotonous, too—because they *all* said the same things, and expected the same answers—yet in a way, if you never had one——

It was here that Mrs. Amberley answered. And again, though he was now telling himself that he had been an ass to ring up, Major Hurst felt a sudden thrill. He shook his shoulders, as if to prove that he had imagined anything so absurd. But made no attempt to modify the caressing note which perhaps, after so much use, was too strong and fixed a habit.

"Primrose?" he said, though of course he knew who it was. "Bill here."

"Oh," said Mrs. Amberley. "Hullo."

"Busy?"

"Well, no. Not particularly."

"Somebody there, is there?"

"No. Nobody."

"I see. Well, what about a drink, then? Why don't you come down?"

"Well, Bill, I—I don't think I will, perhaps. Not just tonight."

"Snooty?" suggested Major Hurst. He couldn't stand opposition. And then, again, one can be gross yet susceptible, too. Somehow he felt that he still hadn't got all her attention; and that he must have it, even if only to show that he didn't want it.

"Of course not," she was saying. "Just a bit busy. That's all."

A challenge, eh ? Or *had* she got someone else up there ? Major Hurst, though it was quite true that he was already slightly entangled with her successor—whose name doesn't matter, but who lived in a mews, and was really (or so he had come to the conclusion) much more his type—must never be treated like this. It was for *him* to say that he was a bit busy, and never for the party of the second part. It was a matter of pride, and technique, not to mention the importance of proving—whatever his age— that he was still in the prime of life.

So he said: "I'd better come up, then." And if Mrs. Amberley made any reply to this, then he didn't and indeed couldn't hear it, for he had already cut himself off. It would be unworthy of his pride and technique, however, if he hurried upstairs. So he didn't, but finished sipping his drink first. and then went through into his bedroom, where—since nothing is hidden from us—he brushed his hair, and made some faces at himself in a mirror. They were rather martial faces, though it was a long time now since he had been in a battle. And they were rather repulsive, though he appeared on the whole to approve the condition in which they left his features after he had made them. He also jerked back his shoulders, and pulled in his diaphragm, which again seemed to provide him with a certain amount of content. As an actor, in turn, he was now ready, one would say, for an imaginary call-boy. He even left the bedroom with a jaunty and distinctly self-satisfied step. He wasn't tired, one might judge, even after all those years, of playing the same old part.

There was no stage, and no audience, yet, though. He must still ascend in a lift—which he did, after he had first made sure that the entrance-hall was empty. Now he was on the top landing, where it was so dark that, without rehearsal, he could hardly have found the right bell-push. But of course he knew just where it was, or his hand did. He pressed it. But if he expected the door to open at once, then he was mistaken. There was silence after that discreet tinkle. In fact, there was a definite pause.

This wasn't in the script. He didn't want to ring again, in case another door opened; for the breeze-blocks and quick-drying plaster quite frequently led to such results. Nor did he wish to stand here, quite apart from the intense cold. But being not without resource he beat a short tattoo, with his fingers, on the door itself—a rather intimate fragment of rhythm, which at least would be unheard elsewhere—and this time there was a kind of answer. A voice—indeed, the voice that he was awaiting—said: "Who's that ?"

He opened the flap of the letter-slot with his thumb, but of course he wasn't going to stoop. "It's Bill," he said, addressing the orifice with some caution. "Buck up and let me in."

"Oh," said Mrs. Amberley's voice. But she did open the door, and he was inside in a trice, and had closed it, though still with great care. She had all her paint on, if not more than ever. A handkerchief was tied round her head, so that little or no hair could be seen. She was still wearing those rust-coloured, factory slacks, and her fur coat. Major Hurst was a little vexed with her for not having changed, and for not looking prettier or more pleased to see him. For even, in his view, when an affair was as good as over, a woman should still take a little more trouble than this.

He said: "Are you only just back, then ?"

They were in her sitting-room now. "Why ?" she asked. "Is it late ?"

"It's after half-past seven," he said. "Why on earth don't you turn your fire on ? Don't you know the heating's all off ?"

"Is it ?" she said. She looked at him, and looked away again. "Was it you who rang up just now ?" she asked.

"My dear child," said Major Hurst, perching on the edge of her table— for of course he couldn't sit down if she went on standing; "have you been overdoing it or something ? Of *course* I rang up. I thought you might care for a drink. I——"

"Did you ?" said Mrs. Amberley, looking puzzled. "I don't want one, thank you. Did you say it was half-past eight ?"

"No," said the Major, looking a little bewildered himself. "Primrose——"

"I beg your pardon ?"

"Look here—I say—are you ill ?"

"I don't think so," said Mrs. Amberley, yet as though this hardly concerned her. She took a cigarette from a cardboard box, and put it between her lips. "Damn!" she said, looking round again. "I'd forgotten. No matches."

"Here you are," said the Major, leaning forward and clicking his lighter. "Come on," he said, for there was no co-operation.

Mrs. Amberley looked startled. "I'm sorry," she said. But even then she made two bad shots at the flame.

"Primrose!" said the Major, sharply. "What on earth's the matter with you ?"

"Do you want to know ?" asked Mrs. Amberley. "I should have thought," she said, "it was obvious. I mean, of course it was bound to happen. Just——" she gave a foolish little, mirthless laugh—"as you were bound to come bounding up here."

Major Hurst didn't appreciate this play on words. He was also thinking that Mrs. Amberley was looking very nearly ugly to-night; and this again he disliked, because it suggested that his own taste was at fault. A further thought that came to him was that she had been into a bar on the way home; so that although he had just had a stiff drink himself, he looked stern.

"Now, Primrose," he said. "You're tired, you know. Why don't you just hop into bed, and I'll bring you something up from my flat ? Or if there's any soup or anything here that I can warm up for you . . . ."

That's it, he was thinking. He liked the sound of brotherliness and intimacy. It was just as it should be. And that was a wonderful touch about hopping into bed—just the right tone—as though he had never been more than the old family nurse. The fact is, he was thinking, I'm really a marvellous friend.

Indeed, and by no means for the first time in his life, he was so much wrapped up in a performance, and pleased with himself for doing the thing so well, that even when he was interrupted it was still only his own voice that he heard.

But then he was interrupted again. And this time—as is also an old psychological custom—he heard both interruptions at once. They required a complete change of character, too, and for a moment the knowledge of this merely made him look angry.

"Dead ?" he repeated. She had no business to blurt it out like that. What was more, he would have given five pounds to have stayed downstairs. But still—well, naturally—there was an appropriate face to be made. "My dear," he was saying, "if I'd known—if you'd only told me——"

Yes, but how on earth did *she* know ?

"Are you *sure* ?" he asked.

"Quite, thank you," said Mrs. Amberley. "They were good enough to ring me up, you see—though of course I've known it for weeks. Here." She thumped her chest. "So perhaps," she added, conversationally and without a trace of emphasis, "you can imagine how much I loathe you now."

"Eh ?" said Major Hurst.

"One does," said the young woman or young widow. "Obviously——" the voice was rising now—"one hates and despises oneself far more. Not that either of us actually killed him, poor Archie." She gave a very peculiar and alarming look at the word "us," as though she had chosen it specially so as to hurt herself. "Oh, no," she said, "I always knew he was going to die there—even if, for some extraordinary reason, they tried to keep him alive. You can't keep people like Archie in prisons. Oh, no, it just can't be done. They die, you see. They're not there any more. They're not anywhere. So I don't even have to explain to him why I behaved like a bitch——"

"Here, I say!" said Major Hurst. "Steady!"

"——but if you think," added Mrs. Amberley, just as steadily as before, "that you've had anything—anything at *all*—well, you're wrong, you see. You've had *nothing !*"

That's rot, thought Major Hurst. And yet—for of course he was staring at her—she was now looking so painfully if not deliberately ugly that in a way he almost agreed with her. Yes, but on the other hand how *dared* she say she loathed him ?

"Look here——" he began.

"Get out!" said Mrs. Amberley. "You dreary old, tenth-rate taxi-tiger! Can't you see you make me *sick !*"

She tried to move past him—one can hardly say where—but he was genuinely infuriated now. He caught hold of her arm, using nearly all his strength.

"Look here, my girl," he started again. "I can make every allowance——"

She just ground the lighted end of her cigarette into the back of his hand, and he let go with a yelp.

"You devil!" he said. "You little——"

He tried to grab her again. But he couldn't, because she was now laughing at him in the most terrifying manner.

"Primrose!" he shouted. "Stop it!"

"What?" said Mrs. Amberley; but she had stopped. "Quite right," she said, as she threw the cigarette away. "Nothing to laugh at. But if you'd just—kindly—go—to Hell—or wherever you came from—I should be so very, *very* much obliged."

"Well," said Major Hurst, "if that's how you feel——"

"That," said Mrs. Amberley, "is exactly how I feel. And how I shall go on feeling. So don't let's talk any more. Good-night."

"But, honestly, I—— Look here, you're not going to——"

"Oh, no," said Mrs. Amberley. "Far too late now. And, besides, do you think I want *your* name mixed up in it?"

Major Hurst looked considerably, if not doubly, relieved.

"Good-night," said Mrs. Amberley again; and turned her back on him. For two pins, perhaps, her visitor would have started the whole scene again; beginning it now by catching her shoulders and forcing her round. But either the two pins weren't forthcoming, or else he was suddenly as anxious as she was for the scene to be at an end. He stepped forward, but only one step. He paused. He looked fairly ugly himself for a moment. And then, it would appear, he had had enough. If she thought this, or if she thought that, then nothing, in a way, would give him more pleasure than to put her right. He was still feeling rather more than vindictive about that burn on his hand. But he was going, all the same. He was backing away. He was out in the little lobby. He had opened the front door of No. 25. He was in the passage, and had shut it behind him.

"Impossible!" he muttered, as he summoned the lift. "Mad!" he remarked, as it carried him down. But such sympathy as he felt was all for himself, as it always was, and always had been. He had been cheated again, because women, in the end, were always impossible and always mad. They understood nothing. They just took what they could get, and then turned round on you and let you down. Luckily he still had some of that tannic ointment that almost everyone had bought at the outbreak of war, and jolly good stuff it was. But it was quite twenty minutes before he was calm or impatient enough to ring up the woman whose name doesn't matter, and to tell her that he was blue and bored and was coming round.

"But have you eaten anything, Bill?" she asked.

"Oh, I'm all right," he said, with just the right hint of husky pathos. "I'll pick up a snack on the way."

"Oh, Bill—no. These raids! I'm sure I can manage *something*—and I do so hate being alone."

"Angel!" said Major Hurst, and hung up, and looked quite himself again. All the same, he was thinking, I've had enough of this flat. Well, dash it, I've always moved when I wanted to, and of course one gets sick of a place. I'll tell Todman. I'll ring him up in the morning. Well, why the devil should I stay here and be frozen—anyway? Why shouldn't I be a bit more comfortable for a change?

So he set off into the blackness with his mind made up. If it remained made up, there would apparently be another departure, before long, among the tenants of Huddleston House; and some grief, for a while, among its porters. Even now, though, a bachelor—or one ranking as a bachelor—could still find fresh accommodation if he knew the ropes. And if anyone possessed such knowledge, in all that concerned the easier and more indulgent aspects of this earthly existence, it was our old friend Major Hurst.

As for our much younger friend Mrs. Archie Amberley, for a while she stood and stared at nothing. Then she sat and stared at nothing. But though she wished to weep, she couldn't weep; for still no tears would come. It wasn't remorse that she felt; for it was true enough, in her own war-time code of ethics, that she had given nothing, whatever she might desperately and miserably and odiously have done. Yet of course this was punishment and of course it had fallen first on someone else. It would, you see. She had even known that it would. So that if anyone thought she was trying to weep for herself, she wasn't. Of course she didn't mind being lost, and ruined, and damned. What else had she asked for? What else had she ever expected? But the blasted thing was that if you trained yourself not to cry, then you couldn't—though you would have given your soul if you had one—do anything but stare, and occasionally shudder, now. That was the reward; and what a joke it all was, and what a mess she had made of everything, and how ridiculous it was to imagine that if somebody died in a prisoners' camp one would ever see them again.

The sirens went at about nine o'clock that night—for the fourth, or was it the fifth night running?—and the guns began almost at once. But though sometimes the windows quivered, and sometimes there was the pattering sound, and once at least the whole block gave a fearful lurch, Mrs. Amberley just sat where she was with her eyes fixed on nothing. There was no need to call on her immense courage, for this, too, was a habit by now. So far indeed, as she was listening to the infernal rumpus at all, she had a faint sort of hope that it might lead to her personal extinction. But at the same time she knew it wouldn't. And it didn't. It faded away, and presently there were more sirens, howling their other note.

"You see?" said Mrs. Amberley. "There you are." And however

she spent the rest of the night, she was out shopping again quite early in the morning; for even with some ghastly and purposely inexpressive letters to be written, she mustn't and wasn't going to be late at that loathsome bench. No, not even if it should now be her own turn to faint there.

It was in the late afternoon of this same grey day—the last Friday in February—that R.J., looking grey himself, if not greyer than usual, arrived with an ancient hand-bag at Huddleston House. As he had entirely refused to say at what time he was to be expected—and on this occasion hadn't even deigned to explain what business, if any, was bringing him to London at all—Gavin had been unable to do more in the way of a welcome than to leave a spare latchkey with the Party-Leader, and to suggest that R.J. should ask for it whenever he turned up.

So R.J. didn't ask for it, being very unamenable to this or any other form of suggestion; but lugged the hand-bag up to the second floor himself—having a similar distrust, it would seem, of electric lifts—and rang the bell at No. 12. As chance would have it, the sub-tenant of the premises was taking a half-day off from his Ministry—to which he was quite entitled—for the purpose of mauling and rending six novels in one outburst of spleen. In about 1,500 words, that is to say, he was preparing to curse modern fiction in general—this, in fact, would consume nearly half the space—after which, with a passing reference to M. de Charlus, he would fall on the six authors in one fell swoop, would demolish their pretensions and grind them to powder, and would then, perhaps, feel better and more like an author himself. At the moment, however, he was still in the midst of this task; so that he looked not only *farouche* but ferocious as well, as he rose from his desk to open the front door.

R.J., on the other hand, was not only afraid of no man—for as a retired headmaster he need no longer even fear parents—but felt strongly that it was this sub-tenant rather than himself who was the actual intruder. So he didn't smile either ingratiatingly or otherwise—not, indeed, that he was a man who went in for smiling—but just dropped the bag, on the inner side of the threshold, and said: "Where's Gavin?"

"At the office," said D. P. Moulton; and then added, as even he seemed to shrink to a schoolboy again: "I expect, sir."

"Ugh," said R.J., looker grimmer than ever. "I see." You were to judge, perhaps, that his mind was a bit torn in twain, between a son who did any work at all (which was good, but surprising) and a son who had failed to be here to greet him (which was bad, but only to be expected). Then he said: "Ugh" again. Then he rather flabbergasted and affronted D.P. Moulton by handing him his hat and coat; for, roughly speaking, D.P. Moulton had no manners at all. And then he stalked into the long sitting-room, rubbing his hands together with a dry, grating sound.

H

"Very chilly here," he said, with an accusatory air.

"I know," said Derek. "I'm afraid the heat's off——" slight pause, but then he couldn't help it—"sir."

"Why?" asked R.J., taking his stance on the hearth-rug, where the gas-fire was at least doing its rather pitiable best. "Eh?"

"They've burnt all the coke, sir," said Derek, without even a hesitation this time. "Can't get any more."

"Umph," said R.J. "Disgraceful. Quite right, though. Trouble is——" He was interrupted by a powerful sneeze. "There!" he said. "I knew it!"

"I—I beg your pardon, sir?"

"Abominably icy train," said R.J. He blew a loud blast on his nose. "Thought I was in for it. Pretty certain now. Got a cold coming on."

"Oh, I hope not, sir," said Derek, looking owlish and slightly alarmed.

Which of us, said R.J.'s inexorable expression, is more likely to be right? But his voice also said: "Is that tea there?" And Derek jumped, and said "Oh, yes, sir—I'm awfully sorry." After which R.J. was good enough to partake of a slight refection or collation. Mostly, apart from a few more sneezes, in a paralysing kind of silence.

Presently he told Derek that it was time to draw the curtains, and though it wasn't, there was no question of his being disobeyed. If only those six novelists could have seen their assailant now. If only they could have heard R.J. recommending him to get on with his work—as though reviewing for the *Friday Reflector* was no more than a species of prep, with an ex-headmaster as invigilator. In spite of his cold, moreover, R.J. was now smoking a short, charred, and badly obstructed pipe. It bubbled—even more than Derek's. It kept going out. He was perpetually re-lighting it. Again, he was perpetually shooting from the chair which he had selected in order to examine the books with which the room was strewn. This he did by opening them, sniffing at them, and then closing them with a bang and a grunt. He also unnerved his companion by making frequent entries in a small pocket-diary and by reading and re-reading some letters which seemed to crackle far more than any ordinary correspondence. He prowled, too. And ever and anon he put some pertinent, if not impertinent, inquiry about the economics of the flat. The would-be reviewer was now frankly swearing under his breath.

"Look here, sir," he said, as R.J. began snapping his fingers in a singularly disturbing manner; "would you like me to get Gavin on the telephone? Shall I tell him you're here, sir?"

"Oh, no, no, no, no, no," said the guest. "I'm very comfortable, thank you, my boy. Quite a change, being up in London. But," he added, pulling out a big watch and eyeing it with a slight scowl, as though it had better not try to deceive him. "I'll tell you what I *should* like."

"Yes, sir?" said Derek, laying his pen down again.

"If that's a wireless set over there," said R.J., "would you mind turning on the news ? I don't like missing it, you know."

He spoke—and perhaps, in this case, there was no special idiosyncrasy —as if listening to the news was part of his contribution to the war-effort. But of course his companion had to turn the thing on. Somebody said he was Thomas Turnbull this evening, and launched into the familiar rigmarole; assisted, though naturally unaware of this, by a running commentary from R.J. "Good," he said. "Dear, dear," he said. "What's *your* opinion," he asked, "of the position in Russia ?" And then: "Quiet, if you don't mind. Can't you make it a bit louder ?"

So Derek made it a bit louder, though this was hardly necessary considering the row that was going on now from the set in No. 13. Shortly afterwards, in fact, he was instructed to reduce the volume again. "That's better," said R.J., and began coughing so that no one could hear anything. But he recovered, though he seemed distracted at having missed part of an item about the South-West Pacific. He wanted Derek to repeat it. And when he couldn't—well, of course he couldn't—he became fractious and nettled, as though he was the victim of a conspiracy to hide all news. And so it went on, for the full twenty minutes, until suddenly he was saying: "Turn it off ! Turn it off !" in apparent terror that he should be contaminated by anything but a bulletin. At which Derek leapt to oblige him with such complete subservience—though fuming with irritation inside—that he all but collided with Gavin, who had just opened the door.

"Hullo!" said Gavin. "What's up ?"

His contemporary just shot a frantic glance over his shoulder.

"Oh!" said Gavin, and was immediately and almost visibly deflated. "Hullo, father," he said. "I'm sorry I'm so late. I—I hope you've been all right."

"I've caught a cold," said R.J. "Why ? Are you generally back earlier than this ?"

"No," said Gavin, already forced on to the defensive. "As a matter of fact, I'm generally——" He pulled himself up, for of course this wasn't the point. "I say," he set off again, "can't I get you something ? Aspirin, or something to gargle, or——"

"Certainly not," said R.J. "There's no need to make such a fuss."

"Oh," said Gavin, again. "I see." Stubborn old Stoic, he thought. Gosh, he thought, I know those colds, too. He'll probably be here for a week now.

He saw further and frightful complications with Mrs. Mudge. But he also, from the tail of his eye, saw Derek creeping away.

"Where are you going ?" he asked, spinning round.

"Out," said D. P. Moulton. It was quite clear that he meant it, whatever impromptu asylum he was now seeking. Only this morning he had said positively that he would be in, and Gavin, for the first time in weeks, had been counting and relying on his presence. But he was going. In fact, he'd gone. It was barely half-past six, and R.J. never went to bed before eleven. Help! And there was almost bound to be an air-raid as well. If only, thought Gavin, it was his fire-watching night. He was ashamed of himself. He had known, of course, that he was going to feel like this; but not quite so quickly, or thoroughly, or abysmally. He saw a vision of Jemima. But as he was always seeing visions of Jemima, and as on the whole, since that night at the lecture—and despite several brief meetings since then—they had only tended to make him ashamed of himself, too, he was no better off than before. Worse, in fact. Far worse.

"Er——" he said, without the vestige of a notion of what was coming next.

"What ?" said R.J. "Speak up, my boy. I can't hear you."

"Oh," said Gavin. He had an inspiration, after all. "Would you care to look at your room, father ?" he asked.

"Not now," said R.J., as though he had been slightly insulted. "Later; later. Sit down, can't you ? There's plenty of time."

How true. How appallingly true. The period before eleven o'clock tonight might almost be described as eternity. It seemed to stretch out until the crack of doom. Yet even this wasn't all. For it was also attached, by a thousand, unseen filaments, to a thousand previous evenings—all equally awkward and devastating—so that now it had become virtually impossible to break away from tradition. Yes, Gavin saw this very clearly indeed. Again, also, he could see or feel how it was he himself who brought out so much of the worst in R.J.—and even how, if only some frightful spell could be broken, it still wasn't too late to start on a different plane. Yet the spell was there all right. It had altered his voice the moment he entered this room. Inferiority complex ? No; because this meant that you began showing off, and never once had he even dreamt of doing that. Nothing to show off about, he reflected, either. He had a dull father, and he was an exceedingly dull young man. Furthermore, he was a failure. Oh, Jemima! Oh, darling!

"Er—how's Mrs. Woolley ?" he inquired, with an unexampled effort.

R.J. looked darkly suspicious.

"Quite well," he said. "So far as I am aware. Why ?"

"Oh," said Gavin, "I just thought I'd ask."

"Umph," said R.J., as though no one but an idiot could have had such an idea. And that was the end of that.

In the middle of the next effort but one—which is to say after a couple of extremely painful pauses—he was suddenly visited with an idea or fixation himself. Didn't Gavin generally work in the evenings ? Didn't he want to work now ? What ?

"Well, no, R.J. You see, 's a matter of fact, I didn't bring anything back with me, because I thought—well, I thought, with *you* here, you see——"

That sounded offensive and inhospitable, at any rate to Gavin. To R.J. it appeared to suggest—for there was another Umph—that the whole story of his son ever doing any work at all, except possibly, under compulsion, at the office, was an entire fabrication. One could see this written all over him. Or Gavin could.

But he couldn't defend himself. Nor could he suddenly conjure a typescript from nowhere. Nor could he conceive reading it with his father's eye on him. He raged in his mind against Derek, who might at least have drawn some of this fire. Yet why should he? He had borne a good deal of the brunt—one had seen that at a glance—and he was dashed sensible to clear out. But, oh, Gosh!

"Er——"

Entrance of Mrs. Mudge, who had been heavily bribed to return from The Dwellings to-night, so as to prepare, it was to be hoped, some kind of an edible supper. She began laying the table for three, while R.J. stared at her.

"Is your friend coming back, then?" he asked, as she left the room.

Gavin wanted to say: "He isn't my friend. The fact is, we're sick of the sight of each other; only I'm not going to turn out of my own flat, and he won't." Never, indeed, had these truths presented themselves more clearly. But he wasn't quite off his head. So that his actual reply took the form of: "I don't really know."

R.J. was immediately suspicious again.

"Do you mean to say," he asked, "that in these days, with all the difficulty about food——"

Here—fortunately, in a way—he sneezed again. Gavin bounced from his chair.

"All right, my boy. All right. I've told you I don't want anything."

"I know. I mean, I beg your pardon. But, look here——"

"Eh? Where?"

"I've had an idea," said Gavin. And he had, and he couldn't think why he hadn't had it before. Maisie's bottle of whisky. Auld Sandy. If it was still there—but one could never quite know with Mrs. Mudge, though if she had taken it of course one could say nothing—then it wasn't only the answer to his latest rebuff by the Britannia Wine Stores but to several other attempts, during the last few days, to procure a bottle of sherry. What was more, it was supposed to be good for colds, wasn't it? *Eureka*—or let's hope so.

He dashed into the lobby; he rootled in the coat-cupboard; he found it; he hobbled hurriedly into the kitchenette—where for a moment he had some difficulty in circumnavigating Mrs. Mudge, who seemed anything but pleased to see him. But for the moment he was still reckless and inspired. "It's all right, Mrs. Mudge," he said, with astonishing assurance. He peeled off the coloured foil. He removed the cork. He seized a decanter from an upper shelf—where it had been doing nothing since the beginning of the war, but was still, presumably, quite clean enough inside. He dusted it, daringly, with a dish-cloth. He poured the whisky into it. He replaced the glass stopper. He grabbed a tumbler. And returned—though already some of the first enthusiasm for the idea had left him—as fast as he could.

"Here you are, R.J.," he said. "Look what I've found!"

R.J. peered at him between his spectacles and his eyebrows, and one can only say that he looked distinctly suspicious again. The idea, in fact, must now be explained, elaborated, and even defended. Why only one tumbler? Oh, whisky, was it? Why couldn't Gavin have said so? "I thought you told me you didn't like it," he said, with a strong implication —at any rate in Gavin's ears—that he was face to face with a drunkard.

"I *don't*," said Gavin, as patiently as he could. "But it's all I've got, father. I mean, it's all I could get. I thought *you* might like it, perhaps, though I'm sorry——"

"When," asked R.J., magisterially, "have you ever seen *me* touch whisky?"

"Never," said Gavin, as there was no other possible answer. "But I thought perhaps if you had a cold—or if you were tired——"

"I'm not the least tired," said R.J. "Well, yes," he admitted, "a drop or two might be good for my cold, perhaps." Then he was indignant again. "But you don't expect me to swallow it neat, do you?"

"Oh, no," said Gavin. "That's just what I was going to say. You see, I'm afraid I haven't got a siphon; but if you could manage with ordinary water—and if you'd just say 'when'——"

"I'm certainly not going to drink spirits before dinner," said R.J., severely. "Put it down on the table." Gavin obeyed at once. "And look here— aren't you going to wash?"

"Yes, I was just going to, but——"

"I'll go first, then," said R.J. He rose, sneezed, and marched into the lavatory. If Gavin had had two perfectly sound feet, he would still have felt shaken as he awaited his return. I knew it would be like this, he was thinking. It always is. It's never not been. I don't know if he does it on purpose or if he can't help it; and if it comes to that, I still don't think he really detests me. But, oh, my goodness, what a gift he's got for making me feel a worm. How does he do it? *Why* does he do it? I wonder——

Re-enter Mrs. Mudge, equipped once more for the street.

"Hullo, Mrs. Mudge? Yes?"

"What about Mr. Moulton's supper? Are you waiting for him?"

"Oh, no. Not if you're ready." Of course he won't come back, if he's got any sense. "Er—*are* you ready?"

"Just on," said Mrs. Mudge, who was another character who had long since abandoned the use of the word "sir." "You don't want *me* to wait on, do you?"

"Oh, no," said Gavin; though he hadn't thought she would be going

quite so soon. "That's all right, Mrs. Mudge. Oh, half a second——"
he just stopped her in time—"what about my bed-clothes?"

"I thought *you* was going to put 'em out," said Mrs. Mudge. "You
don't want the sofa made up now, do you?"

"Oh. No. Perhaps not. But I—I'd rather like to know where they
are."

"Where I put 'em," said Mrs, Mudge, with almost frank contempt.
"On the chair in your room."

"Oh. I see." Rather lucky I didn't push R.J. in there before I'd
shifted them. Better shift them now, perhaps. Drop 'em behind the
sofa. That's the idea. I say, I hope my blasted foot isn't going to pack up.
Oh, and I wonder what——

He called quickly. "Mrs. Mudge!"

She'd heard him, of course. But of course she wouldn't come back
when she was half-way out of the front door. It closed with determination.
He realised that he had said nothing about breakfast, and must now guess
in what order he was to serve whatever she had left in the kitchenette. Not
that he blamed her for wanting to get back, when at any moment——

Even this half-finished thought had been prophetic. The sirens had
begun wailing again. Oh, lord!

R.J. came out of the lavatory.

"Sirens," he said.

"I'm afraid so," said Gavin. "Would you like to——"

" 'Afraid'?" said R.J. "I don't like that word, my boy."

Oh, all right. Stay up here, then; you're as safe as anywhere else, and
I don't know how to heat up a meal that's got cold.

But then suddenly these thoughts became even more indignant, and he
just had to speak up for himself.

"I didn't mean it like that, father——" though I should be an ass if I
wasn't afraid. "I only meant——"

"All right, my boy. All right. There's no need to argue."

"I'll get the food in," said Gavin, with as much calm as he could muster.
"Are you sure you won't have a drink first? Oh, and I must wash, too.
Shan't be a jiffy, R.J."

He moved the decanter and tumbler invitingly, and withdrew. When he
returned, with what he hoped was the soup—and not some perquisite of
Mrs. Mudge's that had been left to cool—R.J. had poured out about a
thimbleful of the whisky, and was sniffing at it with a doubtful look.

"Is it all right?" asked Gavin.

"It's a long time," said R.J., "a very long time, since I touched the stuff."

This was hardly a reply. Any boy who had answered the headmaster
of St. Eustace's like that would have had what is known as very short shrift.
Gavin, however, even if he thought of this, didn't point it out. He put the

two cups of soup down (Mrs. Mudge having recently broken the last soup-plate), and offered his guest some bread.

"Not bad," said R.J., rolling the thimbleful round his tongue, and again not exactly returning a direct reply. He helped himself to a spot more, still without water. It didn't occur to Gavin that he was nervous, though his own nerves were a little taut; as always, if for no other reason, when the sirens had ceased warbling, and half the distant traffic seemed suddenly to be silenced, while the remainder was obviously going as fast as it dared. No guns yet, though, or sounds of aerial engines. Good; so far. But he wouldn't say so—not wishing to have any further misunderstanding about courage. He tasted the soup, and it *was* soup. R.J. tasted it, too, and appeared satisfied. All was still quiet on the Huddleston front.

"Of course——" said R.J., abruptly.

"Er——" said Gavin at the same moment.

This seemed to silence them both, too. Gavin, that is to say, withdrew from the contest, and R.J. didn't attempt to go on with it. They just absorbed the soup, which didn't take very long; and then the host must rise up again.

"Shan't be a second," he said. He took the cups back into the kitchenette, and put them on the draining-board. He examined the top and inside of the gas-cooker, and discovered a choice of vegetables a(ncient potatoes and greyish greens), which he very nearly served with Mrs. Mudge's rapidly-toughening Welsh rabbit. At the last moment however, he spotted two plates on the folding shelf which were obviously the real second course. They had slices of something on them which a vegetarian would have rejected, and which had probably come in a tin from the United States, but were otherwise a bit hard to describe. This meant that he must transfer the vegetables and put the Welsh rabbit back. It also meant that he scorched his fingers. But he reappeared in the end.

"I'm afraid——" he began. And broke off. Chiefly, perhaps, because he had again just remembered the effect of this phrase last time. But also from a certain amount of surprise. Ought he to *tell* R.J. that a tumbler full of almost neat whisky—— No, of course not. Quite out of the question. It was inconceivable that he shouldn't know this, however many years might have elapsed since he last drank the stuff. Besides, this was all theory. He really knew nothing about whisky himself. He put down the plates with a feeling that he had just had another narrow escape. And suddenly the sirens were giving their steadfast shriek.

"Ah!" said R.J. "All Clear. Do you hear it? I was beginning wonder if the brutes meant business to-night."

"That's right, sir," said Gavin, after an effort to say something more adequate. "Let's hope——" He stopped.

"Eh?" said R.J. "Don't mumble like that."

"I'm sorry, father. I—I hope you can eat this."

"My dear boy," said R.J., "I'm used to roughing it."

Snubbed again, thought Gavin; but to do him justice his foot was now aching like fun.   He was also remorseful, though of course he hadn't actually pointed out that an All-Clear at about eight o'clock was no sign, in these times, of a quiet night.   Yet he was remorseful enough to think how ghastly it must be to be old.   And then again, with another reaction, how ghastly it was when old people went on as if the war was a kind of pantomime. Well, of course they couldn't help being spectators.   But "brutes," you know. And then, of course: What have *I* done ?   Nothing.   And we both know it.

He was extremely depressed now.   But R.J., though his cold seemed to be gathering power every moment, was also developing a strange streak of garrulity.   It even survived the Welsh rabbit.   He's talking to me, thought Gavin, as if I was Claud.   But though of course he couldn't answer in the same vein, R.J. was just sweeping him aside now when he attempted to answer at all.   Again, unless Gavin was very much mistaken, this forceful soliloquy on world affairs was becoming a little confused.   Names which even the listener identified as belonging to the previous war kept intruding themselves.   At first R.J. had brushed these away, as if they were persistent bluebottles.   But they kept coming back.   One couldn't pretend that they weren't getting a bit blurred.   It suddenly struck Gavin, as he glanced at the decanter, that if R.J. wasn't tight now—which was still hardly to be believed—then at least he had lowered a pretty fair thundering dose.

He tried to reject this idea.   He felt impious; ashamed; and more nervous than ever.   But he was thinking of Noah now.   He couldn't help it.

Coffee!   That was the stuff.   Besides, dash it, he should have offered it him anyhow.

"I say—father—you'll have coffee, won't you ?"

"Don't erupt," said R.J., with rather more than elision.   He was looking flushed.   He had also either sunk down rather oddly in his chair or had somehow definitely become smaller.   The objective witness, on whom we have called once or twice before, might have summed up Cold plus Fatigue plus War-strain plus Sirens plus Septuagenarianism plus profound practical inexperience of Auld Sandy.   Even Gavin had a notion that quite a number of these factors were involved.   But he was scared.   For his contemporaries had always appeared larger, if anything, when in a corresponding condition. Had he by any chance poisoned his father ?   Had Maisie betrayed him ? Was Auld Sandy, in fact, some fearful form of hooch ?

Two points shone out.   First, he must try and get his father to bed. Secondly, if he even suggested such a thing, R.J. would undoubtedly refuse to go.   He had also just time to reflect that even when you had dreaded an evening, Fate always had a surprise up her sleeve.   He had expected to be exasperated and humiliated, but not in his very wildest fancy had he supposed that it would turn out like this.

"I say—father——"

"Coffee?" said R. J. "Cer'nly not. Siddown! Listen-a-me." He leant forward. He wagged a forefinger as if about to make some tremendously important statement. But then it was as if the forefinger itself was the obstacle. He glared at it. He glanced helplessly at Gavin. He gave such a deep sigh that it was almost a groan.

"Not ill," he said, hoarsely but distinctly. "Jus' tired. Jus'——" he shut his eyes, and his head began lolling—" 'straordinarily—tired."

"Come on, then," said Gavin, gently and kindly, though he still didn't dare mention bed. "Let me help you up, father."

"Eh ?"

"This way. I'll get your bag."

It was years, as he suddenly realised, since he had even touched the old boy. But there was no resistance as he suffered himself to be led, and at times almost lifted, towards the smaller bedroom.

"There we are!" said Gavin, lowering him on to the bed. "Shan't be a moment, father. *You're* all right. Aren't you ?"

"Bathroom," said R. J. Guernsey, looking a bit cross-eyed.

"Oh, yes. Of course. Sorry. Come on, then."

Back again.

"There you are, father. Is that all right ?"

"Lea' me 'lone."

"Yes, of course."

Noah ? Shut up, you swine. Where's this blasted bag now ? Dammit, it's locked. No, it isn't. Oh, lord, look at his night-shirt!

"All right, father. This way! Just coming!"

They were both in the little bedroom again.

"Now, then, father—you mustn't get cold, you know. Here—let me help you."

It was like helping to undress an ancient and obstructive baby. But it was clearly essential. And still the exhausted host must keep up a kind of nursery patter.

"There you are, father. That's more like it. All right; I've got it. Never mind about your shoes. How are you feeling ?" No answer. "That's fine." My hat, what a night! I say, oughtn't I to *force* him to have a couple of aspirins ? Thank God, Derek's not back.

Another idea. "Look here, father, just stay there a second, and I'll fill your hot-water bottle. Just boil a kettle."

"Don't——" said R.J., passionately; and stopped.

"But, father, you need it. It'll do you good. It'll help your cold, father. It'll——"

And then Gavin stopped, too. He had never seen such an expression, though it was true, also, that it was years since he had seen R.J. without his spectacles, and this was the first time, so far as he could remember, that he had ever seen him in bed. But there was more than that to it.

It was myopic, but it was petrifying.   What on earth was going to happen next ?

"Father! I say—are you——"

"Don't keep calling me Father!" said R.J., in the most forcible manner, and with a complete though almost certainly passing return to his ordinary enunciation. He was a little old man—for again he seemed to have both shrunk and aged—in bed in a striped night-shirt. But he looked fierce, and indeed formidable for a moment, as he raised his head, and then thumped it back on the pillow.

Gavin was still standing with the empty hot-water bottle, and gaping.

"Why—why not ?" he was compelled to inquire.

"Because," said R.J., more thickly now, and shutting his eyes, and letting his cold and Auld Sandy surge over him again; "because," he said, "I'm *not* your father. Never have been. That good 'nough reason ?" He thrashed a bit under the blankets. "Siddown, can't you ?" he added. "Tell you the truth. Far berrer. *Et praevalebit*—eh ?"

Gavin's scalp was tingling as he slumped on to the only chair in the little room—regardless of the fact that it was already occupied by the bulk of his visitor's clothes. And his visitor went on talking—quite distinctly enough for all practical purposes. And even if one ought to try and stop him—well, one couldn't. No, it just couldn't be done.

CHAPTER XIV

IT WAS WHILE THAT SECOND BLAST OF THE SIRENS WAS STILL SOUNDING, WHILE Mr. and Mrs. Champion were on their way up from the so-called Shelter again, while the so-called Fire-Guards—who consisted this evening of characters mostly unknown to us, under the deputy leadership of the lanky, long-nosed Freeth—were on the point of dispersing, and while Mrs. Tuke was just emerging from No. 2 with a slightly impatient Lulu, that one of the swing doors in the hall suddenly flapped, and that Mr. J. A. Musselberg, after three nights' absence, returned to Huddleston House. He was still wearing the green hat and ox-blood overcoat. He was still carrying the little suit-case with which he had set out. He looked neat, clean, and calm, if not exactly attractive. And as his dark eyes swept over the group which his unexpected arrival had silenced and even turned, metaphorically speaking, into so many graven images, there was no trace of embarrassment to be detected in their mysterious depths. He even said: "Good-evening," and there was a kind of croak, but no more, from one of the less completely ossified spectators. But the cage of the lift was standing at the ground floor. He opened a gate. He stepped into it. He closed two gates. He pressed a button. And as the cage ascended, with the customary moaning sound, Mr. Musselberg was wafted from sight.

It was clear, in other words, that the story of Mr. Musselberg's imprison-
ment was a myth, and that even his detention was now over. Indeed, in
the general stupefaction and revulsion of sentiment it was even felt by some
that he might merely have been assisting the authorities. He didn't look
as if he had been subjected to the rigour of the law, in even its mildest form.
He had looked plump and assured. You would have said that he had
returned from no more than a business trip, for all that his appearance
conveyed. It was confusing. To some, indeed, it was acutely disappointing,
whether they happened to bear him any personal ill-will or not. They looked
back to the dawn of the legend, though already this was slightly obscured
by the affair of the radiators and the succession of raids, and tried to cling to
those plain-clothes policemen. Yet even these seemed to fail them now.
After all, only Popham had seen them. And nothing, as they suddenly
realised, was more possible than that Popham should have made some kind
of bloomer.

They listened now, still under the spell of that sturdy apparition, so that
still--cold as it was—they must linger in this entrance-hall. Their eyes
couldn't follow the rising cage as it passed out of sight. But they heard
it stop. They heard the gates being opened, and one of them being closed
again. And they knew just how long it should normally take to reach the
door of No. 14. The apparition would have a key, of course. But surely
there would be some sort of sound, some startled cry of rejoicing or welcome,
when Mr. Musselberg returned, as you might say, from a living grave. They
were almost counting on this, but they didn't get it. No sound, whatsoever,
came down the shaft. And indeed, even if they had all levitated themselves
to the second-floor landing, there would still have been nothing to hear.

Mr. Musselberg did let himself in. They were right about that. But
as he had already telephoned to his wife about six hours ago—telling her
that Jack had fixed it, but that he must still catch up with some business
before he came home—Mrs. Musselberg wasn't the least surprised to see
him. Perhaps she wouldn't have been surprised to see him in any case,
for never had she doubted for one moment who would win this round.
Jake, of course. He had said so when he had taken his departure, and when
had he ever been wrong ? These things happened, and were bound to happen,
from time to time. They were traditional, one might almost say. But
if you were prepared, and kept your wits—which was traditional, too—there
was never any reason for panic. You answered some questions, and wasted
some time, and then—unless you were a fool—they thanked you or at the
very worst they warned you; and that was the end. It had to be, when they
were tied hand and foot by their own regulations, and you were restrained
by none. You remained a suspect ? But you had been born a suspect.
Just, and for the same reason, as you had been born with a sharper brain.
Later, unless it ceased to be sharp, which was extremely unlikely, this would
take you to a level where the very scale and magnitude of your operations

would provide a complete defence. You knew this, for again you had been born with the knowledge. And if you had chosen the right sort of wife, she naturally knew it, too.

So there was no demonstration at No. 14, though there was a most appetising smell of cooking. Mr. Musselberg, that is to say, embraced Mrs. Musselberg—even before he removed his green hat. But having done so, he just rubbed his hands, and said: "Good." And then, inflating his out-size nostrils: "Don't say you've got hold of a duck!"

"I have, though," said Mrs. Musselberg, with modest pride. "And salmon to start with. And the lobster sauce you liked that time. Well, dear, you told me to do my best."

"You've done it," said her husband, approvingly. He smacked her where Lieutenant R. G. Margetson, R.N., had so provokingly smacked his sister, but Mrs. Musselberg seemed wholly pleased. "Maggie!" he called out, in the same gay spirit. "I'm ready for the doings when you are." And then, to his wife again: "Come on, then. You and me'll have a little drink. Or maybe a couple. So?"

Such was Mr. Musselberg's happy homecoming, of which we are privileged to give you a brief glimpse. But down in the hall the disillusioned Fire-Guards were again dispersing now, with no more than a shrug and a mutter; for perhaps, it was beginning to strike them, they—and Popham, of course—had made rather a risky mistake; and anyhow this was no place, or temperature, in which to remain even a moment longer than they need. Even Mrs. Tuke, though her eyes had all but started from her head, now yielded to Lulu's persuasion, and allowed herself to be drawn, with some vigour, into the Stygian street. She felt the absence of her daughter keenly, for Sylvia, surely—who had virtually, and rightly, put the hounds on Mr. Musselberg's trail—would have known what to make of this very short absence and swift return. As Sylvia would and did when she came in (being off duty tonight) from a meal with a couple of girl friends called Pepper and Hobbs. "Don't be so stupid, mater," she would say, almost at once. "Of course he's only out on bail."

But he wasn't. He was out, so far as anyone could be said to be out in these days, with no vestige of an undertaking to go back. He was free, so far as anyone was free. The Law had snapped its jaws at him, but it hadn't even torn the edge of his ox-blood overcoat. And the Tukes, it would seem, must either start once more with a fresh idea, or else gnash their own teeth in vain. But in the former event one would advise them to be fairly prompt. For though neither Mr. nor Mrs. Musselberg had any sensibility about rumours attaching to their name, even a slight set-back, in their philosophy, must be followed by a corresponding advance. And it might very well be that, if spared and when the right moment came, they, too, would give a month's notice to Mr. Todman and the Syndicate, and would skip lightly away into a more central and fashionable flat.

They were still eating duck, though, and quaffing their drinks, as the scene again changes to a room which we haven't personally inspected since a day, quite a number of weeks ago, when Miss Marsham returned from a solitary, Sunday walk. Now it is, of course, still a Friday, and a rather later hour than last time. But Miss Marsham is once more alone.

Perhaps, and let us hope so, she has been more successful tonight than on that previous occasion in providing herself with a meal. If so, and, indeed, in any case, she would appear to have finished it and cleared it away; but of course it is a bit early to be thinking of bed yet, so that again, after another day's work for the State, she has got out her mending, and sews as she sits on the floor. But though there is a deep and now constant ache in her heart, it has no longer the very slightest connection with the absence of Bugs. Nor has Bugs let her down tonight, by telephoning at the last moment with some urgent and breathless excuse. On the contrary, it was this morning, at breakfast, that she announced—with a curious mixture of offhandedness and defiance—that she would be dining with Mr. Haggerston-Hawksworth. The objective observer, in fact, might have thought this and that. As for instance, that if she hadn't come to some decision, she was at least in a discriminatory mood. With more knowledge, again, he might have reflected that a time must come for girls like Miss Bryony Bretton when they see themselves, not, indeed, as others see them, but at least from an altered angle. Such girls or young women might *sense* a lost power over another girl or young woman, though still there was no open revolt. Then they might say to themselves: "Hullo! This needs examining. What is happening to *me* that has produced this change in her?" And then: "Good heavens, am I losing my other powers?"

There might be a shaft of light then. It might not reveal the whole truth—which can never be revealed—but a picture, in this case, not altogether untrue. Of a girl who can get almost any young gentleman to give her a brief good time; but has done this so often that for the moment she is suddenly sick of it. It isn't a picture, in fact, so much as a vista; and at the far end—past all the young gentlemen, alive or dead now, who have been attracted and have then slipped away—there is a mirror, with a glimpse of herself. It tells her that she has never for one instant been in love; that she has made, indeed, rather a mess of things all round; that if the vista grows longer a stage must be reached where the image in the mirror will be something at which she can now hardly bear to look. It will have shrunk, too, not only by the law of optics. It will be getting older. It may not be quite so pretty. But if one averts one's eyes, and turns, as one has so often turned, to the willing and unquestioning admiration of another girl, who has done so much until now to soothe, to flatter, and to shore up one's pride—will she still be there? Or how much longer will she be there? Have I, the first girl may now ask herself, been such a fool, after all, as to miss the bus? It is then, for girls who have toyed with love and have indeed made rather a mess of things, that another glimpse can present itself, in the shape of a Mr. Haggerston-Hawksworth.

They may have mocked at him until now, and though a gentleman he is hardly young. But there isn't only a tradition among such tribes as the Musselbergs. There is a very strong instinct elsewhere, as well, to seek what one wants and to get it. So if one wants to be reassured of one's own importance, as one does when one reaches this point; if one is tired of a game at which, as has suddenly become much too clear, one has always failed; and particularly, perhaps (for this was at the bottom of it all), if a devoted slave shows signs, however faint as yet, of regaining her freedom—well, then, the time has arrived for facing these facts and for catching a bus after all.

Is this rough on the Haggerston-Hawksworths? Not necessarily, we should say. For in the first place of course they should have settled this sort of matter at least ten years ago; in the second place, though it may have been the war that has jolted this one out of his rut, he has certainly meant business for quite a long time, and if he didn't he could easily escape; while in the third place—if all goes reasonably well—he will not only be provided with a remarkably beautiful wife, but one, we should say (having studied these things), who will love anyone to whom she is actually married. We see her, indeed—once the feat is achieved—not only developing a fresh source of pride, but becoming (for of course she can't change altogether) extremely possessive once more. Look round. Think of your own friends. Think of Mr. and Mrs.——

But no. No names, on second thoughts, if you don't mind. Of course you have spotted the couple we mean; or possibly several couples. But that will do. We have said quite enough. For in the first place, again, we don't *know* as yet—well, not positively, that's to say—that this marriage will ever come off. And in the second place one has got to be careful, by Jove, about putting real names in a book.

Yet, anyhow, Miss Bretton was out again, undeterred by this week of bombing; and was dining—at not *quite* the restaurant that she would have chosen, perhaps, but she didn't say so—with Mr. Haggerston-Hawksworth. While it might also be mentioned, as a further indication of something, we feel, that although she hadn't entirely removed all colouring matter from her finger-nails, they were now much more pink than scarlet. In the language of nails, in other words, it would seem that she was already prepared to meet one of Mr. Haggerston-Hawksworth's suspected prejudices half-way. He might have taken this as encouragement, if he hadn't been so nervous about giving dinner to a member of his staff at all. Yet though easy to mock at, he was equally suited—if you took this line—to be regarded as rather a pet. He was thirty-eight, while Bugs, though older than the girl whom she called Echo, was still barely twenty-four. He was also, one is bound to admit, just a trifle bald. But his category and attainments were such that he was as safe from the call-up as any Under-Secretary of State. He also had a house, though it was now occupied by soldiers and might never be the same again, not far from Cromer. So Bugs was continuing to bowl him over tonight, and because he was such a change from her previous squires was on the whole rather enjoying the process. But the girl whom she called Echo was alone, and sewing on the hearthrug, when somebody rang the bell.

She got up, with a lap-full of patched *crêpe-de-Chine*, which she hastily and modestly hid. She shook her head, which did something rather essential to her hair. And still wearing a thimble, still wondering who this caller might be, and hoping that it wouldn't prove to be Mr. Everard, she moved gracefully, though in high-heeled slippers, towards the sitting-room door. A further sign of speculation might be seen in that lifted eyebrow, still below a forehead as smooth as glass. She looked thinner than when we first saw her—which must now be quite four months ago—and she was anything but a bolster then. The winter had done this, and the war, and the diet which was alleged to be keeping everyone in such radiant health. But she was also—unless again this was a case where any four months could produce the same subjective effect—looking notably prettier. Of course, Bugs wasn't there, which still might help; for still, when Bugs was there, any stranger would look at her first. Yet the girl Jemima *was* pretty. There need be no qualification now. Indeed, she was even more than this; for she was in love, and not very happy—being under the illusion that she wasn't loved in return. And though in a number of cases this makes you look plainer than ever, there are yet striking exceptions where it has quite another result. In our cold-blooded way, in fact, we should say that Miss Marsham, on this even colder, February evening, was a sight for extremely sore eyes.

The eyes, however, which met hers as she now opened the front door were merely owlish. They belonged, that is to say, to D. P. Moulton, of the Ministry of Propaganda and the *Friday Reflector*, who had been dining alone at the Royal Oak. Here he had absorbed some swipes of a very low alcoholic content—so that he was completely sober. But he had then become bored with the society in the bar (not that he had attempted to speak to anyone, nor that anyone had spoken to him); yet still feeling reluctant to return to the society of R. J. Guernsey, Esq., M.A. (Oxon.), he had had the happy thought, as he re-entered this block some time after the sounding of the All Clear, of pushing the button in the lift marked 3 instead of the button marked 2; and of paying a visit, though for no particular purpose, on the girls in No. 15.

Undoubtedly if he had known that only one girl was at home, he would have preferred that girl to be Bugs; for though she had long since discarded any thought of him as an escort or prey—since she knew now that he was as mean as he was uncouth—yet still, from habit, perhaps, she played just a part of her game. It had flattered him, though he remained owlish. It had even made him believe—which was a fantastic idea—that he was a bit of a dog. One should be particularly careful, perhaps, with Proustians who have no other experience, for they can't have learnt much about life. They are inhibited, and a bit twisted, and if they do break out they may do so in a rather turbulent way. Bugs, however, had never read Proust. Nor had she met a man like D. P. Moulton before. So she put some ideas into his head, as they say; for Beauty can always do that. Now, having roused them, she was dining with Mr. Haggerston-Hawksworth. And suddenly, as that front door swung open, the conviction struck D. P. Moulton— who wasn't only delighted to be able to keep away from R.J., but was still slightly exhilarated by the All Clear—that Echo (as he still thought of her) was really curiously attractive, too.

This caused him to say: "Hullo," in a rather eerie manner, and to stare rather hard as he said it. So Miss Marsham said: "Hullo," too; and thought how all the time—or all the time since the bell had rung—she had really been hoping that it was Gavin. It might be added that if she found herself in a position where young men could call on her at as late an hour as this, with a good chance of discovering her alone, then this, too, was a point that the war-makers had overlooked. That she had done nothing herself to invite it. And that if it accidentally approximated to conditions in an ideal commonwealth, then, thanks to the war-makers, there was no other resemblance; the fact being, indeed, that in a number of cases it led to much, if not all, that earlier generations would have expected. See statistics, if you think otherwise; though personally we have every confidence in Jemima, and in an immense quantity of other tormented young persons, too.

But not much—and in truth our bias has for some time been clear—in D. P. Moulton; who, though no Lothario in practice, could be even more tiresome, perhaps, when he momentarily imagined that he was. His approach, at such junctures, was largely synthetic, and utterly lacking in charm. But it could also be mulish, to quite an unpleasant degree.

He looked past Miss Marsham now, into the empty sitting-room, and he said: "What's happened to Bugs?"

"She's out," said Jemima. "Did you want her?"

"Not really," said Derek, in his dead sort of voice. "But if you don't mind, I think I'll come in."

"Oh," said Jemima, who certainly didn't want him, but could never be rude. "Well, yes. Do."

So he came in, and she left him to shut the front door; which he appeared to do—with an elbow, as he removed his coat. Owing, however, either to original economy on the part of the Syndicate or to an effect of that so-called land-mine, it was seldom a door that closed permanently without a further push. In other words, as he followed his hostess, it gently unlatched itself and remained a few inches ajar. But he had shut the inner door now, and was quite unaware of this. While Jemima was feeling far too much exasperated and disappointed to give the matter a thought.

"You see," said Derek, proceeding towards the hearth, "Gavin's got his old father down there. You've never met him, have you?"

"No," said Jemima; but she was rather interested, all the same. "What's he like?" she asked.

"Appalling," said her visitor, dropping on to the little sofa. "He's a beak, you know. Or he was one."

"A what?"

"A schoolmaster, then. Had a place of his own, I believe. St. Somebody's. Prep school. But I tell you, he's a man to avoid."

"Why?" asked Jemima, curiosity proving a little stronger than loyalty.

"Because," said Derek, "he treats everyone like a schoolboy. I had a couple of hours of him—and I can tell you that's more than enough—before Gavin came in. So I left 'em. Well, he's not *my* father."

"Oh," said Jemima. Poor Gavin, she was thinking; I knew there was something like that, though he's never said so. In an excess of sympathy, accompanied, of course, by that uncontrollable brimming of the eyes, she even felt some slight pity for Derek; though she wished he had sought refuge elsewhere. "Is he staying the night, then?" she asked.

"Yes," said Derek. "Worse luck." He finished lighting the cigarette that he had just plucked from his case, having asked no permission to do so. "Old Gavin," he said, "has got to sleep on a shake-down. Can't say *I* should much like it."

He looked up, as Miss Marsham said: "Oh," again. He saw those liquescent orbs, and though it never occurred to him that he had contributed to the effect, it wasn't one that displeased him. He didn't even associate them with tears, for which he could imagine no reason; yet they gave him a rather rare and perhaps dangerous feeling of strength.

"Why don't you sit down?" he asked, patting the other half of the sofa. "You were sewing, weren't you?" For he had spotted the thimble now, as well as the old chocolate-box, with its reels and scissors and so forth, that was still on the floor. "Why don't you go on?" he said. "I like it."

Nothing wrong with these words, perhaps, though it wasn't his flat. But the tone was wrong. The owlish stare was wrong. Awkwardly enough, he was playing or attempting to play the sultan now; and Miss Marsham, though only faintly aware of this pose, felt bound to resist it.

"I don't think I will," she said. "I'd practically finished." She took off the thimble. She bent—which she could do in one dip, without bending her knees—to pick up the old chocolate-box. Bother! she was thinking, but I don't *want* him to stare at my things. And I *hadn't* practically finished; I'd only just begun. And he's *just* the sort of person who'll stay here for *hours* now—however dull I am.

She sat down on the end of her disguised bed.

"Oh, I say!" said D. P. Moulton. "You can't sit there."

"Why not ? I'm quite comfortable."

"Nothing to lean against," said Derek, leaning back in great comfort himself. "Here!" He patted the seat of the sofa again. I'll just look a fool, thought Jemima, if I make a fuss. And I'd look a fool if I sat behind him, on the arm-chair. But why *should* I stay here till my backbone aches ? I'm not afraid of him. It's only that he's rather disgusting.

So she moved over, though if the sofa had been longer she would have been better pleased. Her guest seemed quite quiet, though. What on earth, she began wondering, am I supposed to do with him now ? She glanced at him again. He was now staring past her.

"I say, Echo," he remarked, "is that thing a bed ?"

It seemed, as she now saw, too, that she must have twitched the cover when she got up from it. The answer to his question, in fact, was perfectly apparent.

"Yes," she said, nevertheless. "Well, it's a sort of divan arrangement, I mean."

"I see." But nothing could be more solemn. "Who sleeps on it ? You or Bugs ?"

"Well, I do, 's a matter of fact. I say—Derek."

"Hullo ?" He wrenched those artificially-enlarged eyes round again.

"I wish I could offer you a drink," said Miss Marsham; "but there just isn't any. At least—— Well, I suppose you wouldn't care for some cocoa ?" She half-rose.

"Sit down," said D. P. Moulton. "No, thanks. Stay here."

"Oh,"said Jemima, subsiding. But then he suddenly got up himself. He was peering at the mantelshelf; or, rather, at the photographs and other articles displayed on it.

"Are all these chaps your friends ?" he asked, swinging round without shifting his feet.

"No," said Jemima, truthfully enough. "Well, I mean, I've met some of them; but they're Bugs's really."

"I see," said her guest, with the same rather forensic air. He swung back again. "And these cards," he went on, now scrutinising the invitations to the bottle-parties. "Do you belong to all these places ?"

"Well——" Yes, but why *should* I sound like a sort of waif and stray ? "Well, no—not *all*." Only to two, as a matter of fact, and as I've only been there with Jonathan—which was how they got hold of my name, I suppose —and as I've never sent them any money, I don't really know that I *do* belong.

"I see," said the guest, again. And this time, having first thrown the end of his cigarette behind the electric fire—whence Smashums would certainly never retrieve it—he swivelled right round, and stood facing his hostess. "What are they *like* ?" he asked. "What do you *do* there ?"

On second thoughts, as it would appear, he then executed another movement that brought him back on to the sofa; but no longer quite so much at his own end of it. It was impossible, however—or so Miss Marsham felt—to draw any attention to this matter; though she did contract just a little.

"Oh, *you* know," she was saying. "They're rather stuffy. And one dances. And—and—well, sometimes there's a sort of little cabaret."

"Like in Paris?" asked D. P. Moulton, though one rather doubts if he was thinking of Proust.

"I don't know," said Jemima. "I've never been there."

"Well, but you know what I mean. Are they—— Do they—— Well, what they call 'strip-tease,' I believe, and all that? Is that the sort of thing?"

She wanted to laugh at him, for of course there had been nothing of the kind, and he had sounded so ridiculously pompous. But then she didn't want to laugh at him, or to laugh at all, for she hated this sort of conversation, and he'd no business to start it; and if she laughed, it would be like admitting that she didn't mind. She recalled some of the other occasions when he had got, or tried to get, like this. Bugs could have dealt with him—though she had rather let him run on, as a matter of fact. I wish, thought Jemima, I'd told him I was just going to bed. But he'd only have argued, I suppose; and it *is* rather early.

She parted her lips to say something, and closed them again. For she had just become aware that his left arm was along the back of the sofa. In other words, his left hand was just behind her. She sat forward, as naturally as she could; but she knew she had been a little too quick.

"What's the matter?" he asked.

"Oh, Derek—please—— I mean, of course it was kind of you to come in——" (what a lie!)—"but you see—— Well, I don't want to—— I mean—— Oh, don't *glare* like that!"

She stood up; but he stood up, too. It seems possible that in the part that he was now playing—admittedly without preparation, and with very little idea, one would say, of construction or plot—he still saw himself in a rather erroneous light. Yet here was a situation in which—poor devil, if you like —he had frequently imagined himself. He had no wish to retreat from it. On the contrary, he was most anxious to see what would happen next. Moreover, in his conceit, or ignorance, or temporary madness, he had taken that allusion to his glare or stare as proof of the very accuracy of the novels which he had so often damned. Their authors—poor devils, too, perhaps— were always paying tribute to the power of the masculine eye. This saved them time, of course. One quite sees their point. For if they followed what happens, nine times out of ten, in real life, no one would have had patience to wait for the promised climax, and their books would have run to an inordinate number of words.

But the critic had overlooked this. The critic was now a character in a novel himself. His eye was hypnotic; he had just been told so. And the obvious, and interesting, and suddenly irresistible thing to do next was what (so he had quite falsely gathered) men of this rather fabulous type were always doing to girls. In fact, as it now struck him with a good deal of force, this was really a wonderful chance.

So he began by seizing one of Miss Marsham's wrists; and she jerked it away, saying: "*Please* don't be silly, Derek!"

He then made a grab at the other wrist, and missed it. But as he said nothing himself—this was the really alarming part—but continued to look pale, owlish, and dogged, Miss Marsham now performed a swift, lateral movement, and escaped round the back of the sofa.

"Now, Derek," she was saying, though her upper lip was quivering in the most unhelpful manner; "you *mustn't* do this sort of thing. You *know*," she added, though not completely convinced of this, "you'd only be sorry." And she said: "Please!" again. And D. P. Moulton, looking rather more flushed at this point, set forth in a clumsy pursuit.

That is to say that it was he who was behind the sofa now, while his quarry was back on the hearth-rug. This is *too* awful, she was thinking. It's disgusting, she was thinking. This is the last straw. I can't stand it. I—— Oh, bother! Here he comes again.

She broke loose into more open country nearer the window. But she wished she hadn't. She wished now that she had chosen to go running round the sofa all night; for there was no protection here, and weedy as he was, he was obviously much the stronger. She picked up a small chair as a weapon of defence. He tried to snatch it away from her; but as she didn't let go, she was whirled right round, so that their positions were again reversed. It was Derek, in other words, who was now facing the door. And it was Derek who saw it fly open—which it did very abruptly indeed.

He said: "Oh!", and stepped back. For it was Gavin—looking almost unrecognisably buoyant and elated—who came bursting and charging in.

"Gavin!" said Jemima, and put down the chair.

"Hullo," said the new arrival, looking slightly taken aback. He turned towards the sub-tenant of No. 12. He was on the point of saying: "I didn't know you were here;" which was the truth, and it was this that had just momentarily curbed his excitement. But as he opened his mouth, he saw D. P. Moulton cower. And then D. P. Moulton was slinking swiftly along the wall. And then, with a rush, he was past him. And then, it is to be presumed, he picked up his hat and coat outside. But while Gavin was still registering a good deal of bewilderment—so much, indeed, that not a syllable of that projected and now obsolete sentence emerged—there was a slam from the front door, and it was as clear that the latch had engaged this time as that the first caller had gone. So that if anyone has been expecting a third and more sanguinary contest than that between Mr. Everard and the pale chemist, or the one between Mr. Barker and Captain Tubbs, then we fear they will be disappointed. For on this occasion not even a blow was struck.

But Gavin wasn't disappointed, though he was still bewildered. He said: "I say—what on earth's up?"

"Nothing," said Jemima, still panting a little. "I suppose—— I mean, perhaps——"

Invention gave out. Also, her eyes were again swimming and brimming. Luckily, however, she was interrupted at this point, and Gavin was still gazing at the door.

"Extraordinary," he said. He closed it. This seemed to remind him of something. "I say," he went on, "perhaps I oughtn't to have barged in like that——"

"Oh, Gavin——"

"——but, you see, your front door wasn't properly shut. Um . . ." He looked extremely thoughtful, though his mind was still in more than a little confusion. He brightened. "Well," he added, "he's gone, anyhow. And I—I can't stay very long myself. But—— Where's Bugs?"

"Out," said Jemima.

He swung round. He seemed to have recovered all that original and still startling ebullience.

"Good!" he said. And then, suddenly: "I say—do I look very odd?"

"No, Gavin." But again this wasn't exactly the truth. "Why—why have you got to go?"

"Because my father——"

It was the speaker who interrupted himself this time. He gave a start and, to Miss Marsham, a quite unaccountable laugh. And then what was for the moment an equally unaccountable scowl.

"I say—Jemima—don't tell me that Derek—well, that he was trying any sort of——"

"Oh, Gavin, it's all over. It was nothing. Well, I think he *was;* but, you see, you came in, and——"

"My God!" said Gavin. "I'll settle his hash." He surged towards the door again. And again he stopped. "Did he kiss you?" he asked, penetratingly.

"No. Oh, no!"

"Sure?"

"Yes—absolutely, Gavin. You—you stopped him."

"Did I, by Jove! Well, he's going out for good in the morning, anyhow. Oh, yes, he is. You see, something's happened. I must go back in a minute, too; but—— Here—sit down."

He took her arm—it was the first time that he had even touched her, but in this case there was no attempt at resistance—and planted her back on the sofa. Then he sat down beside her—firmly. Then there must have been a moment's weakness, for he said:—

"You're not in love with him—are you?"

"I hate him!" said Jemima. "Oh, Gavin—I just can't *stand* him!"

"Nor can I," said her companion. "Gosh, I wish I'd dotted him one. Never mind, though. Too late now—and not my style, perhaps. But he's going; if I have to *kick* him out. I say—I *adore* the way your eyebrow goes up like that."

"Oh, Gavin—do you?" This was beyond brimming; but what in the world had come over him?

"Yes."

A slight silence here. The girl couldn't tell, of course, that at this moment her translated visitor—albeit with no conscious intention of doing anything of the sort—had just summoned up a triple vision. Jock, Ronald, and Charles—his dead friends—had just appeared to him. He wanted to explain something; but then *why*—when either they were dead indeed or already understood? And if they understood, they were backing him. Perhaps, he was suddenly thinking, it was *they* who had inspired—how odd!—yes, Maisie at the Royal Oak, in the first place——

All this in not more than three seconds. And then his voice went on, and he went hurrying after it.

"——why I really came up here. You see, I'd *got* to tell you. Never mind why, for a second. Of course I'd be a cad if I told anyone else. But you're safe, you see. You're *you*. And it may put you off—God knows! —but you see, Jemima—— Here, gimme your hand." He took it, and there was a discharge of more than electricity; but he hung on, and the hand was still there. "You see—well, the most *extraordinary* thing's just happened."

"Has it?" said Miss Marsham, with every possible sound of sympathy— mystified as she still was.

"Yes. You see, all my life I've been sort of *terrified* of my father. He wasn't cruel. But I knew, from the very beginning, that I wasn't what he really wanted. If I'd had more guts—— But then I hadn't, I suppose. Jemima, he got me down, though I don't think he ever meant to. I was a disappointment, you see. I was a failure. I——"

"Oh, Gavin—no. You *couldn't* have been!"

He squeezed her hand. "I *was*," he said. "I just scraped through things. I never did anything clever. He just *paralysed* me—poor old boy. Even in this blasted war, you see, just *look* what I went and did; and just *imagine* what he must have felt."

"It wasn't his foot," said Jemima. "Gavin—you *mustn't* talk like that!"

"I'm not," said Gavin, more strangely than ever. "And you're quite right. It *wasn't* his foot. That's the whole point." He turned still further towards her, with a look that she had never yet seen. "Tomorrow," he said, "from what I know of myself, I shall be shy again—and dull, and dreary, and everything else. Bu tonight—oh, never mind *why* he told me, and of course if he's forgotten in the morning that's probably far the best thing.

I shan't say anything. But there's a reason why I've got to tell *you*. I'm madly in love with you, darling, *darling* Jemima; but I haven't only got a foot that takes off; I'm a——"

"Gavin!"

"Eh?"

"What—what did you say just then? Gavin—I don't mind twopence about your foot—except that it's so horrible for *you*. Of *course* I don't. I'm so *thankful* you're out of it all. I—I'm that sort of girl. I can't help it. I—— Oh, you *did* say it—didn't you?"

"What? Yes, I did. And it's true. But half a second——"

"Why?"

"Well, darling——" He had to gulp then, but her hand was still there, and perhaps, while there was still a dog's chance, he might just as well say it again. "Darling——" (good!)—"I—— Well, that isn't all, you see. No, listen—*please!* Of course it's the most wonderful thing that's ever happened, in a way; but the fact is—well, he was tired, and he had a cold, and I gave him some whisky, and he's not really used to it, and he started telling me, and I didn't stop him, and the truth is . . ."

"Go on!" For what else could one possibly say?

"I'm *going* on. I've got to. Jemima—angel!—he was nearly fifty, and he was in love with my mother—I think she was a kind of governess or something at a big house near by—and then the last war started, and *she* was in love with a much younger man; and he was a soldier, and she was going to have a baby, and he was killed, before they could get married —I don't even know his name yet, but it doesn't matter—and my father married her, if you see what I mean; and I'm the baby; and nobody knows; and she died, when I was about one; and he brought me up, and—— Well, don't you see? It's terrific, I mean! It explains everything, and I'm as proud as Hell of him now. But we're not even relations. It's the most frightful load off my mind. Only——" and away went all that exuberance again, though he still clung on to her hand—"I wanted to marry you—terribly —more than anything else in the world. I couldn't tell you, until this extraordinary thing happened. But now it has—and now I *have* told you —well, there it is. You see, it's not only my foot."

She was almost blinded by the brimming now. Seldom, if indeed ever, had there been such a lump in her throat. But she was doing her utmost to speak.

"You mean—oh, Gavin—you mean——"

He tried to help her out.

"That's right," he said. "I'm a—— Well, I'm illegitimate." And he would have taken his hand away, if she hadn't seized it in both of hers.

"Is that *all* you mean?" she asked.

"Yes," he said. "But it's enough—isn't it?"

"Enough for what?"

"Enough to put you off, I should think."

"Gavin!"

"Eh ?"

"Don't you *dare* ever say that again! It's not *your* fault.   And if *that's* why you told me that you—that you were fond of me, I'm *thankful!*   You *know* it's made you happier——"

"Oh, I admit that."

"Well, then, of *course* it's made me happier, too."

"Has it ?" said Gavin, suddenly realising again what an astonishing evening this was.   "Is that—is that why you're crying ?" he asked.

"Yes, of cuc-course.   What a stupid question."

"Would you like my handkerchief ?"

"Yes, please."

He offered it her with his free hand.   Or, rather, he took it from his pocket and was about to offer it her, when either he changed his mind or they both had the same idea at exactly the same moment.   His arms went round her, as she melted towards him.   Her face, tears and all, was against his cheek. He kissed her eyes.   He kissed her nose.   He kissed her lips.   And the last kiss was the longest.   So long, indeed, that—alas!—being only human, they had presently to leave off so as to breathe.

"Delicious!" said one of them, for they were temporarily indistinguishable.

"Heavenly!" said the other.

They tried it again, and it was even better, perhaps, than before.

And then : "I can't hear," she was saying, "if you roar in my ear like that."

He withdrew a few inches.

"I said, will your family mind ?   They'll have to be told, I suppose."

"Of *course* they won't have to be told," she said   "It's got nothing to do with—— Oh.   I see what you mean.   You mean, just about me being —oh, Gavin!—engaged.   Oh, Gavin, they'll adore you!   Only they might just ask about money—quite nicely, you know."

"So might you," said Gavin, still holding her fast.   "And I can tell you I've got enough for both of us—at least, I think I have.   And I'll tell you why, what's more, though I've only just found out.   It was my real father— you know, I can't help wondering if he's listening to us now, but if he is, I bet he's bucked; I mean, *he* left all he had to my mother—in a sort of secret way, so the other one said—and she never touched it, and *she* left it all for me—only it was more by them, because I did'nt get it till I was grown-up. So that's why I'm a partner in Dingle and Frisby; I mean, I bought the job; and—— Oh, darling!"

"What ?   I'm sure if I say 'partner,' they won't want to know anything more."

"Won't they ?   No, I was thinking of something else.   Have I rushed you ?"

"No.   Yes.   But I liked being rushed."

"Did you? My gosh, I can't believe anything. But—well, here's something I've just thought of that won't interest you in the very least."

"Oh, do tell me!"

"My cousin Claud."

"What, the one you don't like?"

"Why, who told you that?"

"You did, Gavin. In the street. When you were telling me about your poor foot."

"Oh. Did I? Well, you see, he's *not* my cousin. It's marvellous! Perhaps *you're* my cousin." He eyed her. "No, you're not," he decided. "I just *know* you're not. But it *is* marvellous, darling—even if it oughtn't to be. I mean—morals apart—and by the way, I'm an exceedingly moral chap myself—just *imagine* if you had a father who'd always got you down; and if you suddenly found he wasn't your father at all; and that as well as that he'd really been rather an absolute hero. I mean, think of it. Saving somebody's name, and putting up, for years and years, with a child that wasn't your own. Poor old R.J. You know, I feel a worm, darling. I can see all his good points suddenly. I admire him enormously. I can see the funny side of him without being maddened any more. And the touching side. You know, I don't think he *could* upset me now. Only I wonder . . ."

"What, Gavin?"

"Well, how much he'll remember in the morning."

"You—you mean, he's asleep now?"

"Well, yes. Just dropped off, like a wizened old baby, with his mouth wide open. That was when I felt I *must* tell you, you see. Only I did more than that, didn't I?"

"Yes, Gavin. Gavin—are you sure you meant to?"

"Pooh!" said young Mr. Guernsey, for though perhaps he had no name now, there is not much else to call him. "What a footling question, my own, precious, darling Jemima. Are *you* sure—that's the real point—that you don't mind getting married—oh, gosh, what a wonderful thought!—to a——"

She put her hand over his mouth; the hand, that is to say, that he wasn't still holding.

"You're you," she said, though she had forgotten that she was quoting his own words. "Nobody can alter that."

Prickles were running all over him, as he grasped her slim waist.

"I say—do you want me to cry, too?" he asked.

"If you like, darling."

But he didn't. The fact was that, though deeply stirred, he was far and away too happy. Besides, he was thinking too much, as might be judged from his silence. He was thinking of the last war, which had brought him, as he suddenly saw, into being. He was thinking of his mother, whom he had never known, with an almost painful sensation of pity. It was impossible to think clearly of his father, for obvious reasons; in a sense, also, he had no wish, just yet, to return to the position of having any father at all; but most positively he had forgiven—if it was for him to forgive—a ghost who had tried to atone.

He thought of R.J., and knew now, whatever the morning might bring, that they could never be on the old terms again.

And then he thought of the girl who was here by his side. And this, of course—though no one could have done less to deserve her—was a thought that swamped everything else.

"Jemima," he said.

"Yes, Gavin ?"

"Nothing. I was only thinking how lucky I am, and how sweet you are."

"I see. Poor Gavin."

"Poor ? Nothing of the sort. Not now."

She left it at that. She wanted to hold this moment; and, besides, if she explained how ordinary she was, how awful it would be if he believed her. So again they were both silent; though now, as they both gradually became aware, the room itself was filled with a good deal of sound. How long it had been going on, they had no idea. But the nightly chorus of loud-speakers had started again, and the same voice was booming through walls, and floor, and ceiling. They could hear what it was saying, too, as by sheer insistence it forced itself into their ears. In fact, though they were thinking and dreaming still, they were also half-consciously listening.

". . . at a meeting in his constituency today," said the tones of Thomas Turnbull once more, from which the microphone had removed, as scrupulously as ever, any hint that his mind was involved, "Mr. Wilfred Buzzard, Minister of Interference, said that the enemy was now hemmed in on all sides, and knew that the hour of his final defeat was approaching. 'But,' added Mr. Buzzard, 'it is up to us all, for that very reason, to increase our effort. There must be no complacency——' "

Here, abruptly and without the faintest warning, all the loud-speakers ceased functioning at the same moment—almost as though Mr. Turnbull had been felled to the earth with a bludgeon. But the sets still hummed, and the true cause was quite clear enough. People with outside aerials, or people in other parts of the country, could still, if they chose, hear the rest of Mr. Buzzard's remarks. But here, among the ageing equipment in Huddleston House, there was sudden and complete silence, as one miracle of Man's invention was quelled by another. As radio-diffusion yielded to radio-location. And, indeed, though one occupant of the sofa had just time to say: "Oh, lord—here they come again!", there was barely an instant tonight before this view was still further confirmed. The sirens were at it now, far, near, rising and falling, in a monotonous rendering of half—and by no means the more popular half—of their all too familiar repertory. The closer and, as always, the slightly later ones set off, it is true, with a distinct suggestion that they were originating rather than imitating the sound. "Here—

listen to *me*," they seemed to be saying. "How do you like *this* version?" Yet by the second or third howl, at the very most, they appeared to abandon their claim. That hint of personality evaporated, and they were just howling for howling's sake, like dogs baying the moon.

Only there wasn't a moon, as the Londoners well knew. There was just a pitch-black vault overhead, resounding already—for clearly, again, it was to be a real performance this time, and a prompt one, too—with the distant thump of guns. There was also the well-known scurrying of footsteps in the street outside; the noise of the cars that were spurting, in the customarily urgent fashion, along the main road; and of course—even while the further sirens were sulkily ceasing their song—the hoarse and angry cry, from this street again, of: "Put out that light!" Everything, in fact, as you might say, was now set for another and a pretty blithering exhibition of how the Great Powers—as they described themselves—conducted their quarrels.

"Oh, Gavin," said Miss Jemima Marsham, "what an awful nuisance." And then, for even now, it would seem, she could think of others: "I say— what about your father? Well, I mean, your . . ."

"Oh, of course we've got to call him that," said Gavin, who was on his feet now, for at least they both belonged to him, though only one was of flesh and blood. And he thought: We! That's a wonderful word. "But I don't know," he added, "that I oughtn't really——"

"Yes, of course you must. You can't leave him alone down there. I mean, if this wakes him up and he wants you——"

"That's what I was thinking," said Gavin. "Poor old blighter. I—I suppose you couldn't come, too?"

They heard the lift moaning now, for naturally the Champions were on their way down again to the Shelter.

'I don't think I'd better," said Jemima. She wrinkled her nose, and the eyebrow went up. "Well, you might have to explain me, and I don't know that this is *quite* the best time. Besides, there might be Derek."

"Blast him," said Gavin, in a preoccupied manner. "And yet I simply loathe leaving you."

"I loathe your going," said the girl whom he loved so much. "But I still think you must. Perhaps——"

She had been going to point out that if his father, or alleged father, was still asleep, and if the raid died down, then perhaps he could return. But at this moment there was such a salvo from the nearer guns—with squeals, barks, bellowings, bumps, and roars—that her gentle voice, even before she broke off, was completely drowned. She was on her feet, too, though, now. Indeed, she had risen so hastily that she had stepped out of those slippers; or it may be that during a previous embrace they had fallen off. So that now, as Gavin's arms went round her again, he was astonished to discover how small she had become; and how light, for as his heart beat wildly, he lifted her right off the floor.

"There!" he said, as at last he put her down again. "Hell!" he said. "Now I must beat it. But for God's sake," he added, as people were always adjuring each other in these strange and on the whole, one would say, by no means complacent days, "take care of yourself."

She just smiled at him; and he still seemed to see her smiling, as he plunged into the murky, icy corridor, and then dutifully turned—with a queer look of triumph and awe—to descend the stairs.

Here, too, we retire from the scene ourselves; or it may be that the steel, and concrete, and bricks, and breeze-blocks, and quick-drying plaster, have suddenly at this point become solid and impermeable again; that the Asmodean eye can no longer see through roof or walls, and even into the minds of those who dwell beyond them. There has been a flash of another magic—if not brighter, then it is to be hoped more lasting, than the flames now blazing in the London sky; and as, for us, the sound of bombs and gun-fire fades away, we know that the time has come to say farewell. Perhaps, though we were unaware of this before, the spell which has revealed so much was only offered to us on certain terms. We were to wait, and watch, and listen, until someone was happy. And then either our power would leave us, or we should be released.

Suddenly, however, there can be no doubt that it has left us; so that now, for all that we have seen, and heard, and learnt, henceforth we can only guess.

It may be, once more, for instance, that this was the night when the 2,000-kilo H.E. bomb fell fair and square on the roof of Huddleston House, and burst in the lift-shaft, and wiped out the whole cast. Or there may have been no such night. Or a few months later a flying-bomb may have cut out and dropped in the same manner, with possibly a more selective form of massacre. Or, if this didn't happen, there might be a rocket. Or an aerial who-knows-what? Or perhaps, again, though the building itself may have survived, the demand for official accommodation—whether for soldiers, temporary Civil Servants, or specially imported refugees—may have hurled all the residents forth from their flats, and from Bessingham House as well. Any of these things may have come to pass. We just don't know.

Nor do we know—assuming that he was alive in the morning—how much R. J. Guernsey, Esq., M.A. (Oxon.), remembered of the previous evening when he eventually awoke. Nothing, perhaps. Or everything. It's quite an interesting point. If we may guess, though, we should say that he remembered something; and that presently, if not at first, he would have few regrets. We should say that he, also, might be happier than he had been in the past; with an heir, if not a son, who no longer feared him, and even held him in deep admiration, too. Did Gavin discover his true father's name? Possibly, if he wished to; as he might when he got over the first rapturous sense of freedom. His bride, we should say, might feel a certain curiosity on this subject, if only for her own private information. And brides, as is of course well known, are restrained by no scruples at all.

We can't doubt, though, that she was a bride soon enough, if the bombs allowed, for engagements, where there is no other obstacle, are short in war-time; and quite right, too. We are afraid, however, that whether she moved from No. 15 into No. 12 or not—and whether D. P. Moulton departed with a kick or, as on the whole seems more likely, without it—this wouldn't necessarily excuse her from attendance at the Ministry of Redirection. Or not just yet.

It must be guess-work, too, as to when, if ever, Gavin's ex-cousin Claud succeded in disentangling the curiously confused rights and wrongs, indebted-ness or liability, and other outstanding points at issue in the case of an officer who loses a foot in a civilian capacity, and gets a new one before the military mandarins have decided what forms should be filled in. We have a theory that if Claud had left the whole thing alone, this confusion—rich as it already was—might have remained under some slight control. But we can offer no forecast as to the month, or even year, when the case will be finally closed. Not, we should imagine, that his client will care very much. For we picture his client as concerned in much simpler, and infinitely more pleasant affairs.

Then there's Bugs. Odd girl; if not exactly unique. We didn't much like her at first, in spite of her looks. And yet—under the influence of Jemima, no doubt—it seems that we can bear her no grudge. Again, though, we can't give you the date of her wedding, nor swear that it ever took place. But if it did, and somehow we still rather think it did, we wish both Mr. and Mrs. Haggerston-Hawksworth nothing but sunshine and joy. Why not? For what harm have they ever done us? Or what odds would it make if we didn't?

Yet still, now the spell is loosed, we can only guess. We don't know what happened to Mr. Vardas, though to tell the truth we don't much mind. We don't know what happened to Miss Pattinson, though we trust that she re-covered her flat. We should like also to think that Miss Kenton-Hinksey was eventually restored to health, for though she was odd, too, we always rather admired her, and feel strongly that she deserves better luck. And Mrs. Amberley? What a problem! Do you think time can solve it? Well, we hope so—though again we don't know—for no one should dare to judge Primrose Amberley unless they are prepared to submit to judgment themselves.

Mr. Everard? And Mrs. Everard, and little Cyril? Oh, they'll be all right. We're not worrying about them. We're much more anxious about poor Mrs. Margetson, whose slight stupidity we may have failed to conceal, but whose heart, without question—for all her very natural distaste for bombs—was made of the staunchest stuff. Did she ever get her watch back, we wonder? Or her son? Or her exiled husband? Was she ever